The
QUEST OF THE FOUR

The
QUEST OF THE FOUR

BY

JOSEPH A. ALTSHELER

AUTHOR OF "THE LAST OF THE CHIEFS,"
"THE YOUNG TRAILERS," ETC.

A STORY OF THE COMANCHES AND BUENA VISTA

Amereon House

TO THE READER
It is our pleasure to keep available uncommon titles and to this end, at the time of publication, we have used the best available sources. To aid catalogers and collectors, this title is printed in an edition limited to 300 copies. —— **Enjoy!**

AMEREON HOUSE
the publishing division of
Amereon Ltd.
PO Box 1200
Mattituck, New York 11952-9500

Copyright, 1939, by Sallie B. Altsheler
Printed in the United States of America

CONTENTS

CHAPTER	PAGE
I.—The Meeting of the Four	1
II.—The March of the Train	20
III.—At the Ford	41
IV.—On Watch	58
V.—The Comanche Village	77
VI.—The Medicine Lodge	96
VII.—The Great Sleep	113
VIII.—New Enemies	129
IX.—The Fiery Circle	150
X.—Phil's Letter	168
XI.—With the Army	186
XII.—The Pass of Angostura	203
XIII.—A Wind of the Desert	219
XIV.—Buena Vista	233
XV.—The Woman at the Well	261
XVI.—The Castle of Montevideo	276
XVII.—The Thread, the Key, and the Dagger	292
XVIII.—The Hut in the Cove	310
XIX.—Arenberg's Quest	326
XX.—The Silver Cup	344
XXI.—The Note of a Melody	359
XXII.—Breakstone's Quest	377

The QUEST OF THE FOUR

THE QUEST OF THE FOUR

CHAPTER I

THE MEETING OF THE FOUR

A TALL boy, dreaming dreams, was walking across the Place d'Armes in New Orleans. It was a brilliant day in early spring, and a dazzling sunlight fell over the city, gilding the wood or stone of the houses, and turning the muddy current of the Mississippi into shimmering gold. Under such a perfect blue sky, and bathed in such showers of shining beams, New Orleans, a city of great and varied life, looked quaint, picturesque, and beautiful.

But the boy, at that moment, thought little of the houses or people about him. His mind roamed into the vast Southwest, over mountains, plains, and deserts that his feet had never trod, and he sought, almost with the power of evocation, to produce regions that he had never seen, but which he had often heard described. He had forgotten no detail of the stories, but, despite them, the cloud of mystery and romance remained, calling to him all the more strongly because he had come upon a quest the most vital of his life, a quest that must lead him into the great unknown land.

He was not a native of New Orleans or Louisiana. Any one could have told at a glance that the blue eyes, fair hair, and extreme whiteness of skin did not belong to the Gulf coast. His build was that of the Anglo-Saxon. The height, the breadth of shoulder and chest, and the whole figure, muscled very powerfully for one so young, indicated birth in a clime farther North—Kentucky or Virginia, perhaps. His dress, neat and clean, showed that he was one who respected himself.

Phil Bedford passed out of the Place d'Armes, and presently came to the levee which ran far along the great river, and which was seething with life. New Orleans was then approaching the zenith of its glory. Many, not foreseeing the power of the railroad, thought that the city, seated near the mouth of the longest river of the world, into which scores of other navigable streams drained, was destined to become the first city of America. The whole valley of the Mississippi, unequalled in extent and richness, must find its market here, and beyond lay the vast domain, once Spain's, for which New Orleans would be the port of entry.

Romance, too, had seized the place. The Alamo and San Jacinto lay but a few years behind. All the states resounded with the great story of the Texan struggle for liberty. Everybody talked of Houston and Crockett and Bowie and the others, and from this city most of the expeditions had gone. New Orleans was the chief fountain from which flowed fresh streams of men who steadily pushed the great Southwestern frontier farther and farther into the Spanish lands.

It seemed to Phil, looking through his own fresh, young eyes, that it was a happy crowd along the levee. The basis of the city was France and Spain, with an American superstructure, but all the materials had been bound into a solid fabric by their great and united defense against the British in 1815. Now other people came, too, called by the spirit of trade or adventure. Every nation of Europe was there, and the states, also, sent their share. They came fast on the steamers which trailed their black smoke down the yellow river.

THE MEETING OF THE FOUR

The strong youth had been sad, when he came that morning from the dingy little room in which he slept, and he had been sad when he was walking across the Place d'Armes, but the scene was too bright and animated to leave one so young in such a state of mind. He bought a cup of hot coffee from one of the colored women who was selling it from immense cans, drank it, exchanged a cheerful word or two of badinage, and, as he turned away, he ran into a round man, short, rosy, and portly. Phil sprang back, exclaiming:

"Your pardon, sir! It was an accident! All my fault!"

"No harm done where none iss meant," replied the stranger, speaking excellent English, although with a strong German accent. It was obvious, even without the accent, that he was of German birth. The Fatherland was written all over his rotund figure, but he was dressed in the fashion of the Southwest—light suit, light shoes, and a straw hat.

It was a time when chance meetings led to long friendships. On the border, a stranger spoke to another stranger if he felt like it. One could ask questions if he chose. Partnerships were formed on the spur of the moment. In the vast army that was made up of the children of adventure, formality was a commodity little in demand. The German looked rather inquiringly at the boy.

"From farther North, iss it not so?" he asked. "Answer or be silent. Either iss your right."

Phil laughed. He liked the man's quaint manner and friendly tone, and he replied promptly:

"I was born in Kentucky, my name is Philip Bedford, and I am alone in New Orleans."

"Then," said the German, "you must be here for some expedition. This iss where they start. It iss so. I can see it in your face. Come, my young friend, no harm iss done where none iss meant."

THE QUEST OF THE FOUR

Phil had taken no offense. He had merely started a little at the shrewd guess. He replied frankly:

"I'm thinking of the West, Texas and maybe New Mexico, or even beyond that—California."

"It iss a long journey to take alone," said the German, "two thousand, three thousand miles, and not one mile of safe road. Indians, Mexicans, buffaloes, bears, deserts, mountains, all things to keep you from getting across."

"But I mean to go," said Phil firmly.

The German looked at him searchingly. His interest in Phil seemed to increase.

"Something calls you," he said.

Phil was silent.

"No harm iss done where none iss meant," continued the German. "You have told me who you are, Mr. Philip Bedford, and where you come from. It iss right that I tell you as much about myself. My name iss Hans Arenberg, and I am a Texan."

Phil looked at him, his eyes full of unbelief, and the German laughed a little.

"It iss so," he said. "You do not think I look like a Texan, but I am one by way of Germany. I—I lived at New Braunfels."

Arenberg's voice broke suddenly, and then Phil remembered vaguely—New Braunfels, a settlement of German immigrants in Texas, raided by Comanches, the men killed, and the women carried off! It was one of those terrible incidents of the border, so numerous that the new fast crowded the old out of place.

"You come from New Braunfels! You are one of the survivors of the massacre!" he exclaimed.

"It iss so," said the German, his eyes growing somber, "and I, too, wish to go far into the West. I, too, seek something, young Mr. Philip Bedford, and my road would lie much where yours leads."

The two looked at each other with inquiry that

THE MEETING OF THE FOUR

shaded into understanding. Arenberg was the first to speak.

"Yes, we could go together," he said. "I trust you, and you trust me. But two are not strong enough. The chances are a thousand to one that neither of us would find what he iss seeking. The Mexicans wish revenge on the Texans, the Comanches raid to the outskirts of San Antonio. Pouf! Our lives would not be worth that! It must be a strong party of many men!"

"I believe you are right," said Phil, "but I wish to go. I wish to go very much."

"So do I," said Arenberg. "It iss the same with both of us, but suppose we wait. Where do you live?"

Phil no longer hesitated to confide in this chance acquaintance, and he replied that he was staying in a house near the Convent of the Ursuline Nuns, where a little room sheltered him and his few belongings.

"Suppose," said Arenberg, "that I join you there, and we save our expenses. In union there iss strength. If you do not like my suggestion say so. No harm iss done where none iss meant."

"On the contrary, I do like it," said Phil heartily. "It seems to me that we can help each other."

"Then come," said Arenberg. "We will go first to my place, where I will pay my own bill, take away what I have, and then we will join forces at yours. Iss it not so?"

Arenberg was staying at one of the inns that abounded in New Orleans, and it took him only a half hour to pack and move, carrying his baggage in his hand. Phil's room was in a large, rambling old house, built of cypress wood, with verandas all about it. There an American widow kept boarders, and she had plenty of them, as New Orleans was overflowing with strangers. The room was small and bare, but it was large enough, as Phil's baggage, too, was limited. A cot was put in for Arenberg, and the two were at home.

THE QUEST OF THE FOUR

The day was now drawing to a close, and the two ate supper with a strange company in the large dining-room of the boarding house. Phil, a close observer, noted that six languages were spoken around that more or less hospitable board. He understood only his own, and a little French and Spanish, but the difference in sound and intonation enabled him to note the others. One of the men who sat opposite him was a big fellow with glistening gold rings in his ears, evidently a West Indian of somewhat doubtful color, but he was quiet, and ate dextrously and skillfully with his knife. A sallow young Mexican with curling black mustaches complained incessantly about his food, and a thin New Englander spoke at times of the great opportunities for capital in the Southwest.

Phil and Arenberg, who sat side by side, said little, but both watched all the other guests with interested eyes. The one who held Phil's gaze the longest was a smoothly shaven young man on the other side of the table. It was the difference between him and the others that aroused Phil's curiosity. He sat very erect, with his square shoulders thrown back, and he never spoke, except to accept or reject the food passed by colored girls. His eyes were blue, and his face, cut clear and strong, betokened perception and resolve. Phil believed that he could like him, but his attention by and by wandered elsewhere.

Philip Bedford had not felt so nearly content for many days. The making of a new friend was a source of strength to the boy, and he felt that he had taken a step forward in his great search. Fresh confidence flowed like good wine into his veins. He had friendly feelings toward all those around the table, and the room itself became picturesque. He ate of strange dishes, French or Spanish, and liked them, careless what they were. A mild breeze came through the open windows, and the outlines of buildings were softened in the dusk. Within

THE MEETING OF THE FOUR

the room itself six candles in tall candlesticks, placed at regular intervals on the table, cast a sufficient light. Two young colored women in red calico dresses, and with red turbans on their heads, kept off the flies and mosquitoes with gorgeous fans of peacock feathers, which they waved gently over the heads of the guests. Phil became deeply conscious of the South, of its glow and its romance.

The guests, having a sufficiency of food, left the table one by one. The young man with the smooth face was among the first to go. Phil noticed him again and admired his figure—tall, slender, and beautifully erect. He walked with ease and grace, and his dress of plain brown was uncommonly neat and well fitting. "I should like to know that man," was Phil's thought.

After dinner the boy and Arenberg sat on the veranda in the dusk, and talked in low voices of their plans. They deemed it better to keep their intentions to themselves. Many expeditions were fitting out in New Orleans. Some were within the law, and some were not. Wise men talked little of what was nearest to their hearts.

"If we go into the West—and we are going," said Phil, "we shall need weapons—rifles, pistols."

"Time enough for that," said Arenberg. "If we have the money, we can arm ourselves in a day. Weapons are a chief article of commerce in New Orleans."

An hour later they went up to their room and to bed. Phil carried his money on his person, and most of his other belongings were in a stout leather bag or valise, which was fastened with a brass lock. It was necessary for him to open the bag to obtain some clean linen, and as Arenberg's back was turned he took out, also, a small paper, yellow and worn. He opened it for the thousandth time, choked a sigh, and put it back. As he relocked the bag and turned, he noticed that Arenberg also had been looking at something. It seemed to be a photograph, and the German, after returning it to his own bag, gazed absently out of the window. His face, which at other times was obviously made for smiles and cheeriness, was heavy with grief. A flood of sympathy rushed over Philip Bedford. "I wonder what it is he seeks out there," the boy thought as he looked unconsciously toward the West. But he had too much delicacy of mind to say anything, and presently Arenberg was himself again, speaking hopefully of their plans as they prepared for bed.

Phil slept soundly, except for one interval. Then he dreamed a dream, and it was uncommonly vivid. He saw Hans Arenberg rise from his cot, take from his bag the small object which was undoubtedly a photograph, go to the window, where the moonlight fell, and look at it long and earnestly. Presently his chest heaved, and tears ran down either cheek. Then his head fell forward, and he dropped the photograph to his breast. He stood in that stricken attitude for at least five minutes, then he put the photograph back in the bag, and returned to his cot. In the morning Phil's recollection of the dream was very vivid, but Arenberg was cheery and bright.

The boy and the man ate breakfast together in the dining-room, a breakfast of oranges—Phil had never seen an orange until he came to New Orleans—cakes and butter and coffee. Only a few of the diners of the evening before were present when they went into the room, but among them was the young man with the shaven face and the firm chin. Phil liked him even better in the morning light. His seemed the kindly face of a man with a strong and decided character. Their eyes met, and the stranger smiled and nodded. Phil smiled and nodded back. After breakfast Phil and Arenberg went out upon the veranda. The man was already there, smoking a cigarette.

"Fine morning," he observed easily. "One could not ask anything better than these early spring days in New Orleans. In the North we are still in the grasp of snow and ice."

THE MEETING OF THE FOUR

Phil and Arenberg also sat down, as the way was now opened for conversation.

"Then you are from the North, I suppose," said Phil.

"Yes," replied the stranger, "from the State of New York, but I am traveling now, as you see. My name is Middleton, George Middleton."

He paused, meditatively blew a whiff of smoke from the little Spanish cigarrito, and added:

"I'm not for long in New Orleans. I'm thinking of a journey in the West."

"Nobody goes there unless he has a very good reason for going. Iss it not so? No harm iss done where none iss meant," said Arenberg, in a tone half of apology and half of inquiry.

Middleton laughed and took another puff at his cigarrito.

"Certainly no harm has been done," he replied. "You are right, also, in saying that no one goes into the West unless he has an excellent reason. I have such a reason. I want to look for something there."

Phil and the German exchanged glances. They, too, wished to look for something there. So! Here was a third man seeking to embark upon the great journey. But it was no business of theirs what he sought, however curious they might feel about it. Phil took another look at Middleton. Surely his was a good face, a face to inspire trust and courage.

"We wish to go across Texas and New Mexico, also," he said, "but we've been delaying until we could form a party."

"You've two at least," said Middleton, "and you now have the chance to make it three. Why not do so?"

"We will," said Arenberg. "It iss a case where three are company, and two are not so much. Our firm is now Middleton, Bedford, Arenberg & Co."

"Do not put me first," said Middleton. "We must all be on exactly the same plane. But I hope, friends,

9

that you trust me as much as I trust you. I think I know truth and honesty when I see them."

"We do!" said Phil and Arenberg together and emphatically.

The three shook hands, and that single act bound them into a solemn compact to stand by one another through all things. They did not waste words. Then the three went into the town, walking about among the inns and on the levee to hear the gossip of New Orleans, and to learn what chance there was of a large party going into the West. On the way Middleton told them of some things that he had learned. He was not sure, but a large wagon train might start soon for Santa Fé, in the far Mexican land of New Mexico. It was to be a trading expedition, carrying much cloth, metal goods, and other articles of value to this, the greatest of Mexico's outlying posts.

"It will be a numerous train," said Middleton, "perhaps too numerous, as it may arouse the suspicion of the Mexicans. The relations of the States and Mexico are none too good. There is trouble over Texas, and who can tell what will happen a thousand miles in the depths of the wilderness?"

"Nobody," said Arenberg. "Who should know better than I?"

He spoke with such sudden emphasis that Middleton opened his mouth as if he would ask a question, but changed his mind and was silent.

"Then it is your opinion, Mr. Middleton," said Phil, "that we should join this train?"

"If nothing better offers. All such expeditions are loosely organized. If we should wish to leave it we can do so."

"It iss well to keep it in mind," said Arenberg. "No harm can be done where none iss meant."

They entered a large inn kept by a Frenchman. Many men were sitting about drinking or smoking. Middleton

THE MEETING OF THE FOUR

ordered lemonade for the three, and they sat at a small table in the corner, observing the life of the place. Phil's attention was presently attracted to another small table near them, at which a single man sat. His gaze would not have lingered there, had it not been for this man's peculiar appearance. His age might have been thirty-five, more or less, and his figure was powerful. His face was burned almost black by a sun that could not have been anything but ardent, but his features and his blue eyes showed him to be American of a fair race. His clothes were poor, and he looked depressed. Yet the stranger was not without a certain distinction, an air as of one who did not belong there in an inn. Something in the blue eyes told of wild freedom and great spaces. He interested Phil more than anybody else in the room. He felt that here was another man whom he could like.

The talk about them drifted quite naturally upon the subject of the West, what Texas was going to do, what Mexico was going to do, the great trail toward the Pacific, and the prospect of trouble between the United States and Mexico. The shabby man raised his head and showed interest. His eyes began to glow. He was not more than three feet away, and Phil, prompted by a sort of instinct, spoke to him.

"It seems that all eyes turn toward the West now," he said.

"Yes," replied the stranger, "and they're right. It's out there that the great things lie."

He moved his hand with a slight but significant gesture toward the setting sun.

"I've been there once," he said, "and I want to go back."

"A man takes his life in his hands when he travels that way," said Phil.

"I know," replied the stranger, "but I'm willing to risk it. I must go back there. I want to look for something, something very particular."

THE QUEST OF THE FOUR

Phil started. Here was a fourth who sought some darling wish of his heart in that far mysterious West. He felt a strange influence. It seemed to him a sign, or rather a command that must be obeyed. He glanced at Middleton and Arenberg, who had been listening, and, understanding him perfectly, they nodded.

"We three are going into the West, also, on errands of our own," said Phil. "Why not join us? Three are good, but four are better."

"It iss a fair proposition," added Arenberg. "No harm iss done where none iss meant."

"We make the offer," said Middleton, "because on such a journey one needs friends. If you do not think you can trust us, as our acquaintance is so short, say so."

The man examined them keenly, one by one. Phil, looking with equal keenness at him, saw that, despite shabbiness of dress and despondency of manner, he was not a common man. In truth, as he looked, the depression seemed to be passing away. The stranger raised his head, threw back his shoulders, and the blue eyes began to glow.

"You look all right to me," he said. "A man has got to make friends, and if you trust me I don't see why I can't trust you. Besides, I'm terribly anxious to go back out there, and my reason is mighty good."

"Then shall we consider it a bargain?" said Middleton.

"You may count me one of the band as long as you will have me," said the stranger with hearty emphasis, "and I suppose I oughtn't to come in as an unknown. My name is Breakstone, William Breakstone, though I am always called Bill Breakstone by those who know me. Bill Breakstone seems to run off smoother."

He smiled in the most ingratiating manner. The sudden acquisition of friends seemed to have clothed him about with sunlight. All the others felt that they had made no mistake

THE MEETING OF THE FOUR

"I'm a rover," said Bill Breakstone in round, cheerful tones. "I've been roaming all my life, though I'm bound to say it hasn't been to much purpose. As you see me now, I haven't got nearly enough to buy either a rifle or a horse for this big trip on which you're asking me to go, and on which I'm wanting to go terrible bad."

"Never mind, Mr. Breakstone—" began Middleton, but he was interrupted.

"I'm Breakstone or Bill to those that feed with me," said the new man, "and I'm Mr. Breakstone to those that don't like me or suspect me."

"All right," said Middleton with a laugh, "it's Breakstone for the present. By and by we may call you Bill. I was going to tell you, Breakstone, that we four go in together. We furnish you what you need, and later on you pay us back if you can. It's the usual thing in the West."

"You're right, my lord," said Bill Breakstone, "and I accept. It gives me pleasure to be enrolled in your most gallant company, and, by my troth, I will serve you right well."

Middleton looked at him in amazement, and Bill Breakstone broke into a mellow, infectious laugh.

"I don't talk that way all the time," he said. "It merely bursts out in spots. You may not believe it, when you look at me, but I studied for the stage once, and I've been an actor. Now and then the old scraps come to the end of my tongue. All's well that end's well, and may that be the fate of our expedition."

"Come," said Middleton, after telling his own name and that of his friends to Breakstone, "we'll go to our quarters and make a place for you. Phil and Arenberg are in a room together, and you shall share mine."

"Lead on!" said Bill Breakstone.

The four left the inn. Bill Breakstone was as poor as he described himself to be. He owned only the worn suit of clothes in which he stood, a pistol, and a pair of saddle bags, seeming to contain some linen, of which he took good care.

"Prithee, young sir," he said to Phil, "I would fain guard well the little that I have, because if I lose the little that I have, then what I have shall be nothing. Do I argue well, Sir Ivanhoe?"

"It's conclusive," said Phil. He took greatly to this man who had become in an hour the life of their little band, a constant source of cheerful patter that invigorated them all. Middleton bought him a new suit of clothes, gave him some money, which he promised earnestly to return a hundredfold, and then they went forth to inquire further into the matter of the trading expedition for Sante Fé. But their attention was diverted by the arrival of a large steamboat that had come all the way from Pittsburgh loaded with passengers. A particular group among the arrivals soon became the center of their interest.

The members of the group were Mexicans, and they were evidently people of distinction, or, at least, position. The first among them was middle-aged, fat, and yellow, and dressed in garments much brighter in color than Americans wear. Indeed, as a wind somewhat chill swept over the river, he threw around his shoulders a red serape with a magnificent border of gold fringe. But a young man who walked by his side made no acknowledgment to the wind. It was he whom Phil watched most. Some people inspire us at once with hostility, and Phil had this feeling about the stranger, who bore himself in a manner that had more than a tinge of sneering arrogance.

The young man was obviously of the Spanish race, although his blood might run back to Northern Spain, as he was tall and very strongly built, and his complexion inclined to fairness, but Phil believed him to be of Mexican birth, as he showed the shade of change that the New World always made in the old. He wore the uniform of

THE MEETING OF THE FOUR

a captain in the Mexican army. Mexican uniforms were not popular in the States, but he bore himself as if he preferred the hostility of the crowd to its friendship. His insolent gaze met Phil's for an instant, and the boy gave it back with interest. For a few moments these two who had never met before, who did not know the names of each other, and who might never meet again, stared with immediate hostility. Eye plumbed the depths of eye, but it was the Mexican who looked away first, although he let his lips curl slightly into a gesture with which he meant to convey contempt.

Middleton had observed this silent drama of a few moments, and he said quietly:

"You do not know, Philip, who these men are?"

"No," replied the boy, "but I should like to know."

"The stout, elderly man is Don August Xavier Hernando Zucorra y Palite, who is at the head of a special Mexican embassy that has been at Washington to treat with our government about the boundary of Texas—you know there has been trouble between the States and Mexico over the Texan boundary—and the younger is Pedro de Armijo, his nephew, and the nephew, also, of Armijo, the governor of New Mexico, where we are planning to go."

"I fancied from his manner," said Bill Breakstone, "that young Armijo was the President of Old Mexico and New Mexico both. I have called you Sir Knight, and My Lord Phil, but our young Mexican is both His Grace and His Royal Highness. By my halidome, we are indeed proud and far above that vile herd, the populace."

"Well, he will not bother us," said Arenberg. "If you run after trouble you will find it coming to meet you."

Middleton watched the Mexicans with uncommon interest until they passed out of sight. Arenberg, a shrewd and penetrating man himself, said:

"You are interested in them, Mr. Middleton?"

THE QUEST OF THE FOUR

"I am," replied Middleton frankly, "and I know, too, that the errand of Zucorra to Washington has been a failure. The relations of the United States and Mexico are no better."

"But that won't keep us from going across to the Pacific, will it, Cap?" said Bill Breakstone briskly. "You don't mind if I call you Cap, do you, Mr. Middleton? You are, in a way, our leader, because you are most fit, and the title seems to suit you."

"Call me Cap if you wish," replied Middleton, "but we are all on equal terms. Now, as we have seen the Mexicans, and, as there is nothing more here to attract us, we might go on up the levee."

"Prithee, we will suit the deed to the word," said Bill Breakstone, "but do not run into that drunken Indian there, Phil. I would not have thy garments soiled by contact with this degraded specimen of a race once proud and noble."

Phil turned a little to one side to avoid the Indian of whom Breakstone spoke. The levee was littered with freight, and the red man huddled against a hogshead of tobacco from far Kentucky. His dress was partly savage and partly civilized, and he was sodden with dirt and drink. But, as Breakstone spoke, he raised his head and flashed him a look from fiery, glowing eyes. Then his head sank back, but the single glance made Breakstone shiver.

"I felt as if I had received a bullet," he said. "Now what did the noble savage mean by giving me such a look? He must have understood what I said. Ah, well, it mattereth not. He looked like a Comanche. It has been wisely said, let the cobbler stick to his last, and there is no last in New Orleans for Mr. Cobbler Comanche."

"You didn't suppose he understood you," said Arenberg, "and no harm iss done where none iss meant."

Phil looked back at the Comanche, but there was nothing heroic about him. He was huddled lower than

THE MEETING OF THE FOUR

ever against the tobacco hogshead. Certainly there was no suggestion of the dauntless warrior, of the wild horseman. Phil felt a curious little thrill of disappointment.

He looked in the same place the next day for the Comanche, but he did not see him, and then, in the excitement of great preparations, he forgot the Indian. The New Mexico expedition was about to become a fact, and the little band of four were promptly received as members. On all such perilous trips strong and well-armed men were welcome.

The outfit would embrace about sixty wagons and two hundred men, and the goods they carried would be of great value. Phil and his comrades paid for the right to put their extra supplies in one of the wagons, and then they equipped themselves with great care. They bought four good horses, four fine rifles, made by the famous Dickson, of Louisville, four double-barreled pistols of long range, knives and hatchets, a large quantity of ammunition, an extra suit apiece of stout deerskin, four small pocket compasses, and many other things which seem trifles in a town, but which are important in the wilderness.

It took them but a few days to make their purchases, but it was at least three weeks before the train started. The Mexicans, meanwhile, had stayed about a week at the chief hotel, and then had left on a steamer for their own country. Phil heard that there had been much talk about the high-handed manner of young Armijo, and that he had been extremely disagreeable to all about him. The older man, Zucorra, who was milder and more diplomatic, had sought to restrain him, but with no success. It was a relief when they were gone.

The boy, still curious about the Comanche, looked for him once more on the levee. More hogsheads of tobacco and sugar were there, but the Indian was not leaning against any of them. At last he found him in one of the inns or taverns frequented by sailors and roustabouts, a rough place at any time, and crowded then with men from the ships and boats. The Indian was sitting in a corner, huddled down in a chair, in much the same attitude of sloth and indifference that he had shown when leaning against the hogshead. Phil saw that when he stood up he would be a tall man, and his figure, if it were not flabby, would be powerful.

Phil was intensely interested. The Indian had always appealed to his romantic imagination, and, now that he saw one of the race close at hand, he wished to learn more. He sat down near the man, and, not knowing what else to say, remarked that it was a fine day. The Comanche raised his head a little, and bent upon Phil a look like that he had given to Breakstone. It was a piercing glance, full of anger and hatred. Then the glowing eyes were veiled, and his head dropped back on his arms. He did not utter a word in reply.

The innkeeper, who had noticed the brief incident, laughed.

"Don't you try to get up a conversation with Black Panther, my boy," he said. "He ain't what you would call a pow'ful talker."

"No, I suppose he wouldn't talk anybody to death," said Phil. "What is he?"

"He's a tame Comanche, an' he's been loafing around New Orleans for two or three months—learnin' the white man's vices, 'specially the drinkin' of fire water, which he keeps first on the list. You can see what it's done for him—taken all the pith right out of him, same as you would take it out of a length of elder to make a pop gun. I reckon New Orleans ain't no place for an Indian. Hello, what's the matter with Black Panther?"

The Indian uttered a short, savage exclamation that startled every one in the place, and sprang to his feet. His long coal black hair was thrown back from his face, and he seemed to be alive in every fiber. The eyes were like two points of fire.

THE MEETING OF THE FOUR

"Black Panther was a great warrior and a chief," he said. "He has been a dog in the white man's town, and he has burned his brain with fire water until it is like that of a little child. But he will be a great warrior and a chief again. Now, I go."

He gathered a tattered old blanket around his shoulders, and, holding himself erect, stalked in savage dignity out of the place.

"Now, what in thunder did he mean?" exclaimed the astonished innkeeper.

"I think he meant just what he said," replied Phil. "He is going away from New Orleans. He certainly looked it."

So far as he knew, the assertion was true, because, as long as he remained in the city, he neither saw nor heard anything further of the Comanche. But the time for his own departure was soon at hand, and in the excitement of it he forgot all about the Comanche.

CHAPTER II

THE MARCH OF THE TRAIN

THE train made an imposing appearance with its sixty wagons and its horsemen, numerous and well armed. It was commanded by a middle-aged trader of experience, Thomas Woodfall, who had already made several trips to Sante Fé, and the hopes of all were high. They carried, among other things, goods that the señoras and señoritas of Santa Fé would be eager to buy, and much gain might be obtained. But every one of the four who rode so closely together thought most in his heart of that for which he sought, and in no instance was the object of search the same.

But they were cheerful. Whatever were past griefs or whatever might be those to come, the present was propitious and fair. The Southern spring was not yet advanced far enough to drive the cool tang out of the air by daylight, while at night fires were needed. It rained but little, and they marched steadily on through crisp sunshine.

"I trust that the good Sir Roland is pleased," said Bill Breakstone to Phil. "Fresh air in the lungs of youth produces exhilaration."

"It's fine," said Phil, with emphasis.

"But we may yet come to our Pass of Roncesvalles. Bethink you of that, Sir Roland. They say that it's an ill wind that blows nobody good, and I say that it's a good wind that blows nobody ill. The rain will rain, the snow will snow, the wind will blow, and what will poor rabbit do then?"

THE MARCH OF THE TRAIN

"Get into his little nest, cover himself up warm and dry, and wait until it passes," replied Phil.

"Right, Master Philip. Go up to the head of the class," said Bill Breakstone in his usual joyous tones— Phil always thought that Bill had the cheeriest voice in the world—"I'm glad to see you taking thought for the future. Now our good friend Hans, here, would not have made such an apt reply."

"Perhaps not, and I do not mind your saying so, Herr Bill Breakstone," said Arenberg, smiling broadly. "No harm iss done where none iss meant."

"A fit answer from a loyal representative of the Hohenstauffens, the Hohenzollerns, and the Katzenellenbogens," chanted Bill Breakstone.

"Ah, Herr Breakstone, it iss that you are one happy man," said Arenberg. "I wonder that you go to find something, when you have the joy of living anywhere."

"But I do go to find something," said Breakstone, suddenly becoming grave. Phil noticed that he puckered up his eyes and gazed far into the West, as if he would see already that for which he sought.

They traveled for several days among plantations in a low damp country, and then they passed suddenly beyond the line of cultivation into a drier region of low hills and small prairies. Phil was pleased with the change. If they were going into the wilderness, he was anxious to reach it as soon as possible, and this, beyond a doubt, was the edge of the unknown. The first night that he heard the scream of a panther in the woods he felt that they were leaving all civilization behind, and that, save for the train, the world of men was blotted out.

Yet it was very pleasant as long as the weather remained dry, and the early spring was certainly doing its best. It was a succession of crisp days and cool nights, and Phil liked the steady advance by day through new lands, and the rest in the evening, when they built fires for the cooking and to fend off the chill. They usually drew the wagons up in a circle in one of the little prairies, and then went to the forest near by for wood that belonged to whomsoever took it. Phil and Bill Breakstone were always active in this work.

"It gives me an appetite for supper," said Breakstone. "I would have you to know, Sir Philip of the Forest, that sitting long hours on a horse which carries me luxuriously along, the horse doing all the work and I doing none, tends to laziness and fat. I need this exercise to put me in proper trim for the luscious repast that awaits us."

"I don't need anything to whet my appetite," replied Phil, as he laughed. "To tell you the truth, Bill, I'm always hungry."

"Do not grieve or have fears for the larder, Sir Philip of the Hungry Countenance. There is an abundance of food in the wagons, and we also shall soon be in a good game country. Unless my eye and hand have lost their cunning, a fat deer shall speedily be roasting over the coals."

The four kept close together, and they usually gathered around the fire at which Thomas Woodfall, the leader, sat. Woodfall had shown a decided respect and liking for Middleton, and, following the custom which Breakstone had established, always addressed him as Cap, short for Captain. Phil and Breakstone had been particularly active gathering wood that evening, and it had been Phil's task and pleasure, when it was all put in a heap, to light it. Now he was watching the little flames grow into big ones, and the yellow light turn to blazing red. He listened, also, as the flames hissed a little before the wind, and the dry boughs snapped and crackled under the fiery torch. Middleton regarded him with kindly approval.

"A good boy," he said to Woodfall. "A lad with fine instincts and a brave spirit."

"And a mighty handy one, too," said Woodfall.

THE MARCH OF THE TRAIN

"I've noticed how he works. He's as big and strong as a man, and I never saw anybody else who was just prized down like a hogshead of tobacco, crowded full of zeal."

"I think it likely he will need it all before our journey is over," said Middleton.

"It's probable," repeated Woodfall, "but I'll ask you, Cap, not to speak it. It may be that this expedition was begun at the wrong time. I had heard, and the owners had heard, that the troubles with Mexico were quieting down, but it seems that, instead of doing so, they are getting livelier."

"I shall certainly say nothing about it to our people here," replied Middleton. "Cheerful hearts are the best, and we may have trouble with neither Mexicans nor Indians."

Phil himself was not thinking at that moment of either yellow or red foes. His fire had grown into a mighty pyramid, and, as the dead wood burned fast, it soon sank down into a great mass of glowing coals. Then he, Breakstone, and Arenberg boiled coffee in big iron pots, and cooked bread and many slices of bacon. The night was cool and nipping, but the coals threw out an abundance of heat. A delicious aroma arose and spread far. Everybody came forward with tin cup and tin plate, and helped himself. Phil took his filled plate in one hand, his filled cup in the other, and sat down on a fallen log with Breakstone and Arenberg.

"In my time, and as an ornament to the stage," said Bill Breakstone, "I have eaten some bountiful repasts. I have feasted as a prince, a duke, or some other lordling. I have been the wrestler in the Forest of Arden with *Rosalind* and *Celia*. I have had my head deep in the mug of sack, as *Sir John Falstaff*, but most of those magnificent repasts depended largely upon the imagination. Here I am neither prince nor duke, but the food is real, and the air is so good that one might even bite a chip with a certain pleasure. Excuse me, Sir Philip of the Forest, while I even drain the coffee-cup."

He took it all down at one draught, and a beatific glow overspread his face. Arenberg regarded him with admiration.

"Ach, Mein Herr Breakstone, but you are one cheerful man!" he said. "You never do any harm, because none iss meant. When you drink the coffee you make me think of the German in the old country drinking beer, and you like it as well."

"I snatch the joys of the flying day, or, rather, night, and think not of the ills of the morrow," replied Breakstone. "Somebody somewhere said something like that, and, whoever he was, he was a good talker. To-morrow, Phil, I think I may get a chance to show you how to shoot a deer."

"I hope so," said Phil eagerly. He, too, was luxuriating, and he was fully as cheerful as Bill Breakstone. The great beds of coal threw a warm, luminous glow over all the circle enveloped by the wagons. Everybody ate and felt good. The pleasant hum of pleasant talk arose. Outside the wagons the tethered horses cropped the short young grass, and they, too, were content. Not far away the forest of magnolia, poplar, and many kinds of oak rustled before the slight wind, and the note that came from it was also of content.

Phil, after he had eaten and drunk all that he wished, and it was much, lay on the ground with his back against the log and listened to the talk. He heard wonderful tales of adventure in the West Indies and on the South American coast, of fights in Mexico and Texas, when the little bands of Texans won their independence, of encounters with raiding Comanches, and of strange stone ruins left by vanished races in the deserts of the Far West. He was fascinated as he listened. The spirit of romance was developed strongly within him. It was, indeed, a most adventurous search upon which he was embarked,

THE MARCH OF THE TRAIN

and this spirit, strong, enduring, hardened to meet all things, was what he needed most.

As the fires died down, and the warmth decreased, he wrapped his blanket around himself, and now and then dozed a little. But he still felt very content. It seemed to him that it was uncommon fortune to have joined such an expedition, and it was a good omen. He must succeed in his great search.

"Well, Sir Roland, what is it?" said Bill Breakstone at last. "Do you want to sleep in the wagon or on the ground here? The good Knight Orlando, who for the present is myself, means to choose the ground."

"No stuffy wagon for me on a night like this," rejoined Phil sleepily. "I am going to sleep just where I lie."

He settled back more comfortably, put his arm under his head, and in a few moments was in the deep, dreamless sleep of youth and health. Bill Breakstone quickly followed him to that pleasant land of Nowhere. Then Arenberg and the Captain were soon entering the same region. The fires sank lower and lower, the sound of breathing from many men arose, the horses outside became quiet, and peace settled over the wilderness camp.

Phil slept far into the night, he never knew how far, but he believed it was about half way between midnight and morning. When he awoke it was very dark, and there was no noise but that of the breathing men and the rustling wind. Just why he, a sound sleeper, had awakened at that time he could not say. But he had eaten largely, and he was conscious of thirst, a thirst that could be quenched easily at a little spring in the wood.

The boy rose, letting his blanket drop to the ground, and glanced over the sleeping camp. Despite the darkness, he saw the forms of recumbent men, and some coals that yet glimmered faintly. Around them was the dark circling line of the wagons. No regular watch was kept.

as they were yet far from dangerous country, and, passing between two of the wagons, Phil went toward the spring, which was about three hundred yards away.

It was a nice cold spring, rising at the base of a rock, and running away in a tiny stream among the poplars. Phil knelt and drank, and then sat upon an upthrust root. The desire for sleep had left him, and his mind turned upon his great search. He took the paper from the inside pocket of his coat, unfolded it, and smoothed it out with his fingers. It was too dark for him to read it, but he held it there a little while, then folded it up again, and returned it to its resting place. He was about to rise again and return to the camp, but something moved in the thicket. It might have been a lizard, or it might have been the wind, but he was sure it was neither. The sound was wholly out of harmony with the note of the night.

Phil remained sitting on the upthrust root, but leaned against the trunk to which the root belonged. His figure blended darkly against the bark. Only an eye of uncommon acuteness would note him. The slight stirring, so much out of tune with all the wilderness noises, came again, and, despite his strength and will, both of which were great, Phil felt ice pass along his spine, and his hair rose slightly. That uncanny hour at which evil deeds happen held him in its spell. But he did not move, except for the slipping of his hand to the pistol in his belt, and he waited.

Slowly a dark face formed itself in the bushes, and beneath it was the faint outline of a human figure. The face was malignant and cruel, a reddish copper in color, with a sharp, strong chin, high cheek-bones, and black glowing eyes. These eyes were bent in a fierce gaze upon the circle of wagons. They did not turn in Phil's direction at all, but the face held him fascinated.

It seemed to Phil that he had seen that countenance before, and as he gazed he remembered. It was surely

THE MARCH OF THE TRAIN

that of Black Panther, the Comanche, but what a startling change. The crouching, fuddled lump of a man in tattered clothes, whom he had seen in New Orleans, had been transformed when the breath of the wilderness poured into his lungs. He fitted thoroughly into this dark and weird scene, and the hair on Phil's head rose a little more. Then the head, and the figure with it, suddenly melted away and were gone. There was no strange stirring in the thicket, nothing that was not in accord with the night.

The ice left Phil's spine, the hair lay down peacefully once more on his head, and his hand moved away from the pistol at his belt. It was like a dream in the dark, the sudden appearance of that Medusa head in the bushes, and he was impressed with all the weight of conviction that it was an omen of bad days to come. The wind whispered it, and the quiver in his blood answered. But the men in the train might laugh at him if he told that he had merely seen an Indian's face in the bushes. The thing itself would be slight enough in the telling, and he did not wish to be ridiculed as a boy whose fears had painted a picture of that which was not. But he walked warily back, and he was glad enough when he repassed between two of the wagons, and resumed his old place. Middleton, Arenberg, and Bill Breakstone all slept soundly, and Phil, wrapped in his blanket, sought to imitate them. But he could not. He lay there thinking until the low band of scarlet in the east foreshadowed the day. He rose and looked once more over the camp. The last coal had died, and the dark forms, wrapped in their blankets, looked chill and cold. But the red dawn was advancing, and warmth came with it. One by one the men awoke. The horses stirred. Phil stood up and stretched his arms. Middleton, Bill Breakstone, and Arenberg awoke. They had slept soundly and pleasantly all through the night.

"'Tis a fine couch, this Mother Earth," said Bill

Breakstone, "finer than cloth of gold, if it be not raining or snowing, or the winds be not nipping. Then, in such event, I should take the cloth of gold, with a snug tent over it."

"I have slept well, and I awake strong and refreshed," said Arenberg simply. "It iss all I ask of a night."

"I have not slept well," said Phil, "at least I did not during the latter part of the night."

There was a certain significance in his tone, and the others looked at him. Only they were near, and Phil said in a low tone:

"I awoke in the night, and I was restless. I walked down to the spring for a drink, and I saw a face in the bushes, the face of a man who was watching us."

"Ah!" said Middleton, a single monosyllable, long drawn. But his tone expressed interest, not surprise. He looked at the boy as if he expected to hear more.

"I saw the face clearly," continued Phil. "It was changed, wonderfully changed in expression, but I knew it. I could not be mistaken. It was that Comanche, called Black Panther, whom we saw in New Orleans. He was dirty and degraded there, but he did not seem so last night."

"I am glad that you told this, Phil," said Middleton. "It was a lucky chance that awakened you and sent you to the spring."

"Once I thought I would not speak of it at all," said the boy. "I was afraid they would say it was only a dream or a creation of my fancy."

"I'm sure that you really saw it," said Middleton, "and I will speak with Mr. Woodfall. The time has come when we must be cautious."

The camp was now wholly awake, and the men began to light the fires anew, and take their breakfasts. Middleton talked with Mr. Woodfall, and, as the latter kept it no secret, the news soon spread throughout the train. Philip Bedford, prowling about in the dark, had seen an

THE MARCH OF THE TRAIN

Indian in the woods near by, an Indian who seemed to be watching them.

The news was variously received, because there were many kinds of men in this train. Some took it seriously; others were disposed to laugh, and to hint, as Phil had feared, that it was fancy or a dream; and others cared nothing about it. What was a single wandering warrior to them? But the leader compelled a more careful advance. Scouts were sent ahead, and others rode on the flanks. Phil and his comrades shared in this duty, and that very day he and Bill Breakstone and Arenberg were among those who rode ahead.

It was not an easy duty, because they were now in thick forest, with much swampy ground about. Dark funereal cypresses abounded in the marshy soil, and gloomy moss hung from the live oaks. A deer sprang up, and Phil pulled down his rifle, but Breakstone would not let him shoot.

"Not now, Phil," he said. "We must not shoot at chance game when we are scouting. My talk may not sound like it, but I know something of wilderness life. One can never be too cautious, whether on the plains or in the woods. Things may happen. Wait for them. As the poet saith, 'One crowded hour of glorious life is worth a world without a name.'"

"Say that again," said Arenberg.

"One crowded hour of glorious life is worth a world without a name."

"It sounds good. It iss good. I will remember it," said the German.

But as two or three days passed with no sign of trouble, the face that Phil had seen in the bushes was forgotten or ignored. It was a light-hearted crowd, used to wild life and adventure, and these men, drawn from different parts of the globe, occupied with to-day, took little thought of to-morrow's dangers. The weather remained beautiful. Days and nights were dry, and they were again on good firm earth, which made the way of the wagons easy. Phil, instructed by Bill Breakstone, stalked and shot a deer, a fine, fat buck, which gave a slice for everybody in the train, and which brought him compliments. In fact, he was already a general favorite, and he did not mind when they jested now and then about the face in the bushes, and told him that he was a seer of visions. He was rapidly becoming an adept in the forest life, to which he took naturally, and in Bill Breakstone he had no mean tutor. Breakstone soon showed that he was a scout and trailer of the first quality, although he did not explain why he had spent so many years in the wilds.

"It's partly gift, and partly training, Sir Philip of the Youthful Countenance and of the Good Blue Eye," he said. "If you just teach yourself to see everything and to hear everything about you, and never forget it, you've got most of the lesson. And you, Phil, with good eyes, good ears, a quick mind, and a willing heart, ought to come fast toward the head of the class."

Phil flushed with pleasure. In the task that he had set for himself he greatly needed forest lore, and it was a keen satisfaction to know that he was acquiring it. He redoubled his efforts. He always noted carefully the country through which they passed, the configuration of the earth, and the various kinds of trees and bushes. At night he would often ask Bill Breakstone to question him, and from his superior knowledge and longer training to point out a mistake whenever he might make it. Bill was a severe teacher, and he criticised freely whenever Phil was wrong. But he admitted that his pupil was making progress. Arenberg was smoking his pipe at one of their sittings, and, taking it out of his mouth, he remarked:

"No harm iss done where none iss meant. Now what I wish to ask you, Herr Breakstone, and you, young Herr Philip, would you remember all your lessons if you were on foot on the prairie, unarmed, and a wild Comanche warrior were riding at you, ready to run his lance through you?"

"I don't know," replied Phil frankly, "but I hope such a time will never come."

"That's the rub," said Arenberg meditatively. "It iss good to know all the rules, to do all you can before, but it iss better to think fast, and act right when the great emergency comes. It iss only then that you are of the first class. I say so, and I say so because I know."

Only Phil noticed the faint tone of sadness with which his words ended, and he glanced quickly at the German. But Arenberg's face expressed nothing. Once more he was pulling calmly at his pipe. Bill Breakstone gave his words hearty indorsement.

"You're right," he said. "The Grand Duke of Germany speaks the truth. I've embodied that piece of wisdom in a little poem, which I will quote to you:

> "You may lead a horse to the water,
> But you cannot make him drink.
> You may stuff a man with knowledge,
> But you cannot make him think.

"Part of that is borrowed, and part of it is original, but, combining the two parts, I think it is a little masterpiece."

Arenberg took out his pipe again, and regarded Bill Breakstone with admiration.

"It iss one great man, this Herr Bill Breakstone," he said. "He makes poetry and tells the truth at the same time."

"Thanks, most puissant lord," said Breakstone, "and now, the lesson being over, Phil, I think we might all of us go to sleep and knit up a few raveled sleeves of care."

"We might take to the wagon," said Middleton. "If I'm any judge of weather, Phil, the beautiful spell that we've had is coming to an end."

THE QUEST OF THE FOUR

"You're right, Cap," said Breakstone. "I noticed that when the sun set to-day it looked redder than usual through a cloud of mist, and that means rain. Therefore, *Orlando* deserts his little Forest of Arden, and betakes himself to the shelter of the curved canvass."

Phil deemed it wise to imitate him, and the four found places in the large wagon among their goods, where they had the shelter of the canvas roof, although the cover was open at either end to allow the clean sweep of the air. Phil, as usual, slept well. Five minutes was about all he needed for the preparatory stage, and tonight was no exception. But he awoke again in the middle of the night. Now he knew full well the cause. Low thunder was rumbling far off at the edge of the earth, and a stroke of lightning made him wink his sleepy eyes. Then came a rush of cold air, and after it the rain. The big drops rattled on the curving canvas roof, but they could not penetrate the thick cloth. Phil raised himself a little, and looked out at the open ends, but he saw only darkness.

Meanwhile the rain increased and beat harder upon the roof, which shed it like shingles. Phil drew his blanket up to his chin, rested his head and shoulders a little more easily against a bag of meal, and never had a greater sense of luxury in his life. The beat of the rain on the canvas was iike the patter of the rain on the roof of the old home, when he was a little boy and lay snug under the eaves. He had the same pleasant sense of warmth and shelter now. The storm might beat about him, but it could not touch him. He heard the even breathing of his comrades, who had not awakened. He heard the low thunder still grumbling far off in the southwest, and the lightning came again at intervals, but he sank gently back to slumber.

When he awoke the next morning the rain was still falling, and the whole world was a sodden gray. The air, too, was full of raw chill, despite the southern lati-

THE MARCH OF THE TRAIN

tude, and Phil shivered. It was his first impulse to draw the blanket more tightly, but he resolutely put the impulse down. He threw the blanket aside, slipped on his coat and boots, the only apparel that he had removed for the night's rest, and sprang out into the rain, leaving his comrade still asleep.

Not many of the men were yet up, and Phil went at once into the forest in search of fallen wood, which was always abundant. It was not a pleasant task. For the first time he felt the work hard and disagreeable. Mists and vapors were rising from the wet earth, and the sun did not show. The rain came down steadily, and it was cold to the touch. It soaked through the boy's clothing, but he stuck to his task, and brought in the dead wood by the armful. At the third load he met Bill Breakstone, who hailed him cheerily.

"Well, you do make me ashamed of myself, Sir Knight of the Dripping Forest," he said. "When we awoke and found you already up and at work, we concluded that it was time for us to imitate so good an example. Ugh, how cold this rain is, and we five hundred miles from an umbrella!"

Phil was compelled to laugh, and then the laugh made him feel better. But it was a morning that might well oppress the bravest. The wet wood was lighted with extreme difficulty, and then it smoked greatly under the rain. It was hard to do the cooking, and breakfast was not satisfying. But Phil refused to make any complaint. With the rain in his face, he spoke cheerfully of sunshine and warm dry plains.

"We ought to strike the plains of Texas to-morrow or the next day," said Bill Breakstone. "I've been through this region before, and I don't think I'm mistaken. Then we'll get out of this. If it's a long lane that has no turning, it's one just as long that has no end."

They started late, and deep depression hung over the train. The men no longer sang or made jokes at the expense of one another, but crouched upon their horses or the wagon seats, and maintained a sullen silence. Phil was on horseback, but he dried himself at one of the fires, and with the blanket wrapped around his body he was now fairly well protected. It was hard to maintain a pleasant face, but he did it, and Middleton, whom all now usually called Cap, looked his approval.

They advanced very slowly through thickets and across small streams, with mists and vapors so dense that they could see but little ahead. They did not make more than seven or eight miles that day, and, wet and miserable, they camped for the night. The guard was still maintained, and Phil was on duty that night until twelve. When midnight came he crawled into the wagon, depressed and thoroughly exhausted. But he slept well, and the next morning the rain was over. The mists and vapors were gone, and a beautiful sun was shining. All of Phil's good spirits came back as he sprang out of the wagon and looked at the drying earth.

The whole camp was transformed. The cooking fires burned ruddily and with a merry crackle. The men sang their little songs and made their little jokes. They told one another joyously that they would be out of the forest soon and upon the open prairies. They would be in Texas—Texas, that wonderful land of mystery and charm; Texas, already famous for the Alamo and San Jacinto. The fact that this Texas was filled with dangers took nothing from the glow at their hearts. Phil shared in the general enthusiasm, and cried with the others, "Ho for Texas!"

Arenberg's face became very grave.

"Do not be carried away with the high feelings that run to the head," he said. "No harm iss done where none iss meant, but it iss a long road across Texas, and there iss no mile of it which does not have its dangers. Who should know better than I?"

"You speak the truth," said Middleton. "I often

THE MARCH OF THE TRAIN

think of that Comanche, Black Panther, whose face Phil saw in the thicket."

"You are right to speak of it," said Bill Breakstone. "I have been in the West. I have spent years there. I have been in places that no other white man has ever seen, and just when you think this West, beyond the white man's frontier, is most peaceful, then it is most dangerous. *Hamlet*, Prince of Denmark, was a dreamy kind of fellow, but when the time came he was a holy terror."

Phil was impressed, but in a little while it seemed to him that it could scarcely be so. The threat contained in Black Panther's face was fading fast from his mind, and danger seemed to him very far. His exuberance of spirit was heightened by the easy journey that they now had through a forest without any undergrowth. The wagons rolled easily over short, young grass, and the thick boughs of the trees overhead protected them from the sun.

"Do you know the country, Bill?" asked Middleton.

"I think so," replied Breakstone. "Unless I'm mightily mistaken, and I don't think I am, this forest ends in four or five miles. Then we come right out on the genuine Texas plain, rolling straight away for hundreds of miles. I think I'll take Phil here and ride forward and see if I'm not right. Come, Phil!"

The two galloped away straight toward the West, and, as the forest offered no difficulties, they were not compelled to check their speed. But in less than an hour Breakstone, who was in advance, pulled his horse back sharply, and Phil did the same.

"Look, Phil!" exclaimed Breakstone, making a wide sweep with his hands, while face and eyes were glowing, "See, it is Texas!"

Phil looked. None could have been more eager than he was. The hill seemed to drop down before them sheer, like a cliff, but beyond lay a great gray-green waving sea, an expanse of earth that passed under the horizon, and that seemed to have no limit. It was treeless, and the young grass had touched the gray of winter with fresh green.

"The great plains!" exclaimed Phil. He felt an intense thrill. He had at last reached the edge of this vast region of mystery, and to-morrow they would enter it.

"Yes, the great plains," said Bill Breakstone. "And down here, I think, is where our wagons will have to pass. He turned to the left and followed a gentle slope that led to the edge of the plains. Thus, by an easy descent, they left the forest, but when they turned back Phil's eye was caught by a glittering object:

"Look, Bill!" he exclaimed. "See the arrow! What does it mean?"

An arrow with a deeply feathered shaft had been planted deep in an oak tree. Evidently it had been fired from a bow by some one standing on the plain, and it was equally evident that a powerful hand had drawn the string. It stood out straight and stark as if it would stay there forever. Bill Breakstone rode up to it and examined it critically.

"It's a Comanche arrow, Phil," he said, "and, between you and me, I think it means something:

"An arrow I see
Stuck in a tree,
But what it does mean
Has not yet been seen—

"Especially when it's coupled with the fact that you saw Black Panther's face in the thicket. I may have an imaginative mind, Sir Philip of the Forest, soon to be Sir Philip of the Plain, but this arrow I take to be our first warning. It tells us to turn back, and it may have been fired by Black Panther himself, late Knight of the Levee and of Strong Drink."

"Will we turn back?" asked Phil somewhat anxiously.

THE MARCH OF THE TRAIN

Bill Breakstone laughed scornfully.

"Do you think a crowd like ours would turn back for a sign?" he asked. "Why, Phil, that arrow, if it is meant as a threat, is the very thing to draw them on. It would make them anxious to go ahead and meet those who say they must stop. If they were not that kind of men, they wouldn't be here."

"I suppose so," said Phil. "I, for one, would not want to turn back."

He rode up to the tree, took the arrow by the shaft, and pulled with all his might. He was a strong youth, but he could not loosen it. Unless broken off, it was to stay there, a sign that a Comanche warning had been given.

"I knew you couldn't move it," said Bill Breakstone. "The Indians have short bows, and you wouldn't think they could get so much power with them, but they do. It's no uncommon thing for a buck at close range to send an arrow clear through a big bull buffalo, and it takes powerful speed to do that."

They rode back, met the advancing line of wagons, and told what they had seen, to which the men themselves, as they came to the edge of the prairie, were able to bear witness. Yet they were not greatly impressed. Those who believed that it meant a challenge gayly accepted it as Breakstone had predicted.

"Let the Comanches attack, if they will," they said, shaking their rifles. Even the face of the quiet Middleton kindled.

"It's a good spirit our men show," he said to the three who were his chosen comrades, "but I knew that they would never turn back because of an Indian threat."

The train advanced slowly down into the plain, and then began its march across the vast, grayish-green expanse. The traveling was very easy here, and they made seven or eight miles over the rolling earth before they stopped at sunset. Phil, looking back, could still see the dark line of the hilly country and the forest, but before him the prairie rolled away, more than ever, as the twilight came, like an unknown sea.

The camp was beside a shallow stream running between low banks. They built their fires of cottonwood and stunted oaks that grew on either side, and then Phil saw the darkness suddenly fall like the fall of a great blanket over the plains. With the night came a low, moaning sound which Bill Breakstone told him was merely the wind blowing a thousand miles without a break.

Phil took his turn at guard duty the latter half of that night, walking about at some distance from the camp, now and then meeting his comrades on the same duty, and exchanging a word or two. It was very dark, and the other sentinels were not in the best of humor, thinking there was little need for such a watch, and Phil by and by confined himself strictly to his own territory.

Although his eyes grew used to the darkness, it was so heavy that they could not penetrate it far, and he extended his beat a little farther from the camp. He thought once that he heard a light sound, as of footsteps, perhaps those of a horse, and in order to be certain, remembering an old method, he lay down and put his ear to the ground. Then he was quite sure that he heard a sound very much like the tread of hoofs, but in a moment or two it ceased. He rose, shaking his head doubtfully, and advanced a little farther. He neither saw nor heard anything more, and he became convinced that the footsteps had been those of some wild animal. Perhaps a lone buffalo, an outlaw from the herd, had been wandering about, and had turned away when the human odor met his nostrils.

He returned toward the camp, and something cold passed his face. There was a slight whistling sound directly in his ear, and he sprang to one side, as if he had narrowly missed the fangs of a rattlesnake. He

THE MARCH OF THE TRAIN

heard almost in the same instant a slight, thudding sound directly in front of him, and he knew instinctively what had made it. He ran forward, and there was an arrow sticking half its length in the ground. The impulse of caution succeeded that of curiosity. Remembering Bill Breakstone's teachings, he threw himself flat upon the ground, letting his figure blend with the darkness, and lay there, perfectly still. But no other arrow came. Nothing stirred. He could not make out among the shadows anything that resembled a human figure, although his eyes were good and were now trained to the work of a sentinel. Once when he put his ear to the earth he thought he heard the faint beat of retreating hoofs, but the sound was so brief and so far away that he was not sure.

Phil felt shivers, more after he lay down than when the arrow passed his cheek. It was the first time that a deadly weapon or missile had passed so close to him, fired perhaps with the intent of slaying him, and no boy could pass through such an experience without quivers and an icy feeling along the spine.

But when he lay still awhile and could not detect the presence of any enemy, he rose and examined the arrow again. There was enough light for him to see that the feathered shaft was exactly like that of the arrow they had found in the tree.

He pulled the weapon out of the ground and examined it with care. It had a triangular head of iron, with extremely sharp edges, and he shuddered again. If it had struck him, it would have gone through him as Bill Breakstone said the Comanche arrows sometimes went entirely through the body of a buffalo.

He took the arrow at once to the camp, and showed it to the men who were on guard there, telling how this feathered messenger—and he could not doubt that it was a messenger—had come. Woodfall and Middleton were awakened, and both looked serious. It could not be any play of fancy on the part of an imaginative boy. Here was the arrow to speak for itself.

"It must have been the deed of a daring Comanche," said Middleton with conviction. "Perhaps he did not intend to kill Phil, and I am sure that this arrow, like the first, was intended as a threat."

"Then it's wasted, just as others will be," said Woodfall. "My men do not fear Comanches."

"I know that," said Middleton. "It is a strong train, but we must realize, Mr. Woodfall, that the Comanches are numerous and powerful. We must make every preparation, all must stay close by the train, and there must be a strict night watch."

He spoke in a tone of authority, but it fitted so well upon him, and seemed so natural that Woodfall did not resent it. On the contrary, he nodded, and then added his emphatic acquiescence in words.

"You are surely right," he said. "We must tighten up everything."

This little conference was held beside some coals of a cooking fire that had not yet died, and Phil was permitted to stand by and listen, as it was he who had brought in the significant arrow. The coals did not give much light, and the men were half in shadow, but the boy was impressed anew by the decision and firmness shown by Middleton. He seemed to have an absolutely clear mind, and to know exactly what he wanted. Phil wondered once more what a man of that type might be seeking in the vast and vague West.

"I'll double the guard," said Woodfall, "and no man shall go out of sight of the train. Now, Bedford, my boy, you might go to sleep, as you have done your part of a night's work."

Phil lay down, and, despite the arrow so vivid in memory, he slept until day.

CHAPTER III

AT THE FORD

AS Phil had foreseen, his latest story of warning found universal credence in the camp, as the arrow was here, visible to all, and it was passed from hand to hand. He was compelled to tell many times how it had whizzed by his face, and how he had found it afterward sticking in the earth. All the fighting qualities of the train rose. Many hoped that the Comanches would make good the threat, because threat it must be, and attack. The Indians would get all they wanted and plenty more.

"The Comanche arrow has been shot,
For us it has no terror;
He can attack our train or not,
If he does, it's his error,"

chanted Bill Breakstone in a mellow voice, and a dozen men took up the refrain: "He can attack our train or not, if he does, it's his error."

The drivers cracked their whips, the wagons, in a double line, moved slowly on over the gray-green plains. A strong band of scouts preceded it, and another, equally as strong, formed the rear-guard. Horsemen armed with rifle and pistol rode on either flank. The sun shone, and a crisp wind blew. Mellow snatches of song floated away over the swells. All was courage and confidence. Deeper and deeper they went into the great plains, and the line of hills and forest behind them became dimmer and dimmer. They saw both buffalo and antelope grazing, a mile or two away, and there was much grumbling because Woodfall would not let any of the marksmen go in pursuit. Here was game and fresh meat to be had for the taking, they said, but Woodfall, at the urgent insistence of Middleton, was inflexible. Men who wandered from the main body even a short distance might never come back again. It had happened too often on former expeditions.

> "Our leader's right.
> A luckless wight
> Trusting his might
> Might find a fight,
> And then good night,"

chanted Bill Breakstone, and he added triumphantly:

"That's surely good poetry, Phil! Five lines all rhyming together, when most poets have trouble to make two rhyme. But, as I have said before, these plains that look so quiet and lonely have their dangers. We must pass by the buffalo, the deer, and the antelope, unless we go after them in strong parties. Ah, look there! What is that?"

The head of the train was just topping a swell, and beyond the dip that followed was another swell, rather higher than usual, and upon the utmost crest of the second swell sat an Indian on his horse, Indian and horse alike motionless, but facing the train with a fixed gaze. The Indian was large, with powerful shoulders and chest, and with an erect head and an eagle beak. He was of a bright copper color. His lips were thin, his eyes black, and he had no beard. His long back hair fell down on his back and was ornamented with silver coins and beads. He wore deerskin leggins and moccasins, sewed with beads, and a blue cloth around his loins. The rest of his body was naked and the great muscles could be seen.

The warrior carried in his right hand a bow about one half the length of the old English long bow, made of the tough bois d'arc or osage orange, strengthened and rein-

AT THE FORD

forced with sinews of deer wrapped firmly about it. The cord of the bow was also of deer sinews. Over his shoulder was a quiver filled with arrows about twenty inches in length, feathered and with barbs of triangular iron. On his left arm he carried a circular shield made of two thicknesses of hard, undressed buffalo hide, separated by an inch of space tightly packed with hair. His shield was fastened by two bands in such a manner that it would not interfere with the use of the arm, and it was so hard that it would often turn a rifle shot. Hanging at his horse's mane was a war club which had been made by bending a withe around a hard stone, weighing about two pounds, and with a groove in it. Its handle of wood, about fourteen inches in length, was bound with buffalo hide.

Apparently the warrior carried no firearms, using only the ancient weapons of his tribe. His horse was a magnificent coal black, far larger than the ordinary Indian pony, and he stood with his neck arched as if he were proud of his owner. The Indian's gaze and manner were haughty and defiant. It was obvious to every one, and a low murmur ran among the men of the train. Phil recognized the warrior instantly. It was Black Panther, no longer the sodden haunter of the levee in the white man's town, but a great chief on his native plains. Phil looked at Middleton, who nodded.

"Yes," he said, "I know him. He has, of course, been watching us, and knows every mile of our march. Unless I am greatly mistaken, Phil, this is the third warning."

Woodfall had ridden up by the side of Middleton, and the latter said that Black Panther would probably speak with them.

"Then," said Woodfall, "you and I, Mr. Middleton, will ride forward and see what he has to say."

Phil begged to be allowed to go, too, and they consented. Woodfall hoisted a piece of white cloth on the end of his rifle, and the Indian raised his shield in a gesture of understanding. Then the three rode forward. The whole of the wagon train was massed on the swell behind them, and scores of eyes were watching intently for every detail that might happen.

The Indian, after the affirmative gesture with the shield, did not move, but he sat erect and motionless like a great bronze equestrian statue. The blazing sunlight beat down upon horse and man. Every line of the warrior's face was revealed—the high cheek-bone, the massive jaw, the pointed chin, and, as Phil drew nearer, the expression of hate and defiance that was the dominant note of his countenance. Truly, this Black Panther of the slums had undergone a prairie change, a wonderful change that was complete.

Woodfall, Middleton, and Phil rode slowly up the second swell, and approached the chief, for such they could not doubt now that he was. Still he did not move, but sat upon his horse, gravely regarding them. Phil was quite sure that Black Panther remembered him, but he was not sure that he would admit it.

"You wish to speak with us," said Middleton, who in such a moment naturally assumed the position of leader.

"To give you a message," replied Black Panther in good English. "I have given you two messages already, and this is the third."

"The arrows," said Middleton.

"Yes, the Comanche arrows," continued the chief. "I thought that the white men would read the signs, and perhaps they did."

"What do you wish of us?" said Middleton. "What is this message which you say you now deliver for the third time?"

The chief drew himself up with a magnificent gesture, and, turning a little, moved his shield arm with a wide sweeping gesture toward the West.

"I say, and I say it in behalf of the great Comanche

AT THE FORD

nation, 'Go back.' The country upon which you come belongs to the Comanches. It is ours, and the buffalo and the deer and the antelope are ours. I say to you turn back with your wagons and your men."

The words were arrogant and menacing to the last degree. A spark leaped up in Middleton's eye, but he restrained himself.

"We are but peaceful traders going to Santa Fé," he said.

"Peaceful traders to-day, seizers of the land to-morrow," said the Comanche chief. "Go back. The way over the Comanche country is closed."

"The plains are vast," said Middleton mildly. "One can ride hundreds of miles, and yet not come to the end. Many parts of them have never felt the hoof of a Comanche pony. The plains do not belong to the Comanches or to anybody else."

"They are ours," repeated the chief. "We tell you to go back. The third warning is the last."

"If we still come on, what would you do?" said Middleton.

"It is war," replied Black Panther. "You will not reach Santa Fé, and you will not go back to New Orleans. The Comanches will welcome you to their plains with the arrows from their bows and the bullets from their rifles."

"Be it so," said Middleton, continuing his calm, even tone. "We have not come so far merely to turn back. The Comanche welcome of bullets and arrows may greet us, but we are strong men, and for any welcome that may be given to us we shall always repay. Is it not so, Mr. Woodfall?"

Woodfall nodded.

"Give that answer to your tribe," said Middleton, speaking in firm tones, and looking the chief squarely in the eyes. "We have started to Santa Fé, and there we go. The Comanche nation has not enough warriors to turn us back."

THE QUEST OF THE FOUR

A spark of fire seemed to leap from the chief's eye, but he made no other demonstration.

"I have given you the third and last warning," he said. "Now I go."

He raised the shield in a sort of salute, and, without a word, turned and rode away. The three sat on their horses, looking at him. When he had gone about two hundred yards he paused a moment, fitted an arrow to his bow, shot it almost straight up into the air, and then, uttering a long fierce whoop, galloped away over the plain.

The Indian's cry was sinister, ominous of great dangers, and its meaning sank deeply on Phil's heart. A peculiar shiver ran down his backbone, and the little pulses in his temples began to beat. He did not doubt for a moment that the warning of the Comanche was black with storm. He watched the sinister figure becoming smaller and smaller, until it turned into a dark blur, then a dot, and then was seen no more in the vast, gray-green expanse.

The incident seemed to have sunk deep into the minds of the other two, also, and they rode gravely and in silence back to the train, which was now drawn up in one great group on the crest of the swell. The men, keen borderers most of them, had divined the significance of what they saw, but they crowded around the three for more definite information. Woodfall told them briefly. He knew their temper, but he thought it best to put the question and to put it fairly.

"Men," he said, "we are undoubtedly threatened with an attack. The Comanches are numerous, brave, and cunning. I will not conceal from you those facts. A fight with them will mean loss to us, and, even if we win that fight, as I am sure we will, they will attack again. Now, if any want to turn back, let them do so. All who wish to go back, say 'I'."

He paused. There was a dead silence throughout the

AT THE FORD

train. The corners of Woodfall's lips curved a little into a slow smile.

"Those who wish to go on, Comanche or no Comanche, say 'Yes,'" he cried.

A single "Yes" was thundered out from scores of throats, and many of the more enthusiastic raised their rifles and shook them.

"I thought so," said Woodfall quietly, and then he added in a louder voice: "Forward!"

Fifty whips cracked like so many rifle shots. The wagons creaked and moved forward again, and by their side rode the armed horsemen. They descended the slope, rose to the crest of the next swell, where the Comanche horseman had stood, and then passed on, over wave after wave into the unbroken gray-green expanse of the West. There was nothing before them but the plains, with a bunch of buffalo grazing far off to the right, and a herd of antelope grazing far off to the left. The ominous spell that the Indian had cast seemed to have vanished with him so far as the great majority of the men were concerned. But Phil and his immediate comrades did not forget.

"The words of that Indian, as you have delivered them to me, linger in my mind, young Sir Philip of the Plains," said Bill Breakstone, "but I am glad he took the trouble to give us a warning. A stitch in time may save the lives of nine good men.

> "Give me the word
> That harm you mean,
> Then my good sword
> I take, I ween.

"At least that poem is short and to the point, Sir Philip. And now I think me that to-morrow about the noon hour, if we should maintain our present pace, we cross a river known variously to the different Indian tribes, but muddy, deep, and flowing between high banks. The crossing will be difficult, and I ought to tell Woodfall about it."

"By all means," said Middleton, "and I can tell you, Breakstone, that I already wish we were safely on the other side of that river."

They camped that night in the open plain. There was a good moonlight, but the watch was doubled, the most experienced frontiersmen being posted as sentinels. Yet the watchers saw nothing. They continuously made wide circles about the camp, but the footprint of neither man nor horse was to be seen. The day dawned, cold and gray with lowering skies, and, before the obscure sun was an hour above the plain, the train resumed its march, Woodfall, Middleton, Breakstone, Phil, and Arenberg riding in a little group at the head.

"How far on do you say is this river?" asked Woodfall.

"We should strike it about noon," replied Breakstone, repeating his statement of the day before. "It is narrow and deep, and everywhere that I have seen it the banks are high, but we ought to find somewhere a slope for a crossing."

"Is it wooded?" asked Middleton.

"Yes, there are cottonwoods, scrub oaks, bushes, and tall grass along either bank."

"I'm sorry for that," said Woodfall.

Phil knew perfectly well what they meant, but he kept silent, although his heart began to throb. The other three also fell silent, and under the gray, lowering sky the spirits of the train seemed to sink. The men ceased to joke with one another, and no songs were sung. Phil heard only the tread of the horses and the creak of the wagons.

An hour or two later they saw a dim black line cutting across the plain.

"The trees along the banks of the river," said Bill Breakstone.

AT THE FORD

"And they are still two or three miles away," said Woodfall

The leader rode among his men and spoke with them. The train moved forward at the same speed, drawing itself like a great serpent over the plain, but there was a closing up of the ranks. The wagons moved more closely together, and every driver had a rifle under his feet. The horsemen rode toward the head of the train, held their rifles across the pommels of their saddles, and loosened the pistols in their holsters. Phil was conscious of a deep, suppressed excitement, an intensity of expectation, attached to the dark line of trees that now rose steadily higher and higher out of the plain.

An old buffalo hunter in the train now recalled the river, also, and, after studying the lay of the land carefully, said that they would find a ford about two miles north of the point toward which the head of the train was directed. The course was changed at once, and they advanced toward the northwest.

"Do you think anything is going to happen, Bill?" asked Phil, speaking for the first time.

"Do you feel kind of tingly in your blood?" asked Breakstone, not replying directly.

"I tingle all over," said Phil frankly.

"I'm tingling a bit myself," said Breakstone, "and I've spent a good many years in the wilderness. Yes, Phil, I think something is going to happen, and I think you and me and the Cap and Arenberg ought to stick together."

"That is well spoken," said Middleton. "We are chosen comrades, and we must stand by one another. See how the trees are drawing nearer."

The black line now stood up level with the earth, and the trees became detached from one another. They could also see the thick undergrowth hiding the river, which seemed to flow in a deep gash across the plain. Middleton took from his saddlebags a pair of strong glasses, and, as they rode on, examined the double line of trees with the minutest scrutiny. Then he lowered the glasses, shaking his head.

"I can't make out anything," he said. "Nothing moves that I can see. There is no sign of human life."

"The Comanche iss cunning," said Arenberg. "Harm iss done where harm iss meant, but I for one am willing to meet him."

The mild German spoke in such a tone of passion that Phil was startled and looked at him. Arenberg's blue eyes shone with a sort of blue fire, and he was unconsciously pressing his horse ahead of the others. It was evident, even to one as young as Phil, that he was stirred to his utmost depths. The boy leaned over and whispered to Breakstone:

"He must have some special cause to hate the Comanches. You know he was in that massacre at New Braunfels."

"That's so," said Breakstone,

> "When you feel the savage knife,
> You remember it all your life."

"These mild men like Arenberg are terrible when they are stirred up, Phil. 'Still waters run deep,' which sounds to me rather Irish, because if they are still they don't run at all. But it's good all the same, and, between you and me, Phil, I'd give a lot if we were on the other side of this river, which has no name in the geographies, which rises I don't know where, which empties into I don't know what, and which belongs to I don't know whom. But, be that as it may, lay on, Macduff, and I won't be the first to cry 'Hold, enough!'"

The train took another curve to the northward, approaching the ford, of which the old scouts told. The swells dipped down, indicating a point at which the banks of the river were low, but they could still see the double

AT THE FORD

line of trees lining either shore, and the masses of bushes and weeds that extended along the stream. But nothing stirred them. No wind blew. The boughs of the cottonwoods, live oaks, and willows hung lifeless under the somber sky. There was still no sign of human presence or of anything that lived.

But the men of the train did not relax their caution. They were approaching now up a sort of shallow trough containing a dry sandy bed, down which water evidently flowed during the wet season into the river. It, also, for the last half mile before it reached the main stream, had trees and bushes on either shore. Middleton suggested that they beat up this narrow strip of forest, lest they walk straight into an ambush. Woodfall thought the idea good, and twenty men scouted the thickets. They found nothing, and many in the train began to feel incredulous. That Comanche had been a mere boaster. He was probably still galloping away over the prairie, putting as much distance as he could between himself and the Santa Fé train. But Middleton yet distrusted. He seemed now to be in every sense the leader of the train, and he did it so quietly and with such indirection that Woodfall took him to be an assistant, and felt no offense. At his prompting, strong bodies of skirmishers were thrown forward on either bank of the dry creek bed, and now, increasing their pace somewhat, they rapidly drew near the river.

It still seemed to Phil that nothing could happen. It was true that the skies were gray and somber, but there was no suggestion of an active and hostile presence, and now the river was only a hundred yards away. From his horse's back he could see the surface of the stream—narrow, muddy, and apparently deep. But on the hither shore there was a gradual slope to its waters, and another of the same kind on the farther bank seemed to lead up among the trees.

"It ain't so deep as it looks," said an old frontiersman. "'Bout four feet, I should say. It'll just 'bout hit the bottoms o' our wagon beds."

The stream itself was not more than twenty yards wide. One could pass it in a few minutes, if nothing was thrown across the way, and Phil now began to feel that the unspoken alarm was false. But just when the feeling became a conviction and the wagons were not more than twenty yards from the river, he saw something gleaming in the brush on the far shore. It was the dyed feather of an eagle, and it made a blood red spot against the green bushes. Looking closely Phil saw beneath the feather the light copper face of an Indian, and then he knew that the Comanches were there.

Scarcely a second after he saw the coppery face, a hurricane of arrows whistled from the covert on the far shore. The short shafts of the Comanches filled the air. Mingled with them was the sharp crashing of rifles, and bullets and arrows whistled together. Then came the long yell of the Comanches, from scores of throats, high pitched, fierce, defiant, like the scream of a savage beast about to leap upon its prey. In spite of all his resolution, Phil felt that strong shiver in every nerve from head to heel. Some of the shafts were buried to the feather in the bodies of the horses and mules, and a terrible tumult arose as the animals uttered their screaming neigh and fought and kicked in pain and terror. Nor did the men escape. One, pierced through the throat by a deadly barb, fell lifeless from his horse. Another was stricken in the breast, and a dozen were wounded by either arrows or bullets.

The train was thrown into confusion, and the drivers pulled back on their lines. Sure death seemed to hover in front of them. The greatest danger arose from the wounded and frightened horses, which plunged and struggled and tried to break from their harness, but the hands on the lines were strong, and gradually they were reduced to order. The wagons, also, were driven back a little, and then the triumphant Comanches sent forth their war whoop again and again. The short shafts once more flew in showers, mingled as before with the whistling of the bullets, but most of the missiles, both arrows and bullets, fell short. Now the Comanches appeared thickly among the bushes, chiefly on foot, their horses left at the edge of the timber, and began to make derisive gestures.

It seemed to Phil that the crossing of the river was impossible in the face of such a fierce and numerous foe, but Middleton and Woodfall had been conferring, and suddenly the Cap, to use his more familiar name among the men, whirled off to the south at the head of a hundred horsemen. He waved his hand to his three partners, and they galloped with the band.

"There must be another crossing, not as good as this, but still a crossing," said Bill Breakstone. "If at first you don't succeed, then try, try again."

This flanking movement was hidden from the Comanches on the other shore by the belt of timber on the side of the train, and the horsemen galloped along rapidly in search of a declivity. Phil's heart was thumping, and specks floated before his eyes, but he was well among the foremost, and he rode with them, stride for stride. Behind him he heard the crackle of rifle shots, the shouts of the Comanches, and the defiant replies of the white men.

"Keep a good hold on your rifle, Phil!" shouted Bill Breakstone in his ear. "If the gods whisper truly to me, we will be in the water soon, and, by my faith, you'll need it."

The Captain uttered a shout of joy. They had come to a place where the bank sloped down to the river and the opposite shore was capable of ascent by horses.

"Into the river, men, into the river!" he shouted. "The horses may have to swim, but we can cross it! We must cross it before the main Indian force comes up!"

The whole troop galloped into the water. Middleton shouted to them to keep their rifles dry, and every man held his above his head or on his shoulder. The muddy water splashed in Phil's face, but he kept by the side of Breakstone, and in a few moments both their horses were swimming.

"Let the horse have his head, Phil," said Breakstone. "He'll make for the nearest land, and you can use both your hands for the work that we now have to do."

Phil dropped the rein, and the horse swam steadily. They were now about the middle of the stream, which was wider here than at the ford. Two or three brown faces suddenly appeared in the brush on the bank in front of them, and the savage cry arose. Comanche skirmishers had discovered the flank movement, but the white troop was already more than half way across. Bullets were fired at the swimming men and horses. Some struck in flesh, but others dashed up jets of yellow foam.

"On! On!" cried Middleton. "We must gain the bank!"

"On! On!" cried Phil, borne on by excitement. "We must gain the bank!"

He was carried away so much by the fire and movement of the moment that he did not feel fear. His blood was tingling in every vein. Myriads of red specks danced before him. The yellow water splashed all about him, but he did not notice it. An arrow whizzed by his cheek, and two bullets struck near, but he continued to urge his horse, which, gallant animal, was already doing his best. Some of the white men, even from the unsteady position of a swimming horse's back, had begun to fire at the Indians in the brush. Phil heard Bill Breakstone utter a deep sigh of satisfaction as he lowered the muzzle of his rifle.

"Got one," said Bill. "It's good to be zealous, but that Comanche ought to have known more than to run square against a rifle bullet."

The feet of Phil's horse touched earth, and he began

AT THE FORD

to wade. Everything now depended upon an instant or two. If they could gallop up the declivity before the Comanches could arrive in force they would secure a great advantage. But the Comanches were coming rapidly, and the fire from their bows and rifles increased. The white men, now that their position was steadier, also fired more rapidly. Phil sent a bullet at a bronze figure that he saw darting about in the undergrowth, but he could not tell whether or not he had hit.

"On!" shouted Middleton. "Give them no chance! Rush the slope!"

They were out of the river now, and in among the bushes and weeds. But they did not stop there. Dripping with the yellow water, streaked sometimes with red, they rode straight at the Comanches, shouting and firing with both rifles and pistols. The Indian skirmishers gave way, and, jumping upon their ponies, galloped down the stream to the main ford. The white men uttered a cry of exultation. They were now on the western bank, and the flank movement was a complete success.

"Follow them!" shouted Middleton. "We must press home the attack upon the main body!"

Ahead of them the Comanches, bent low on their mustangs, were galloping over the plain. Behind came the white men, hot with the fire of battle and urging on their horses. Phil, Bill Breakstone, and Arenberg rode knee to knee, the boy between. He was wet from head to foot with splashed water, but he did not know it. A bullet had touched the tip of one ear, covering it with blood, but he did not know that, either. There was no cruelty in his nature, but just now it thrilled with battle. He sought a shot at the flying Comanches, but they were too far away.

"Hold your fire," said Bill Breakstone. "The battle is not over yet by any means. A job that's half finished isn't finished at all."

They heard now the shots at the ford above them and

a tremendous shouting. Evidently the two forces were firing at each other across the stream, and the wagons did not yet dare the passage. A few moments later they saw the smoke of the rifles and brown figures darting about in the thickets.

"Now, boys!" shouted Middleton. "All together! A great cheer!"

A mighty shout was poured forth from three score throats, and Middleton waved his felt hat about his head. From the eastern bank came an answering cry, and the signal was complete. Woodfall and the others with the train knew that their comrades were across, and now was the time for them to force the passage. Phil saw the white tops of the wagons shake. Then the wagons themselves rolled slowly forward into the water, with horsemen in front of them and on the flanks, firing at the Indians on the bank. The Comanches sent a shower of bullets and arrows upon the advancing line, but in another instant they were compelled to turn and defend themselves. Middleton and his victorious troop were thundering down upon them.

The attack upon their flank came so swiftly that the Comanches were taken by surprise. As their own skirmishers fled, the white force galloped in upon their heels. Yet these bold warriors, kings of the plains, victors in many a battle over other tribes and Mexicans, fought with a courage and tenacity worthy of their race and traditions. They were marshaled, too, by a chief who had returned to his own, the great Black Panther, and by able assistants.

Middleton's daring men met a storm of arrows and bullets, but they charged on, although some saddles were emptied. They were at the edge of the timber now, and the mounted white men poured in a deadly fire. The sound of the shots became a steady, incessant crackle. Puffs of smoke arose, and, uniting, formed a canopy of vapor. The odor of gunpowder spread and filled the nos-

AT THE FORD

trils of the combatants. Shots, the trampling of hoofs, the cries of the wounded and dying rung upon the drums of their ears.

It was a terrific medley, seemingly all confusion, but really fought with order by skilled leaders. Black Panther had one half of his warriors to face the wagons and horsemen in the river and the other half faced south to beat off Middleton's troop, if it could. He himself passed from one to another, encouraging them by every art that he knew, and they were many.

But it was Middleton's men who gave the deathblow. They struck so hard and so often that it was continually necessary for Black Panther to send more of his warriors to the defense of his flank. The firing upon the wagons and horsemen in the river slackened, and they rushed forward. The horsemen gained the bank, and, at the same time, Middleton's men charged with greater fire than ever. Then the horsemen from the ford rushed up the ascent and joined in the attack. Compressed between the two arms of a vise, the Comanches, despite every effort of Black Panther and his chiefs, gave way. Yet they did not break into any panic. Springing on their horses, they retired slowly, sending back flights of arrows and bullets, and now and then uttering the defiant war whoop.

Meanwhile, the last of the wagons emerged from the river, and was dragged up the ascent. Although the Comanches might yet shout in the distance, the crossing was won, and everybody in the train felt a mighty sense of relief.

CHAPTER IV

ON WATCH

THE wagons drew up in a great square on the open plain, but just at the edge of the timber, and the men, breathless, perspiring, but victorious, dropped from their horses. The Comanches still galloped to and fro and shouted in the distance, but they kept well out of rifle shot, and Phil, although it was his first battle, knew that they would not attack again, at least not for the present. They had been driven out of an extremely strong position, ground of their own choosing, and nothing remained to them but to retire.

The boy stood by the side of his horse, holding the bridle in one hand and the rifle in the other. He was still trembling from the excitement of forcing the ford and the battle among the trees, but the reddish mist before his eyes was gradually clearing away. He let the bridle rein drop, and put his hand to his face. It came away damp and sticky. He looked at it in an incurious way to see if he were wounded, but it was only dust and the smoke of burned gunpowder, kneaded together by perspiration. Then he felt cautiously of his body. No bullet or arrow had entered.

"Unhurt, Phil?" boomed out the voice of Bill Breakstone beside him. "So am I, and so is Middleton. Arenberg got a scratch, but he's forgotten it already. But, I trow, Sir Philip of the River, that was indeed a combat while it lasted!

"The Comanches shot
With spirit hot,
But now, they're not.

"You can't say anything against that poem, Phil; it's short and to the point. It's true that the Comanches are not entirely gone, but they might as well be. Let 'em shout out there in the plain as much as they choose, they're going to keep out of rifle range. And I congratulate you, Phil, on the way you bore yourself through your first 'baptism of fire.'"

"I thank you, Bill," said Phil, "but the fact is, I don't know just how I bore myself. It's been more like a dream than anything else."

"That's likely to happen to a man the first time under fire, and the second time, too, but here we are on the right side of the river and ready for a breathing spell."

Phil threw the reins over his horse's neck, knowing that the latter would not leave the camp, and set to work, helping to put everything in order, ready for fight or rest, whichever the Comanches chose to make it. The wagons were already in a hollow square, and the wounded, at least twenty in number, laid comfortably in the wagons, were receiving the rude but effective treatment of the border. Seven or eight had been killed, and three or four bodies had been lost in the current of the stream. They were now digging graves for the others. Little was known of the slain. They were wandering, restless spirits, and they may or may not have been buried under their own names. They had fallen in an unknown land beside an unknown river, but their comrades gave all due honor as they put them beneath the earth. Middleton said a few words over the body of each, while others stood by with their hats off. Then they smoothed out the soil above them as completely as possible, in order that their graves might be lost. They took this precaution lest the Comanches come after they had gone, take up the bodies, and mutilate them.

When the solemn task was done, the men turned away to other duties. They were not discouraged; on the contrary, their spirits were sanguine. The gloom of the burial was quickly dispelled, and these wild spirits, their fighting blood fully up, were more than half willing for the Comanches to give them a new battle. It was such as these, really loving adventure and danger more than profit, who steadily pushed forward the southwestern frontier in the face of obstacles seemingly insuperable.

Their position at the edge of the wood, with the strong fortification of the wagons, was excellent, and Middleton and Woodfall, after a short consultation, decided to remain there until morning, for the sake of the wounded men and for rest for all. Phil worked in the timber, gathering up fallen fuel for fires, which were built in the center of the hollow square, and he found the work a relief. Such a familiar task steadied his nerves. Gradually the little pulses ceased to beat so hard, and his head grew cool. When enough dead wood had been brought in, he took another look at the western horizon. Comanches could still be seen there, but they no longer galloped about and shouted. A half dozen sat motionless on their ponies, apparently looking at the white camp, their figures, horse and rider, outlined in black tracery against the blood-red western sun. Phil had a feeling that, although beaten at the ford, they were not beaten for good and all, and that the spirit of Black Panther, far from being crushed, would be influenced to new passions and new attack. But, as he looked, the Comanche horsemen seemed to ride directly into the low sun and disappear. The hard work that had kept him up now over, he felt limp, and sank down near one of the fires.

"Here, Phil, drink this," said Bill Breakstone, handing him a cup of hot coffee. "It has been a pretty hard day on the nerves, and you need a stimulant."

Phil swallowed it all, almost at a draught—never had coffee tasted better—and his strength came back rapidly. Breakstone, also, drank a cup and sat down beside the boy.

"Here comes Arenberg," he said in a low tone to Phil.

ON WATCH

"That German was a very demon to-day. He got right into the front of the charge, and after his rifle was empty he clubbed it and brought down one of the Comanches."

Phil looked up. Arenberg's face was still set in a stern, pitiless mask, but when his eyes caught the boy's he relaxed.

"It iss a good day well spent," he said, throwing himself down by the side of the two. "We never could have forced the ford if we had not made that flank movement. Harm wass meant by both sides and harm wass done. But it iss over now. How does the young Herr Philip feel?"

"Pretty good now," replied Phil, "but I've had my ups and downs, I can tell you. A little while ago I felt as if there were no backbone in me at all."

Food was now cooked, and, after eating, the three relapsed into silence. Presently Middleton, also, joined them, and told them that very thorough preparations had been made to guard against a surprise. Sentinels on horseback were already far out on the plain, riding a watchful round which would be continued all through the night.

"It is easy to guard against surprise on that side," said Middleton, "but snipers may creep down the river bank in the timber. We must keep our best watch there."

"I'll go on duty," said Philip promptly.

"Not yet," replied Middleton. "You may be needed late in the night, in which case we'll call on you, but our most experienced borderers don't think the Comanches will come back."

"You can never trust them," said Arenberg earnestly.

"We don't mean to," said Middleton. "Now, Phil, I'd advise you to wrap yourself in your blanket and go to sleep. On a campaign it's always advisable to sleep when you're off duty, because you never know when you will get the chance again."

THE QUEST OF THE FOUR

It seemed to Phil that it was impossible to sleep, after so much excitement and danger, but he knew that Middleton was speaking wise words, and he resolved to try. There were yet hours of daylight, but, putting his blanket beneath him, he lay before one of the fires with his arm under his head and closed his eyes. He would open them now and then to see the yellow flames, the figures of the men moving back and forth, and the circle of wagons beyond. He could not make himself feel sleepy, but he knew that his nerves were relaxing. Physically he felt a soothing languor, and with it came a mental satisfaction. He had helped to win his first battle, and, like the older and seasoned men around him, the victory encouraged him to bid further defiance to the Comanches or anything else that threatened.

These reflections were so grateful that he found himself able to keep his eyes shut longer. It was not so much of an effort to pull the eyelids down, and when, at intervals steadily growing more distant, he opened his eyes, it was to find the fires and figures of the men becoming dim, while the circling line of the wagons beyond was quite lost. At last the eyelids stayed down of their own accord, and he floated away into a sleep that was deep, sweet, and refreshing.

Others in the camp slept, also, some in the wagons and some on the ground, with saddles for pillows. Those whose duty it was to watch paid no attention to them, but beat up the brush incessantly, and kept up their endless circles on the plains. The somber clouds that had obscured the morning floated away, driven back by a late afternoon sun of uncommon splendor. The gray-green plains turned to a brilliant red and gold; the willows, cottonwoods, and oaks seemed sheathed in gold, every bough and twig; the muddy river took on rich and gleaming tints, and then suddenly the sun was gone, leaving all in darkness, save for the smoldering fires.

Phil slept soundly hour after hour. He was so exhausted physically and mentally that the relaxation was complete. No dream good or bad came to trouble him, and Breakstone, who observed his peaceful face, said to Middleton:

"Talk about knitting up the raveled sleeve of care. That boy is knitting up both sleeves at the same time, and he is knitting them fast."

"He is a good lad," said Middleton, "and a brave one, too. It was his first battle, but he certainly bore himself well. Now I wonder what search is bringing him out here into the wilderness."

"And I guess he, too, often wonders the same about us."

"Just as I have wondered it about you, and as you have wondered it about me."

"But we find it best—every one of us—to keep our search to ourselves for the present."

"It is surely best."

The two men looked at each other rather significantly, and then talked of other things.

Phil was awakened at midnight to take his turn at the watch. The night, as it is so often on the plains of Texas, even in summer, was cold, and he shivered a little when he drew himself out of his warm blankets. The fires were nearly out, leaving only a few coals that did not warm, and few figures were moving except outside the circle. His body told Phil that he would much rather sleep on, but his mind told him with greater force that he must go ahead and do his duty with a willing heart, a steady hand, and a quick eye. So he shook himself thoroughly, and was ready for action. His orders were to go in the timber a little to the northward and watch for snipers. Three others were going with him, but they were to separate and take regular beats.

Phil shouldered his rifle and marched with his comrades. They passed outside the circles of wagons, and stood for a few moments on the bare plain. Afar off they saw their own mounted sentinels who watched to the westward, riding back and forth. The moon was cold, and a chill wind swept over the swells, moaning dismally. Phil shivered and was glad that he had a watch on foot in the timber. His comrades were willing to hasten with him to that shelter, and there they arranged their beats. The belt of timber was about a hundred yards wide, with a considerable undergrowth of bushes and tall weeds. They cut the hundred yards into about four equal spaces, and Phil took the quarter next to the river. He walked steadily back and forth over the twenty-five yards, and at the western end of his beat he regularly met the next sentinel, a young Mississippian named Welby, whom Phil liked. They exchanged a few words now and then, but, save their low tones, the monotonous moaning of the wind among the trees, and an occasional sigh made by the current of the river, which here flowed rather swiftly, there was no sound. On the opposite bank the trees and bushes reared themselves, a wall of dark green.

The chill of the night grew, but the steady walking back and forth had increased the circulation and warmed the blood in Phil's veins, and he did not feel it. His long sleep, too, had brought back all his strength, and he was full of courage and zeal. He had suffered a reaction after the battle, but now the second reaction came. The young victor, refreshed in mind and body, feared nothing. Neither was he lonely nor awed by the vast darkness of night in the wilderness. The words that he spoke with Welby every few minutes were enough to keep him in touch with the human race, and he really felt content with himself and the world. He had done his duty under fire, and now he was doing his duty again.

He paused a little longer every time he came to the river, and forcing his mind now to note every detail, he was impressed by the change that the stream had under-

ON WATCH

gone. There was a fine full moon, and the muddy torrent of the day was turned into silver, sparkling more brightly where the bubbles formed and broke. The stream, swollen doubtless by rains about its source, flowed rapidly with a slight swishing noise. Phil looked up and down it, having a straight sweep of several hundred yards either way. Now and then the silver of its surface was broken by pieces of floating débris, brought doubtless from some far point. He watched these fragments as they passed, a bough, a weed, or a stump, or the entire trunk of a tree, wrenched by a swollen current from some caving bank. He was glad that he had the watch next to the river, because it was more interesting. The river was a live thing, changing in color, and moving swiftly. Its surface, with the objects that at times swept by on it, was a panorama of varied interest.

Besides Welby he saw no living creature. The camp was hidden from him completely by the trees and bushes, and they were so quiet within the circle of the wagons that no sound came from them. An hour passed. It became two, then three. Vaporous clouds floated by the moon. The silver light on the river waned. The current became dark yellow again, but flowing as ever with that soft, swishing sound. The change affected Phil. The weird quality of the wilderness, clothed in dark, made itself felt. He was glad when he met Welby, and they lingered a few seconds longer, talking a little. He came back once more to the river, now flowing in a torrent almost black between its high banks.

He took his usual long survey of the river, both up and down stream. Phil was resolved to do his full duty, and already he had some experience, allied with faculties naturally keen. He examined the opposite bank with questioning eyes. At first it had seemed a solid wall of dark green, but attention and the habit of the darkness now enabled him to separate it into individual trees and bushes. Comanches ambushed there could easily shoot across the narrow stream and pick off a white sentinel, but he had always kept himself well back in his own bushes, where he could see and yet be hidden.

His gaze turned to the river. Darker substances, drift from far banks, still floated on its surface. The wind had died. The branches of the trees did not move at all, and, in the absence of all other sound, the slight swishing made by the flowing of the river grew louder. His wandering eyes fastened on a small stump that was coming from the curve above, and that floated easily on the surface. Its motion was so regular that his glance stayed, and he watched it with interested eyes. It was an independent sort of stump, less at the mercy of the current than the others had been. It came on, bearing in toward the western bank, and Phil judged that if it kept its present course it would strike the shore beneath him.

The black stump was certainly interesting. He looked farther. Four feet behind it was floating another stump of about the same size, and preserving the same direction, which was a diagonal line with the current. That was a coincidence. Yet farther was a third stump, showing all the characteristics of the other two. That was remarkable. And lo! when a fourth, and then a fifth, and then a sixth came, a floating line, black and silent, it was a prodigy.

The first black stump struck lightly against the bank. Then a Comanche warrior, immersed hitherto to the chin, rose from the stream. The water ran in black bubbles from his naked body. In his right hand he held a long knife. The face was sinister, savage, and terrible beyond expression. Another of the stumps was just rising from the stream, but Phil fired instantly at the first face, and then sprang back, shouting, "The Comanches." He did not run. He merely sheltered himself behind a tree, and began to reload rapidly. Welby came running through the bushes, and then the others, drawn by the shout. In a minute the timber was filled with armed men.

ON WATCH

"What is it? What is it? What did you shoot at?" they cried, although the same thought was in the minds of every one of them.

"The Comanches!" replied Phil. "They came swimming in a line down the river. Their heads looked like black stumps on the water! I fired at the first the moment he rose from the stream! I think it was their plan to ambush and kill the sentinels!"

Bill Breakstone was among those who had come, and he cried:

"Then we must beat them off at once! We must not give them a chance to get a footing on the bank!"

They rushed forward, Phil with them, his rifle now reloaded, and gazed down at the river. They heard no noise, but that slight swishing sound made by the current, and the surface of the stream was bare. The river flowed as if no foreign body had ever vexed its current. Fifty pairs of eyes used to the wilderness studied the stream and the thickets. They saw nothing. Fifty pairs of ears trained to hear the approach of danger listened. They heard nothing but the faint swishing sound that never ceased. A murmur not pleasant to Phil, arose.

"I've no doubt it was a stump, a real stump," one of the older men said.

A deep flush overspread Phil's face.

"I saw a Comanche with long black hair rise from the water," he said.

The man who had spoken grinned a little, but the expression of his face showed that doubt had solidified into certainty.

"A case of nerves," he said, "but I don't blame you so much, bein' only a boy."

Phil felt his blood grow hot, but he tried to restrain his temper.

"I certainly saw a Comanche," he said, "and there were others behind him!"

"Then what's become of all this terrible attack?" asked the man ironically.

"Come! Come!" said Woodfall. "We can't have such talk. The boy may have made a mistake, but the incident showed that he was watching well, just what we want our sentinels to do."

Phil flushed again. Woodfall's tone was kindly, but he was hurt by the implication of possible doubt and mistake. Yet Woodfall and the others had ample excuse for such doubts. There was not the remotest sign of an enemy. Could he really have been mistaken? Could it have been something like a waking dream? Could his nerves have been so upset that they made his eyes see that which was not? He stared for a full minute at the empty face of the river, and then a voice called:

"Oh, you men, come down here! I've something to show you!"

It was Bill Breakstone, who had slipped away from them and gone down the bank. His voice came from a point at least a hundred yards down the stream, and the men in a group followed the sound of it, descending the slope with the aid of weeds and bushes. Bill was standing at the edge of a little cove which the water had hollowed out of the soft soil, and something dark lay at his feet.

"I dragged this out of the water," he said. "It was floating along, when an eddy brought it into this cove."

They looked down, and Phil shut off a cry with his closed teeth. The body, a Comanche warrior, entirely naked, lay upon its back. There was a bullet hole in the center of the forehead. The features, even in death, were exactly those that the boy had seen rising from the water, sinister, savage, terrible beyond expression. Phil felt a cold horror creeping through all his bones, but it was the look of this dead face more than the fact that he had killed a man. He shuddered to think what so much malignant cruelty could have done had it gained the chance.

ON WATCH

"Well, men," said Bill Breakstone quietly, "was the story our young friend here told such stuff as dreams are made on, or did it really happen?"

"The boy told the truth, and he was watching well," said a half dozen together.

The old frontiersman who had so plainly expressed his disbelief in Phil—Gard was his name—extended his hand and said to the lad:

"I take it all back. You've saved us from an ambush that would have cost us a lot of men. I was a fool. Shake hands."

Phil, with a great leap of pride, took the proffered hand and shook it heartily.

"I don't blame you, Mr. Gard," he said. "Things certainly looked against me."

"The Comanches naturally took to flight when their leader was killed," said Woodfall. "They could not carry through such an attempt without surprise, but good eyes stopped them."

Phil's heart leaped again with pride, but he said nothing. They climbed back up the slope, and the guard in the timber was tripled for the short time until day. Phil was told that, as he had already done so much, he might go off duty now.

He was glad enough to seek rest, and so rapidly was he becoming used to danger that he lay down calmly before one of the fires and went to sleep again. He awoke two or three hours later to a crisp fresh morning, and to the news that the train would promptly resume its advance, whether or not Comanches tried to bar the way. With the intoxicating odor of victory still in their nostrils, the hardy frontiersmen were as willing as ever for another combat. But the enemy had disappeared completely. A brilliant sun rose over the gray-green swells, disclosing nothing but a herd of antelope that grazed far to the right.

"The antelope mean that no Comanches are near,"

said Arenberg. "The warriors will now wait patiently and a long time for a good opportunity. Sometimes much harm iss done where much iss intended."

"That is so," chanted Bill Breakstone.

> "Over the plains we go,
> Our rifles clear the way.
> The Indians would say no.
> Our band they cannot stay.

"As I have often remarked before, Phil, my poetry may be defective in meter and some other small technicalities, but it comes to the point. That, I believe, was the characteristic of Shakespeare, also. I agree, too, with Arenberg, that the Comanches will not trouble us again for some time. So, I pray thee, be of good cheer, Sir Philip of the Merry Countenance, Knight of the Battle beside the Unknown River, Slayer of Comanches in the Dark, Guardian of the Public Weal, et cetera, et cetera."

"I am cheerful," said Phil, to whom Breakstone was always a tonic, "and I believe that we can beat off the Comanches any time and every time."

"Jump on your horse," said Breakstone, a little later; "we're all ready."

Phil leaped into the saddle with one bound. The train moved forward, and he and Breakstone joined Middleton and Arenberg at its head. Middleton had powerful glasses, and he swept the plain far ahead, and to right and left. His gaze finally settled on a point to the southwest. The others followed his look with great interest, but the naked eye could see nothing but the rolling gray-green plains and the dim blue horizon beyond. Middleton looked so long that at last Bill Breakstone asked:

"What do you see?"

"I do not see anything that I can really call living," replied Middleton, "but I do see a knoll or slight elevation on the plain—what would be called farther north a butte—and on that knoll is a black blur, shapeless and unnamable at this distance."

"Does the black blur move?" asked Bill Breakstone.

"I cannot tell. It is too far even for that, but from it comes a beam of brilliant light that shifts here and there over the plain. Take a look, Bill."

Breakstone eagerly put the glasses to his eyes, and turned them upon the knoll.

"Ah, I see it!" he exclaimed. "It's like a ball of light! There it goes to the right! There it goes to the left! Now it falls in our direction! What in the name of Shakespeare's thirty-five or forty plays is it, Cap?"

"Let me have the glasses, I want another look," replied Middleton.

His second look was a long one taken in silence. At last he replied:

"It's a signal, lads. I've seen the Comanches talk to one another in this way before. A Comanche chief is sitting on his horse on top of that knoll. He holds a rounded piece of looking-glass in the hollow of his hand, and he turns it in such a way that he catches the very concentrated essence of the sun's rays, throwing a beam a tremendous distance. The beam, like molten gold, now strikes the grass on top of a swell off toward the north. It's a secret just how they do it, for not yet has any white man learned the system of signals which they make with such a glass. Ah!"

The "Ah!" came forth, so deep, so long drawn, and so full of meaning that Phil, Arenberg, and Bill Breakstone exclaimed together:

"What is it?"

"I would not have known that the black blur on top of the knoll was a chief on horseback if I had not been on the Texas plains before," replied Middleton, "but now I can make out the figures of horse and man, as he is riding around and around in a circle and riding very rapidly."

THE QUEST OF THE FOUR

"What does that mean?" asked Phil.

"It means danger, not to us, but to the Comanches. The warrior is probably signaling to a band of his tribe who are meditating attack upon us that we are too strong."

"Then it must be some fresh band," said Bill Breakstone, "because the one that had the little encounter with us yesterday knew that already."

"I take it that you're right," said Middleton, smiling and closing the glasses. "The second band won't molest us—not to-day."

"That seems to be a very effective way of signaling," remarked Phil.

"On the plains, yes," said Middleton. "It is astonishing how far such a vivid beam of light will carry, as the crest of the knoll was too high for it to be intercepted by the swells."

Middleton told Woodfall what they had seen. The leader's chin stiffened a little more, and the wagons went on at the same pace, trailing their brown length across the prairie.

About ten o'clock the march became difficult, as they entered a town, but such a town! Its inhabitants were prairie dogs, queer little animals, which darted down into their burrows at the approach of the horsemen and wagons, often sharing the home with a rattlesnake. But the horsemen were now compelled to proceed with exceeding care, as the horses' feet often sank deep down in the dens. Stumbles were frequent and there were several falls. Wagon wheels, also, sank, and the advance became so difficult that Woodfall halted the train and sent Phil and some others to find a way around the town.

They rode five or six miles to the south, and still the singular town stretched away, apparently endless. Then they came back and rode five or six miles to the north with the same result. Acting upon the advice of Middleton, Woodfall, after hearing these reports, decided to go straight on through the town. It was known that such towns had been found twenty-five miles long, and this might be as large. So they went directly ahead. The riders dismounted and led their horses. Three times Phil killed coiling rattlesnakes with the butt of his rifle, but he did not seek to molest any of the prairie dogs.

They moved very slowly, and it was three hours before they crossed the prairie dog town, leaving behind them some destruction, but not more than they could help.

"Well, Sir Philip of the Prairie Dogs, what name are you going to give to the populous community through which we have just passed?" asked Breakstone.

"I suppose Canine Center will do as well as any other," replied Phil.

"A wise selection, my gay youth," replied Bill Breakstone. "But these animals, properly speaking, are not dogs, they are more like rats. I'm glad we've passed 'em. It isn't pleasant to have your horse put his foot in one of their dens and shoot you over his head. The good hard plain for me."

He cantered forward, and Phil cantered with him, raising his head and breathing the pure air that blew over such vast reaches of clean earth. He felt the blood leaping in his veins again from mere physical happiness. He began to whistle gayly, and then to sing "Open thy lattice, love," a song just coming into favor, written by the man who became yet more famous with "Old Kentucky Home" and "Suwanee River." Phil had a fine, fresh, youthful voice, and Breakstone listened to him as he sang through two verses. Then he held up his hand, and Phil stopped.

"What's the trouble?" asked the boy.

"I don't object to your song, Phil, and I don't object to your singing, but it won't be a good time for love to open the lattice; it will be better to close it tight. Don't you feel a change in the air, Phil? Just turn your face to the northwest, and you'll notice it."

THE QUEST OF THE FOUR

Phil obeyed, and it seemed to him now that the air striking upon his cheek was colder, but he imagined that it was due to the increasing strength of the wind.

"I do not care if the wind is a little cold." he said. "I like it."

> "The wind is cold,
> And you are bold;
> The sky turns gray
> You're not so gay;
> And by and by
> For sun you'll sigh,"

chanted Bill Breakstone, and then he added:

"See that gray mist forming in a circle about the sun, and look at that vapor off there in the northwest. By George, how fast it spreads! The whole sky is becoming overcast! Unroll your blanket, Phil, and have it ready to wrap around you! The whole train must stop and prepare!"

Bill Breakstone turned to give his warning, but others, too, had noticed the signals of danger. The command to stop was given. The wagons were drawn rapidly into a circle, and just as when the danger was Indians, instead of that which now threatened, all the horses and mules were put inside the circle. But now all the men, also, took their station inside, none remaining outside as guard.

The wind meanwhile rose fast, and the temperature fell with startling rapidity. The edge of the blast seemed to be ice itself. Phil, who was helping with the corral of wagons, felt as if it cut him to the bone. He fully appreciated Bill Breakstone's advice about the blanket. The day also was swiftly turning dark. The sun was quite gone out. Heavy clouds and masses of vapor formed an impenetrable veil over all the sky. Now, besides the cold, Phil felt his face struck by fine particles that stung. It was the sand picked up by the wind, perhaps hundreds of miles away, and hurled upon them in an enveloping storm.

ON WATCH

Phil pulled down his cap-brim and also sheltered his eyes as much as he could with his left arm.

"It's the Norther," cried Breakstone. "Listen to it!"

The wind was now shrieking and howling over the plains with a voice that was truly human, only it was like the shout of ten thousand human beings combined. But it was a voice full of malice and cruelty, and Phil was glad of the companionship of his kind.

The cold was now becoming intense, and he rapidly drew the blanket about his body. Then he suddenly bent his head lower and completely covered his eyes with his arm. It was hailing fiercely. Showers of white pellets, large enough to be dangerous, pounded him, and, as the darkness had now increased to that of night, he groped for shelter. Bill Breakstone seized him by the arm and cried:

"Jump into the wagon there, Phil! And I'll jump after you!"

Phil obeyed with the quickness of necessity, and Breakstone came in on top of him. Middleton and Arenberg were already there.

"Welcome to our wagon," said Arenberg, as Phil and Breakstone disentangled themselves. "You landed on one of my feet, Phil, and you landed on the other, Bill, but no harm iss done where none iss meant."

Phil cowered down and drew his blanket more closely around him, while the hail beat fiercely on the arched canvas cover, and the cold wind shrieked and moaned more wildly than ever. He peeped out at the front of the wagon and beheld a scene indescribable in its wild and chilling grandeur. The darkness endured. The hail was driven in an almost horizontal line like a sheet of sleet. The wagons showed but dimly in all this dusk. The animals, fortunately, had been tethered close to the wagons, where they were, in a measure, protected, but many of them reared and neighed in terror and suffering.

THE QUEST OF THE FOUR

One look satisfied Phil, and he drew back well under cover.

"How often does this sort of thing happen in Texas?" he asked Arenberg.

"Not so often," replied the German, "and this Norther, I think, is the worst I ever saw. The cold wind certainly blows like der Teufel. These storms must start on the great mountains far, far to the north, and I think they get stronger as they come. Iss it not so, Herr Breakstone?"

"Your words sound true to me, Sir Hans of the Beer Barrel," replied Breakstone. "I've seen a few Northers in my time, and I've felt 'em, but this seems to me to be about the most grown-up, all-around, healthy and frisky specimen of the kind that I ever met."

Phil thought that the Norther would blow itself out in an hour or two, but he was mistaken. Several hours passed and the wind was as strong and as cold as ever. The four ate some cold food that was in the wagon, and then settled back into their places. No attempt would be made to cook that day. But Phil grew so warm and snug in his blanket among the baggage, and the beating of the rain on the stout canvas cover was so soothing, that he fell asleep after awhile. He did not know how long he slept, because when he awoke it was still dark, the wind was still shrieking, and the other three, as he could tell by their regular breathing, were asleep, also. He felt so good that he stretched himself a little, turned on the other side, and went to sleep again.

CHAPTER V

THE COMANCHE VILLAGE

THE Norther did not blow itself out until noon of the next day. Then it ceased almost as abruptly as it had begun. The wind stopped its shrieking and howling so suddenly that the silence, after so long a period of noise, was for awhile impressive. The clouds fell apart as if cut down the middle by a saber, and the sun poured through the rift.

It was like a fairy transformation scene. The rift widened so fast that soon all the clouds were gone beyond the horizon. The sky was a solid blue, shot through with the gold of the warm sun. The hail melted, and the ground dried. It was spring again, and the world was beautiful. Phil saw, felt, and admired. Bill Breakstone burst into song:

> "The Norther came,
> The Norther went.
> It suits its name,
> Its rage is spent.

"From the looks of things now," he continued, "you wouldn't think it had been whistling and groaning around us for about twenty-four hours, trying to shoot us to death with showers of hail, but I'd have you to know, Sir Philip of the Untimely Cold and the Hateful Storm, that I have recorded it upon the tablets of my memory. I wouldn't like to meet such a Norther when I was alone on the plains, on foot, and clad in sandals, a linen suit, and a straw hat."

"Nor I," said Phil with emphasis.

Now they lighted fires of buffalo chips which were abundant everywhere, and ate the first warm food that they had had since the day before at noon. Then they advanced four or five miles and encamped on the banks of a creek, a small stream of water flowing in a broad, sandy bed. Phil and some of the others scouted in a wide circle for Comanches, but saw no signs, and, as he had slept so late that day, the boy remained awake most of the night. There was a good moonlight, and he saw dusky slinking forms on the plain.

"Coyotes," said Bill Breakstone. "At least, most of them are, though I think from their size that two or three of those figures out there must be timber wolves. If I'm right about 'em, it means that we're not far from a belt of forest country."

"I hope you're right," said Phil. "I'm getting tired of plains now, and I'd like to see trees and hills again, and also water that runs faster and that's less muddy than these sluggish and sandy creeks."

Bill Breakstone threw back his head and laughed with unction.

"That's the way with fellows who were born in the hills," he said. "Wherever you go, sooner or later you'll pine for 'em again. I'm one of that lot, too."

"Yes, it's so," admitted Phil. "I like the great plains, the vastness, the mystery, and the wonderful air which must be the purest in the world, that's always blowing over them, but for a real snug, homey feeling give me a little valley in the hills, with a brook of green-white water about six inches deep running down it, and plenty of fine trees—oak, beech, hickory, elm, walnut, and chestnut—growing on the slopes and tops of the hills."

"A pretty picture, Sir Philip of the Brook, the Hill, the Valley, and the Tree," said Bill Breakstone, "and maybe we will see it soon. As I told you, timber wolves indicate trees not far off."

THE COMANCHE VILLAGE

But the chief event that day was buffaloes and not timber. They ran into a vast herd, traveling north with the spring, and killed with ease all they wanted. The bodies were cut up, and the wagons were filled with fresh meat. There was a momentary quandary about the hides, which they wished to save, a process that required immediate curing, but they were unwilling to stop for that purpose on the plain. Two of the scouts came in at sundown with news that the timber was only three or four miles ahead, and the whole train pushed forward, reaching it shortly after nightfall.

The wagons stopped just within the edge of the timber, but Phil, Breakstone, Arenberg, and Middleton rode on, the night being so clear and bright that they could see almost as well as by day. The first range of hills was low, but beyond lay others, rising perhaps two hundred feet above the level of the plain. The timber on all the hills and the valleys between was dense and heavy, embracing many varieties of hard wood, elm, hackberry, overcup, ash, pecan, and wild china. There were also the bushes and vines of the blackberry, gooseberry, raspberry, currant, and of a small fox grape, plentiful throughout the mountains of Texas. The fox grape grew on a little bush like that of the currant, and growing in abundance was another bush, from two to six feet in height, that would produce wild plums in the autumn.

"It's a good country, a fine country," said Bill Breakstone. "A man could live all the year around on the food that he would find in this region, buffalo and antelope on the plains, deer and maybe beaver in here, and all sorts of wild fruits."

Phil nodded. He was reveling in the hills and timber. The moonlight fell in a vast sheet of silver, but the foliage remained a solid mass of dark green beneath it. A tremulous little wind blew, and the soft sound of fresh young leaves rubbing together came pleasantly. A faint noise like a sigh told of a tiny stream somewhere trickling over the pebbles. Phil opened his eyes as wide as he could and drew in great gulps of the scented air. Big bronze birds, roused by the tread of the horsemen, rose from a bough, and flew away among the trees. They were wild turkeys, but the lad and his comrades were not seeking game just then. Bill Breakstone, who was in advance, stopped suddenly.

"Come here, Sir Philip of the Hilly Forest," he cried, "and see what uncle has found for his little boy."

Phil rode up by his side and uttered a little gasp of admiration. As he sat on his horse, he looked into a ravine about two hundred feet deep. Down the center of the ravine dashed a little mountain river of absolutely clear water. It was not more than twenty feet wide, but very deep. As Breakstone said, "it ran on its side," but it ran along with much murmur and splash and laughter of waters. Often as the swift current struck the stony sides of the ravine it threw up little cascades of foam like snow. The banks themselves, although of stone, were covered most of the way with clustering vines and short green bushes. The crest of the farther bank was wooded so heavily with great trees that they were like a wall. Farther down, the stream descended with increased swiftness, and a steady murmuring noise that came to them indicated a waterfall. The brilliant moonlight bathed the river, the hills, and the forest, and the great silence brooded over them all. Middleton and Arenberg also came, and the four side by side on their horses sat for awhile, saying nothing, but rejoicing in a scene so vivid and splendid to them, after coming from the monotony of the great plains.

"I'd like to drop off my horse after a hot day's ride," said Bill Breakstone, "and have some of that river run over me. Wouldn't that be a shower-bath for a tired and dusty man!"

"It's likely to be ice-cold," said Middleton.

"Why so?" asked Phil.

THE COMANCHE VILLAGE

"Because it rises somewhere high up. There must be mountains to the northward, and probably it is fed most of the year by melting snows. I think Bill would have enough of his bath very quickly."

"If I get a chance, and there is any way to get down to that stream, I may try it to-morrow," said Bill threateningly.

"Meanwhile, we'll ride back and tell what we've seen," said Middleton.

"Isn't there any danger of Indian ambush in the timber?" asked Phil.

"I don't think so," replied Middleton. "The Comanches are horse Indians, and keep entirely to the plains. The other tribes are too much afraid of the Comanches to remain near them, and in consequence the edge of a hilly stretch such as this is likely to be deserted."

They rode back to the wagons and found that the cooking fires were already lighted, and their cheerful blaze was gleaming among the trees. Everybody else, also, was delighted at being in the timber, where clear water flowed past, and most of the wounded were able to get out of the wagons and sit on the grass with their comrades. Woodfall decided that it was a good place in which to spend a few days for rest, repairs, and the hunting of game, as they wanted other fresh meat besides that of the buffalo.

The next morning they began to cure the buffalo hides that they had already obtained. A smooth piece of ground, exposed all day to the rays of the sun, was chosen. Upon this the skin was stretched and pegged down. Then every particle of the flesh was scraped off. After that, it was left about three days under the rays of the sun, and then it was cured. Twenty-five skins were saved in this manner, and, also, by the same method of drying in the sun, they jerked great quantities of the buffalo meat.

THE QUEST OF THE FOUR

But Middleton, Arenberg, Breakstone, and Phil turned hunters for the time. They found that the hill region was very extensive, timbered heavily, and abundant in game. They hunted wholly on foot, and found several places where the ravine opened out, at which they could cross the little river by walking, although the water rose to their waists.

They had great luck with the game, shooting a half dozen splendid black-tailed deer, a score of wild turkeys, and many partridges, quail, and grouse. Bill Breakstone, according to his promise, bathed in the river, and he did it more than once. He was also joined by his comrades, and, as Middleton had predicted, they found the water ice-cold. No one could stand it more than five minutes, but the effect was invigorating.

A great deal of work was done at the camp. The axles of wagons were greased, canvas ripped by wind or hail was sewed up again, clothing was patched, and the wounded basked in sun or shade. Two of these had died, but the rest were now nearly well. All except two or three would be fit to resume their duties when they started again.

Woodfall, knowing the benefit of a complete rest, still lingered, and Phil and his friends had much time for exploration. They combined this duty with that of the scouting, and penetrated deep into the hills, watching for any Comanches who might stray in there, or for the mountain tribes. Once they came upon several abandoned lodges, made partly of skins and partly of brush, but they were falling in ruins, and Bill Breakstone reckoned they were at least two years old.

"Wichitas, Wacos, Kechies, and Quapaws live around in the hills and mountains," he said, "and this, I take it, was a little camp of Kechies, from the looks of the lodges. Two or three groups of them may be lingering yet in this region, but we haven't much to fear from them."

THE COMANCHE VILLAGE

Woodfall, intending at first to make the stay only four or five days, decided now to protract it to ten or twelve. The journey to Santa Fé was one of tremendous length and hardship. Moreover, a buffalo hunter, straying in, told them that the Comanches were very active all over the Texas plains. Hence the Santa Fé train would need all its strength, and Woodfall was anxious that every one of the wounded should be in fighting condition when they left the timber. Therefore the delay.

Phil was glad of the added stay in the hills. He was developing great skill as a hunter and a trailer, and he and his comrades wandered farther and farther every day into the broken forest region toward the north. Oftenest he and Bill Breakstone were together. Despite the difference in years, they had become brothers of the wilderness. In their scoutings they found available pathways for horses over the hills and among the great trees, and, starting one morning, they rode far to the north, covering thirty or forty miles. Phil was interested in some high mountains which showed a dim blue ahead, and Breakstone was carefully examining the rock formations. But as night came on they found that the hills were dropping down, and the mountains seemed to be about as blue and as far ahead as ever.

"I should judge from these signs," said Breakstone, "that there is a valley or narrow plain ahead, between us and the mountains. But we'll look into that to-morrow. It isn't good to be riding around in the dark over hills and through thickets."

They found a little grassy open space, where they tethered their horses, leaving them to graze as long as they wished, and, lighting no fire, they ate jerked buffalo meat. Then they crept into snug coverts under the bushes, wrapped their blankets about them, and fell asleep. Phil opened his eyes at daylight to find Breakstone already awake. The horses were grazing contentedly. The trees and bushes were already tipped with fire by the gorgeous Texas sun.

"Sir Philip of the Bushes," said Bill Breakstone, "you just lie here and chew up a buffalo or two, while I go ahead and take a look. As I said last night, these hills certainly drop down into a plain, and I want to see that plain."

"All right," said Phil, "I'll stay where I am. It's so snug in this blanket on a cool morning that I don't care to move anyhow, and I can eat my breakfast lying down."

He drew out a freshly jerked strip of buffalo meat, and another very tender portion of a black-tailed deer that he himself had shot, and fell to it. Bill Breakstone, his rifle held conveniently at his side, slid away among the bushes. Phil ate contentedly. The sun rose higher. The morning was absolutely still. The horses seemed to have had enough grass, and lay down placidly on their sides. It occurred to Phil that he, too, had eaten enough, and he put the remainder of the food back in his hunter's knapsack. Then he began to get drowsy again. It was so very still. He thought once of rising and walking about, but he remembered Breakstone's advice to lie still, and, against his will, he kept it. Then his drowsiness increased, and, before he was aware of it he was asleep again.

When Phil awoke the second time, he threw off his blanket and sprang to his feet in surprise. The sun was high up in the blue arch. It must be at least ten o'clock in the morning, and Bill Breakstone had not come back. The horses were on their feet and were grazing again. They were proof that nothing had disturbed the glade. But Bill Breakstone was not there. Nor had he come back and gone away again. If he had done so, he would have awakened the boy. He had been absent three or four hours, and Phil was alarmed.

The boy stood up, holding his hand on the hammer of

THE COMANCHE VILLAGE

his rifle. This beautiful day, with its blue skies above and its green forest below, oppressed him. It was so still, so silent, and Bill Breakstone had vanished so utterly, just as if he had been turned into thin air by the wave of a magician's wand! The boy was alone in the wilderness for the first time. Moreover, he felt the presence of danger, and the queer little shiver which often comes at such moments ran through his blood. But the shiver passed, and his courage rose. He had no thought of going back to the camp to report that Bill Breakstone was missing. No, he would find him himself. That was his duty to his comrade.

The boy waited a little longer, standing there in the shade with his rifle ready, and eyes and ears intent. He stood thus for a quarter of an hour, scarcely moving. The brilliant sunshine poured down upon him, bringing out every line of the strong young figure, illuminating the face which was thrown a little forward, as the blue eyes, gazing intently through the undergrowth, sought some evidence of a hostile presence. Finally the eyes turned to the horses which were grazing calmly in the full circle of their long lariats. Phil decided that such calm on their part signified the absence of any enemy. If either man or beast came near they would raise their heads.

Then Phil moved forward through the bushes, putting into use all his new skill and caution. The bushes closed softly behind him, and he entered a slope covered with great trees without undergrowth. His eyes could range forward several hundred yards, but he saw nothing. He advanced for a few minutes, steadily descending, and he was tempted to shout his loudest or fire off his rifle as a signal to the derelict Bill Breakstone that it was time for him to come back. But he resisted both temptations, and soon he was glad that he had done so. The slope was very gradual, and he traveled a full two miles before he came to the edge of the woods and saw before him the plain that Bill Breakstone had predicted. He took one look, and then, springing back, sank down in the covert of the bushes.

Before Phil lay a fairly level plain about a mile in width and of unknown length, as in either direction it passed out of sight among the hills. In the center of it was a shallow but wide creek which perhaps flowed into the nameless river. The valley was very fertile, as the grass was already rich and high, despite the earliness of spring.

At the widest point of the valley stood a large Indian village, two hundred lodges at least, and Phil could not doubt that it was a village of the Comanches. Hundreds of ponies, grazing in the meadows to the north, and guarded by boys, proved that they were horse Indians, and no other tribe dared to ride where the Comanches roamed.

Phil could see far in the dazzling sunlight, and all the normal activities of human life, that is, of wild life, seemed to prevail in the Comanche village. Evidently the warriors had been on a great buffalo hunt. Perhaps they had struck at another point the same herd into which the train had run. Over a wide space buffalo hides were pegged down. Old squaws were scraping the flesh from some with little knives, while others, already cleaned, were drying in the sun. Vast quantities of buffalo meat were being jerked on temporary platforms. Little Indian boys and girls carried in their hand bones of buffalo or deer, from which they ate whenever they felt hungry. Everywhere it was a scene of savage plenty and enjoyment, although signs of industry were not wholly lacking, even among the warriors. Many of these, sitting on the grass, were cleaning their rifles or making new bows and arrows. Now and then one would make a test, sending into the air an arrow which some little boy was glad to run after and bring back. At another point a number of boys were practicing at a target with small bows and blunt-headed arrows. Two warriors on their ponies came up the valley, each carrying before him the

THE COMANCHE VILLAGE

body of a black-tailed deer. They were received with shouts, but soon disappeared with their spoils among the lodges, which were made universally of the skin of the buffalo. Down at the end of the village some warriors, naked to the breech cloth, danced monotonously back and forth, while an old man blew an equally monotonous tune on a whistle made of the bone of an eagle.

Phil, lying close in his covert, watched with absorbed eyes, and with mind and vision alike quick and keen, he took in every detail. The warriors were tall men, with intelligent faces, aquiline noses, thin lips, black eyes and hair, and but little beard. The hair grew very long, as they never cut it, and in many cases it was ornamented with bright beads and little pieces of silver. They wore deerskin leggins or moccasins, and a cloth of some bright color, bought from American Mexican traders, wrapped around the loins. The body from the loin cloth upward was naked, but in winter was covered with a buffalo robe. The women were physically very much inferior to the men. They were short and with crooked legs. Moreover, they wore their hair cut close, being compelled to do so by tribal law, the long-haired Comanche men and the short-haired Comanche women thus reversing the custom of civilization. Both men and women wore amulets. The Comanches, like most Indian tribes, were great believers in dreams, and the amulets were supposed to protect them from such as were bad.

Phil's roving eye lighted upon a small frame structure built of slight poles, the only one in the village not of hides. Such a building was always to be found in every Comanche village, but he did not know until later that it was a combined medicine lodge and vapor bath house. It was spherical in shape, and securely covered with buffalo hides. When a warrior fell seriously ill, he was seated in his lodge, beside several heated stone ovens, on which water was thrown in profusion. Then, while a dense, hot vapor arose, the shaman, or medicine man, practiced incantations, while men outside made music on whistles or the Indian drums. The hot bath was often effective, but the Comanche ascribed at least a part of the cure to the medicine man's incantations. Young Comanche men, also, often took a vapor bath before going on the war path, thinking that it had power to protect them from wounds.

Then Philip saw to the right a far larger building than that of the vapor bath, although it was made of dressed skins with just enough poles to support it. This was the medicine lodge of the Comanche village, a building used for important purposes, some of which Phil was to learn soon.

The boy did not doubt that his comrade had been taken, and, unless killed, was even now a captive in the Comanche village. He might be held in that huge medicine lodge, and the boy's resolution strengthened to the temper of steel. He could not go back to the train without Bill Breakstone; so he would rescue him. He did not yet have any idea how, but he would find a way. There were depths of courage in his nature of which he himself did not know, and springing from this courage was the belief that he would succeed.

While he yet lay in the covert he saw a band of Indians, about a dozen in number, riding up the valley. They were apparently visitors, but they were welcomed with loud cries. The leader of the band, a large man with brilliant feathers in his hair, replied with a shout. Then a horseman rode forth to meet him. Even at the distance Phil recognized the horseman as Black Panther. He, too, was arrayed in his finest, and, as a great crowd gathered, the two chiefs slowly approached each other. When their horses were side by side, Black Panther leaned over in his saddle, put his head on the other's shoulder, clasped his arms around his chest, and gave him a tremendous squeeze. The stranger returned the salute in kind, and then the two, amid great shouts of

THE COMANCHE VILLAGE

approval, rode among the lodges, disappearing from Phil's sight.

Phil watched awhile longer, but he saw nothing except the ordinary life of the village. Then he went back to the glen in which the horses were tethered. They were still grazing, and Bill Breakstone had not returned. Phil led them down to a little brook, let them drink, and then, after some thought, took off the lariats, coiled them around the saddles, and turned the animals loose. He believed they would stay in the glen or near it, as the pasturage was good, and the water plentiful, and that they could be found when needed.

Having attended to the horses, he returned to the edge of the forest and sat himself down to think out the plan of his great adventure.

It was his intention to enter the Comanche village without detection, and, hard as such a task seemed to him, it was even harder in reality. No race more wary than the Comanches ever lived. Besides the boys who habitually watched the ponies, they had regular details of warriors as herdsmen. Other details served as sentries about the village, and the adjacent heights were always occupied by scouts. All these guards were maintained night and day. Phil could see some of them now patrolling, and, knowing that any attempt of his would be impossible in the daylight, he waited patiently for night. He had with him enough food to last for a day or two, and, choosing a place in the dense covert, he lay down. He called up now all the wilderness lore of Breakstone, Arenberg, Middleton, and the others in the train. He knew that he must restrain all impulsiveness until the appointed time, and that he must lie without motion lest the keen eyes of wandering warriors should see the bushes above him moving in a direction other than that of the wind. He also laid his rifle parallel with his body, in the position in which it could be used most quickly, and loaded the pistol. It was hardest of all to lie perfectly

THE QUEST OF THE FOUR

still. He wished to turn over, to crawl to a new place, and his bones fairly ached, but he restrained himself. Naturally a youth of strength and determination, his mind took the mastery over his body, and held it fast and motionless among the bushes.

It was well that he controlled himself so completely. Indians came near the edge of the woods, and once some boys passed, driving a herd of ponies. But he crouched a little closer, and they went on. The day was fearfully long. The high sun poured down a shower of vertical beams that reached him even in the shelter of the bushes. The perspiration stood out on his brow, and his collar clung to his neck. He envied the freedom of the Comanches in the villages and the easy way in which they went about the pleasure of savage life. More warriors, evidently hunters, came in. Some bore portions of the buffalo, and others were loaded with wild turkeys.

In these hard hours the boy learned much. He had passed safely through battle. But there one was borne up by the thrill and excitement of the charge, the firing and shouting and the comradeship of his fellows. Here he was alone, silent and waiting. Enduring such as that, his will achieved new powers. A single day saw the mental growth of a year or two.

The sun passed the zenith and crept slowly down the western heavens. Welcome shadows appeared in the east, and the far lodges of the Comanches grew misty. Phil thought now that the village would sink into quiet, but he noticed instead a great bustle, and many people going about. Squaws bore torches which made a bright core of flame in the increasing dusk, and Phil was quite sure now that something unusual was going to occur. It seemed to him that the whole population of the village was gathering about the great medicine lodge. It must be the beginning of some important ceremony, and the time to enter the Comanche village was propitious. He inferred that on such an occasion the guard would be

THE COMANCHE VILLAGE

relaxed, at least in part, and as he heard the sound of hundreds of voices chanting monotonously he prepared for his great adventure.

The twilight faded, and the night came in its place, thick and dark. The sound of many voices, some singing, some talking, came clearly through the crisp, dry air. The core of light before the medicine lodge increased, and, by its radiance, he saw dusky figures hastening toward it to join the great group gathered there.

Phil took off his cap and hid it in the bushes. He would be bareheaded like the Comanches, wishing to look as much like them as possible. Fortunately his hair had grown somewhat long, and his face was deeply tanned. Once he thought of stripping to the waist in Comanche fashion, but his body, protected from the sun, was white, and he would be detected instantly.

He spent a little time flexing and stretching his muscles, because, when he first rose to his feet, he could scarcely stand, and the blood, choked up in the arteries and veins, tingled for lack of circulation. But the stiffness and pain soon departed, and he felt stronger than ever before in his life. Then he started.

He advanced boldly into the plain, bent very low, stopping at times to look and listen, and, also, to rest himself. More than once he lay flat upon the ground and allowed his muscles to relax. Once he saw upon his right two Indian warriors standing upon a knoll. They were a part of the night guard, and their figures were outlined duskily against the dusky sky. Their faces were not disclosed. But Phil knew that they were watching —watching with all the effectiveness of eye and ear for which the Indian is famous. At this point he crawled, and, in his crawling, he was so nearly flat upon his stomach that his advance was more like a serpent's than that of anything else.

He left the patrol behind, and then he saw another on his left, and much nearer to him, two more warriors, who did not occupy any knoll, but who merely walked back and forth on the flat plain. They were between him and the great fire, and he saw them very distinctly, tall men of light copper color, with high cheek-bones and long black hair. Both were armed with rifles, of which the Comanches were beginning to obtain a supply, and their faces in the glow of the firelight seemed very savage and very cruel to Phil. Now he flattened himself out entirely, and moved forward in a slow series of writhings, until he had passed them. There was an icy rim around his heart until he left these two behind, but when they were gone in the darkness his courage leaped up anew.

He now reached the eastern end of the village and crept among the lodges. They were all deserted. Their occupants had gone to witness the ceremony that was now at hand, whatever it might be. Not a woman, not a child was left. Phil stood up straight, and it was an immense relief to him to do so. It was a relief to the spirit as well as the body. He felt like a human being again, and not some creeping animal, a human being who stands upon his two feet, a human being who has a brain with which he thinks before he acts. It was strange, but this mere physical change gave him a further supply of courage and hope, as if he had already achieved his victory.

He passed between two lodges and saw a gleam beyond. It was the surface of the wide but shallow creek, showing through the dusk. The banks were five or six feet high, and there was a broad bed of sand extending on either side of the water.

Phil glanced up the stream, and saw that it flowed very close to the medicine lodge. An idea sprang up at once in his alert brain. Here was his line of approach. He dropped softly down the bank, taking his chance of quicksand, but finding instead that it was fairly firm to the feet. Then, hugging the bank, he advanced with noiseless tread toward the medicine lodge. Chance and his own quick mind served him well. His feet did not

THE COMANCHE VILLAGE

sink more than a few inches in the sand, and the bank continued at its uniform height of about six feet. He continued slowly, pausing on occasion to listen, because he could see nothing in the village. But occasional stray beams from the fires, passing over his head, fell upon the creek, lingering there for a moment or two in a red glow. Above him on the bank, but some distance back, the fires seemed to grow, and the monotonous beat of the singing grew louder. Phil knew that he was now very near the medicine lodge, and he paused a little longer than usual, leaning hard against the sandy bank with a sort of involuntary impulse, as if he would press his body into it to escape observation.

He looked up and saw two or three boughs projecting over the bank. Then the medicine lodge was some distance away, perhaps fifteen or twenty yards, and, therefore, the adventure would increase in peril! Another glance at the boughs reassured him. Perhaps there was a little grove between the creek and the medicine lodge, and it would afford him hiding! The largest of the boughs, amply able to support his weight, was not more than three or four feet above the bank, and, climbing cautiously the sandy slope, he grasped it and drew himself up. Then he slid along it until he came to the crotch of the tree, where he crouched, holding his rifle in one hand.

He was right in his surmise about the grove, although it was narrower than he had supposed, not more than seven or eight yards across at the utmost. But the trees were oak, heavy-limbed and heavy-trunked, and they grew close together. Nevertheless, the light from some of the fires showed through them, and at one side loomed the dark mass of the medicine lodge. As nearly as he could see, it was built directly against some of the trees. He crawled from his tree to the one next to it, and then to a third. There he stopped, and a violent fit of shuddering seized him. The trees were occupied already.

THE QUEST OF THE FOUR

On boughs so near that he could touch them rested a platform of poles about eight feet long and four feet wide. The poles were tied tightly together with rawhide thongs, and over them were spread leaves, grass, and small boughs. Upon these couches rested two long figures wrapped tightly in buffalo hide. They were the bodies of the dead. Farther on were other platforms and other bodies. Phil knew what the dark objects were. He had read and heard too much about Indian life to be mistaken, and, despite his power of will over self, he shuddered again and again. He surmised that these might be temporary burial platforms, as they were usually put in isolated places away from the village, but here they were, and now it occurred to him that their presence would be to his advantage. Superstition is strong among the Comanches, and they would not walk under the trees that supported the burial platforms on their boughs.

He advanced from bough to bough until he came directly against the skin walls of the great medicine lodge. There he lay along a strong and horizontal bough with his body pressed close to the wall, and a human eye ten feet away would not have seen him. Just above Phil's head was a place where two of the buffalo hides had not been sewn closely together, and the light from within shone out. He raised his head, widened the place with his knife, and looked down into the medicine lodge.

The boy beheld an extraordinary scene. From the roof of the lodge hung a joss or image, with the profile of a man, rudely carved from a split log. One side of the face was painted white, and the other black. Beneath it was a circular space about twenty feet in diameter, roped off and surrounded by a great crowd of people. Old squaws held aloft torches of pine or other wood that cast a ruddy light over eager and intense faces.

A great medicine dance was about to be held; and now the shaman, or chief medicine man, an old, dark Indian named Okapa, who for the present took precedence

THE COMANCHE VILLAGE

over both Black Panther and his visitor, who was the great chief Santana, was preparing to begin. Phil could see Okapa clearly as he stood alone in the center of the cleared circular space, carrying in his hands a short, carved stick, like a baton. It is hard to judge an Indian's age, but Phil Bedford believed that this man must be at least seventy. Nevertheless, despite his deeply lined and seamed face, he was erect and strong. But it was a cruel face, with thin, compressed lips, a large hooked nose, and jet black eyes that smoldered with dark fire. It was a face to inspire fear, and it was all the more ominous when the light of many torches fell upon it, tinting it a deeper and darker red.

Okapa raised his hand. Save for the tense breathing of the multitude there was silence in the lodge. Phil, forgetful of all danger, pressed more closely against the buffalo skin to see.

CHAPTER VI

THE MEDICINE LODGE

OKAPA uttered a name. A young warrior, bare to the waist, stepped forward, entering the circular space within the ropes. He called a second name, and a second warrior responded in like manner, then a third and fourth, and so on until his list was complete with twelve. These were to be the dancers. One was chosen for every one hundred persons—men, women, and children—in the band. Therefore, this village had a population of twelve hundred.

The dancers, all young men, stood close together, awaiting the signal. They had been taking strange compounds, like drugs, that the Indians make from plants, and their eyes were shining with wild light. Their bodies already moved in short, convulsive jerks. Any dancer who did not respond to his name would have been disgraced for life.

After a few moments Okapa called six more names, with a short delay after every one. Six powerful warriors, fully armed with rifle, tomahawk, and knife, responded, and took their position beside the ropes, but outside the ring. They were the guard, and the guard was always half the number of the dancers.

Now the breathing of the multitude became more intense and heavy, like a great murmur, and Okapa handed to every one of the dancers a small whistle made of wood or bone, in the lower end of which was fastened a single tail feather of the chaparral cock or road runner, known to the Indians as the medicine bird. The dancers put

THE MEDICINE LODGE

the little whistles in their mouths, then the shaman arranged them in a circle facing the center. The crowd in the medicine lodge now pressed forward, uttering short gasps of excitement, but the guards kept them back from the ropes.

To the boy at the slit between the buffalo skins it was wild, unreal, and fantastic beyond degree, some strange, mysterious ceremony out of an old world that had passed. He saw the bare chests of the warriors rising and falling, the women as eager as the men, a great mass of light coppery faces, all intense and bent forward to see better. He knew that the air in the medicine lodge was heavy, and that its fumes were exciting, like those of gunpowder. Parallel with the dancers, and exactly in the center of their circle, hung the hideously carved and painted joss or wooden image. The twelve looked fixedly at it.

The shaman, standing on one side but within the circle, uttered a short, sharp cry. Instantly the twelve dancers began to blow shrilly and continuously upon their whistles, and they moved slowly in a circle around and around toward the right, their eyes always fixed upon the joss. The multitude broke into a wild chant, keeping time to the whistles, and around and around the dancers went. The shaman, stark naked, his whole body painted in symbols and hieroglyphics, never ceased to watch them. To Philip's eyes he became at once the figure of Mephistopheles.

It was difficult for Phil afterward to account for the influence this scene had over him. He was not within the medicine lodge. Where he lay outside the fresh cool air of the night blew over him. But he was unconscious of it. He saw only the savage phantasmagoria within, and by and by he began to have some touch of the feeling that animated the dancers and the crowd. An hour, two hours went by. Not one of the men had ceased for an instant to blow upon his whistle, nor to move slowly around and around the wooden image, always to the right. The dance, like the music, was monotonous, merely a sort of leaping motion, but no warrior staggered. He kept his even place in the living circle, and on and on they went. Perspiration appeared on their faces and gleamed on their naked bodies. Their eyes, wild and fanatical, showed souls steeped in superstition and the intoxication of the dance.

Many of those in the crowd shared in the fierce paroxysm of the hour, and pressed forward upon the ropes, as if to join the dancers, but the armed guard thrust them back. The dancers, their eyes fixed on the joss, continued, apparently intending to go around the circle forever. The air in the lodge, heavy with dust and the odors of oil and paint and human beings, would have been intolerable to one just coming from the outside, but it only excited those within all the more.

Phil's muscles stiffened as he lay on the bough, but his position against one of the wooden scantlings that held the buffalo skins in place was easy, and he did not stir. His eyes were always at the slit and he became oppressed with a strange curiosity. How long could the men maintain the dancing and singing? He was conscious that quite a long time had passed, three or four hours, but there was yet no faltering. Nor did the chant of the crowd cease. Their song, as Phil learned later, ran something like this:

> "The Comanche goes forth to war,
> His arrow and bow he takes,
> The shaman's blessing is on his head.
> His eye is keen and his arm is strong;
> He rides the plain like the wind;
> His spirit is hot as the touch of fire.
> The foeman fights but his strength fails;
> His scalp hangs at the Comanche's belt."

There were four or five verses of this, but as soon as they were all sung, the singers went back to the beginning and sang them again and again in endless repeti-

THE MEDICINE LODGE

tion, while the twelve little whistles shrilled out their piercing accompaniment. The wind began to blow outside, but Phil did not feel it. Heavy clouds and vapors were drifting past, but he did not notice them, either. Would this incantation, for now it was nothing else, go on forever? Certainly the shaman, naked and hideously painted, presided with undiminished zest at this dance of the imps. He moved now and then about the circle of dancers, noting them sharply, his eye ready for any sign of wavering, whether of the spirit or the body.

Phil observed presently some shifting in the crowd of spectators, and then a new face appeared in the coppercolored mass. It was the face of a white man, and with a little start the boy recognized it as that of Bill Breakstone. It may seem singular, but he felt a certain joy at seeing him there. He had felt sure all the while that Breakstone was a prisoner, and now he had found him. Certainly he was in the midst of enemies. Nevertheless, the boy had gone a step forward in his search.

Breakstone was not bound—there was no need of it, a single white man in such a crowd—and Phil thought he could see pallor showing through his tan, but the captive bore himself bravely. Evidently he was brought forward as a trophy, as the chant was broken for a moment or two, and a great shout went up when he approached, except from the dancers, who circled on and on, blowing their whistles, without ceasing. Okapa walked over to Breakstone and brandished a tomahawk before his face, making the sharp blade whistle in front of his nose and then beside either cheek. Phil held his breath, but Bill Breakstone folded his arms and stood immovable, looking the ferocious shaman squarely in the face. It was at once the best thing and the hardest thing to do, never to flinch while a razor edge of steel flashed so close to one's face that it felt cold as it passed.

Two or three minutes of such amusement satisfied the shaman, and, going back inside the ropes, he turned his attention again to the dancers. It was now much past midnight, and the slenderest and youngest of the warriors was beginning to show some signs of weakness. The shaman watched him keenly. He would last a long time yet, and if he gave up it would not occur until he fell unconscious. Then he would be dragged out, water would be thrown over him, and, when he recovered, he would be compelled to resume dancing if the shaman ordered it. Sometimes the dancers died of exhaustion. It was well to be in the good graces of the shaman.

But Phil was now watching Bill Breakstone, who was pressing back in the crowd, getting as far as possible from the ropes that enclosed the dancers. Once or twice he saw Breakstone's face, and it seemed to him that he read there an intention, a summoning of his faculties and resolution for some great attempt. The mind of a man at such a time could hold only one purpose, and that would be the desire to escape. Yet he could not escape single-handed, despite the absorption of the Comanches in the medicine dance. There was only one door to the great lodge, and it was guarded. But Phil was there. He felt that the hand of Providence itself had sent him at this critical moment, and that Bill Breakstone, with his help, might escape.

He watched for a long time. It must have been three or four o'clock in the morning. The whistling, shrill, penetrating, now and then getting horribly upon his nerves, still went on. The wavering warrior seemed to have got his second wind, and around and around the warriors went, their eyes fixed steadily upon the hideous wooden face of the joss. Phil believed that it must be alive to them now. It was alive to him even with its ghastly cheek of black and its ghastly cheek of white, and its thick, red lips, grinning down at the fearful strain that was put upon men for its sake.

Phil's eyes again sought Breakstone. The captive had now pushed himself back against the buffalo skin

THE MEDICINE LODGE

wall and stood there, as if he had reached the end of his effort. He, too, was now watching the dancers. Phil noted his position, with his shoulder against one of the wooden pieces that supported the buffalo hide, and the lad now saw the way. Courage, resolution, and endurance had brought him to the second step on the stairway of success.

Phil sat on the bough and stretched his limbs again and again to bring back the circulation. Then he became conscious of something that he had not noticed before in his absorption. It was raining lightly. Drops fell from the boughs and leaves, but his rifle, sheltered against his coat, was dry, and the rain might serve the useful purpose of hiding the traces of footsteps from trailers so skilled as the Comanches.

He dropped to the ground and moved softly by the side of the lodge, which was circular in shape, until he came to the point at which he believed Bill Breakstone rested. There was the wooden scantling, and, unless he had made a great mistake, the shoulder of the captive was pressed against the buffalo hide on the left of it. He deliberated a moment or two, but he knew that he must take a risk, a big risk. No success was possible without it, and he drew forth his hunting-knife. Phil was proud of this hunting-knife. It was long, and large of blade, and keen of edge. He carried it in a leather scabbard, and he had used it but little. He put the sharp point against the buffalo hide at a place about the height of a man, and next to the scantling on the left. Then he pressed upon the blade, and endeavored to cut through the skin. It was no easy task. Buffalo hide is heavy and tough, but he gradually made a small slit, without noise, and then, resting his hand and arm, looked through it.

Phil saw little definite, only a confused mass of heads and bodies, the light of torches gleaming beyond them, and close by, almost against his eyes, a thatch of hair.

That hair was brown and curling slightly, such hair as never grew on the head of an Indian. It could clothe the head of Bill Breakstone and none other. Phil's heart throbbed once more. Courage and decision had won again. He put his mouth to the slit and whispered softly:

"Bill! Bill! Don't move! It is I, Phil Bedford!"

The thatch of brown hair, curling slightly at the ends, turned gently, and back came the whisper, so soft that it could not have been heard more than a foot away:

"Phil, good old Phil! You've come for me! I might have known it!"

"Are they still looking at the dance?"

"Yes, they can't keep their eyes off it."

"Then now is your only chance. You must get out of this medicine lodge, and I will help you. I'm going to cut through the buffalo hide low down, then you must stoop and push your way out at the slash, when they're not looking."

"All right," said Bill Breakstone, and Phil detected the thrill of joy in his tone. Phil stooped and bearing hard upon the knife, cut a slash through the hide from the height of his waist to the ground.

"Now, Bill," he whispered, "when you think the time has come, press through."

"All right," again came the answer with that leaping tone in it.

Phil put the knife back in its scabbard, and, pressing closely against the hide beside the slash, waited. Bill did not come. A minute, another, and a third passed. He heard the monotonous whistling, the steady chant, and the ceaseless beat of the dancer's feet, but Breakstone made no sound. Once more he pressed his lips to the slit, and said in the softest of tones:

"Are you coming, Bill?"

No answer, and again he waited interminable minutes. Then the lips of the buffalo skin parted, and a shoulder appeared at the opening. It was thrust farther, and a head and face, the head and face of Bill Breakstone, followed. Then he slipped entirely out, and the tough buffalo hide closed up behind him. Phil seized his hand, and the two palms closed in a strong grasp.

"I had to wait until nobody was looking my way," whispered Breakstone, "and then it was necessary to make it a kind of sleight-of-hand performance. I slipped through so quick that any one looking could only see the place where I had been."

Then he added in tones of irrepressible admiration:

"It was well done, it was nobly done, it was grandly done, Sir Philip of the Night and the Knife."

"Hark to that!" said Phil, "they miss you already!"

A shout, sharp, shrill, wholly different from all the other sounds, came from within the great medicine lodge. It was the signal of alarm. It was not repeated, and the whistling and wailing went on, but Phil and Breakstone knew that warriors would be out in an instant, seeking the lost captive.

"We must run for it," whispered Breakstone, as they stood among the trees.

"It's too late," said Phil. Warriors with torches had already appeared at either end of the grove, but the light did not yet reach where the two stood in the thick darkness, with the gentle rain sifting through the leaves upon them. Phil saw no chance to escape, because the light of the torches reached into the river bed, and then, like lightning, the idea came to him.

"Look over your head, Bill," he said. "You stand under an Indian platform for the dead, and I under another! Jump up on yours and lie down between the mummies, and I'll do the same here. Take this pistol for the last crisis, if it should come!"

He thrust his pistol into his companion's hand, seized a bough, and drew himself up. Bill Breakstone was quick of comprehension, and in an instant he did likewise. Two bodies tightly wrapped in deerskin were about three feet apart, and Phil, not without a shudder, lay down between them. Bill Breakstone on his platform did the same. They were completely hidden, but the soft rain seeped through the trees and fell upon their faces. Phil stretched his rifle by his side and scarcely breathed.

The medicine dance continued unbroken inside. Okapa, greatest shaman of the Comanches, still stood in the ring watching the circling twelve. The symbols and hieroglyphics painted on his naked body gleamed ruddily in the light of the torches, but the war chief, Black Panther, and the other great war chief, Santana, had gone forth with many good warriors. The single cry had warned them. Sharp eyes had quickly detected the slit in the wall of buffalo skin, and even the littlest Indian boy knew that this was the door by which the captive had passed. He knew, too, that he must have had a confederate who had helped from the outside, but the warriors were sure that they could yet retake the captive and his friend also.

Black Panther, Santana, and a dozen warriors, some carrying torches, rushed into the grove. They ran by the side of the medicine lodge until they came to the slit. There they stopped and examined it, pulling it open widely. They noticed the powerful slash of the knife that had cut through the tough buffalo hide four feet to the ground. Then they knelt down and examined the ground for traces of footsteps. But the rain, the beneficent, intervening rain, had done its work. It had pushed down the grass with gentle insistence and flooded the ground until nothing was left from which the keenest Comanche could derive a clue. They ran about like dogs in the brake, seeking the scent, but they found nothing. Warriors from the river had reported, also, that they saw nobody.

It was marvelous, incomprehensible, this sudden van-

THE MEDICINE LODGE

ishing of the captive and his friend, and the two chiefs were troubled. They glanced up at the dark platforms of the dead and shivered a little. Perhaps the spirits of those who had passed were not favorable to them. It was well that Okapa made medicine within to avert disaster from the tribe. But Black Panther and Santana were brave men, else they would not have been great chiefs, and they still searched in this grove, which was more or less sacred, examining behind every tree, prowling among the bushes, and searching the grass again and again for footsteps.

Phil lay flat upon his back, and those moments were as vivid in his memory years afterward as if they were passing again. Either elbow almost touched the shrouded form of some warrior who had lived intensely in his time. They did not inspire any terror in him now. His enemies alive, they had become, through no will of their own, his protectors dead. He did not dare even to turn on his side for fear of making a noise that might be heard by the keen watchers below. He merely looked up at the heavens, which were somber, full of drifting clouds, and without stars or moon. The rain was gradually soaking through his clothing, and now and then drops struck him in the eyes, but he did not notice them.

He heard the Comanches walking about beneath him, and the guttural notes of their words that he did not understand, but he knew that neither he nor Bill Breakstone could expect much mercy if they were found. After one escape they would be lucky if they met quick death and not torture at the hands of the Comanches. He saw now and then the reflection of the torch-lights high up on the walls of the medicine lodge, but generally he saw only the clouds and vapors above him.

Despite the voices and footsteps, Phil felt that they would not be seen. No one would ever think of looking in such places for him and Breakstone. But the wait was terribly long, and the suspense was an acute physical strain. He felt his breath growing shorter, and the strength seemed to depart from his arms and legs. He was glad that he was lying down, as it would have been hard to stand upon one's feet and wait, helpless and in silence, while one's fate was being decided. There was even a fear lest his breathing should turn to a gasp, and be heard by those ruthless searchers, the Comanches. Then he fell to calculating how long it would be until dawn. The night could not last more than two or three hours longer, and if they were compelled to remain there until day, the chance of being seen by the Comanches would become tenfold greater.

He longed, also, to see or hear his comrade who lay not ten feet away, but he dared not try the lowest of whispers. If he turned a little on his side to see, the mummy of some famous Comanche would shut out the view; so he remained perfectly still, which was the wisest thing to do, and waited through interminable time. The rain still dripped through the foliage, and by and by the wind rose, the rain increasing with it. The wet leaves matted together, but above wind and rain came the sound from the medicine lodge, that ceaseless whistling and beating of the dancers' feet. He wondered when it would stop. He did not know that Comanche warriors had been known to go around and around in their dance three days and three nights, without stopping for a moment, and without food or water.

After a long silence without, he heard the Comanches moving again through the grove, and the reflection from the flare of a torch struck high on the wall of the medicine lodge. They had come back for a second search! He felt for a few moments a great apprehension lest they invade the platforms themselves, but this thought was quickly succeeded by confidence in the invisibility of Breakstone and himself, and the superstition of the Indians.

THE MEDICINE LODGE

The tread of the Comanches and their occasional talk died away, the lights disappeared from the creek bed, and the regions, outside the medicine lodge and the other lodges, were left to the darkness and the rain. Phil felt deep satisfaction, but he yet remained motionless and silent. He longed to call to Breakstone, but he dreaded lest he might do something rash. Bill Breakstone was older than he, and had spent many years in the wilderness. It was for him to act first. Phil, despite an overwhelming desire to move and to speak, held himself rigid and voiceless. In a half hour came the soft, whispering question:

"Phil, are you there?"

It was Breakstone from the next tree, and never was sound more welcome. He raised himself a little, and drops of rain fell from his face.

"Yes, I'm here, Bill, but I'm mighty anxious to move," he replied in the same low tone.

"I'm tired of having my home in a graveyard, too," said Bill Breakstone, "though I'll own that for the time and circumstances it was about the best home that could be found this wide world over. It won't be more than an hour till day, Phil, and if we make the break at all we must make it now."

"I'm with you," said Phil. "The sooner we start, the better it will please me."

"Better stretch yourself first about twenty times," said Bill Breakstone. "Lying so long in one position with the rain coming down on top of you may stiffen you up quite a lot."

Phil obeyed, flexing himself thoroughly. He sat up and gently touched the mummy on either side of him. He had no awe, no fear of these dead warriors. They had served him well. Then, swinging from a bough, he dropped lightly to the ground, and he heard the soft noise of some one alighting near him. The form of Bill Breakstone showed duskily.

THE QUEST OF THE FOUR

"Back from the tombs," came the cheerful whisper. "Phil, you're the greatest boy that ever was, and you've done a job that the oldest and boldest scout might envy.

"I was a captive,
The Indians had me;
Phil was adaptive,
Now they've lost me.

"I composed that rhyme while I was lying on the death platform up there. I certainly had plenty of time —and now which way did you come, Phil?"

"Under the shelter of the creek bank. The woods run down to it, and it is high enough to hide a man."

"Then that is the way we will go, and we will not linger in the going. Let the Comanches sing and dance if they will. They can enjoy themselves that way, but we can enjoy ourselves more by running down the dark bed of a creek."

They slipped among the wet trees and bushes, and silently lowered themselves down the bank into the sand of the creek bottom. There they took a parting look at the medicine lodge. It showed through a rift in the trees, huge and dark, and on either side of it the two saw faint lights in the village. Above the soft swishing of the rain rose the steady whistling sound from the lodge, which had never been broken for a moment, not even by the escape of the prisoner and the search.

"I was never before so glad to tell a place good-by," whispered Bill Breakstone.

"It's time to go," said Phil. "I'll lead the way, as I've been over it once."

He walked swiftly along the sand, keeping well under cover of the bank, and Bill Breakstone was close behind him. They heard the rain pattering on the surface of the water, and both were wet through and through, but joy thrilled in every vein of the two. Bill Breakstone had escaped death and torture; Phil Bedford, a boy, had rescued him in face of the impossible, and they certainly had full cause for rejoicing.

"How far down the creek bed do you think we ought to go?" asked Breakstone.

"A quarter of a mile anyway," replied Phil, "and then we can cut across the plain and enter the forest."

Everything had been so distinct and vivid that he remembered the very place at which he had dropped down into the creek bed, when he approached the medicine lodge, and when he came to it again, he said: "Here we are," springing up at one bound. Breakstone promptly followed him. Then a figure appeared in the dusk immediately in front of Phil, the figure of a tall man, naked save the breech cloth, a great crown of brightly colored feathers upon his head. It was a Comanche warrior, probably the last of those returning from the fruitless search for the captive.

The Comanche uttered the whoop of alarm, and Phil, acting solely on impulse, struck madly with the butt of his rifle. But he struck true. The fierce cry was suddenly cut short. The boy, with a shuddering effect, felt something crush beneath his rifle stock. Then he and Bill Breakstone leaped over the fallen body and ran with all their might across the plain toward the woods.

"It was well that you hit so quick and hard," breathed Breakstone, "but his single yell has alarmed the warriors. Look back, they are getting ready to pursue."

Phil cast one hurried glance over his shoulder. He saw lights twinkling among the Comanche lodges, and then he heard a long, deep, full-throated cry, uttered by perhaps a hundred throats.

"Hark to them!" exclaimed Breakstone. "They know the direction from which that cry came, and you and I, Phil, will have to make tracks faster than we ever did before in our lives."

"At any rate, we've got a good start," said Phil.

They ran with all speed toward the woods, but behind

them and in other directions they heard presently the beat of hoofs, and both felt a thrill of alarm.

"They are on their ponies, and they are galloping all over the plain," said Bill Breakstone. "Some of them are bound to find us, but you've the rifle, and I've the pistol!"

They ran with all their might, but from two or three points the ominous beat of hoofs came closer. They were devoutly glad now of the rain and the shadowed moon that hid them from all eyes except those very near. Both Phil and Breakstone stumbled at intervals, but they would recover quickly, and continue at undiminished speed for the woods, which were now showing in a blacker line against the black sky.

There was a sudden swift beat of hoofs, and two warriors galloped almost upon them. Both the warriors uttered shouts at sight of the fugitives, and fired. But in the darkness and hurry they missed. Breakstone fired in return, and one of the Indians fell from his pony. Phil was about to fire at the other, but the Comanche made his pony circle so rapidly that in the faint light he could not get any kind of aim. Then he saw something dark shoot out from the warrior's hand and uncoil in the air. A black, snakelike loop fell over Bill Breakstone's head, settled down on his shoulders, and was suddenly drawn taut, as the mustang settled back on his haunches. Bill Breakstone, caught in the lasso, was thrown to the ground by the violent jerk, but with the stopping of the horse came Phil's chance. He fired promptly, and the Comanche fell from the saddle. The frightened mustang ran away, just as Breakstone staggered dizzily to his feet. Phil seized him by the arm.

"Come, Bill, come!" he cried. "The woods are not thirty yards away!"

"Once more unto the breach, or rather the woods!" exclaimed the half-unconscious man. "Lead on, Prince Hal, and I follow! That's mixed, but I mean well!"

THE MEDICINE LODGE

They ran for the protecting woods, Breakstone half supported by Phil, and behind them they now heard many cries and the tread of many hoofs. A long, black, snake-like object followed Bill Breakstone, trailing through the grass and weeds. They had gone half way before Phil noticed it. Then he snatched out his knife and severed the lasso. It fell quivering, as if it were a live thing, and lay in a wavy line across the grass. But the fugitives were now at the edge of the woods, and Bill Breakstone's senses came back to him in full.

"Well done again, Sir Philip of the Knife and the Ready Mind," he whispered. "I now owe two lives to you. I suppose that if I were a cat I would in the end owe you nine. But suppose we turn off here at an angle to the right, and then farther on we'll take another angle. I think we're saved. They can't follow us on horses in these dense woods, and in all this darkness."

They stepped lightly now, but drew their breaths in deep gasps, their hearts throbbing painfully, and the blood pounding in their ears. But they thanked God again for the clouds and the moonless, starless sky. It could not be long until day, but it would be long enough to save them.

They went nearly a quarter of a mile to the right, and then they took another angle, all the while bearing deeper into the hills. From time to time they heard the war cries of the Comanches coming from different points, evidently signals to one another, but there was no sound of footsteps near them.

"Let's stop and rest a little," said Bill Breakstone. "These woods are so thick and there is so much undergrowth that they cannot penetrate here with horses, and, as they know that at least one of us is armed, they will be a little wary about coming here on foot. They know we'd fight like tigers to save ourselves. 'Thrice armed is he who hath his quarrel just,' and if a man who is trying to save his life hasn't got a just quarrel, I don't know who has. Here's a good place."

They had come to a great oak which grew by the side of a rock projecting from a hill. The rain had been gentle, and the little alcove, formed by the rock above and the great trunk of the tree on one side, was sheltered and dry. Moreover, it contained many dead leaves of the preceding autumn, which had been caught there when whirled before the winds. It was large enough for two, and they crept into it, not uttering but feeling deep thanks.

CHAPTER VII

THE GREAT SLEEP

WHEN Phil drew the warm leaves about him he felt a mighty sensation of relief, accompanied by a complete mental and physical relaxation. The supreme tension of the spirit that had borne him up so long was gone now, when it was needed no longer, and he uttered a deep sigh of content. Bill Breakstone put a hand upon his shoulder.

"Phil," he said simply, "I owe you so much that I can't ever repay it."

"Your chance will come," replied the boy. "You'll probably do more for me than I've ever done for you."

"We'll see," said Bill Breakstone. "I'm thinking, Phil, that this is about the best hiding place we could have found, so we'll just lie quiet, as we'll see the edge of the day inside of half an hour."

The two remained perfectly still. Yet they could hear for awhile their own strained breathing, and Phil felt his heart constrict painfully after his long flight. But the breathing of both grew easier. In a short while it was normal again. Then they saw a touch of gray in the east, the rain ceased like a dissolving mist, a silver light fell over the forest, turning presently to gold, and it was day in the east.

Some of the sunbeams entered the thick jungle of forest where they lay, touching the leaves and grass here and there with gold, but in most places the shadows still hovered. Phil and Breakstone looked at their surroundings. They had left no trail in coming there, and the bushes about them were so dense that even Indian eyes ten feet away could not have seen them.

The sunlight was deepening. Birds in the trees began to sing. All the beings of the wilderness, little and big, awoke to life. Trees and grass dried swiftly under the strong fresh wind. Bill Breakstone glanced at his youthful comrade.

"Phil," he said, "I'll take the rifle, and you go to sleep. You've had a harder time than I have, and, when you wake up, I'll tell you how I was captured."

"I think I'll do it, Bill," said the boy, putting his arm under his head and closing his eyes. The strain was gone from his nerves now, and sleep came readily. In three minutes he was oblivious of Comanches and all else that the world contained. Bill Breakstone could have slept if he had tried, but he did not try. Under a manner nearly always light and apparently superficial he concealed a strong nature and much depth of feeling. It seemed to him that at the last moment a hand had been stretched out to save him from the worst of fates. It seemed to him, also, that it must have been a sort of inspiration, the direction of a supreme will, for Phil to have come to him at such a time. It was a brave deed, a wonderful deed, and it had been brilliantly successful.

The light was strong, and Bill Breakstone looked down at the boy who was a younger brother to him now. He saw that the strain upon Phil had been great. Even while he slept his face was very white, except where fatigue and suspense had painted it black beneath the eyes. Phil Bedford had done more than his share, and it was now for him, Bill Breakstone, to do the rest. He slipped the muzzle of the rifle forward in order that it might command the mouth of the hollow, and waited. He would have pulled more leaves and brush before the entrance, but he knew that any disturbance of nature would attract the eye of a passing Comanche, and he allowed everything to remain exactly as it had been.

THE GREAT SLEEP

He lay comfortably among the leaves, and for a long time he did not stir. Phil breathed regularly and easily, and Bill saw that he would be fully restored when he awoke. Bill himself thought neither of hunger nor thirst, the tension was too great for that, but he never ceased to watch the sweep of trees and brush. It was half way toward noon when he saw some bushes about ten yards in front of him trembling slightly. He became at once alert and suspicious. He drew himself up in the attitude of one who is ready for instant action, slipping the muzzle of the rifle a little farther forward.

The bushes moved again, and something came into view. Bill Breakstone sank back, and his apprehension departed. It was a timber wolf, gray and long. A dangerous enough beast, if a man alone and unarmed met a group of them, but Bill, with the rifle, had no fear. The wolf sniffed the odor of flesh, sniffed again, knew that it was the odor of human flesh, and his blood became afraid within him. Bill Breakstone laughed quietly, but the boy slept placidly on. The incident amused Bill, and, therefore, it was welcome. It broke the monotony of the long quiet, and, just when he was laughing noiselessly for the fourth time over the wolf's discomfiture, the bushes moved again. Bill, as before, slipped the muzzle of his rifle farther forward and waited. A slight pungent odor came to his nostrils. The bushes moved more than before, although without noise, and a great yellow body came into view. The eyes were green, the claws sharp and long, and the body lithe and powerful. It was a splendid specimen of the southwestern puma, a great cat that could pull down a deer. But Bill Breakstone was still unafraid. He raised the rifle and aimed it at the puma, although he did not press the trigger.

"I can kill you, my friend, with a single bullet," he murmured, "but the report of that rifle would probably bring the Comanches upon us. Therefore, I will look you down."

THE QUEST OF THE FOUR

The puma paused in doubt and indecision, restlessly moving his tail, and staring with his great green eyes until they met the gray eyes of the human creature, looking down the sights of the rifle barrel. That steady, steel-like gaze troubled the puma. He was large and powerful. He could have struck down the man at a single blow, but the heart within that mass of bone and muscle became afraid. The green eyes looked fearfully into the gray ones, and at last turned aside. The great beast turned stealthily, and slid into the thicket, at first slowly, and then in a run, as the terror that he could not see crowded upon his heels.

Bill Breakstone had laughed several times that morning, but now he laughed with a deep unction.

"I'm proud of myself," he murmured. "It's something to outlook a panther, but I don't know that I'd have looked so straight and hard if I hadn't had the rifle ready, in case the eyes failed. Now I wonder who or what will be the next invader of our premises."

His wonder lasted only until noon, when the sun was poised directly overhead, and the open spaces were full of its rays. Then, as light as the beasts themselves had been, two Comanches walked into full view. Bill Breakstone was as still as ever, but his hand lay upon the trigger of the rifle.

The Comanches were not a pleasant sight to eyes that did not wish to see them. They were powerful men, naked save for the waist cloth, their bodies painted with many strange symbols and figures. Although most of their tribe were yet armed with bows and arrows, each carried a fine rifle. Their faces were wary, cunning, and cruel. They were far more to be dreaded than wolf or panther. Yet Bill Breakstone at that moment felt but little fear of either. He was upheld by a great stimulus. The boy who slept so peacefully by his side had saved him in the face of everything, and, if the time had come, he would do as much for Phil. He felt himself, with the

THE GREAT SLEEP

rifle and pistol, a match for both warriors, and his breathing was steady and regular.

The warriors stopped and stood in the bush, talking and pointing toward the east. Bill Breakstone surmised that they were talking about him and Phil, and it was likely from their pointing fingers that they believed the fugitives had gone toward the east. As Bill watched them, his suspense was mingled with a sort of curiosity. Would some instinct warn them that Phil and he lay not ten yards away? The woods were vast, and they and all their comrades could not search every spot. Would this be one of the spots over which they must pass?

It took two minutes to decide the question, and then the warriors walked on toward the east, their brown bodies disappearing in the foliage. Bill drew a mighty breath that came from every crevice and cranny of his lungs. He did not know until then how great his suspense had been. He sank back a little and let the rifle rest softly on the leaves beside him. He glanced at Phil. His face was less drawn now, and much of the color had come back. While Bill awaited the crisis, his finger on the trigger, the sleeping boy had grown stronger. Bill decided that he would let him sleep on.

Bill Breakstone had been through much. He, too, began to feel sleepy. The dangers of animal and man had come and passed, leaving his comrade and him untouched. His nerves were now subdued and relaxed, and he felt a great physical and mental peace. The day, too, was one calculated to soothe. The air was filled with the mildness of early spring. A gentle wind blew, and the boughs and bushes rustled together, forming a sound that was strangely like a song of peace.

But Bill Breakstone was a man watchful, alert, a sentinel full of strength and resolution. He would not sleep, no, not he, not while so much depended upon him, yet the song among the leaves was growing sweeter and gentler all the time. He had never felt such a soothing quiet in all his life. The complete relaxation after so much danger and tension was at hand, and it was hard for one to watch the forest and be troubled about foes who would no longer come. Yet he would remain awake and keep faithful guard, and, as he murmured his resolution for the fifth time, his drooping eyelids shut down entirely, and he slept as soundly as the boy who lay by his side, his chest rising and falling as he breathed long and regularly.

Phil Bedford and Bill Breakstone slept all that afternoon. It was a mighty sleep, the great sleep following complete mental and physical exhaustion, the sleep that comes at such times to strong, healthy beings, in whom the co-ordination of brain, muscle, and nerve is complete.

By some unconscious method of keeping time they breathed in perfect unison, and the gentle wind, which all the while was blowing through the leaves, kept time with them, too. Thus the evening shortened. Hour by hour dropped into the sandglass of time. The two, rivals of the ancient seven of famous memory, slept on. Both the wolf and the puma, driven by curiosity, came back. They crept a little nearer than before, but not too near. They felt instinctively that the mighty sleepers, mightily as they slept, could yet be awakened, and the smell of man contained a quality that was terrifying. So they went away, and, an hour after they were gone, the same two Comanches, naked to the waist, painted hideously in many symbols and decorations, and savage and cruel of countenance, came back in their places. But Bill Breakstone and Phil lay safe in the leaves under the bank, sleeping peacefully without dreams. So far as the Comanches were concerned, they were a thousand miles away, and presently the two warriors disappeared again in the depths of the forest, this time not to return.

Time went on. The two slept the great sleep so quietly that all the normal life of the woods about them was resumed. Woodpeckers drummed upon the sides of

THE GREAT SLEEP

the hollow trees, a red bird in a flash of flame shot among the boughs, quail scuttled in the grass, and a rabbit hopped near. Midafternoon of a cloudless day came. The sun shot down its most brilliant beams, the whole forest was luminous with light. The Comanches ceased their search, confident that the fugitives were gone now beyond their overtaking, and returned to their villages and other enterprises, but Breakstone and Phil slept their great sleep.

Twilight came, and they were still sleeping. Neither had stirred an inch from his place. The little animals that hopped about in the thickets believed them dead, they were so quiet, and came nearer. Night came on, thick and dark. An owl in a tree hooted mournfully, and an owl in another tree a half mile away hooted a mournful answer. Phil and his comrade did not hear, because they still lay in their great sleep, and the doings of the world, great or small, did not concern them.

Phil awoke first. It was then about midnight, and so dark in the alcove that he could not see. His eyes still heavy with sleep and his senses confused, he sat up. He shook his head once or twice, and recollection began to come back. Surely the daylight had come when he went to sleep! And where was Bill Breakstone? He heard a regular breathing, and, reaching out his hands, touched the figure of his comrade. Both had slept, and no harm had come to them. That was evident because he also touched the rifle and pistol, and they would have been the first objects taken by a creeping enemy. But surely it could not have been a dream about his going to sleep in the daylight! He remembered very well that the sun was rising and that there were golden beams on the bushes. Now it was so dark that he could see only a few faint stars in the sky, and the bashful rim of a moon. He sat up and gave Bill Breakstone a vigorous shake.

"Bill," he said, "wake up! It's night, but what night I don't know!"

THE QUEST OF THE FOUR

Bill Breakstone yawned tremendously, stretched himself as much as the narrow space would allow, and then slowly and with dignity sat up. He, too, was somewhat confused, but he pretended wisdom while he was trying to collect his senses. The two could barely see each other, and each felt rather than saw the wonder in the other's eyes.

"Well," said Bill Breakstone at last, "I'd have you to know, Sir Philip of the Dream and the Snore, though I can't prove that you've done either any more than I can prove that I haven't done both, that we're the genuine and true Babes in the Wood, only we've waked up. Here we've been asleep, maybe a week, maybe a month, and the pitying little birds have come and covered us up with leaves, and we've been warm and snug, and the wild animals haven't eaten us up, and the bad men, that is to say the Comanches, haven't found us. How do you feel, Phil?"

"Fine, never better in my life."

"That describes me, also, with beautiful accuracy. We'll never know, maybe, how long we've slept, whether one day, two days, or three days, but a good spirit has been watching over us; of that I'm sure.

>"Phil and Bill,
>To sleep they went;
>Phil and Bill
>From sleep they came.
>Phil and Bill,
>They had no tent;
>But Phil and Bill,
>They are true game.
>Phil and Bill,
>The leaves, a bed,
>Phil and Bill,
>They took no ill.
>That's Phil and Bill.

"I don't think that's a bad poem, Phil, considering the short time I've had for its composition, and you'll

THE GREAT SLEEP

observe that, with a modesty not common among poets, I've put you first."

"It's all right for the time," said Phil, "but don't do it too often. But, Bill, I'd trade a whole slab of poetry for an equal weight in beef or venison. I'm beginning to feel terribly hungry."

"I'd make the trade, too," said Bill Breakstone, "and that's not holding poetry so cheap, either. It's pleasant for the Babes in the Wood to wake up again, but there's a disadvantage; you've got to eat, and to eat you've got to find something that can be eaten. I'm like King Richard, 'A horse! A horse! My kingdom for a horse!' But I wouldn't ride that horse; I'd eat him."

"What time o' night would you say it is, Bill?"

Bill Breakstone attentively studied the few stars to be seen in the extremely dusky heavens.

"I'd say it was somewhere between six o'clock in the evening and six o'clock in the morning, with the emphasis on the 'somewhere.' I wonder what's happened around in these woods since we went to sleep last week, Phil; but I suppose we'll never know."

Bill stood up, and with his fingers combed the leaves out of his hair.

"Phil," he said, "I'll tell you the story of my life for the last day or two. It doesn't make a long narrative, but while it was happening it was tremendously moving to me. When I left you I skipped along through the edge of the woods and came to the plain. Then I saw the Indian village and the Indian horses grazing on the meadows. I looked them over pretty thoroughly, concluded I didn't like 'em, and started back to tell you about 'em. I thought I was mighty smart, but I wasn't smart enough by half."

"What happened?"

"Just as I turned around to start upon my worthy mission, three large, unclothed Comanches laid rude hands upon me. I didn't have much chance, one against three, and surprise on their side, too. They soon had me by the neck and heels, and carried me off to their village, where they gave me the welcome due to a distinguished stranger. Black Panther was especially effusive. He wanted to know all about me and my friends, if any, perchance, were near by. It was the same band that had attacked our wagon train and that was beaten off. Their scouts had warned them that we were on the other side of the big forest, but they were afraid to attack again. I gathered from what Black Panther said—he understands English, and I understand some Comanche—that they believed me to be lost, strayed, or stolen—that is, I had wandered away in some manner, or had been left behind. The chief tried to get all sorts of information out of me, but I didn't have any to tell. Finding that I was born dumb, he began to talk about punishments."

"What were they going to do to you, Bill?"

"There was a lot of lurid talk. I say 'lurid' because I seem to remember something about flames. Anyway, it was to be unpleasant, and I suppose if you hadn't come, Phil, at the right time, I shouldn't ever have had the great sleep that I've enjoyed so much, at least not that particular kind of sleep. Phil, it looks to me as if you came when I called, and I'm not joking, either."

"We'll put that aside," said Phil, "and hunt something to eat."

"Yes, it's our first duty to provision this army of two," said Bill Breakstone, "and I think we can do it. The woods are full of game, but we'll have to wait till morning for a shot. As for the Indians hearing the reports of our rifles, we must take the chance of that, but I don't think they'll roam very far from the village, and we'll spend the rest of the night going toward the point where we left the wagon train, which is directly away from the Comanches. Toward morning we'll sit down by the bank of a stream if we can find one, and wait for the game to come to drink."

THE GREAT SLEEP

"That seems to me to be our best plan," said Phil.

Both had a good idea of direction, and, despite the darkness, they advanced in a fairly straight line toward the point they sought. But they found it rough traveling through the thick undergrowth, among briers and across ravines and gulleys. Meanwhile, old King Hunger, bristling and fearsome, seized them and rent them with his fangs. There was no resisting. They must even suffer and stand it as best they could.

"I think it's at least a thousand hours until day," said Bill Breakstone at last. "Do you know, Phil, I've got to the point where I'd enjoy one of those stage banquets that I've often had. You don't really eat anything. The plates are empty, the glasses are empty, and, empty as they all are, they're generally whisked away before you can get a good long look at them. But there's something soothing and filling about them anyway. Maybe it's an illusion, but if an illusion is of the right kind, it's just the right kind of thing that you ought to have."

"An illusion may be all right for you, Bill," returned Phil, "but what about some of those dinners you can get in New Orleans. Oyster soup, Bill; fish fresh from the gulf, Bill; nice old Virginia ham, Bill; stuffed Louisiana turkey, Bill; a haunch of venison, Bill; fried chicken, Bill; lamb chops, Bill; and a lot of other things that money can buy in New Orleans, Bill?"

"If you weren't my best friend, Phil, and if you hadn't just saved my life, I might make an attack upon you with the intent of bodily harm. You surely make me sour with your talk about the whole provision train that can be bought in New Orleans with money. Hear that old owl hooting! He's just laughing at us. I'd stop and shoot him if we had light enough for a shot."

"Never mind the owl, Bill," said Phil. "Perhaps when we get that good juicy deer we're looking for we can hoot back at him, if we feel like it."

THE QUEST OF THE FOUR

"That's so," said Bill, although he said it gloomily.

They advanced in silence another hour, and then Phil, who was a little in advance, stopped suddenly. He had seen the gleam of water, and he pointed it out to his comrade.

"A spring," said Bill Breakstone, "and it's been trampled around the edges by many hoofs and paws."

He stooped and tasted the water. Then he uttered a mighty sigh of satisfaction.

"A salt spring, too," he said. "We're in luck, Phil. I see our breakfast coming straight toward us at this spring, walking briskly on four legs. The wild animals always haunt such places, and if we don't have savory steaks before the sun is an hour high, then I'm willing to starve to death. We must find an ambush. Here it is! Luck's a funny thing, Phil. It goes right against you for awhile, and nothing seems able to break it. Then it turns right around and favors you, and no fool thing that you do seems to change it. But I guess it evens up in the long run."

They found a dense clump of bushes about twenty yards from the salt spring, and sat down among them.

"There's no wind at all," whispered Bill Breakstone, "so I don't think that any animal eager for his salt drink will notice us. I've got my heart set on deer, Phil, and deer we must have. Now which of us shall take the rifle and make the shot? The rifle is yours, you know, and you have first choice."

But Phil insisted upon the older and more experienced man taking the weapon, and Breakstone consented. Then they lay quiet, eagerly watching every side of the spring. The darkness soon thinned away, and the bushes and trees became luminous in the early morning light.

"Something will come soon," said Breakstone.

They waited a little longer, and then they heard a rustling among the bushes on the far side of the spring. The bushes moved, and a black-tailed deer, a splendid

THE GREAT SLEEP

buck, stepped into the opening. He paused to sniff the air, but nothing strange or hostile came to his nostrils. The deadly figure, crouching in the bushes with the loaded rifle at his cheek, might have been a thousand miles away, for all the deer knew.

Phil and Bill Breakstone might have admired the deer at another time, but now other emotions urged them on. The deer stepped down to the water. Breakstone looked down the sights, and Phil trembled lest he should miss. He tried to look along the barrel himself and see what spot Bill had picked out on the animal's body. Then he watched the marksman's finger curl around the trigger and at last press hard upon it. The flash of flame leaped forth, the report sounded startlingly loud in the clear morning, and the deer jumped high in the air.

But when the big buck came down he ran into the forest as if he had not been touched. Phil uttered a gasp of despair, but Bill Breakstone only laughed.

"Don't you fret, Phil," he said. "My heart was in my mouth, but my bullet didn't miss. He's hit hard, and we've got nothing to do but follow him by the plain trail he'll leave. We'll come to our breakfast in less than ten minutes."

Phil soon saw that Breakstone was right. The trail on the other side of the salt spring was plain and red, and presently they found the great stag in a thicket, lying upon his side, stone dead. Bill Breakstone was an adept at cleaning and dressing, and soon the ugly work was over. They always carried matches, and Phil quickly lighted a fire of dry sticks that burned up rapidly and that soon made a fine heap of glowing coals.

"Now," said Breakstone, "we'll cook and eat, then we'll cook and eat again, then we'll cook and eat once more."

"And I don't care very much whether Comanches heard the rifle shot or not," said Phil. "It seems to me that when I eat as much as I want I can whip the whole Comanche nation."

"I feel that way, too," said Bill Breakstone, "but the Comanches didn't hear. I know it in my bones. Didn't I tell you about that streak of luck? Luck's coming our way now, and the streak will last for awhile."

They cut long twigs, sharpened them at the ends, and fried over the coals strips of the deer, which gave out such a rich aroma as they sputtered that the two could scarcely restrain themselves. Yet they did it, they remained white men and gentlemen, and did not guzzle.

"Phil," said Bill, before he took a single bite, "I remember about that dinner in New Orleans you were talking of so long ago. I remember about those beautiful oysters, those splendid fish from the gulf, the gorgeous Virginia ham, the magnificent Louisiana turkey; yes, I remember all those magnificent fripperies and frummeries, but it seems to me if they were all set down before us, spread on a service of golden plate, they wouldn't be finer than what is now awaiting us."

"Bill," said Phil with deep emphasis and unction, "you never spoke truer words in your life."

"Then lay on, Macduff, and the first who cries 'hold, enough'—well, he won't be much of a trencherman."

They fell to. They did not eat greedily, but they ate long and perseveringly. Strip after strip was fried over the coals, gave out its savory odor, and disappeared. Phil occasionally replenished the fire, adding to the bed of coals, but keeping down the smoke. Bill, stretching his long body on the ground and then propping himself up on his elbow, concluded that it was a beautiful world.

"Didn't I tell you our luck would hold for awhile?" he repeated. "Since we got into the woods, things have come easy. A good bed put itself right in our way, then a deer walked up and asked to be eaten.

> "The deer
> It was here.
> One shot—
> In our pot.

THE GREAT SLEEP

"We haven't any pot, but you can use things in a metaphorical sense in order to get your rhyme. That's what poetry is for."

"I'm beginning to feel satiated," said Phil.

" 'Satiated' is a good word," said Bill Breakstone, "but it isn't used much on the plains. Still, I'm beginning to feel that way myself, too, and I think we'd better begin to consider the future, which is always so much bigger than the present."

"We must find our horses."

"Of course, and after that we must find the train, which will be our chief problem. It may be where we left it or it may have gone on, thinking that we had been killed by some outlying party of Comanches. But I don't believe Middleton and Arenberg would move without us. They may now be somewhere in these woods looking for us."

"Can you figure out the direction of the valley in which we left our horses?"

Breakstone studied the sun attentively.

"It's southeast from here," he replied, "and I fancy it's not more than three or four miles. Two likely lads like you and me ought to find it pretty soon, and, nine chances out of ten, the horses will be there. We'll take some of the best portions of the deer with us, and start at once."

They chose the choicest pieces of the meat and started, now strong of body and light of heart. Phil's own judgment about the direction agreed with Breakstone's, and in less than an hour they saw familiar ground.

"I'm a good prophet to-day," said Breakstone. "I've got the gift for a few hours at least. I predicted truly about the deer, and now I am going to predict truly about the horses. We'll have them by the bridle inside of half an hour."

In fifteen minutes they were in the little valley, in three minutes they found the horses grazing peacefully, and in two more minutes they caught them.

THE QUEST OF THE FOUR

"We've done the work and with ten minutes to spare," said Bill Breakstone, triumphantly, "and now, Phil, another wonderful change in our fortunes has come. If a camel is the ship of the desert, then a horse is the boat of the plains, the long boat, the jolly boat, the row boat, and all the rest of them. Now for the wagon train!"

"Now for the wagon train!" repeated Phil.

CHAPTER VIII

NEW ENEMIES

THE two were in splendid spirits. They had escaped great dangers, and they were on horseback once more. It is true, they were somewhat short on armament, but Breakstone took Phil's pistol, while the latter kept the rifle, and they were confident that they could find game enough on the plains until they overtook the wagon train. The horses themselves seemed glad of the companionship of their old masters, and went forward readily and at an easy pace through the woods. They soon found the path by which they had come, and followed it until they crossed the river and reached the site of the camp. But the trail toward the plain lay before them broad and easy.

"They can't have gone long," said Breakstone. "They may have thought that we were merely loitering behind for some purpose of our own and would soon overtake them. A whole train isn't going to linger about for two fellows well mounted and well armed who are supposed to know how to take care of themselves. But, Sir Philip of the Youthful Countenance, I don't think that Middleton and Arenberg would go ahead without us."

"Neither do I," said Phil with emphasis. "I as good as know that they're looking for us in these woods, and we've got to stay behind and find them, taking the risk of Comanches."

"Wherein I do heartily agree with you, and I'm going to take a chance right now. It is likely that the two, after fruitless searches for us, would return here at intervals, and, in a region like this, the sound of a shot will travel far. Fire the rifle, Phil, and it may bring them. It's often used as a signal. If it brings the Comanches instead, we're on our horses, and they're strong and swift."

Phil fired a shot, but there was no response. He waited half an hour and fired a second time, with the same result. After another half hour, the third shot was fired, and, four or five minutes later, Breakstone announced that he heard the tread of hoofs. It was a faint, distant sound, but Phil, too, heard it, and he was confident that it was made by hoofs. The two looked at each other, and each read the question in the other's eye. Who were coming in reply to the call of that third rifle shot, red men or white?

"We'll just draw back a little behind this clump of bushes," said Breakstone. "We can see a long way through their tops, and not be seen until the riders come very close. Then, if the visitors to this Forest of Arden of ours, Sir Philip, are not those whom we wish to see, it's up and away with us."

They waited in strained eagerness. The sounds grew louder. It was certain, moreover, that the riders were coming straight toward the point at which the rifle had been fired.

"Judging from the hoofbeats, how many would you say they are?" asked Phil.

"Not many. Maybe three or four, certainly not more. But I'm hoping that it's two, neither more nor less."

On came the horsemen, the hoofbeats steadily growing louder. Phil rose in his stirrups and gained a further view. He saw the top of a soft hat and then the top of another. In a half minute the faces beneath came into view. He knew them both, and he uttered a cry of joy.

"Middleton and Arenberg!" he exclaimed. "Here they come!"

"Our luck still holds good," said Bill Breakstone.

NEW ENEMIES

He and Phil galloped from behind the bushes and shouted as warm a welcome as men ever had. They received one equally warm in return, as Middleton and the German urged their horses forward. Then there was a mighty shaking of hands and mutual congratulations.

"The train left yesterday morning," said Middleton, "but we couldn't give you up. We scouted all the way across the forest and saw the Comanches on the other side. There was nothing to indicate anything unusual among them, such as a sacrifice of prisoners, and we hoped that if you had been taken by them you had escaped, and we came back here to see, knowing that if you were able you would return to this place. We were right in one part of our guess, because here you are."

"And mighty glad we are to be here," said Bill Breakstone, "and I want to say to you that I, Bill Breakstone, who may not be of so much importance to the world, but who is of vast importance to himself, would not be here at all, or anywhere else, for that matter, if it were not for this valiant and skillful youth, Sir Philip Bedford, Knight of the Texas plains."

"Stop, Bill," exclaimed Phil blushing. "Don't talk that way."

"Talk that way! Of course I will! And I'll pile it up, too! And after I pile it up and keep on piling it up, it won't be the whole truth. Cap, and you, Hans, old fellow, Phil and I were not taken together, because Phil was never taken at all. It was I alone who sat still, shut my eyes, and closed my ears while I let three of the ugliest Comanche warriors that were ever born walk up, lay violent hands on me, harness me up in all sorts of thongs and withes, and carry me off to their village, where they would have had some red sport with me if Phil hadn't come, when they were all mad with a great dance, and taken me away."

Then he told the story in detail, and Phil, shy and blushing, was compelled to receive their compliments, which were many and sincere. But he insisted that he merely succeeded through good luck, which Bill Breakstone warmly denied.

"Well, between the two of you, you have certainly got out of it well," said Middleton, "and, as we are reunited, we must plan for the next step. We can easily overtake the train by to-morrow, but I'm of the opinion that we'll have to be very careful, and that we must do some scouting, also. Arenberg and I have discovered that the Comanche warriors are on the move again. Their whole force of warriors seemed to be getting ready to leave the village, and they may be planning, after all, a second attack upon the train, a night surprise, or something of that kind. We, too, will have to be careful lest we run into them."

"Then it may be for the good of the train that we were left back here," said Phil, "because we will return with a warning."

"It may be the hand of Providence," said Arenberg, "since the Comanches did no harm where much was intended."

As both Middleton and Arenberg were firmly convinced that the plain would be thick with Comanche scouts, making their passage by daylight impossible, or at least extremely hazardous, they decided to remain in the woods until nightfall. They rode a couple of miles from the camp, tethered their horses in thick bushes, and, sitting near them, waited placidly. Phil Breakstone, and Arenberg talked in low tones, but Middleton sat silent. Phil noticed presently that "The Cap" was preoccupied. Little lines of thought ran down from his eyes to the corners of his nose.

Phil began to wonder again about the nature of Middleton's mission. Every one of the four was engaged upon some great quest, and none of them knew the secret of any of the others. Nor, in the rush of events, had they been left much time to think about such matters.

NEW ENEMIES

Now Phil again studied Middleton more closely. There was something in the unaccustomed lines of his face and his thoughtful eye indicating a belief that for him, at least, the object of the quest might be drawing nigh. At least, it seemed so to the boy. He studied, too, Middleton's clean cut face, and the sharp line of his strong chin. Phil had noticed before that this man was uncommonly neat in his personal appearance. It was a neatness altogether beyond what one usually saw on the plains. His clothing was always clean and in order, he carried a razor, and he shaved every day. Nor did he ever walk with a slovenly, lounging gait.

Phil decided that something very uncommon must have sent him with the Santa Fé train, but he would not ask; he had far too much delicacy to pry into the secret of another, who did not pry into his own.

Middleton and Arenberg had ample food in their saddlebags and Phil and Breakstone combined with it their stock of deer meat. Nothing disturbed them in the thicket, and at nightfall they mounted and rode out into the plain

"I know something about this country before us," said Breakstone. "It runs on in rolling swells for a march of many days, without any streams except shallow creeks, and without any timber except the fringes of cottonwoods along these creeks."

"And I know which way to go in order to overtake the train," said Middleton. "Woodfall said that they would head straight west, and we are certainly good enough plainsmen to keep our noses pointed that way."

"We are, we surely are," said Bill Breakstone, "but we must keep a good watch for those Comanche scouts. They hide behind the swells on their ponies, and they blend so well with the dusky earth that you'd never notice 'em until they had passed the signal on to others that you were coming and that it was a good time to form an ambush."

THE QUEST OF THE FOUR

There was a fair sky, with a moon and some clear stars, and they could see several hundred yards, but beyond that the whole horizon fused into a dusky wall. They rode at a long, swinging pace, and the hoofs of their horses made little noise on the new spring turf. The wind of the plains, which seldom ceases, blew gently in their faces and brought with it a soft crooning sound. Its note was very pleasant in the ears of Philip Bedford. In the saddle and with his best friends again, he felt that he could defy anything. He felt, too, and perhaps the feeling was due to his physical well-being and recovered safety, that he, also, was coming nearer to the object of his quest. Involuntarily he put his left hand on his coat, where the paper which he had read so often lay securely in a little inside pocket. He knew every word of it by heart, but when the time came, and he was alone, he would take it out and read it again. It was this paper that was always calling to him.

They rode on, crossing swell after swell, and, after the first hour, the four did not talk. It was likely that every one was thinking of his own secret.

They came about midnight to a prairie creek, a stream of water two or three yards wide and a few inches deep, flowing in a bed of sand perhaps fifteen yards across. A thin fringe of low cottonwoods and some willows grew on either shore. They approached warily, knowing that such a place offered a good ambush, and realizing that four would not have much chance against a large Comanche war band.

"But I don't think there is much danger," said Bill Breakstone. "If the Comanches are up to mischief again, they're not looking for stray parties; their mind is on the train, and, by the way, the train has passed along here. Look down, and in this moonlight you can see plainly enough the tracks of a hundred wheels."

"The horses are confident," said Middleton, "and I think we can be so, too."

NEW ENEMIES

The horses were advancing without hesitation, and it soon became evident that nothing was concealed among the scanty lines of trees and bushes.

"Look out for quicksands," said Arenberg. "It iss not pleasant to be swallowed up in one of them and feel that you have died such a useless death."

"There is no danger," said Phil, whose quick eye was following the trail of the wagons. "Here is where the train crossed, and if the wagons didn't sink we won't."

The water being cold and entirely free from alkali, the horses drank eagerly, and their riders, also, took the chance to refill their canteens, which they always carried strapped to their saddle bows. They also rested awhile, but, when they remounted and rode on, Middleton noticed a light to the northward. On the plains then, no man would pass a light without giving it particular attention, and the four sat on their horses for some minutes studying it closely. They thought at first that it might be a signal light of the Comanches, but, as it did not waver, they concluded that it must be a camp fire.

"Now I'm thinking," said Bill Breakstone, "that we oughtn't to leave a camp fire burning away here on the plains, and we not knowing anything about it. It won't take us long to ride up and inspect it."

"That is a truth," said Middleton. "It is not a difficult matter for four horsemen to overtake a wagon train, but we'll first see what that fire means."

"It iss our duty to do so," said the phlegmatic German.

They rode straight toward the light, and their belief that it was a camp fire was soon confirmed. They saw the red blaze rising and quivering, and then dusky figures passing and repassing before it.

"We're yet too far away to tell exactly what those figures are," said Bill Breakstone, "but I don't see any sign of long hair or war bonnets, and so I take it that they are not Comanches, nor any other kind of Indians, for that matter. No warriors would build so careless a fire or wander so carelessly about it.

"They are white men," said Middleton with conviction, as he increased his horse's pace. "Ah, I see now! Mexicans! Look at the shadows of their great conical hats as they pass before the fire."

"Now I wonder what they're doing here on Texas soil," said Bill Breakstone.

Middleton did not answer, but Phil noticed that the look in his eyes was singularly tense and eager. As they drew near the fire, which was a large one, and the hoofbeats of their horses were heard, two men in Mexican dress, tall conical broad-brimmed hats, embroidered coats and trousers and riding boots, bearing great spurs, came forward to meet them. Phil saw another figure, which had been lying on a blanket by the fire, rise and stand at attention. He instantly perceived, even then, something familiar in the figure.

The four rode boldly forward, and Middleton called out:

"We are friends!"

The two Mexicans who were in advance, rifle in hand, stood irresolutely, and glanced at the man behind them, who had just risen from his blanket.

"You are welcome," said this man in good English but with a strong Mexican accent. "We are glad for anybody to share with us our camp fire in this wilderness. Dismount, Señores."

Then Phil knew him well. It was Pedro de Armijo, the young Mexican whom he had seen with the Mexican envoy, Zucorra, in New Orleans, one whom he had instinctively disliked, one whom he was exceedingly astonished to see at such a time and place. Middleton also recognized him, because he raised his cap and said politely:

"This is a pleasant meeting. You are Captain Pedro de Armijo, who came to our capital with His Excellency

NEW ENEMIES

Don Augustin Xavier Hernando Zucorra on a mission, intended to be of benefit to both our countries. My name is Middleton, George Middleton, and these are my friends, Mr. Breakstone, Mr. Arenberg, and Mr. Bedford."

De Armijo gave every one in turn a quick scrutinizing look, and, with flowing compliment, bade them welcome to his fireside. It seemed that he did not remember Middleton, but that he took for granted their former meeting in Washington. Phil liked him none the more because of the polite words he used. He was not one to hold prejudice because of race, but this Mexican had a manner supercilious and conceited that inspired resentment.

"It seems strange, Señor Middleton," said de Armijo, "that we should meet again in such a place on these vast plains, so far from a house or any other human beings, plains that were once Mexican, but which you now call yours."

De Armijo glided over the last words smoothly, but the blood leaped in Phil's temples. Middleton apparently took no notice, but said that he and his comrades were riding across the plains mainly on an exploring expedition. As there was some danger from Comanches, they were traveling partly by night, and, having seen the camp fire, they had come to investigate it, after the custom of the wilderness.

"And, now that you have found us," said de Armijo with elaborate courtesy, "I have reason to believe that you would run into Comanche horsemen a little farther on. They would not harm us Mexicans, with whom they are at peace, but for you Americans they would have little mercy. Stay with us for the remainder of the night."

He smiled, showing his white teeth, and Middleton smiled back as he replied:

"Your courtesy is appreciated, Captain de Armijo.

We shall stay. It is pleasant, too, to welcome a gallant Mexican officer like yourself to American soil."

The eyes of de Armijo snapped in the firelight, and the white teeth were bared again. Phil knew that he resented the expression "American soil." Mexico still maintained a claim to Texas—which it could not make good—and he felt equally confident that Middleton had used it purposely. It seemed to him that some sort of duel was in progress between the two, and he watched it with overwhelming curiosity. But de Armijo quickly returned to his polite manner.

"You speak the truth," he said. "It is I who am your guest, not you who are mine. It was Mexican soil once, and before that Spanish—three centuries under our race—but now gone, I suppose, forever."

Middleton did not reply, but approached the fire and warmed his hands over the blaze. The night was cold and the flames looked cheerful. The others tethered their horses, and all except the two who had met the Americans took their places by the fire. The Mexicans were six in number. Only de Armijo seemed to be a man of any distinction. The others, although stalwart and well armed, were evidently of the peon class. Phil wondered what this little party was doing here, and the conviction grew upon him that the meeting had something to do with Middleton's mission.

"I am sorry," said de Armijo, "that we do not even have a tent to offer you, but doubtless you are accustomed to sleeping under the open sky, and the air of these plains is dry and healthy."

"A blanket and a few coals to warm one's feet are sufficient," said Middleton. "We will avail ourselves of your courtesy and not keep you awake any longer."

Both Breakstone and Arenberg glanced at Middleton, but they said nothing, wrapping themselves in their blankets, and lying down, with their feet to the fire. Phil did the same, but he thought it a strange proceed-

NEW ENEMIES

ing, this apparently unguarded camping with Mexicans, who at the best were not friends, with the possibility of Comanches who were, at all times, the bitterest and most dangerous of enemies. Yet Middleton must have some good reason, he was not a man to do anything rash or foolish, and Phil awaited the issue with confidence.

Phil could not sleep. The meeting had stirred him too much, and his nerves would not relax. He lay before the fire, his feet within a yard of the coals, and his head in the crook of his arm. Now and then he heard a horse move or stamp his hoofs, but all the men were silent. De Armijo, lying on a blanket and with a fine blue cavalry cloak spread over him, seemed to be asleep, but as he was on the other side of the fire Phil could not see his eyes. Middleton was nearer, and he saw his chest rising and falling with the regularity of one who sleeps.

It all seemed very peaceful, very restful. Perhaps de Armijo's hospitality was real, and he had wronged him with his suspicions. But reason with himself as he would, Phil could not overcome his dislike and distrust. Something was wrong, and something was going to happen, yet much time passed and nothing happened. De Armijo's eyes were still shaded by his cloak, but his long figure lay motionless. Only a few live coals remained from the fire, and beyond a radius of twenty feet lay the encircling rim of the darkness. At the line where light and dark met, crouched the two peons with their rifles across their knees. It was Phil's opinion that they, too, slept in this sitting posture. Surely de Armijo and his men had great confidence in their security, and must be on the best of terms with the Comanches! If so, it might increase the safety of the little American party, also, but the boy yet wondered why Middleton had stopped when they were all so eager to reach the wagon train and warn it of the new danger.

Phil stirred once or twice, but only to ease his position, and he did it without noise. His eyes were shaded by the brim of his soft hat, but he watched the circle about the fire, and most of all he watched de Armijo. An interminable period of time passed, every second growing to ten times its proper length. Phil was as wakeful as ever, but so much watching made the figures about the fire dim and uncertain. They seemed to shift their places, but the boy was still resolved to keep awake, although everybody else slept through the night. His premonition was yet with him, his heart expanded, and his pulse beat faster.

The remaining coals died one by one. The circle of light, already small, contracted still more, became a point, and then vanished. Everything now lay in the dark, and the figures were merely blacker shapes against the blackness. Then, after that long waiting, with every second and minute drawn out tenfold, Phil's premonition came true. Something happened.

De Armijo moved. He moved ever so slightly, but Phil saw him, and, lying perfectly still himself, he watched him with an absorbed attention, and a heart that had increased its beating still further. De Armijo's body itself had not moved, it was merely one hand that had come slowly from under the covering of the cloak, and that now lay white against the blue cloth. A man might move his hand thus in sleep, but it seemed to Phil that the action was guided by a conscious mind. Intent, he watched, and presently his reward came. The other hand also slid from beneath the cloak, and, like its fellow, lay white against the blue cloth. Now both hands were still, but Phil yet waited, confident that more would come. It was all very quiet and slow, like the craft and cunning of the Indian, but Phil was willing to match it with a patience and craft of his own.

At last the whole figure of de Armijo stirred. Phil saw the blue cloak tremble slightly. Then the man raised his head ever so little and looked about the dark circle. Slowly he let the head fall back, and the figure became still again. But the boy was not deceived. Already every suspicion had been verified in his mind, and his premonition was proved absolutely true.

Pedro de Armijo raised himself again, but a little higher this time, and he did not let his head and body drop back. He looked about the circle with a gaze that Phil knew must be sharp and scrutinizing, although it was too dark for him to see the expression of his eyes. The Mexican seemed satisfied with his second examination, and then, dropping softly on his hands and knees, he crept toward Middleton. It occurred to Phil afterward that this approach toward Middleton did not surprise him. In reality, it was just what he had expected de Armijo to do.

The boy was uncertain about his own course, and, like one under a spell, he waited. The dusky figure of de Armijo creeping toward Middleton had a sinuous motion like that of a great snake, and Phil's hand slipped down to the hammer of his rifle, but he would not fire. He noticed that de Armijo had drawn no weapon, and he did not believe that murder was his intention.

Middleton did not move. He lay easily upon his right side, and Phil judged that he was in a sound sleep. De Armijo, absorbed in his task, did not look back. Hence he did not see the boy who rose slowly to a sitting posture, a ready rifle in his hands.

Phil saw de Armijo reach Middleton's side and pause there a moment or two. He still drew no weapon, and this was further proof that murder was not in the Mexican's mind, but Phil believed that whatever lay between these two was now at the edge of the crisis. He saw de Armijo raise his hand and put it to Middleton's breast with the evident intention of opening his coat. So he was a thief! But the fingers stopped there as Phil leveled his rifle and called sharply:

"Hands up, de Armijo, or I shoot!"

The startled Mexican would have thrown up his

hands, but he did not have time. They were seized in the powerful grasp of Middleton, and he was pulled downward upon his face.

"Ah, would you, de Armijo!" cried Middleton in exultant tones. "We have caught you! Good boy, Phil, you were watching, too!"

"All the others were up in an instant, but Breakstone and Arenberg were too quick for the Mexicans. They covered them with their rifle muzzles before their antagonists could raise their weapons.

"Throw down every gun and pistol!" said Breakstone sternly. "There, by the log, and we'll see what's going forward!"

Sullenly the Mexicans complied, and then stood in a little huddled group, looking at their fallen leader, whom Middleton still held upon the ground, but who was pouring out muffled oaths from a face that was in the dirt.

"Take his pistols, Phil," said Middleton, and the boy promptly removed them. Then Middleton released him, and de Armijo sat up, his face black as night, his heart raging with anger, hate, and humiliation.

"How dare you attack me in my own camp! You whom we received as guests!" he cried.

"We did not attack you," replied Middleton calmly. He had risen to his feet, and he towered over the Mexican like an accusing judge. "It is you who attacked us, or me, rather, and you intended, if you did not get what you wanted with smooth fingers, to use violence. You cannot deny that, Captain Pedro de Armijo of the Mexican army; there were at least two witnesses of your act, Philip Bedford and myself."

De Armijo looked down at the ground, and seemed to commune with himself for a few moments. Then he stood at his full height, brushed the traces of dirt from his clothes, and gave Middleton a look of uncompromising defiance and hostility. All at once it struck Phil that this was a man of ability and energy, one who could be a bitter and dangerous enemy.

"You are right in part, Captain Middleton," said de Armijo slowly. "I was seeking to take the maps, letters, and instructions that you carry inside your tunic, next, perhaps, to your very flesh. They would be valuable possessions to us, and it was my duty, as a captain in the Mexican army, to take them if I could, from you, a captain in the American army."

Phil started and looked anew at Middleton. A captain in the American army! This was why he had walked with that upright carriage! This was why he had been so particular about his personal appearance! He began to see a little way.

"We, too, have our channels of information," said de Armijo, "and I knew that you had embarked upon a mission in the West to learn our movements and forces upon the border, and our temper and disposition with regard to great matters that are agitating both Mexico and America."

"It is true, all that you say," replied Middleton tranquilly. "I am Captain George Middleton of the American regular troops, and, at the request of our War Department, I undertook the hazardous mission of which you speak."

"You will go no farther with it," said de Armijo.

"How can you keep me from it?"

"I cannot—perhaps, but events can—events have. You do not know, but I do, Captain Middleton, that there is war between your country and mine."

"Ah!" exclaimed Middleton, and, despite the darkness, Phil saw a sudden flush spring into his face.

"It is not only war," continued de Armijo, "but there has been a heavy battle, two of them, in fact. Your troops met ours at Palo Alto on May eighth, and again on the following day at Resaca de la Palma."

"Ah!" exclaimed Middleton again, the exclamation

being drawn up from the very depths of his being, while the flush on his face deepened. "And you know, I suppose, which won?"

It was a peculiar coincidence that the moon's rays made their way at that moment through clouds, and a bright beam fell on the face of Pedro de Armijo. Phil saw the Mexican's face fall a little, despite all his efforts at self-control. De Armijo himself felt this change in his countenance, and, knowing what it indicated to the man who asked the question, he replied without evasion:

"I regret to say that the fortunes of war were against the deserving. Our brave general, Ampudia, and our gallant troops were compelled to retire before your general, Taylor. At least, so say my hasty advices; perhaps they are wrong."

But Phil could see that de Armijo had no such hope. The news was correct, and the boy's heart thrilled with joy because the first victories had fallen to his own people.

"I would not have told you this," continued de Armijo, "had you not caught me in an attempt to take your papers. Had it been peace, 'steal' would have been the word, but since it is war 'steal' turns to enterprise and zeal. Had I not believed you ignorant that the war has begun, and that I might make more profit out of you in our hands than as a fugitive, or at least as one who might have escaped, I should have opened fire upon you as you approached. Perhaps I made a mistake."

"All of us do at times," said Middleton thoughtfully.

"Well spoken," said de Armijo. He lighted a cigarette and took a few easy puffs.

"Well, Captain Middleton," he said at length, "the problem is now yours, not ours. You have taken it out of our hands. What are you going to do with us?"

"It seems to me," said Captain Middleton, "that this problem, like most others, admits of only one solution. You are our prisoners, but we cannot hold you. Our own situation prevents it. We could kill you, but

NEW ENEMIES

God forbid a single thought of such a crime. We will take your arms and let you go. You will not suffer without your arms, as your Comanche friends are near, a fact which you know very well."

"We accept your terms," said de Armijo, "since we must, and with your permission we will mount our horses and ride away. But it is to be understood, Captain Middleton, and you, young Mr. Bedford, and the rest of you, that we part as enemies and not as friends."

"As you will," said Middleton. "I recognize the fact that you have no cause to love us, and perhaps the sooner we both depart from this spot the better it will be for all."

"But we may meet again on the battlefield; is it not so?" said de Armijo.

"That, I cannot tell," replied Middleton, "but it is not unlikely."

Breakstone and Arenberg still stood by the captured arms, but, without casting a glance at either the arms or their guardians, de Armijo signaled to his men, and they mounted and rode away.

"Adios!" he called back in Spanish, although he did not turn his face.

"Adios!" said Middleton in the same tone.

They did not move or speak until they heard the hoofbeats die away, and then it was Bill Breakstone who first broke the silence.

"That certainly came out well," he said. "The curtain came down on a finer finish than the first act indicated. I confess that I didn't know your plan, Captain—I don't call you Cap any more—but I trusted you, and I confess, also, that I fell asleep. It was you and Sir Philip of the Active Mind and the Watchful Eye who did most of the work.

> "It was in Tex.
> We met the Mex.
> They spoke so high,
> But now they cry.

Or, at least, they ought to cry when they think how we turned the tables on them. Now, Captain, I suppose we must be up and doing, for those fellows, as you said, will go straight to the Comanches, and if we linger here our scalps will be of less value to ourselves than to anybody else.'

"It is quite true," said Captain Middleton. "We must reach the train as soon as possible, because the danger to it has increased with our own. But even more important than that is the great change that must be made. Woodfall cannot go on now, since the whole Southwest will be swept by bands of Mexican and Indian horsemen.'

"What must the train do?" asked Phil in anxiety, because this concerned him very nearly.

"It must turn south and join the American army on the Rio Grande. Most of the things that it carries will be of value to our troops, and Woodfall will clear as much profit there as at Santa Fé, which is now a city in arms against us. In this case the path of comparative safety and honor is also the path of profit. What more could Woodfall ask?"

"He's a brave man, and brave men are with him," said Bill Breakstone. "You won't have to ask him twice."

Phil's heart had throbbed with joy at Middleton's answer. His quest was always in his mind. He had feared that they might turn back, but now it suited him as well to join the American army as to go on toward Santa Fé. The quest was a wide one. But Arenberg suppressed a sigh.

"Let's be starting," said Middleton. "We'll take their arms with us. They're of value, and Bill, moreover, is without a rifle or musket."

Breakstone, who had been examining the weapons, uttered a cry of joy.

"Here is a fine rifle," he said. "one of the best

NEW ENEMIES

American make. I wonder how that Mexican got it! The rest are not so good."

"Take the fine one, Bill," said Middleton, "and we will pack up the rest and ride."

They were out of the woods in a few minutes, and again rode rapidly toward the west. It was an easy task to pick up the great wagon trail again, even in the dark of the night, as the grass and soil were trodden or pressed down over a width of fully two hundred yards. The country rolled lightly. Bill Breakstone thought that a range of hills lay toward the north, but in the night they could not see.

"I hope that we'll overtake Woodfall before day," said Middleton, "because I've an idea that de Armijo and the little band with him are not the only Mexicans hereabouts. He would not come so far North without a considerable force, and I suspect that it is his intention to capture our train, with the aid of the Comanches."

"We can beat them off," said Breakstone confidently.

"If our people are warned in time," said Middleton.

"Much harm iss meant," said Arenberg, speaking for the first time, "but we may keep much from being done. Our most dangerous enemies before the daylight comes are the Comanches. They have already learned from de Armijo that we are here, and it iss like as not that they are now between us and the train."

Middleton looked at his watch, holding it in the moon's rays.

"It is two hours until day," he said, "and the trail is rapidly growing fresher. We may yet get through before the ring closes. Ah, there they are now!"

A hand's breadth of fire suddenly leaped up in the north, and burned there like a steady torch. Far in the east, another but fainter appeared and burned, and a third leaped up in the south. But when they looked back in the west they saw none.

"Fortune rides on our cruppers so far," said Middleton. "We are on the side of the circle which yet has the open segment. Push on, my boys!"

Phil's knees involuntarily pressed against the side of his horse, and that strange sensation, like icy water running down the spine, came again. Those three lights speaking to one another in the darkness and across great distances were full of mystery and awe. But he rode without speech, and he looked most of the time at the lights, which remained fixed, as if what they said could not be changed.

Middleton, who was in advance, suddenly reined in his horse, and the others, stopping, also, noticed that just in front of them a depression ran across the plain.

"It's an arroyo or something like it," said Bill Breakstone, "but the wagons have crossed it anyhow."

They followed the trail to the other side and then saw that it continued almost parallel with the broad gully.

"Why shouldn't we take to the gully?" said Phil. "It has a smooth bottom, it is wide enough for us, riding two abreast, and it will give us shelter."

"A good idea," said Middleton.

They turned back into the arroyo, and found an easy road there. The banks were several feet high, and, as the dusk still hung on the plain, they increased their speed, counting each moment worth one man's life. They came soon to a place where the gully was shallower than usual, and then they saw two or three faint lights in the plain before them, apparently about a half mile away. Middleton raised a warning hand, and they stopped.

"Those are the lights of the train," he said. "They undoubtedly have scouts out, and of course they have seen the signals of the Comanches and the Mexicans, just as we have, but they do not know as much as we do. I think we had better go down the arroyo as far as we can, and then, if the alarm is sounded by our enemies, gallop for it."

NEW ENEMIES

"It iss our choice because there iss none other," said Arenberg.

They continued, but more slowly, in order to make as little noise as possible. They had covered more than half the distance when Phil saw a faint line of gray on the horizon line in the east. The next moment against the background of gray appeared a horseman, a man of olive skin, clad in sombrero, bright jacket, embroidered trousers, and boots with great spurs. He carried a weapon like a spear, and Phil knew at once that he was a Mexican lancer, no doubt a sentinel.

The man saw them, and, instead of attempting to use his lance, snatched a pistol from his belt and fired point blank. The bullet passed by Middleton's face, and, like a flash, Bill Breakstone replied with a bullet from his rifle. The Mexican went down, but from three points of the compass came cries, the shouts of the Mexicans and the long war whoop of the Comanches.

"Forward for your lives!" cried Middleton, and, dashing out of the arroyo, they galloped at full speed toward the wagon train.

CHAPTER IX

THE FIERY CIRCLE

THE thin gray light in the east broadened into a bar as the hoofbeats of the four thundered over the plain. From left to right came shouts, the yells of the Indians and the fierce cries of the Mexicans.

"Bend low," cried Middleton, "and we may escape their bullets!"

Phil lay almost upon his horse's neck, but it was an unconscious act. He was thrilling with excitement, as the four horsemen almost clove the morning mist, and rode on swift hoofs straight toward the wagon train. Then came the rattling of rifles and whistling of arrows from either side. "Ping!" the bullets sang in his ear and "Ping!" the arrows sang, also. He remembered afterward that he wished, if he were hit at all, to be hit by a bullet instead of an arrow; an arrow sticking in one's flesh would be very cumbersome and painful. But neither arrow nor bullet struck true. Their ride was too sudden and swift, and the light too faint to permit good aim to the Mexicans and Comanches. Yet Phil heard confused sounds, shouted commands, and the noise of hurrying feet. He saw dark faces appearing in the mist on either side, and he also saw the outlines of wagons through the same mist in front. Then he saw men, rifle in hand, who seemed to rise out of the plain in front of the wagons. Two of the men raised their rifles and took aim at the galloping horsemen.

"We are friends, and we bring you warning!"

THE FIERY CIRCLE

shouted Middleton in a tremendous voice. "Don't fire upon us!"

But the men and three others who appeared near them pulled the trigger. Phil did not hear the ping of the bullets, and now he realized that they fired not at his comrades and himself but at those who pursued. A death-cry and yells of rage came from behind them, but in another minute they were within the line of sentinels and were springing from their horses, ready to take their part in the combat that they expected.

All the morning mists were driven away at that moment by the sun, as if a veil had been lifted, and the whole plain stood out clear and distinct under a brilliant sky. Before them were the wagons, drawn up in a circle in the customary fashion of a camp, the horses and mules in the center, and the men, arms in hand, forming an outer ring for the wagons. But from the northeast and the southeast two lines were converging upon them, and Phil's heart kindled at the sight.

The line in the northeast was made up of red horsemen, four hundred Comanches, naked to the waist, horribly painted, and riding knee to knee, the redoubtable chiefs, Santana and Black Panther, at their head. The line in the southeast was composed of Mexican cavalry, lancers splendidly mounted, the blades of their lances and their embroidered jackets glittering in the sun. They made their horses prance and cavort, and many in the first rank whirled lariats in derision.

A tall figure strolled forward and welcomed Middleton and his comrades. It was Woodfall, his face flushed somewhat, but his manner undaunted.

"I'm glad to welcome you back, Mr. Middleton," he said, "and with your comrades, all of them alive and well. But what does this mean? Why do those men ride to attack, when this is the soil of Texas?"

He waved his hand toward the advancing Mexican column.

THE QUEST OF THE FOUR

"They advance against us," replied Middleton, "because this is war, war between the United States and Mexico—we learned that last night from one of their own officers—and there have been two heavy battles on the Rio Grande, both victorious for us."

It was not strange that a sudden cheer burst from the men who heard these words. Woodfall listened to it grimly, and, when it died, he said:

"Then if these Mexicans attack, we'll soon have a third victory to our credit. The Indian bow and the Mexican lance can't break through a circle of riflemen, entrenched behind wagons—riflemen who know how to shoot."

Again that defiant, even exultant cheer rose from the men who heard, and, passing on like a fire in dry grass, it rolled all around the circle of wagons. The Mexicans heard it. They detected the defiant note in it, and, wisely, they checked their speed. The column of Indian warriors also came more slowly. Philip Bedford, hardened in so brief a space to danger and war, did not feel any great fear, but the scene thrilled him like a great picture painted in living types and colors against the background of the earth. There were the red horsemen, the sun deepening the tints of their coppery faces and bringing out the glowing colors of their war bonnets. To the southeast the Mexican column, also, was a great ribbon of light lying across the plain, the broad blades of the lances catching the sun's rays and throwing them back in golden beams.

"A fine show," said Woodfall, "and if those Mexicans had two or three cannon they might wipe us out, but they haven't, and so we're lucky."

"I think I ought to tell you, Mr. Woodfall," said Middleton, "that I'm a captain in the regular army, Captain Middleton, and that I've been making use of your hospitality to find what forces the enemy had in these parts, and what movements he was making. I was sent by our government, and, as you see, I'm finding what I was sent to find."

"I thought there was something military about your cut, Captain," said Woodfall, "and it seems to me to be a good thing that you are with us. If we've helped you without knowing, then you, knowing it, can help us now."

The hands of the two men met in the strong clasp of friendship and trust.

"They're about to move," said Middleton, who practically took command. "I suggest that we go inside the circle of wagons now, and that at least two-thirds of our men devote their attention to the lancers. The Mexicans are brave; we must not forget that."

They went inside at once, where a few men were detailed to see that the horses and mules did not make too great a turmoil, while the rest posted themselves for defense. The wagons were in reality a formidable barrier for an attacking force that did not have artillery. The majority of the Americans lay down under the wagons between the wheels. Phil was under one of them with Bill Breakstone on one side of him and Arenberg on the other. Middleton was elsewhere with Woodfall.

"Much harm iss meant," said Arenberg, "and I would say to you, Philip, although little advice iss needed by you now, not to fire too soon, and to remember, when you take aim, to allow for the fact that they are coming toward us at a gallop."

"That's right," said Bill Breakstone. "Old Hans, here, knows."

"Ach," said Arenberg, uttering a sigh, "I love peace, and I never thought to have a part in cruel Indian and Mexican battles."

It occurred to Phil that the sigh had no reference to the coming combat. The German's face showed sadness, but not a trace of fear. He turned his gaze from Arenberg and fixed it upon the Mexican column which they were facing. He thought that he saw de Armijo in the front rank among the officers in brilliant dress, but he was not sure. The distance was too great. He wondered whether he would shoot at him, if he saw him later in the charge.

The sunlight was intensely bright, such as one sees only on great upland plains, and the Mexican lancers with their horses stood out, like carving, against the background of gold and blue. Phil saw the column suddenly quiver, as if a single movement ran through all. The lances were lifted a little higher, and their blades cast broader beams. A flag fluttered in the front rank and unfolded in the slight wind.

The notes of a trumpet sounded high and clear, the Mexicans uttered a long, fierce shout, the colors shifted and changed, like water flowing swiftly, as the column broke into a gallop and came straight toward the wagons, the plain thundering with the beat of their hoofs. From another part of the compass came a second cry, higher pitched, longer drawn, and with more of the whine of the wolf in it. Phil knew that it came from the Comanches, who were also charging, led by Black Panther and Santana, but he did not take his eyes from the Mexicans.

The two attacking columns began to fire scattering shots, but the defenders of the wagons had not yet pulled a trigger, although many a forefinger was trembling with eagerness.

"It's pretty, but it's a waste, a dead waste," said Bill Breakstone. "I hate to shoot at them, because I've no doubt many a brave young fellow is out there, but we've got to let them have it. Steady, Phil, steady! They're coming close now."

Suddenly they heard the loud shout, "Fire!" It was Middleton who uttered it, and everybody obeyed. A sheet of flame seemed to spurt from the wagons, and the air was filled with singing lead. The entire head of the Mexican column was burnt away. The ground was strewn

THE FIERY CIRCLE

with the fallen. Riderless horses, some wounded and screaming with pain, galloped here and there. The column stopped and seemed to be wavering. Several officers, sword in hand—and now Phil was sure that he saw de Armijo among them—were trying to urge the lancers on. All the Americans were reloading as fast as they could, and while the Mexicans yet wavered, they poured in a second volley. Unable to withstand it, the lancers broke and fled, bearing the officers away with them in their panic.

Phil, Bill Breakstone, and Arenberg crawled from under the wagon and stood on the outside, erect again. There they contemplated for a few moments the wreck that they and their comrades had made. From the Indian point of attack came the sound of retiring shots, and they knew that the Comanches had been quickly repulsed, also.

"It was one of the most foolish things I ever saw," said Bill Breakstone, "to ride right into the mouths of long-barreled, well-aimed rifles like ours. Their numbers didn't help them. What say you, Sir Philip of the Rifle and the Wagon?"

"It seems to me that you're right," replied the boy. "I don't think they'll charge again, nor will the Comanches."

"You're right, too; they've had enough."

The Mexicans and Comanches, having gathered up their wounded, united and remained in a dark cloud beyond rifle shot, apparently intending neither to charge again nor to go away. But the defenders of the train were cheerful. They had suffered no loss, being protected so well, and they were willing enough to meet a second attack delivered in the same fashion. But Middleton and Woodfall had hot coffee and tea served, and then with strong field glasses they observed the enemy.

"I believe they are in great doubt," said Middleton. "They may think they can starve us out, but the Mexicans will not want to wait for so long a process; it is likely that they will prefer going southward to join their main army."

He said these words aloud, where many could hear, but a little while afterward he and Woodfall drew to one side and talked a long time in low tones. Phil could tell by their faces that they were very earnest, and he felt sure that a proposition would be made before long. He called Breakstone's attention to them.

"You're right," said Bill, "they'll have something to say soon, and it will concern all of us. Ah, there comes the Cap—I mean the Captain—now, and he's going to make a speech."

Middleton sprang upon a wagon tongue, and, standing very quiet, looked slowly around the circle of defenders, all of whom bent their eyes upon him. They were a motley group, Americans mostly, but with a scattering of a dozen European nationalities among them. The majority of them were bareheaded, with necks and chests uncovered, and all were stained black or brown with a mixture of perspiration, dust, and burnt gunpowder. The majority of them were young, some but little older than Phil himself. They looked very curiously at Middleton as he stood upon the wagon pole. Already all knew that he was an officer in the regular army. In the distance hung the dark fringe of Mexicans and Comanches, but, for the moment, only the sentinels paid any attention to them.

"Men," cried Middleton, "you have beaten off the attack of the Mexicans and the Comanches, and you can do it again as often as they come! I know that, and so do you!"

He was stopped for a few seconds by a great cheer, and then he resumed:

"We can beat them off, but the road to Santa Fé has now become impossible. Moreover, the nation with which we are at war holds Santa Fé, and to go there would be merely to march into prison or worse. We can't turn back. You are not willing to go back to New Orleans, are you?"

"Never!" they cried in one voice.

Middleton smiled. He was appealing deftly to the pride of these men, and he had known the response before it came.

"Then if we can neither go on to Santa Fé nor turn back to New Orleans," he said, "we must either start to the north or to the south."

He was speaking now with the greatest fervor. His face flushed deeply, and they hung upon his words.

"To the north lies the wilderness," he said, "stretching away for thousands of miles to the Arctic Ocean. To the south there are plains reaching down to a river, broad, shallow, and yellow, and somewhere along that river armies are fighting, armies of our own people and armies of the Mexicans with whom we are now at war. Which way shall we go, north or south?"

"South!" was roared forth in one tremendous voice.

Again Middleton smiled. Again he had known before it came the response that would be spoken.

"Then south it is," he said, "and we make for Taylor's army on the Rio Grande. You will find there a better market for what you carry in your wagons than you would have found at Santa Fé, and you're likely to find something else, also, that I know you won't shirk."

"Fighting!" roared forth that tremendous voice once more.

"Yes, fighting," said Middleton, as he sprang down from the pole and rejoined Woodfall.

"That was clever talk," said Bill Breakstone, "but he knew his ground before he sowed the seed. These are just the sort of lads who will be glad to go south to Taylor, breaking their way through any Mexicans or Indians who may get across their path.

THE QUEST OF THE FOUR

> "He said north
> He said south,
>   What's the choice?
> We spoke forth,
> It was south,
>   With one voice.

And now, unless I'm mightily mistaken, we'll fare forth upon our journey, as the knights of old would say. This is a good camp for defense, but not for siege. It lacks water. You just watch, Phil, and you'll see a wrinkle or two in plains work worth knowing."

The men began to hitch the horses to the wagons, but they were interrupted in the task by a horseman who rode forth from the Mexican column, carrying a white handkerchief on the point of a lance. He was joined by two Indian chiefs riding on either side of him. Phil instantly recognized all three. The white man was Pedro de Armijo, and the Indians were Black Panther and Santana.

"They want a big talk," said Bill Breakstone. "I fear the Greeks bearing gifts, and also a lot of other people who smile at you while they hold daggers behind their backs, but I suppose our side will hear what they have to say."

Middleton and Woodfall were already mounting to ride forth, and Middleton beckoned to Phil.

"Come, Phil," he said. "They are three, and we should be three, also. You can call yourself the secretary of the meeting if you like."

Phil sprang eagerly upon his horse, proud of the privilege and the honor, and rode forth with them. The Mexican and the two Comanches were coming on slowly and gravely. Four hundred yards behind them, Mexicans and Indians, all on horseback, were now gathered in a broad dark line, sitting motionless and watching. Their three envoys sat on their horses midway between the hostile forces, and the three Americans, meeting them there, stopped face to face. De Armijo looked at Middleton and

THE FIERY CIRCLE

smiled slightly, ironically. His bearing was proud, and was evidently meant to be disdainful. One would have thought that he was a victor, receiving an embassy about to sue for peace. Middleton returned his gaze steadfastly, but his face expressed nothing. He looked once at Phil, and the boy thought he saw something singular in the glance, as if he impinged somehow upon the mind of the Mexican, but in a moment the look of de Armijo passed.

"I have come, Captain Middleton," said the young Mexican, "to save bloodshed, if you are willing to listen to reason. You will observe what forces have come against you. We have here a numerous body of Mexican cavalry, the finest in the world, and we have also the flower of the Comanche nation, the bravest of the Indian warriors. In victory, the Mexicans are humane and merciful, but the Indian nature is different. Excited and impassioned, it finds vent in terrible deeds. Therefore, as you are surrounded and cannot escape, we ask you to surrender now, and save the lives of your men."

It was hard for Phil to restrain an exclamation at this piece of presumption, but Middleton received it gravely. His face was still without expression. Nevertheless, his reply was barbed.

"Your demand seems inopportune, Lieutenant de Armijo," he replied. "You can scarcely have forgotten, since it occurred less than an hour ago, the defeat of both your cavalry and your Comanche allies. Perhaps we are unduly confident, but we feel that we can do so again, as often as needed."

De Armijo frowned. He glanced at his Indian comrades. Phil wondered if he had been deceiving them with promises of what the invincible Mexican lancers could and would do. But the two savages made no response. Their coppery faces did not move.

"This, then, is your final answer, Captain Middleton," said de Armijo.

"It is," replied Middleton. "It is not the custom

for victors to surrender. So we bid you good day, Lieutenant de Armijo."

As he spoke, he saluted and turned his horse. Woodfall and Phil saluted and turned with him. The Mexican returned the salute with a gloved hand, but the Indians turned stolidly without a sign. Then the two parties rode away in opposite directions, each to its own men. Phil dismounted at the wagons, and was met by Breakstone and Arenberg with eager questions.

"What did that yellow Mex. want, Sir Philip of the Council?" asked Breakstone.

"As he has just given us such a severe thrashing," replied Phil, "he demanded our immediate and unconditional surrender. He said that if we acceded to this demand only one-tenth of us would be shot, but he made it a special condition that a renowned scout, sharpshooter, white warrior, and talker, one William Breakstone, be shot first and at once, as a terrible example, in the presence of both victor and vanquished. Immediately after him one Hans Arenberg, a very dangerous and bloodthirsty man, was to share the same fate. If we refused this gentle alternative, we were all to be killed, and then scalped by the savages."

"Of course, Sir Philip," said Bill Breakstone, "they've put a just value on me, but I surmise that the jest doth leap from your nimble tongue. Now the truth!"

"De Armijo and the Indian chiefs did really demand our surrender," said Phil. "They said we could not escape. They talked as if they were the victors and we the beaten."

"Now, by my troth, that is a merry jest!" exclaimed Bill Breakstone. "When do we lay down our arms? Is it within the next five minutes, or do we even take fifteen?"

"You can surrender if you want to, Bill," said Phil, "but nobody else has any notion of doing so. The rest,

THE FIERY CIRCLE

I think, are going to march southward at once, Mexicans or no Mexicans, Comanches or no Comanches."

"Well spoken," said Bill Breakstone, "and I will even help in the march."

A roar that might easily have been called a shout of defiance came from the men of the train, when the story of the council was told. Then, with increased zeal, they fell to the work of girding up for the march and battle. The insolent demand of de Armijo added new fire to their courage. Cheerful voices arose, the rattle of bridle-bits, the occasional neigh of a horse, men singing snatches of song, generally lines from sentimental ballads, and the clink of bullets as they were counted and dropped into their pouches. Some of these sounds were of war, but Phil found the whole effect buoyant and encouraging. He caught the spirit, and whistled a lilting air as he, too, worked by the side of Bill Breakstone.

The boy soon saw the plan. Gradually the circle of wagons formed itself into two parallel lines, the noses of the horses or mules almost touching the rear of the wagon in front of them. Outside and on either side, but close to the wagons, rode the armed horsemen, two formidable lines, who, if hard pressed, could take refuge and shelter between the parallel rows of wagons. Moreover, the wagons handled by such cool and skillful men could be turned in a crisis, and even under fire, into a circle again, with the animals in the center. Phil understood the arrangement thoroughly, admired it tremendously, and was sure that the master mind of Middleton had directed everything. He glanced at the Mexicans and Comanches. They were still hovering in a great dark mass about a thousand yards away, and Phil knew that they were watching every movement of the Americans with the most intense curiosity.

Middleton and Woodfall rode to the head of the train. The loud command: "March!" was given. Every driver cracked his whip at the same time, the whole making **a** report like the sudden crash of many rifles, and the train began to move slowly across the plain, every armed man on either side holding his finger on the trigger of his rifle.

Phil was just behind Bill Breakstone, and both of them looked back at the enemy. Phil wondered what the Mexicans and Comanches would do, but he did not believe they would allow the train to depart unmolested, despite the fact that their face had already been well burned. He saw the hostile columns advance at about an even pace with the train, but he judged that there was uncertainty in their ranks. The Americans bore a certain resemblance to a modern armored train, and such men as de Armijo, Black Panther, and Santana were wary, despite their great excess of numbers.

The train moved forward at a slow but steady pace, but now its head was turned almost due south instead of west. Before them rolled the plains as usual, green with a grass not yet dried by the summer suns. Here and there appeared strange flowering shrubs, peculiar to the Texas uplands, but no trees broke the view. The plains rolled away until they died under the horizon of reddish gold that seemed an interminable distance away. There was little sound now but that of the turning wheels, the creaking of the axles, and the hoofbeats of many scores of horses and mules. The men were almost completely silent, and this silence, in itself, was strange, because the very atmosphere was impregnated with war. At any moment they might be in deadly conflict; yet they rode on, saying nothing.

Behind them came the Mexicans and Comanches in a double column, preserving the same distance of about a thousand yards, they, too, riding in silence, save for their hoofbeats. The dead evidently had been left as they fell or put in hasty graves, while the wounded were carried on horses in the rear. Phil looked back again and again at this singular pursuit, which, for the present, seemed no pursuit at all—at least, not hostile. It reminded him of the silent but tenacious manner in which wolves followed a great deer. While fearing his antlers and sharp hoofs, they would hang on and hang on, and in the end would drag down the quarry. Would that be the fate of the train?

"It's pretty good country for traveling," said Bill Breakstone cheerily, "and I don't see that anything is interrupting us. Except that we pass over one swell after another, the road is smooth and easy. What fine grassy plains these are, Phil, and look! yonder are antelopes grazing to the north of us. They've raised their heads to see, if they can, what we are, and what is that crowd behind us. They're just eaten up with curiosity."

Phil saw the herd of antelope come nearer. They were on a swell, in black silhouette against a red sun, and they were exaggerated to three or four times their real size. Phil was something of a philosopher, and he reflected that they were safe in the presence of so many men, because the men were not seeking game, but one another. The train moved on, and the herd of antelope dropped behind and out of sight. Still there was no demonstration from the enemy, who yet came on, in two columns, at the same distance of about a thousand yards, the sunlight gleaming on the lances of both Mexicans and Comanches. It began to seem to Phil as if they would always continue thus. Nevertheless, it was hard on the nerves, this incessant watching, as if one were guarding against a beast that might spring at any moment. Moreover, their force looked so large. But Phil glanced at the long-barreled rifles that the men of the train carried. They had proved far more than a match for muskets and lances.

"Will they attack us?" he asked Arenberg.

"Much harm iss meant," replied the German, "but they will not seek to do it until they think they see a chance. It iss time only that will tell."

The extraordinary march lasted all day. Neither side

committed a single hostile act, and the silence, so far as the men were concerned, was unbroken. The distance of about a thousand yards was preserved, but the Mexicans and Comanches were still there, and it seemed that they did not intend to be shaken off. About sunset they came to one of the shallow prairie streams, this time a mere brook, but with plenty of water for their animals.

"Here we camp," said Bill Breakstone, and almost as he spoke Middleton gave the word. One line of wagons went forward, the other stopped, the two ends joined, and then they swung around in a circle, with the stream flowing down the center of the enclosure. It was all done with so much celerity and so little trouble that the Mexicans and Comanches seemed to be taken by surprise. A few of them rode nearer, and some of the Comanches fired arrows, but they fell far short, and the Americans paid no attention to them.

"We'll take a bite and a drink, Phil," said Bill Breakstone, "a bite of cold meat and a drink of cold water."

"It iss good," said Arenberg. "That iss what we will do."

They had no fuel with which to light fires, but there were lanterns carrying candles in the train, and these were hung on the sides of the wagons facing the inner ring, casting a pleasant light on the men as they passed. But Phil and his two comrades, food in hand, went outside.

"Hope it won't come on too dark," said Breakstone. "A thick night is what we've got to dread. If our friends out there mean to do anything, they'll try it to-night, or I'm mightily fooled."

In the east, where the enemy hung, the twilight had come already and now both Mexicans and Comanches were blurring with the darkness. A lance blade or two gave back a last flash of fire from the setting sun, but in a few more instants the rays ceased to reach them, and they sank into the night of the eastern plain.

THE FIERY CIRCLE

"Feels damp, and that's bad," said Bill Breakstone. "Clouds mean a thick night, and a thick night means a lot of stalking and sniping by those rascals out there. Well, well, lay on, Macduff, and it won't be we who will first cry, 'Hold, enough!'"

The twilight soon deepened into dark, the wind rose a little, and, as Breakstone had feared, it brought with it shifts of rain, light showers only, but cold and very unpleasant. Only a few of the most hardened slept. All the others kept vigilant watch about the wagons. Phil, Breakstone, and Arenberg remained together, and nothing happened until nearly midnight. Then the mixed force of the enemy, creeping near, opened fire from every side, but the American sharpshooters lying down on the ground replied, firing at the flashes. This combat lasted nearly half an hour, and it was more spectacular than dangerous to the defenders.

"This is drawn out rather long and produces nothing, Sir Philip of the Midnight, the Wilderness, and the Rain," said Bill Breakstone, "and with our long range rifles we have the advantage. They're merely wasting good lead. Ah, I think I must have got that fellow! I hope it was one of those sneaking Comanches, and, if so, he deserves it for keeping me here on the ground in the rain, when I ought to be snoozing comfortably in a wagon."

He had fired at a flash about a hundred yards away, and his own fire drew shots from different points. Phil heard bullets whistling over his head, but, as they were hugging the earth very closely, he did not feel any great alarm over such blind shooting.

The firing increased a little presently, and now its effect upon the boy was wholly spectacular. He watched for the points of flame as one would for fireworks. Sometimes the flashes looked blue, sometimes yellow, and sometimes red. At other times they showed variations and new combinations of all three colors.

THE QUEST OF THE FOUR

"Since one has to watch, it's rather pretty, and it breaks the monotony," said Bill Breakstone. "Now, I think our little display of fireworks is ceasing."

Bill was a good prophet, because the firing quickly sank to a few scattered shots, and then to nothing. After that, they lay in the darkness and silence for a long time. Phil was wet and cold, and he longed for a warm blanket and the shelter of a wagon, but he was not one to flinch. As long as those two skilled plainsmen, Breakstone and Arenberg, thought it necessary to remain, he would remain without a complaint. He also expected that some other hostile movement would be made.

At some late hour of the night the boy heard the rapid beat of many hoofs, and then a mass of horsemen showed dimly in the dusk, dark squadrons galloping down upon the train. But the riflemen were ready. The train became at once a living circle of fire. A storm of bullets beat upon the charging horsemen, and fifty yards from the barrier they halted. There they wavered a few moments, while wounded horses screamed with pain, then turned and galloped back as fast as they had come.

"That's the fall of the curtain on the last act," said Bill Breakstone. "They thought to catch us napping, to stampede our horses, or to do something else unpleasant to us that depended on surprise."

Nevertheless, they watched all the remainder of the night, and Phil was devoutly glad when he saw the first touch of rose in the east, the herald of the new day. Before them the plain lay clear, except a fallen horse near by, and there was no sign of the enemy.

"They have had enough," said Bill Breakstone. "The darkness offered them their only chance, and now the sunrise has put them to flight.

"Night,
Fight.
Sun,
Done.

THE FIERY CIRCLE

"That's a short poem, Phil, one of the shortest that I've ever composed, but it's highly descriptive, and it's true."

It was true. Middleton and Woodfall, even when they searched the entire circle of the horizon with powerful field glasses, could find no trace of the enemy.

CHAPTER X

PHIL'S LETTER

NOW began the great march. The whole train was filled with an extraordinary animation. South to Taylor! South to the Rio Grande! South to join the forlorn hope against the Mexican masses! It appealed to them more than Santa Fé had ever appealed. Wild spirits, thrilling with the love of adventure and the hope of battle, they had before them the story of Texas and its gallant and victorious stand against overwhelming numbers. They knew every detail of that desperate and successful struggle, and they felt that they could do as well. Indeed, among them were some who had been mere boys at San Jacinto, and they began to talk of Sam Houston and that glorious war, of Goliad and of the Alamo, when the last man fell.

But while they talked they worked. In their zeal and enthusiasm they forgot that not one man in ten had closed his eyes the night before, and, a half hour after the brief breakfast was finished, they started again. It was a long journey, but they were prepared for it, and they moved steadily onward all through the day. Two or three times single horsemen were seen through the field glasses, but they were so far away none could tell whether they were Indians or Mexicans. Middleton, however, was firmly convinced that they would not be attacked again, at least not by the same forces which had been making so much trouble for them.

"There isn't much profit in hunting us," he said, "we are too difficult game, and the hunter has suffered

PHIL'S LETTER

more damage than the hunted. Moreover, de Armijo will want to join the main Mexican army near the Rio Grande. More glory is to be won there, and, if I mistake not, he is an exceedingly ambitious man. But the Comanches will leave so formidable a foe to snap up wandering hunters or small parties."

Middleton's theory seemed probable, but they did not relax the watch. That night half the men stood guard until midnight, and the other half until morning. The whole night passed in complete peace. There was not a single shot at the sentinels. The only sounds they heard were the lonesome howls of coyotes far out on the plain. Phil, Breakstone, and Arenberg were in the first watch, and they walked back and forth together in a little segment of the circle about thirty yards from the wagons. They talked more than usual, as they shared in the general belief that there would be no further attack, at least, not yet.

The night, in truth, was in sharp contrast with the one that had preceded it. There was no rain and no wind, the sky was just a peaceful blue, cut by the white belt of the Milky Way, and with the great stars dancing in myriad pools of light. Strife and battle seemed far away and forgotten.

"It will take us a long time to reach General Taylor on the Rio Grande or beyond, where he iss likely to be," said Arenberg

"A couple of months, maybe," said Breakstone.

"And then," continued Arenberg, "we do not know how long we will have to stay there. We do not know what great battles we will have to fight, and if we live through it all it may be a year, two years, until we can come back into the North."

"Not so long as that, I think," replied Breakstone.

Phil noticed Arenberg's melancholy tone, and once more he wondered what this man's quest might be. Evidently it did not lie to the south, for to him alone the turning from the old course had caused pain. He could not keep from showing sympathy.

"I feel that all of us will come back sooner or later, Mr. Arenberg," he said, "and we will go on in the way we chose first, and to success."

The German put his hand affectionately on the boy's shoulder.

"There are no prophets in these days," he said, "but now and then there iss a prophecy that comes true, and it may be that our God puts it in the mouth of a boy like you, instead of that of an older man. You strengthen my weak faith, Philip."

His tone was so solemn and heartfelt that the other two were silent. Surely the motive that drew Arenberg into the wilderness was a most powerful one! They could not doubt it. They walked without saying more until it was twelve when Bill Breakstone dropped his rifle from his shoulder with a great sigh of relief.

"It's just occurred to me that I haven't slept a wink for thirty-six hours," he said, "and I'm going to make up for lost time as soon as I can."

"Me, too," said Phil.

"Much sleep iss meant by me, also," said Arenberg.

Phil concluded to sleep in a wagon that night, and, in order to enjoy the full luxury of rest, he undressed for the first time in several days. Then he found a soft place in some bags of meal, covered himself with a blanket, and shut his eyes.

He had a wonderful sense of safety and comfort. After so much hardship and danger, this was like a king's bed, and the royal guards were outside to keep away harm. It was extraordinary how some sacks of flour and an army blanket could lull one's senses into golden ease.

He heard a few noises outside, a sentinel exchanging a word with another, the stamp of a restless horse's hoof, and then, for the last time, the long, lonesome howl of

PHIL'S LETTER

the coyote. A minute after that he was asleep. When he awoke the next day he felt that he was moving. He heard the cracking of whips and the sound of many voices. He sprang up, lifted the edge of the wagon cover, and looked out. There was the whole train, moving along at its steady, even pace, and a yellow sun, at least four hours high, was sailing peacefully in blue heavens. Phil, ashamed of himself, hurried on his clothes and sprang out of his wagon at the rear. The first man he saw was Bill Breakstone, who was walking instead of riding.

"Bill," he exclaimed indignantly, "here I've been sleeping all the morning, while the rest of you fellows have been up and doing!"

"Don't you worry yourself, Sir Philip of the Wagon and the Great Sleep," replied Bill Breakstone grinning. "A good wilderness rover rests when he can, and doesn't rest when he can't. Now you could rest, and it was the right thing for you to do. I haven't been up myself more than half an hour, while Captain Middleton and Arenberg are still asleep. Now, my merry young sir, I hope that will satisfy you."

"It does," replied Phil, his conscience satisfied, "and between you and me, Bill, it seems to me that we have come out of our troubles so far mighty well."

"We have," replied Bill Breakstone emphatically. "The curtain has gone down on act one, with honest and deserving fellows like you and myself on top. Act two hasn't begun yet, but meanwhile the winds blow softly, the air is pure, and we'll enjoy ourselves."

"Have you seen anything of our Comanche and Mexican friends?"

"Not a peep. We're marching in looser order now, because if they came we'd have ample time to form in battle array after we saw them."

But no enemy appeared that day nor the next day, and they rode south for many days in peace. Although eager to reach the Rio Grande as soon as possible, they were too wise to hurry the animals. The steady, measured pace was never broken, and they took full rest at night. They stopped sometimes to kill game and replenish their supplies of food. They found plenty of buffalo, and the most skillful of the hunters also secured all the antelope that they wished. Now and then they crossed a river that contained fish, and they added to their stores from these, also.

They were now far into the summer, but the grass was still green, although the heat at times was great, and rain fell but seldom. The character of the vegetation changed as they went south. Bill Breakstone defined it as an increase of thorns. The cactus stood up in strange shapes on the plain, but along the banks of the creeks they found many berries that were good to the taste. Four weeks after the turn to the south they met two messengers coming from the direction of Santa Fé and bound for the mouth of the Rio Grande. They were American soldiers in civilian dress whom Middleton knew, and with whom it had evidently been a part of his plan to communicate. He received from them important news, over which he pondered long, but, some time after the two men had disappeared under the horizon to the eastward, he spoke of it to Phil, Breakstone, and Arenberg.

"They have heard much," he said, "but it comes largely through Mexican channels. It is said that an American force from one of the Western States is moving on Santa Fé, and that it is likely to fall into our hands. It is said, also, that Taylor's advance into Mexico has been stopped, and that another army under Scott is to go by sea to Vera Cruz, and thence attempt to capture the City of Mexico. I don't know! I don't know what it all means! Can it be possible that Taylor has been beaten and driven back? But we shall see!"

"I know Taylor can't have been beaten," said Phil;

"but I'll be mighty glad when we reach the Rio Grande and find out for sure everything that is going on."

"That's so," said Bill Breakstone.

"News is contrary,
But we'll go;
Our views vary,
But we'll know.

Although we'll have to wait a long time about it, as Texas runs on forever."

The tenor of the messages soon spread through the train, and increased the desire to push on; yet neither Middleton nor Woodfall deemed it wise to give the animals too great a task for fear of breaking them down. Instead, they resolutely maintained their even pace, and bearing now to the eastward, still sought that Great River of the North which is greater in history and political importance than it is in water.

The time, despite the anxieties that they all shared, was not unpleasant to Phil. He enjoyed the free life of the wilderness and the vast plains. He saw how men were knitted together by common hardship and common danger. He knew every man and liked them all; hence, all liked him. He could never meet one of them in after life without a throb of emotion, a sense of great fellowship, and a sudden vivid picture of those days rising before him. He also learned many things that were of value. He knew how to mend any part of a wagon, he understood the troubles of horses, and he could handle a mule with a tact and skill that were almost uncanny.

"I suppose that mules, being by nature contrary animals, *like* Phil," said Bill Breakstone. "I've always behaved decently toward them, but I never knew one yet to like me."

"You want to treat a mule not like an animal but like a human being," said Arenberg. "They know more than most men, anyhow. It iss all in the way you approach them. I know how it ought to be done, although I can't always do it."

Many such talks beguiled the way. Meanwhile Phil could fairly feel himself growing in size and strength, and he longed like the others for the sight of Taylor and his army. The idea of taking part in a great war thrilled him, and it might also help him in his search. Meanwhile, the summer waned, and they were still in Texas. It seemed that they might ride on forever and yet not reach that famous Rio Grande. The grass turned brown on the plains, the nights grew cooler, and two northers chilled them to the bone. Several times they saw Comanches hovering like tiny black figures against the horizon, but they never came near enough for a rifle shot. Twice they met hunters and scouts who confirmed the earlier news obtained from the two messengers from the westward. Taylor, beyond a doubt, had halted a hundred and fifty or two hundred miles beyond the Rio Grande. There was even a rumor that he had been captured. This might or might not be true, but there was no doubt of the fact that an advance on the City of Mexico, due southward by land, was no longer intended. The report that Scott was to lead the army by way of Vera Cruz was confirmed. Middleton was troubled greatly, as Phil could see.

"I don't like the looks of this," he confided to his three most intimate associates, who, of course, were Phil, Bill Breakstone, and Arenberg. "I can't believe that Taylor has been taken—he isn't that kind of a man—but this stripping him of his forces to strengthen Scott will leave him almost unarmed before a powerful enemy."

Phil saw the cogency of his reasoning. Deeply patriotic, his private motives could not rule him wholly in the face of such an emergency. He longed with a most intense longing now for a sight of the Rio Grande. A great battle often hung in such an even balance that a few men might turn the scale. The brave and resolute two

PHIL'S LETTER

hundred with the train were a force not to be despised, even where thousands were gathered. The leaders, also felt the impulse. Despite caution and calculation, the speed of the train was increased. They started a little earlier every morning, and they stopped a little later every evening. Yet there were delays. Once they had a smart skirmish with Mexican guerillas, and once a Comanche force, which did little but distant firing, held them three days. Then a large number of their animals, spent by the long march, fell sick, and they were compelled to delay again.

The summer waned and passed. The grass was quite dead above ground, although the roots flourished below. The cactus increased in quantity. Often it pointed long melancholy arms southward as if to indicate that misfortune lay that way. The great silence settled about them again. There were no Indians, no Mexicans, no scouts, no hunters. Phil's thoughts reverted to his original quest. One day as he sat in the wagon he took the worn paper from the inside pocket of his waistcoat and read it for the thousandth time. He was about to hold it up and put it back in its resting place, when Bill Breakstone, seeking an hour or so of rest, sprang into the wagon, also. It was Phil's first impulse to thrust the paper quickly out of sight, and Bill Breakstone, with innate delicacy, pretended not to see, merely settling himself, with a cheerful word or two, into a comfortable seat. But Phil's second thought was the exact opposite. He withheld his hand and opened the worn and soiled paper.

"This is a letter, Bill," he said, "and you've seen it."

"At a distance," replied Bill Breakstone with assumed carelessness. "Too far for me to read a word of it. Love letter of yours, Phil? You're rather young for that sort of thing. Still, I suppose I'll have to call you Sir Philip of the Lost Lady and the Broken Heart."

"It's not that," said Phil. "This letter tells why I came into the Southwest. Somehow, I've wanted to keep it to myself, but I don't now. Will you read it, Bill? It's hard to make out some of the words, but if you look close you can tell."

He reached out the worn piece of paper.

"Not unless you feel that you really want me to read it," said Breakstone.

"I really want you to do so," said Phil.

Breakstone took the paper in his hands and smoothed it out. Then he held it up to the light, because the writing was faded and indistinct, and deciphered:

"I'm here, Phil, in this stone prison—it must be some sort of an old Spanish castle, I think, in the Mexican mountains. We were blindfolded and we traveled for days, so I can't tell you where I am. But I do know that we went upward and upward, and, when my shoes wore out, rocks sharp like steel cut into my feet. We also crossed many deep gulleys and ravines. I think we went through a pass. Then we came down into ground more nearly level. My feet were bleeding. We passed through a town and we stopped by a well. Then a woman gave me a cup of water. My throat was parched with dust. I knew it was a woman by her voice and her words of pity, spoken in Mexican. Then we came here. I have been shut up in a cell. I don't know how long, because I've lost count of time. But I'm here, Phil, between four narrow walls, with a narrow window that looks out on a mountainside, where I can see scrub pines and the thorny cactus. You're growing up now, Phil, and you may be able to come with friends for me. There's one here that's kind to me, the old woman who brings me my food, and she's loaned me a pencil and paper to write this. I've written the letter, and she's going to smuggle it away somehow northward into Texas, and then it may be passed on to you. I'm hoping, Phil, that it will reach you, wherever you are. If it does I know that you will try to come.   JOHN BEDFORD."

"Look on the other side," said Phil.

PHIL'S LETTER

Bill Breakstone turned it over and read the inscription:

"*To Philip Bedford, Esquire,*
"*Paris,*
"*Kentucky.*"

Tears stood in the boy's eyes, and his hands were trembling. Breakstone waited quietly.

"As you see," said Phil, when he felt that his voice was steady, "the letter came. It's my brother, John, who wrote it. A man riding across the country from Frankfort gave it to me in Paris last year. A flat boatman had brought it up the Kentucky River from its mouth at the Ohio, and when he came to Frankfort he asked if anybody would take it to Paris. A dozen were ready to do it. The flatboatman—his name was Simmons, a mountaineer—knew nothing about the letter. He said it had been given to him at the mouth of the Ohio by a man on a steamer from New Orleans. The other man said it had been dropped in front of him on his table at an inn in New Orleans by a fellow who looked like a Mexican. He thought at first it was just a scrap of paper, but when he read it and looked around for the man, he was gone. He resolved to send the letter on to me if he could, but he doesn't know how many hands it had passed through before it reached him. But it's John's handwriting. I could never mistake it."

The boy's voice trembled now, and the tears rose in his eyes again. Breakstone looked at the paper, turning it over and over.

"The old woman that your brother writes about was faithful," he said at last. "Likely a dozen men or women had it before it was dropped on that table in New Orleans. What was your brother doing in Texas, Phil?"

"He was older than I, and he went to Texas to help in the fighting against Mexico. You know there were raids on both sides long after San Jacinto. You remember the Mier expedition of the Texans, and there were others like it. John and his comrades were taken in one of these, but I don't know exactly which. I have written letters to all the Texas officials, but none of them know anything."

"And of course you started at once," said Bill Breakstone.

"Of course. There was nothing to keep me. We were only two, and I sold what we had, came down the Kentucky into the Ohio, and then down the Mississippi to New Orleans, where I met you and the others. I had an idea that John had been carried westward, and that I might learn something about him at Santa Fé, or at least that Santa Fé might be a good point from which to undertake a search. It's all guesswork anyway, that is, mostly, but when de Armijo told us that war had come I wasn't altogether sorry, because I knew that would take us down into Mexico, where I would have a better chance to look for John. What do you think of it, Bill?"

"Let me look at the letter again," said Breakstone.

Phil handed it back to him, and he read and reread it, turned it over and over again, looked at the inscription, "To Philip Bedford, Paris, Kentucky," and then tried to see writing where none was.

"It's the old business of a needle in a haystack, Phil," he said. "We're bound to confess that. We don't know where this letter was written nor when. Your brother, as he says, had lost count of time, but he might have made a stagger at a date."

"If he had put down any," said Phil, "it was rubbed out before it reached me. But I don't think it likely that he even made a guess. Do you know, Bill, I'm afraid that maybe, being shut up in a place like that, it might, after a long time—well, touch his head just a little. To be shut up in a cell all by yourself for a year, maybe two years, or even more, is a terrible thing, they say."

PHIL'S LETTER

"Don't think that! Don't think it!" said Bill Breakstone hastily. "The letter doesn't sound as if it were written by one who was getting just a little bit out of tune. Besides, I'm thinking it's a wonderful thing that letter got to you."

"I've thought of that often, myself," exclaimed Phil, a sudden light shining in his eyes. "This is a message, a call for help. It comes out of nowhere, so to speak, out of a hidden stone castle or prison, and in some way it reaches me, for whom it was intended. It seems to me that the chances were a million to one against its coming, but it came. It came! That's the wonderful, the unforgettable thing! It's an omen, Bill, an omen and a sign. If this little paper with the few words on it came to me through stone walls and over thousands of miles, well, I can go back with it to the one who sent it!"

His face was transfigured, and for the time absolute confidence shone in his eyes. Bill Breakstone, a man of sympathetic heart, caught the enthusiasm.

"We'll find him, Phil! We'll find him," he exclaimed.

Philip Bedford, so long silent about this which lay nearest to his heart, felt that a torrent of words was rushing to his lips.

"I can't tell you, Bill," he said, "how I felt when that letter was handed to me. Jim Harrington, a farmer who knew us, brought it over from Frankfort. He was on his horse when he met me coming down the street, and he leaned over and handed it to me. Of course he had read it, as it wasn't in an envelope, and he sat there on his horse looking at me, while I read it, although I didn't know that until afterward.

"Bill, I was so glad I couldn't speak for awhile. We hadn't heard from John in two or three years, and we were all sure that he was dead. After I read the letter through, I just stood there, holding it out in my hand and looking at it. Then I remember coming back to earth, when Jim Harrington leaned over to me from his saddle and said: 'Phil, is it genuine?'

" 'It's real,' I replied, 'I'd know his handwriting anywhere in the world.'

" 'What are you going to do, Phil?' he asked.

" 'I'm going to start for Mexico to-morrow,' I said.

" 'It's a powerful risky undertaking,' he said.

" 'I'm going to start for Mexico to-morrow,' I said again.

"Then from his height on the horse he put his hand on my head for a moment and said: 'I knew you'd go, Phil. I know the breed. I was in the War of 1812 with your father, when we were boys together. You're only a boy yourself, but you go to Mexico, and I believe you'll find John.'

"So you see, Bill, even at the very start there was one who believed that I would succeed."

"The signs do point that way," admitted Bill Breakstone. "Every fact is against you, but feeling isn't. I've lived long enough, Phil, to know that the impossible happens sometimes, particularly when a fellow is striving all his might and main to make it happen. What kind of a fellow was this brother of yours, Phil?"

"The finest in the world," replied Phil. "He raised me, Bill, as they say up there in Kentucky. He is four years older than I am, and we were left orphans, young. He taught me about everything I know, helped me at school, and then, when I got big enough, we made traps together, and in the fall and winter caught rabbits. Then I had a little gun, and he showed me how to shoot squirrels. We went fishing in the Kentucky often, and he taught me to ride, too. He was big and strong. Although only a boy himself, he could throw anybody in all the towns about there, but he was so good-natured about it that the men he threw liked him. Then we began to hear about Texas. Everybody was talking about Texas. Many were going there, too. It seemed to us the most

PHIL'S LETTER

wonderful country on earth. John caught the fever. He was going to make fortunes for both of us. I don't know how, but he meant to do it. I wasn't big enough to go with him, but he would send for me later. He went down the river to New Orleans. I had a letter from him there, and another from San Antonio, but nothing ever came after that until this dirty, greasy little piece of paper dropped out of the skies. It was four years between."

"Four years between!" repeated Bill Breakstone, "and we don't know what has happened in all that time. But it seems to me, Phil, that you're right. If this little piece of paper has come straight out of the dark thousands of miles to you, then it's going to be a guide to us back to the place where it started, because, Phil, I'm going to help you in this. I've got a secret errand of my own, and I'm not going to tell it to you just yet, but it can wait. I'm going to see you through, Phil, and we're going to find that brother John of yours, if we have to rip open every prison in Mexico."

His own eyes were bright now with the light of enthusiasm, and he held out his hand, which Phil seized. The fingers of the two were compressed in a strong clasp.

"It's mighty good of you, Bill," said the boy, "to help me, because this isn't going to be any easy search."

"It won't be any search at all for awhile," said Bill Breakstone, "because a great war is shoving in between. We are approaching the Rio Grande now, Phil."

The summer was now gone, and they were well into autumn. The train had come a great distance, more miles than any of them could tell. Cool winds blew across the Texas uplands, and the nights were often sharp with cold. Then the fires of cottonwood, dry cactus, or buffalo chips were very welcome, and it was pleasant to sit before them and speculate upon what awaited them on the other side of the Rio Grande. They had passed beyond the domain of the Comanches, and they were skirting along the edge of a country that contained scattered houses of adobe or log cabins—Mexicans in the former, and Americans in the latter. These were not combatants, but they were full of news and gossip.

There had been a revolution or something like it in Mexico. The report of the American successes, at the beginning, was true. Taylor had defeated greatly superior numbers along the Rio Grande, and, after a severe battle, had taken Monterey by storm. Then the Mexicans, wild with rage, partly at their own leaders, had turned out Paredes, their president, and the famous Santa Anna had seized the power. Santa Anna, full of energy and Latin eloquence, was arousing the Mexican nation against invasion, and great numbers were gathering to repel the little American armies that had marched across the vast wilderness to the Mexican border. This news made Middleton very serious, particularly that about Santa Anna.

"He's been called a charlatan, a trickster, cruel, unscrupulous, and many other things not good," he said one evening as they sat about a fire, "and probably all the charges are true, but at the same time he is a man of great ability. He has intuition, the power to divine the plans of an opponent, something almost Napoleonic, and he also has fire and energy. He will be a very dangerous man to us. He hates us all the more because the Texans took him at San Jacinto. If I remember rightly, two boys looking for stray mules found him hiding in the grass the day after the battle, and brought him in a prisoner. Such a man as he is not likely to forget such a humiliation as that."

"I have seen him with my own eyes," said Arenberg. "He iss a cruel man but an able one. Much harm iss meant, and much may be done."

That ended the German's comment, and, taking his pipe, he smoked and listened. But his face, lighted up by the flames, was sad. It was habitually sad, although

PHIL'S LETTER

Phil believed that the man was by nature cheery and optimistic. But Arenberg still kept his secret.

They learned, also, that there had been an armistice between the Americans and the Mexicans, but that Santa Anna had used all the time for preparations. Then the negotiations were broken off, and the war was to pass into a newer and fiercer phase. Taylor was at Saltillo, about two hundred miles beyond the line, but Scott, who had been on the Rio Grande some time earlier, had taken most of his good officers and troops for the invasion by way of Vera Cruz, and Taylor, with his small remaining force, was expected to stand on the defensive, even to retreat to the Rio Grande. Instead of that, he had advanced boldly into the mountains. Politics, it was said, had intervened, and Taylor was to be shelved. Middleton, usually reserved, commented on this to Phil, Breakstone, and Arenberg, who, he knew, would not repeat his words.

"I've no doubt that this news is true," he said, "and it must be a bitter blow to old Rough and Ready—that's what we call Taylor in the army. He's served all his life with zeal and efficiency, and now he's to be put aside, after beginning a successful and glorious campaign. It's a great wrong that they're doing to Zachary Taylor."

"But we're going to join him anyhow, are we not?" asked Phil.

"Yes, that's our objective. I should have to do so, because my original instructions were to report to him, and they have not been changed. And, with Santa Anna leading the Mexicans, what our Government expects to happen at one place may happen at another."

The train itself was now in splendid condition. All the wounded men had fully recovered. The sick horses and mules were well again. The weather had been good, game was plentiful, their diet was varied and excellent, and there was no illness. Moreover, their zeal increased as they drew near the seat of war, and the reports, some true, some false, and all lurid, came thick and fast. It was hard to keep some of them from leaving the train and going on ahead, but Middleton and Woodfall, by strenuous efforts, held them in hand.

They shifted back now toward the east, and came at last to the Rio Grande. Phil was riding ahead of the train, when he caught the first view of it—low banks, an immense channel, mostly of sand, with water, looking yellow and dangerous, flowing here and there in two or three streams. The banks were fringed but sparsely with trees, and beyond lay Mexico, the Mexico of Cortez and the Aztecs, the Mexico of gold and romance, and the Mexico of the lost one whom he had come so far to find.

It was one of the most momentous events in Philip Bedford's life, this view of Mexico, to which he had come over such a long trail. It was not beautiful, there across the Rio Grande; it was bare, dark, and dusty, with rolling hills and the suggestion of mountains far off to the right. The scant foliage was deep in autumn brown. Human life there was none. Nothing stirred in the vast expanse of desolation. The train was so far behind him that he did not hear the rumbling of the wagon wheels, and he sat there, horse and rider alike motionless, gazing into the misty depths of this Mexico which held so much of mystery and which attracted and repelled at the same time. Question after question throbbed through his mind. Would the Americans succeed in penetrating the mountains that lay beyond? And if so, in what direction was he to go? Which way should he look! It seemed so vast, so inscrutable, that he was appalled. For the first time since he had left that little Paris in Kentucky he felt despair. Such a search as his was hopeless, doomed in the beginning. His face turned gray, his chin sank upon his chest, but then Bill Breakstone rode up beside him, and his loud, cheery voice sounded in his ear.

"Well, here we are at last, Phil," he exclaimed.

PHIL'S LETTER

"We've ridden all the way across Texas, and it must have been a hundred thousand miles. Now we stand, or rather sit, on the shores of the Rio Grande.

> "Behold the river!
> But I don't quiver.
> They call it grand.
> It's mostly sand.

It's no Mississippi, Phil, but it's a hard stream for an outfit like ours to cross. I'm glad that Taylor has already cleared the way. You remember what a fight we had with the Comanches back at the crossing of that other and smaller river."

"I do," said Phil, "but there is nothing here to oppose us, and doubtless we can make the crossing in peace."

CHAPTER XI

WITH THE ARMY

THE crossing of the Rio Grande was a formidable task, and the train could never have accomplished it in the face of a foe, even small in numbers, but no Mexicans were present, and they went about their task unhindered. One of the streams was too deep to be forded, but they cut down the larger trees and constructed a strong raft, which they managed to steer over with long poles. The reluctant horses and mules were forced upon it, and thus the train was carried in safety over the deep water. Nor was the task then ended. It usually took six horses and ten or twelve men to drag a wagon through the sand and carry it up the bank to the solid earth beyond, the way having been carefully examined in advance in order to avoid quicksand.

It took three days to build the raft and complete the passage. Phil had never worked so hard in his life before. He pushed at wagon wheels and pulled at the bridles of mules and horses until every bone in him ached, and he felt as if he never could get his strength again. But the train was safely across, without the loss of a weapon or an animal. They were in Mexico, and they did not deceive themselves about the greatness and danger of the task that lay before them. Phil felt the curious effect which the passage over the border from one country to another usually has on people, especially the young. It seemed to him that in passing that strip of muddy river he had come upon a new soil, and into a new climate—into a new world, in fact. Yet the Texas shore, in reality, looked exactly like the Mexican, and was like it.

"Well, Phil," said Bill Breakstone, "here we are in Mexico. I'm covered with mud, so are you, and so is Arenberg. I think it's Texas and Mexico mud mixed, so suppose we go down, find a clear place in the water, and get rid of it."

They found a cool little pool, an eddy or backwater, where the water standing over white sand was fairly clear, and the three, stripping, sprang in. The water was deep, and Bill plunged and dived and spluttered with great delight. Phil and Arenberg were not so noisy, but they found the bath an equal pleasure. It was an overwhelming luxury to get the sand out of their eyes and ears and hair, and to feel the cool water on bodies hot with the ache and grime of three days' hard work.

"You'd better make the best of it, Phil," said Breakstone. "The part of Mexico that we are going into isn't very strong on water, and maybe you won't get another bath for a year."

"I'm doing it," said the boy.

"And don't you mind the fact," said Bill Breakstone, "that the alligators of the Rio Grande, famous for their size and appetite, like to lie around in lovely cool pools like this and bite the bare legs of careless boys who come down to bathe."

Phil felt something grasp his right leg and pull hard. He uttered a yell, and then, putting his hand on Breakstone's brown head, which was rising to the surface, convulsively thrust him back under. But Breakstone came up three yards away, pushed the hair out of his eyes, and laughed.

"I'm the only alligator that's in the stream," he said, "but I did give you a scare for a moment. You are bound to admit that, Sir Philip, Duke of Texas and Prince of Mexico."

"I admit it readily," replied Phil, and, noticing that

Breakstone was now looking the other way, he dived quietly and ran his finger nails sharply along his comrade's bare calf. Breakstone leaped almost wholly out of the water and cried:

"Great Heavens, a shark is eating me up!"

Phil came up and said quietly:

"There are no sharks in the Rio Grande, Mr. William Breakstone. You never find sharks up a river hundreds of miles from the ocean. Now, I did give you a scare for a moment, you will admit that, will you not, Sir William of the Shout, the Shark, and the Fright?"

"I admit it, of course, and now we are even," said Breakstone. "Give me your hand on it."

Phil promptly reached out his hand, and Breakstone, seizing it, dragged him under. But Phil, although surprised, pulled down on Breakstone's hand with all his might, and Breakstone went under with him. Both came up spluttering, laughing, and enjoying themselves hugely, while Arenberg swam calmly to a safe distance.

"You are a big boy, Herr Bill Breakstone," he said. "You will never grow up."

"I don't want to," replied Bill Breakstone calmly. "When it makes me happy all through and through just to be swimming around in a pool of nice cool water, what's the use of growing up? Answer me that, Hans Arenberg."

"I can't," replied the German. "It isn't in me to give an answer to such a question."

"I suppose we've got to go out at last, dress again, and go back to work," said Breakstone lugubriously. "It's a hard world for us men, Phil."

"One iss not a fish, and, being not a fish," said Arenberg, "one must go out on dry land some time or other to rest, and the some time has now come."

They swam to land, but Bill Breakstone began to plead.

"Let's lie here on the sand and luxuriate for a space,

WITH THE ARMY

Sir Philip of the Rio Grande and Count Hans of the Llano Estacado, which is Spanish for the Staked Plain, which I have seen more than once," said Bill Breakstone. "The sand is white, it is clean, and it has been waiting a long time for us to lie upon it, close our eyes, and forget everything except that we are happy."

"It iss a good idea," said Arenberg. "There are times when it iss well to be lazy, only most men think it iss all the time."

They stretched themselves out on the white sand and let the warm sun play upon them, permeating their bodies and soothing and relaxing every muscle. Phil had not felt so peaceful in a long time. It had relieved him to tell the secret of his quest to Breakstone, who, with his permission, had told it in turn to Middleton and Arenberg, and now that he was really in Mexico with strong friends around him he felt that the first great step had been accomplished. The warm sun felt exceedingly good, his eyes were closed, and a pleasant darkness veiled them, a faint murmur, the flowing of the river, came to his ears, and he floated away with the current.

"Here! here! Sir Philip of the Sleepy Head, wake up. It isn't your first duty to go to sleep when you arrive in Mexico! Besides, it's time we were back at the camp, or they'll think Santa Anna has got us already! Also, you need more clothes than you've got on just now!"

Phil sprang up embarrassed, but he saw Arenberg looking sheepish, also.

"You had good company, Sir Philip of the Sleepy Head," exclaimed Breakstone joyously. "Count Hans of the Snore was traveling with you into that unknown land to which millions have gone and returned, and of which not one can tell anything."

"It iss so," said Arenberg. "I confess my weakness."

They dressed rapidly, and, refreshed and young again, ran back to the train. The twilight was now coming, and the wagons were drawn up in the usual circular formation, with the animals in the middle, and, outside the circle, were burning several fires of dry cactus and cottonwood, around which men were cooking.

"Just in time for supper," said Bill Breakstone. "I was a great rover when I was a boy, but my mother said I took care never to get out of sound of the dinner-bell. It may be funny, but my appetite is just as good in Mexico as it was in Texas."

They ate strips of bacon, venison, and jerked buffalo, with a great appetite. They drank coffee and felt themselves becoming giants in strength. The twilight passed, and a brilliant moon came out, flooding the plain with silvery light. Then they saw a horseman coming toward them, riding directly through the silver flood, black, gigantic, and sinister.

"Now what under the sun can that be?" exclaimed Bill Breakstone.

"You should say what under the moon. It iss more correct," said Arenberg. "I can tell you, also, that it iss a white man, although the figure looks black here—I know by the shape. It iss also an American officer in uniform. I know it because I saw just then a gleam of moonlight on his epaulets. He iss coming to inspect us."

The approach of the stranger aroused, of course, the deepest curiosity in everybody, and in a few moments a crowd gathered to gaze at this man who came on with such steadiness and assurance. His figure, still magnified by the moon, out of which he seemed to be riding, showed now in perfect outline. He carried no rifle, but they could see the hilt of a sword on his thigh. He wore a military cap, and the least experienced could no longer doubt that he was an army officer.

"He knows that we are friends," said Middleton, "or he would not come on so boldly. Unless I mistake much, he sits his horse like a regular officer of the United States cavalry. That seat was learned only at West Point."

WITH THE ARMY

The stranger rode out of the magnifying rays. His horse and himself shrank to their real size. He came straight to the group, leaped to the ground, and, holding the bridle in one hand, lifted his cap with the other in salute. Middleton sprang forward.

"Edgeworth," he exclaimed, "when you came near I thought it was you, but I scarcely dared to hope."

The officer, tall and striking of appearance, with penetrating gray eyes, seized Middleton's hand.

"And it is you, Middleton," he said. "What a meeting for two who have not seen each other since they were at West Point together."

"But it's where we both want to be," said Middleton.

"That is so," said Edgeworth with emphasis, "but I had heard, George, that you were sent on an errand of uncommon danger, and I had feared—I will not hesitate to say it to you now—that you would never come back."

Middleton laughed. He was obviously delighted with this meeting of the comrade of his cadetship. Then he introduced Woodfall and the others, after which he asked:

"How did you know we were friends, Tom? You came on as if you were riding to a garden-party."

"A scout brought news of you," he replied. "We have a small force about twenty miles ahead, and I rode back to meet you, and see what was here."

"We have some good men," said Woodfall, "and they are willing to fight. We've come a good many hundreds of miles for that purpose."

"I believe you," said Edgeworth, running his trained eyes over the crowd. "A finer body of men I never saw, and we need you, every one of you."

"What news?" asked Middleton eagerly.

"Much of it, and all bad. Our government has mixed the situation badly. We've been steadily strengthening Scott, and, in the same proportion, we've been weakening Taylor. There are rumors, I don't know how authentic—

perhaps you have heard them—that Santa Anna is coming north with a great force to destroy us. Taylor is expected to retreat rapidly, but he hasn't done it. You know old Rough and Ready, George."

"I hope to Heaven he won't retreat!" exclaimed Middleton.

"He hasn't. So far he has advanced," said Edgeworth. "But I ride back with you in the morning, boys, and I think great things are going to happen before long. Besides the men with you, Middleton, we've use for everything you've got in the wagons. You won't suffer, Mr. Woodfall."

The train moved the next morning an hour earlier than usual. Wheels were turning before daylight. Hearts were beating high, and they pushed on at great speed now, for wagons, until past sunset. In the middle of the day it was hot, in the evening chill winds blew down from the crests of distant mountains, but at all times, morning, noon, and evening, they marched in a cloud of dust, much of it impregnated with alkali. It annoyed Phil and his comrades terribly, sifting into nose, mouth, ears, and eyes, putting a bitter taste on the palate, and making them long for the sweet waters of the pool in which they had bathed so luxuriously.

The next day was the same; more dust, more alkali, and the deadly monotony of a treeless and sandy plain. But that night it was extremely cold. They were approaching the mountains, the spurs of the Sierra Madre, and the winds were sharp with the touch of ice and snow. Winter, also, had come, and in the night ice formed in the infrequent rivulets on the plain. Now and then they passed little Mexican villages, mostly of the adobe huts, with dirt and children strewed about in great quantities. The children were friendly enough, but the women scowled, and the men were away. Phil did not find the villages picturesque or attractive in any sense, and he was disappointed.

WITH THE ARMY

"I hope this isn't the best Mexico has to show," he said.

"It isn't very inviting," said Bill Breakstone, "you wouldn't look around here for a Forest of Arden or a Vale of Vallombrosa, but this is only the introduction to Mexico. Monterey, which General Taylor took, is a fine city, and so are others farther down. I've seen a lot of them myself. Don't you worry, Phil, you'll find enough to interest you before you get through."

They also picked up some wandering scouts and hunters, who joined them in their march. Several of these brought news. Taylor was at Saltillo, and his force was small. The Mexicans were raiding to the very outskirts of the city, and they looked upon Taylor's army as already destroyed. The American force of about four thousand five hundred men contained less than five hundred regular troops. The others, although good material, were raw volunteers, very few of whom had been under fire.

Phil saw Middleton and Edgeworth talking together very anxiously, and he knew that they were full of apprehensions. It seemed as if Fate itself were playing into the hands of Santa Anna. Occasionally they saw bands of Mexican guerillas hovering on the horizon, but they did not bother with them, keeping straight on for Taylor and Saltillo. The cold still increased, both day and night, and the winds that came from the peaks of the Sierra Madre, now plainly in view, cut to the bone. Phil was glad to take to the wagons for sleep, and to wrap himself in double blankets. It was now well into December, but in two more days they expected to reach Taylor at Saltillo.

The last day of the march came, and every heart in the train beat high with expectancy. Even the army officers, Middleton and Edgeworth, trained to suppression of their emotions, could not restrain their eagerness, and they, with Woodfall and others, rode on ahead of the train. Phil, Bill Breakstone, and Arenberg were in this little group, but the three were at the rear.

"Phil, you were right when you called it a strange looking land," said Bill Breakstone, "and I'm of the opinion that we're going to see strange things in it. Our military friends look none too happy, and as I've eyes and ears of my own I know we're likely to have lively times after Christmas. Did you know that Christmas was not far away, Phil?"

"No, I had forgotten all about it," replied Phil, "but, since you mention it, I remember that it is December. Ah, what is that shining in the sun straight ahead of us, Bill?"

He pointed with his finger and showed the faintest red tint under the horizon.

"That," replied Breakstone, "is a red tile roof on a house in Saltillo, and you're the first to see the town. Good eye, my boy. Now, the others have seen it, also! Look how they quicken the steps of their horses!"

They broke into a gallop as they came into a shallow, pleasant valley, with green grass, the Northern palms, clear, flowing water, and many a neat stone house with its piazzas and patios. The domes of several fine churches rose into view, and then men in uniforms, rifle in hand, stood across the road. Phil knew their faces; these men were never bred in Mexico. Brown they were with the wind and sun of many days, but the features beneath the brown were those of the Anglo-Saxons, the Americans of the North, his own people.

"Halt!" came the sharp order from the commander of the patrol.

Middleton replied for them all, but, as Phil rode past, he leaned over and said to the bronzed leader of the patrol:

"I'm here, Jim Harrington. I told you in Paris that I was coming to Mexico. It's a long road, and you're ahead of me, but I'm here."

WITH THE ARMY

The leader, a thick-set, powerful man of fifty-five, looked up in amazement. At first he had not recognized Phil under his tan and layer of dust, but now he knew his voice.

"Phil Bedford, by all that's wonderful!" he exclaimed. "I didn't think that you and I would ever meet in Mexico, but when the call came I couldn't keep away!"

Then he lowered his tone and asked:

"Any news of John?"

Phil shook his head sadly.

"Not a thing," he replied, "but I'm going to find him!"

"I believe you will," said Harrington, "but your search is going to be delayed, Phil. You'll have to wait for something else that none of us will ever forget. But, Phil you've landed among friends. Lots of the boys that you used to know in Paris and around there are here."

As Phil rode on, the truth of Harrington's words was confirmed. Tan and dust did not keep strong, hearty voices from hailing him.

"Hey, you, Phil Bedford, where did you come from?"

"Is that old Phil Bedford? Did he drop from the clouds?"

"Here, Phil, shake hands with an old friend!"

He saw more than a score of familiar faces. A number of these soldiers were almost as young as himself, and two or three of them were related to him by blood. He had a great sensation of home, an overpowering feeling of delight. Despite strangeness and distance, old friends and kindred were around him. But old friends did not make him forget his new friends, or think any less of them. He introduced Middleton, Bill Breakstone, and Arenberg. Middleton was compelled to hurry to General Taylor with his report, but the other two remained and affiliated thoroughly.

"You camp with us," said Dick Grayson, a distant

cousin of Phil's. "We've got a fine place over here, just back of the plaza. Lots of Kentuckians here, Phil—in fact, more from our state than any other. The rest are mostly from Illinois, Indiana, Arkansas, Mississippi, and Louisiana. We haven't got many regulars, but we've got mighty good artillery, and we're ready to give a good account of ourselves against anybody. You ought to see old Rough and Ready. He's as grim as you please. Just as soon bite a ten-penny nail in two as not. Mad clean through, and I don't blame him, because he's been robbed to strengthen Scott."

Phil and his comrades went readily with Grayson. The wagon train was already scattering through the encampment, the volunteers taking their places here and there, while Woodfall and his associates were arranging for the sale of their available supplies. Phil, Breakstone, and Arenberg owned their horses, and, leading them with the bridles over their arms, they walked along with their new friends. Phil noticed that the town was well built in the Mexican style, with many handsome houses and signs of prosperity. The American invaders had harmed nothing, but their encampment was spread throughout the city.

The group walked by a green little park in which a small fountain was playing. A young Mexican in sombrero, gaudy jacket and trousers sat on a stone bench and idly thrummed a guitar. Several thick-set Mexican women, balancing on their heads heavy jars of water, passed placidly by. A small train of burros loaded with wool walked down another street. There was nothing save the presence of the soldiers to tell of war. It all looked like play. Phil spoke of the peaceful appearance of everything to Dick Grayson. Grayson shrugged his shoulders.

"You cannot tell a thing by its looks in this country," he said. "Mexicans seem nearly always to be asleep, but, as a rule, they are not. You don't see many men about, and it means that they are off with the guerillas, or that they've gone south to join Santa Anna. We haven't done any harm here. We've treated the people in Saltillo a good deal better than their own rulers often treat them, and we're friendly with the inhabitants, but Mexicans are bound to stand with Mexicans, just as Americans stand with Americans. It's natural, and I don't blame 'em for it."

"I'd wager that many a message is carried off to the enemy by these stolid looking women," said Bill Breakstone.

Yet the town itself showed little hostility. Nevertheless, Phil could not keep from feeling that it was thoroughly the enemy of the invader, as was natural. As Bill Breakstone truly said, information concerning the Americans was certainly sent to the Mexican leaders. Everything that the Americans might do in the town would quickly become known to the enemy, while a veil always hung before the Mexican troops and preparations. Nevertheless, the life of the city, save for the reduction in the number of its adult inhabitants, went on as usual.

Some of the officers occupied houses, but all the men and younger officers were in tents, either in the open places of the town or on the outskirts. Phil, Arenberg, and Breakstone spent that night with Dick Grayson and others in a little park, where about twenty tents stood. These were to be their regular quarters for the present, and, as Middleton had foreseen, the reinforcement was welcomed eagerly. They ate an abundant supper, and, the night being cold, a fire was built within the ring of the tents. Here they sat and talked. Besides Dick Grayson, there were "Tobe" Wentworth, Elijah Jones, Sam Parsons, and other old friends of Phil.

As they sat before the cheerful blaze and put their blankets over their backs to shield themselves from the bitter mountain winds, they discussed the war and, after the manner of young troopers, settled it, every one in his own way and to his own perfect satisfaction. "Tobe" Wentworth was not an educated youth, but he was a great talker.

"I could a-planned this war," he said, "an' carried it right out without a break to a finish."

"Why didn't you do it, then?" asked Dick Grayson.

"I did think o' writin' to Washin'ton once," said Tobe calmly, "an' tellin' them how it ought to be done, but I reckoned them old fellows would be mighty set in their ways an' wouldn't take it right. Old men don't like to be told by us youngsters that they don't know much."

"I've got a plan, too," said an Indiana youth named Forsythe.

"What is it?" asked Wentworth scornfully.

"It's a secret. I ain't ever goin' to tell it to anybody," said Forsythe. "I've drawed up my will, an' I've provided that when I die it's to be buried with me, still unread, folded right over my heart."

All laughed, but "Tobe" rejoined:

"Sech modesty is becomin' in Hoosiers, all the more so because it's the first time I ever knowed one of them to display it."

"Did you ever hear about that gentleman from Injiany that went out in the Kentucky Mountains once, drivin' a fine buggy?" asked Forsythe. "He noticed some big boys runnin' along behind him. He didn't think much of it at first, but they kept right behind him mile after mile, but sayin' nothin' an' offerin' no harm. At last his curiosity got the better of him, an' he leaned back and asked: 'Boys, why are you followin' me this way?' Then the biggest of them boys, a long, lean fellow, barefooted and with only one suspender, up and answers: 'Why, stranger, we reckoned we'd run behind an' see how long it would take for your hind wheels to ketch up with your front wheels.'"

"Tobe" Wentworth sat calm and unsmiling until the laughter died. Then he said:

"Any of you fellers know how the people of Injiany got the name of Hoosiers? No? Well, I'll tell you. It's so wild and rough over there, an' them people are so teetotally ignorant an' so full of curiosity that, whenever a gentleman from Kentucky crosses the Ohio and goes along one of their rough roads, up they pop everywhere, and call out to him: 'Who's yer?' meaning 'Who are you?' and that started the word Hoosier, which all over the world to-day means the people from Indiany."

When the second laugh died, Bill Breakstone rubbed his hands together.

"I see that I've fallen upon a merry crowd," he said, "and it is well. The spirit of youth is always delightful, and it leads to the doing of great things."

"You talk like an actor," said Dick Grayson, not as a criticism, but in tones of admiration.

"I talk like an actor," replied Bill Breakstone with majesty, "because I am one."

"You don't say so! You don't mean it!" exclaimed a dozen voices at once.

"I am, or, rather, was," replied Bill with dignity, "although I will admit that I am now engaged in other pursuits."

Most of them still looked at him doubtfully, and Bill, his honor at stake, became the subject of a sudden inspiration.

"I see that some of you suspect my veracity, which is natural under the circumstances," he said. "Now, I said I was an actor, and I'll prove that I'm an actor by acting."

"You don't mean it!" they cried again.

"I will," said Bill Breakstone firmly. "Moreover, I will act from a play by the greatest of all writers. Throw the wood together there and let the blaze spring up. I want you to see me."

A dozen willing hands tossed together the logs which sent up a swift, high flame. The whole circle was lighted brightly, and Bill Breakstone stood up. Phil had never taken seriously his assertion that he had been an actor, but now he suddenly changed his opinion. He stood for a few moments in the full blaze of the light, a tall, slender figure, his face lean and shaven smoothly. His expression changed absolutely. He seemed wholly unconscious of the young soldiers about him, of the palms, or of the stone or adobe houses of the town.

Then, in a tone of martial fervor he began to recite scraps from Shakespeare dealing with war and battle, Macbeth's defiance to Macduff, Richard on the battlefield, and other of the old familiar passages. But they were new to most of those about him, and Breakstone himself, as he afterward said, was stirred that night by an uncommon fire and spirit. Something greater than he, perhaps the effect of time and place, seemed to have laid hold of him. The fire and spirit were communicated to his audience, which rapidly increased in numbers, although he did not see it, so deeply was he filled with his own words, carrying him far back into other lands among the scenes that he described. The applause rose again and again, and always he was urged to go on. As he recited for the sixth time, a thick-set, strong figure appeared at the edge of the throng, and men at once made way for it. The figure was that of a man with gray hair, and with a deep line down either cheek. Breakstone's passing glance caught the face and divined in an instant his identity. The applause, the demand for more, rose again, and after a little hesitation the actor began:

" 'My people are with sickness much encumbered
My numbers lessened, and these few I have,
Almost no better than so many French;
Who, when they were in health, I tell the herald,
I thought upon one pair of English legs
Did walk three Frenchmen, yet
Forgive me, God,
That I do brag thus. This poor air of France
Hath blown that voice in me. I must repent,

WITH THE ARMY

Go, therefore, tell thy master here I am;
My ransom is this frail and worthless trunk,
My army but a weak and sickly guard—'"

He paused a moment, but the man with the gray hair and lined cheeks still stood in an attitude of deep attention, and, skipping some of the lines, he continued:

"'If we may pass we will; if we be hindered
We shall your tawny ground with your red blood
Discolor; and so, Montjoy, fare you well,
The sum of all our answer is but this:
We would not seek a battle as we are;
Nor as we are, we say we will not shun it,
So tell your master.'"

He sat down amid roars of applause and universal approval. Did they not know? Mexicans were boasting already that Taylor would have to surrender to Santa Anna without a battle. Bill Breakstone stole a glance toward the place where the gray-haired man had stood, but he was gone now.

"Did you know that old Rough and Ready himself was listening to you there toward the last?" asked Grayson.

"Is that so?" replied Breakstone. "Well, I'm not ashamed of anything that I said, and now, if I've entertained you boys a little, I'd like to rest awhile. You don't know how hard that kind of work is, whether your work be good or bad."

Rest he certainly should have. They had found too great a treasure, these fighting men in a far land, to let him be spoiled by overwork, and they brought him an abundance of refreshment, also.

Breakstone drank a cup of light wine made in Saltillo, as he lay back luxuriously on a pallet in one of the tents. He felt that he had reason to be satisfied with himself, and perhaps, he, playing the actor, had seized an opportunity, and had made it do what might be an important service in a great campaign.

"What was the last piece that you recited?" asked Grayson. "Somehow it seemed to fit in with our own situation here."

"That," replied Breakstone, "was a speech from King Henry V. He is in France with a small army, and the French have sent to him to demand his surrender. He makes the reply that I have just quoted to you."

There was a thoughtful silence, although they had known his meaning already, and presently Phil and his comrades, making themselves comfortable in their tents, went to sleep. They were formally enrolled among the Kentucky volunteers the next day, and began their duties, which consisted chiefly of patrolling. Phil was among the sentinels stationed the next night on the outskirts of the city.

CHAPTER XII

THE PASS OF ANGOSTURA

IT was almost midwinter now in Mexico, and here, in the northern part of the republic, on the great plateau, it was cold. Phil more than once had seen the snow flying, and far away it lay in white sheets on the peaks of the Sierra Madre. He had obtained a heavy blanket coat or overcoat from the stores, and he was glad enough now to pull it closely around him and turn its collar up about his neck, as he walked back and forth in the chilly blasts. At each end of his beat he met another sentinel, a young Kentuckian like himself, and, for the sake of company, they would exchange a friendly word or two before they parted.

The night was dark, and, with the icy winds cutting him, Phil, after the other sentinel had turned away, felt more lonesome in this far strange land than he had ever been before in his life. Everything about him was unfriendly, the hard volcanic soil upon which he trod, the shapeless figures of the adobe huts on the outskirts of the town, and the moaning winds from the Sierra Madre, which seemed to be more hostile and penetrating than those of his own country. It was largely imagination, the effect of his position, but it contained something of reality, also. It certainly was not fancy alone that peopled the country about with enemies. An invader is seldom loved, and it was not fancy at all that created the night and the cold.

Phil's beat was at the edge of open country, and he could see a little distance upon a plain. He thought. at times, that shadowy figures with soundless tread passed there, but he was never sure. He spoke about it to the sentinel on his right, and then to the sentinel on his left. Each in turn watched with him, but then the shadows did not pass, and he concluded that his fancy was playing him tricks. Yet he was troubled, and he resolved to watch with the utmost vigilance. His beat covered a path leading into the town, while to right and left of him was very difficult country. It occurred to him that anybody who wanted to pass would come his way, and he was resolved that nobody should pass. He examined every shadow, even if it might be that of a tree moved by the wind, and he listened to every sound, although it might be made by some strange Mexican animal.

Thus the time passed, and the fleeting shadows resolved themselves into a figure that had substance and that remained. It took the shape of a man in conical hat and long Mexican serape. He also carried a large basket on one arm, and he approached with an appearance of timidity and hesitation. Phil stepped forward at once, held up his rifle, and called: "Halt!" The man obeyed promptly and pointed to the basket, saying something in Spanish. When Phil looked, he pulled back the cover and disclosed eggs and dressed chickens.

"To sell to the soldiers?" asked the boy.

The man nodded. Phil could not see his face, which was hidden by the broad brim of his hat and the folds of his serape, drawn up around his chin, evidently to fend off the cold. His surmise was likely enough. The Americans had made a good market at Saltillo, and the peons were ready to sell. But he did not like the hour or the man's stealthy approach.

"No come in," he said, trying to use the simplest words of his language to a foreigner. "Orders! Orders must be obeyed!"

The man pointed again to his basket, as if, being in doubt, he would urge the value of a welcome.

THE PASS OF ANGOSTURA

"No come in," repeated Phil. "Go back," and he pointed toward the woods from which the Mexican had come.

The man hesitated, but he did not go. He turned again toward Phil, and at that moment the wind lifted a segment of his wide hat-brim. Phil sprang back in amazement. Despite the dark, he recognized the features of de Armijo, who could have come there for no good, who must have come as a spy or worse.

"De Armijo!" he cried, and sprang for him. But the Mexican was as quick as lightning. He leaped backward, dropped his basket, and the long blade of a knife flashed in the air. It cut through the sleeve of Phil's coat, and the sharp point, with a touch like fire, ran along his arm. It was well for him that he had put on the heavy blanket coat that night, or the blade would have grated on the bone.

The pain did not keep Phil from throwing up his rifle, and de Armijo, seeing that his stroke had not disabled the boy, wheeled and ran. Phil fired instantly, and saw de Armijo stagger a little. But in a moment the Mexican recovered himself and quickly disappeared in the darkness, although Phil rushed after him. He would have followed across the plain, but he knew it was his duty to go no farther, and he came back to meet the other sentinels, who were running toward him at the sound of the shot. Phil quickly explained what had occurred, telling the identity of the man, and adding that he was crafty and dangerous.

"A Mexican officer," said one of them. "No doubt he was trying to enter the town in order to get more complete information about us and our plans than they have yet obtained. He would have remained hidden by day in some house, and he would have slipped out again at night when he had learned all that he wanted. You did a good job, Bedford, when you stopped him."

"You did more than stop him," said another, who

had brought a small lantern. "You nicked him before he got away. See, here's a drop of blood, and here's another, and there's another."

They followed the trail of the drops, but it did not lead far. Evidently the effusion of blood had not been great. Then one of the men, glancing at Phil rather curiously, said:

"He seems to have touched you up, Bedford. Do you know that a little stream of blood is running down your left sleeve?"

Phil was not conscious until then that something moist and warm was dripping upon his hand. In the excitement of the moment he had forgotten all about the slash of the knife, but, now that he remembered it, he felt a sudden weakness. But he hid it from the others, and it passed in a minute or so.

The chief of the patrol ordered him to go back and report to an officer, and this officer happened to be Middleton, who was sitting with Edgeworth in one of the open camps before a small fire. Phil's arm meanwhile had been bound up, although he found that the cut was not deep, and would not incapacitate him. Phil saluted in the new military style that he was acquiring, and of which he was very proud, and said, in reply to Middleton's look of inquiry:

"I have the honor to report, sir, that a spy, a Mexican officer, tried to pass our lines at the point where I was stationed. He was disguised as a peon, coming to sell provisions in our camp. When I stopped him he slashed at me with his knife, although the wound he inflicted was but slight, and I, in return, fired at him as he ran. I hit him, as drops of blood on the ground showed, although I think his wound, like mine, was slight."

Captain Middleton smiled.

"Come, Phil," he said, "you've done a good deed, so hop down off your high horse, and tell it in your old, easy way. Remember that we are still comrades of the plains."

THE PASS OF ANGOSTURA

Phil smiled, too. The official manner was rather hard and stiff, and it was easier to do as Middleton suggested.

"Captain," he said, "I recognized the man, and it was one that we've met more than once. It was de Armijo."

"Ah, de Armijo!" exclaimed the Captain. "He was trying to spy upon us. He is high in the Mexican councils, and his coming here means much. It is lucky, Phil, that you were the one to stop him, and that you recognized him. But he did not love you much before, and he will not love you any more, since you have spilled some of his blood with a bullet."

"I know it," replied Phil confidently, "but I feel able to take care of myself as far as de Armijo is concerned."

"You go to your tent and sleep," said Middleton, "and I'll put another man in your place. You must not get too much stiffness and soreness in that arm of yours. You will be likely to need it soon—also, every other arm that you have."

Phil, not loth, returned to his tent, which he shared with Breakstone and two or three others. Bill awoke, and, after listening to a narrative of the occurrence, dressed and rebound the arm carefully.

"I agree with the Captain that things are coming to a head," he said. "When you see a storm bird like de Armijo around, the storm itself can't be far behind. I'm glad he didn't get a good whack at you, Phil, but, as it is, you're so young and so healthy, and your blood is so pure that it won't give you any trouble. I'll dress it again to-morrow, and in a few days it will be well."

Bill Breakstone's prediction was a good one. In three or four days Phil's wound was entirely healed, and two or three days later he could use his arm as well as ever. The boy, meanwhile, was getting better acquainted with the troops, and, like his comrades, was becoming thoroughly a member of the little army. It was reduced now, by the steady drains to strengthen Scott, to 4,610 men, of whom less than five hundred were regular troops. But the volunteers, nearly all from the west and south, little trained though they might be, were young, hardy, used to life in the open air, and full of zeal. They had all the fire and courage of youth, and they did not fear any number of Mexicans.

But the New Year had come, January in its turn had passed, and the news drifting in from a thousand sources, like dust from the desert, grew more alarming. The army organized by Santa Anna at San Luis Potosi was the largest that had ever been gathered in Mexico, with powerful artillery and a numerous cavalry. Santa Anna himself was at his best, drilling, planning, and filling his officers with his own enthusiasm. In Saltillo itself the people grew bolder. They openly said that it was time for the Americans to run if they would save themselves from the invincible Mexican commander and president. It seemed to many of the Americans even that it would be wise to retreat all the way to the Rio Grande, but the old general, his heart full of bitterness, gave no such order. He had begun the campaign in victorious fashion, and then he had been ordered to stop. He had asked to be allowed to serve as second to Scott in the great campaign that would go forward from Vera Cruz, and that had been refused. Then he had asked that more of his troops, especially the regulars, be left to him, and that, too, had been refused. He was expected to yield the ground that he had gained, and retreat in the face of an overwhelming enemy.

Phil saw General Taylor many times in those days. Any one could see him as he passed about the city and camp, a gray, silent man, with little military form, a product of the West and the frontier, to which Phil himself belonged. It was for that reason, perhaps, that Phil could enter so thoroughly into the feelings of the general, a simple, straightforward soldier who believed himself the victim of politics, a man who felt within him not the

THE PASS OF ANGOSTUR

facility for easy and graceful speech and manners, but the rugged power to do great things. He was very gentle and kind to his men in these days. The soldier who had spent a lifetime on the frontier, fighting Indians and dealing with the roughest of his kind, was now more like the head of a great family, a band knitted all the more closely together because they were in a foreign land confronted by a great danger.

Phil was picking up Spanish fast, and his youth, perhaps, caused the people about the city to make more hints, or maybe threats, to him than they would have made to an older man. Santa Anna had with him the whole might of Mexico. He would be before Saltillo in three days, in two days, to-morrow perhaps. The very air seemed to the boy to be charged with gunpowder, and he had his moments of despondency. But he had been through too much danger already to despair, and he allowed no one to think that at any time he was apprehensive.

Bill Breakstone was, for the present, the best man in the army. No other made acquaintances so fast, no other had such a wonderful flow of cheering words, and he was —or had been—an actor. To many of these youths who had never seen a play he must certainly have been the greatest actor in the world. Nor was he like a prima donna, to be coaxed, and then to refuse four times out of five. He recited nearly every evening in front of his tent, and he did more than any other man to keep the army in good heart. General Taylor and his second, General Wool, said nothing, but the younger officers commented openly and favorably. Thus the last days of January went by, and they were deep into February. The menacing reports still came out of the south, and now it was known definitely that Washington expected Taylor to fall back. Gloom overspread the young volunteers. They had not fought their way so far merely to go back, but orders were orders, and they must be obeyed.

THE QUEST OF THE FOUR

Early in the evening Bill Breakstone was reciting again in front of his tent, and at least two hundred stood about listening. This time he was reciting with great fire and vigor his favorite: "Once more unto the breach, dear friends," and, when he had said it once, there was a vigorous call for it again. Obligingly he began the repetition, but when he was midway in it Middleton strode into the circle and held up his hand. His attitude was so tense, and his air and manner showed so much suppressed excitement that every one turned at once from Breakstone to him. Breakstone himself stopped so short that his mouth was left wide open, and he, too, gazed at Middleton.

"My lads," said Middleton, "an order, an important order has just been issued by the commander-in-chief. You are to prepare at once for breaking camp, and you are to march at daylight in the morning."

Some one uttered a groan, and a bold voice spoke up:

"Do we retreat all the way to the Rio Grande, or do we hide somewhere on the way?"

The speaker could not be seen from the place where Middleton stood, nor would the comrades around him have betrayed him. But Middleton looked in the direction of the voice, and his figure seemed to swell. Phil, who was standing near, thought he saw his eyes flicker with light.

"My lads," said Middleton, and his voice was full and thrilling, "we do not retreat all the way to the Rio Grande, nor do we hide on the way. We do not retreat at all. We march forward, southward, through the mountains to meet the enemy."

A cheer, sudden, tremendous, and straight from the heart, burst forth, and it was joined with other cheers that came from other points in the camp.

"Now make it three times three for old Rough and Ready!" cried Phil in his enthusiasm, and they did it with zeal and powerful vocal organs. Middleton smiled and walked on. Immediately everything was haste and

THE PASS OF ANGOSTURA

excitement. The men began to pack. Arms and ammunition were made ready for the march. Youth looked forward only to victory, thinking little of the risks and dangers. Breakstone smiled to himself and said under his breath the words:

> "We would not seek a battle as we are,
> Nor as we are, we say we will not shun it.
> So tell your master.

"Old Rough and Ready perhaps does not seek a battle, but he is willing to go forward and meet it. Ah! these brave boys! these brave boys!"

Then he turned to Phil and Arenberg, who were among his tent-mates.

"We three must stick together through everything," he said. "We've lost Middleton for the time, because he's got to return to his duties as an officer."

"What you say iss good," said Arenberg.

"It's a bargain," said Phil.

They looked to the horses—they were in the cavalry—and at midnight went to sleep. But they were up before dawn, still full of energy and enthusiasm. As the sun cast its first rays on the cold peaks of the Sierra Madre, they mounted, fully armed and equipped, and marched out of Saltillo, although Taylor left a strong guard in the city, wishing to preserve it as a base.

Phil rode knee to knee with Arenberg and Breakstone, and the thrill that he had felt the night before, when Middleton told the news, he felt again this morning. Horse, foot, and artillery, they were only between four and five thousand men, but the whole seemed a great army to the boy. He had never seen so many men under arms before. Breakstone saw his eye kindling.

"They are stained by travel and tanned by weather, but it's a fine crowd, just as you think it is, Sir Philip of Saltillo. Don't you agree with me, Hans, Duke of the Sierra Madre?"

"It can fight," said Arenberg briefly.

"And that's what it has come out to do."

Phil saw the people of Saltillo watching them as the army left the suburbs and moved on toward the mountains. But the spectators seemed to be silent. Even the children had little to say. Phil wondered what they thought in their hearts. He did not doubt that most of them were sure that this army, or what was left of it, would come back prisoners of Santa Anna. He was glad when they left them behind, and henceforth he looked toward the mountains, which upreared cold peaks in the chilly sunshine of winter. But the air was dazzlingly clear and crisp. Pure and fresh, it filled all on that high plateau with life, and Phil's mood was one that expected only the best.

"We are not going to ride straight over those mountains, are we?" he said to Bill Breakstone.

"No," replied Bill, "we feel pretty nearly good enough for anything, but we will not try any such high jumping as that. There's a pass. You can't see it from here, because it's a sort of knife-cut going down deep into the mountains, and they call it the Pass of Angostura. We'll be there soon."

There was much noise as the army began its march, friend calling to friend, the exchange of joke and comment, wagon drivers and cannon drivers shouting to their horses, and the clanking of arms. But they soon settled down into a steady sound, all noises fusing into one made by an army that continued to march but that had ceased to talk.

Phil studied the mountains as they came nearer. They were dark and somber. Their outlines were jagged, and they had but little forest or verdure. The peaks seemed to him volcanic, presenting a multitude of sharp edges.

As the sun rose higher, the day grew somewhat warmer, but it was still full of chill. The horses blew smoke from their nostrils. Scouts coming out of the passes met them and repeated that Santa Anna was now advancing from San Luis Potosi. Nor had rumor exaggerated his forces. He outnumbered the American army at least five to one, and his front was covered by a great body of cavalry under General Minon, one of the best Mexican leaders.

This news quickly traveled through the columns, and Phil and his friends were among the first to hear it. Breakstone gazed anxiously at the peaks.

"They don't know just how far Santa Anna has come," he said, "but it's mighty important for us going to the south to get through that pass before he, coming to the north, can get through it."

"We'll make it," said Phil, with the sanguine faith of youth. "I don't believe that Santa Anna is yet near enough to dispute the pass with us."

"Likely you are right, Sir Philip of the Brave Heart and the Cheerful Countenance," replied Bill Breakstone. "But we shall soon see for certain. In another hour we will enter the defiles."

Phil said nothing, but rode on with his comrades. The city had now dropped behind them and was far out of sight. On their flanks rode scouts who would be skirmishers if need be. They marched on a level and good road, and about six miles from Saltillo they passed a hacienda and tiny village.

"What village is that?" asked Phil of some one.

"Buena Vista," was the reply.

Phil heard it almost without noticing, although it was a reply to his own question. Yet it was a name that he was destined soon to recall and never to forget. How often for years and years afterward that name came back to him at night, syllable by syllable and letter by letter! Now he rode on, taking no thought of it, and the little village and hacienda lay behind him, sleeping peacefully in the sun. His attention was for the mountains, because they were now entering the defile, the pass of Angostura, which cuts through the spur thrown out by the Sierra Madre. This is lofty, and the way narrowed fast. Nor did the sunlight fall so plentifully there, and the winds grew colder as they whistled through the pass. After the brilliant opalescent air of the plain, they seemed to be riding in a sort of twilight, and Phil felt his spirits droop. Deeper and deeper they went into the cut. Above him loomed the mountains, dark and menacing. Shrub and dwarfed plants clung here and there in the crannies, but the range was bare, and often it was distorted into strange shapes, sometimes like that of the human countenance. The sky showed in a ribbon above, but it had turned gray, and was somber and depressing. Behind came the long line of the army, the wheels of the artillery clanking over the stones.

Once or twice Phil thought he saw figures in sombreros and serapes far up the mountainside, watching them. Mexicans, no doubt, ready to report to Santa Anna the advance of the American army. He expected that some stray shots might be fired down into the pass by these spies or guerillas, but evidently they had other business than merely to annoy, and no bullets came.

Phil's horse stumbled, and the boy saved him from a fall with a quick pull. Arenberg's horse stumbled, also, and Phil noticed that his own was now walking gingerly over a path of solid but dark stone, corrugated and broken into sharp edges. Well might a horse, even one steel-shod, be careful here! Phil knew it was volcanic rock, lava that had flowed down ages ago from the crests of the peaks about them, once volcanoes but extinct long since.

His horse stumbled again, but recovered himself quickly. It certainly was dangerous rock, sometimes sharp almost like a knifeblade, and the shoes of the infantry would be cut badly. Cut badly! A sudden thought sprang up in his brain and refused to be dislodged. It was one of those lightning ideas, based on little things, that carry conviction with them through their very force and swiftness. His free hand went up to the breast of his coat and clutched the spot beneath which his brother's letter lay. He had read a hundred times the words of the captive, telling how his feet had been cut by the sharp stone. Lava might be found at many places in Mexico, but it was along these trails in Northern Mexico that the fighting bands of Mexicans and Texans passed. He reasoned with himself for a few moments, saying that he was foolish, and hoping that he was not, but the idea remained in his head, and he knew that it was fixed there. He leaned over and said, in a husky whisper to Bill Breakstone:

"Bill, have you noticed it! The rock! The lava! How it cuts! How it would quickly slice the sole from the shoe of a captive who had marched far! Bill! Bill, I say, have you noticed it?"

Bill Breakstone looked in astonishment at his young comrade, but he was a man of uncommonly quick perceptions, and in a moment he comprehended.

"I understand," he said. "Your brother's letter and the passage in which he tells of his shoes being cut by the sharp stone while he was led along blindfolded. He may have passed along this very road, Phil. It may be. It may be. I won't say you are wrong."

"What if we are near him now!" continued Phil. "I've often heard you quote those lines, Bill, saying there are more things in heaven and earth than we dream of in our philosophy. I told you before that if the letter could reach me so far away in Kentucky it could also bring me to the place where it was written! I believed it then, Bill, and I believe it now. What if John is here in these mountains, within forty or fifty miles of us, or maybe twenty!"

"Steady, boy, steady!" said Bill Breakstone soothingly. "Your guess may be right. God knows I'm not the one to deny it, but we've got to fight a battle first.

At least, I think so, and for the present we must put our minds on it."

Phil was silent, but his idea possessed him. Often we dwell upon things so long and we seek so hard to have them happen in a certain way that the slightest indication becomes proof. He could not think now of Taylor or Santa Anna, or of a coming battle, but only of his brother between four narrow stone walls, sitting at a narrow window that looked out upon a bleak mountainside. His horse no longer felt the guiding hand upon the bridle rein, but guided himself. Breakstone noticed that the boy's mind was far away, and, his heart full of sympathy, he said nothing for a long time.

They passed after awhile into a narrow valley, down the center of which ran a dry arroyo, fully twenty feet deep, with perpendicular banks. The rest of the valley was crisscrossed with countless gullies worn by winter storms and floods, and the army was compelled to march in a slender file in the bed of the arroyo. Here many of the cavalrymen dismounted and led their horses. The cannon wheels clanked louder than ever.

"I'll be glad when we're through this," said Bill Breakstone. "Seems to me the place was built for a trap, and it's mighty lucky for us that there's nobody here to spring it. Look out, Phil, you'd better watch your horse now! Some of these turnings are pretty rough, and you don't want a thousand pounds or so of horseflesh tumbling down upon you."

Phil came back from his visions and devoted himself to the task before them, one that required the full attention of every man. An entire battery became stuck in a gully that intersected the arroyo. He and other cavalrymen hitched their horses to the guns and helped pull them out. The whole army was now stumbling and struggling over the fearful ground. Every effort was made to save artillery and horses alike from injury. But as they approached its lower end the Pass of Angostura

THE PASS OF ANGOSTURA

became still more difficult. The gullies increased in number, and many of the deep intersecting ravines ran far back into the mountains. A swarm of sure-footed skirmishers on either flank could have done great damage here to the Americans, but the peaks and the lava slopes on either side presented only silence and desolation.

It was a long journey, difficult in the extreme, and attended by thousands of falls, cuts, and bruises, but the army came through the Pass of Angostura at last, marching out upon a series of promontories or ridges, each about a mile long and perhaps a third of a mile across. From these the exhausted troops looked back at the frowning mountains and the deep defile through which they had come.

"That was certainly a job," said Bill Breakstone.

"Yes," said Middleton, who stood near, "but what a place for a defense, the plateau and these promontories running out from it, and all the ravine and gullies behind!"

It is a matter of chronicle that at least fifty officers were saying the same words at almost the same time, and even Phil, without military training, could see the truth of it. Taylor pushed on to Agua Neva, arriving there in the evening. But the next morning the reports of Santa Anna's advance in overwhelming force became so numerous that he fell back with the main army to the mouth of the Pass of Angostura, leaving Marshall with his brave Kentuckians as a rear guard at Agua Neva, and with instructions to make the utmost resistance if they were attacked.

The next night came on somber and cold. It was the evening of February 21, 1847, and the next day would be the birthday of the great Washington, a fact not forgotten by these young volunteers so far from the states in which they were born. This was a land totally unlike their own. Cold black peaks showed in the growing twilight. Around them were the gullies, the ravines, and the arroyos, with the sheets of the ancient black lava. It was like a region that belonged in the far beginning of time.

A great force under Wool, the second in command, was throwing up intrenchments of earth and rock and fortifying the heads of the ravines. Lieutenant Washington, with five heavy guns, was planted in the roadway, or rather trail, in front of all. Other guns were placed on the plateau and promontories, and behind guns and parapets the army went into camp for the night.

"This doesn't look much like Kentucky and the Bluegrass, does it, Phil?" said Grayson, as they drank their coffee.

Phil glanced at the mountains, the crests of which were now hidden in the darkness, and listened to the cold wind moaning through the narrow pass by which they had come. Then he replied:

"It doesn't, by a long sight, and I can tell you that I'm mighty glad I've lots of company here. If I were alone, I'd feel that the ghosts of the old Aztecs and Toltecs were surrounding me in the darkness. It's good to see the fires."

Many fires had been lighted, mostly in the ravines, where they were sheltered from the wind, but Phil had no doubt that the scouts of Santa Anna saw points of light at the mouth of the pass. After his supper he stood upon one of the promontories and strove to pierce the darkness to the south. But he could see nothing. The night hung an opaque veil over the lower country.

CHAPTER XIII

A WIND OF THE DESERT

ALTHOUGH many of the soldiers, the more hardened, had lain down to sleep, Phil did not feel that he could close his eyes. Too many deep emotions stirred his soul. He felt that he was at the verge of a great event, one in which he was to take a part to the full extent of his strength and courage, and there, too, was the sign of the lava, always coming back, always persisting. He might reason with himself and call himself foolish, but he could not dispossess his mind of the idea that it was an omen to show him that he was upon the trail by which that letter had come so vast a distance to him in the little town of Paris.

Every nerve in the boy was astir. He walked back and forth on one of the promontories, looking at the mountains which now in the darkness had become black and full of threats, and trying in vain to soothe and quiet himself so he could lie down like the others and take the rest and forgetfulness that all men need before going into battle. While he was there, Middleton called to him:

"Come, Phil," he said, reverting to his old manner of comradeship, "you ride with us to-night."

"Ride to-night!" replied Phil. "Where?"

"To the south, to meet Santa Anna. I am ordered to take thirty men and keep going until I come into touch with the enemy. I am to have thirty men of my choice, and you, Breakstone, and Arenberg were the first three that I named. You don't have to go unless you wish."

"But I wish!" exclaimed Phil earnestly. "Don't think I'm unwilling, Captain! Don't think it!"

Middleton laughed.

"I don't," he said. "I knew that you would be keen for it. Saddle your horse and look to your arms. We ride in five minutes."

Phil was ready in three, and the thirty troopers rode silently down one of the ravines and into the lower country. Phil looked back and saw the fires of the camp, mere red, yellow, and pink dots of flame. The mountains themselves were fused into a solid mass of black. The troop, arrow headed in shape, with Middleton at the point of the shaft, and Phil, Breakstone, and Arenberg close behind him, rode in silence save for the beat of their horses' hoofs. The wind here did not moan like that in the pass, but it seemed to Phil to be colder, and it had an edge of fine particles that stung his cheeks and eyes.

The night was bright enough to allow of fairly swift riding, and the ground was no longer cut and gullied as at the mouth of the pass. Hence the troopers were not compelled to devote their whole attention to their horses and they could watch the country for sign of an enemy. But they did not yet see any such sign. Phil knew that they were on the road, leading southward to Santa Anna, and he felt sure that if they kept upon it they must soon come upon the Mexican army. Yet the silence and desolation were complete here. The pass had been weird and somber to the full, but there they had thousands of comrades, and the fires in the ravines had been cheering. Now the unlit darkness was all about them, and it still had that surcharged quality that it had borne for Phil when in the pass. Nor did the fine dust cease to sting his face.

"What is it, Bill?" he asked. "Where does it come from, this dust?"

"It's a wind of the desert that stings us, Phil," re-

A WIND OF THE DESERT

plied Breakstone. "It comes vast distances, and I think, too, that it brings some of the fine dust ground off the surface of the lava. Its effect is curious. It's like burnt gunpowder in the nostrils. It seems to heat the inside, too."

"It makes me feel that way," said Phil, "and it seems to be always urging us on."

"An irritant, as it were," said Breakstone, "but I don't think we need it. The event itself is enough to keep us all on edge. Feel cold, Phil?"

"No, I've got a pair of buckskin gauntlets. Fine thing for riding on nights like this."

"So have I. But the night is cold, though. Now we're always thinking of warm weather in Mexico, but we never find a country what we expect it to be. Ah, we're leaving the road. The Captain must think there is something not far ahead."

They turned at a sharp angle from the road, and entered a thin forest. Phil looked back toward the mouth of the pass from which they had come. Everything there was behind an impenetrable black veil. The last point of fire had died, and the mountains themselves were hidden. But he took only a single backward look. The wind of the desert was still stinging his face, and it seemed to arouse him to uncommon fire and energy. His whole attention was concentrated upon their task, and he was eager to distinguish himself in some way. But he neither heard nor saw anything unusual.

They proceeded slowly through the forest, seeking to prevent all but the least possible noise, and came presently to a field in which Indian corn seemed to have grown. But it was bare now, save for the dead stalks that lay upon the ground, and here the troop spread out, riding almost in a single line.

It was Phil, keen of eye and watchful, who first saw a dim red tint under the far southern horizon, and he at once called Middleton's attention. The Captain halted them instantly, and his gaze followed the line of Phil's pointing finger.

"It is Santa Anna's army," he said, "and you, Phil, have the honor of locating it first. The dim band of light which you pointed out is made by their camp fires, which are many. We need not try to conceal that fact from ourselves."

"We take a nearer view, do we not, Captain?" asked Bill Breakstone.

"Of course," replied Middleton, "but be cautious, all of you. It is important to see, but it is equally important to get back to General Taylor with the tale our eyes may tell."

They rode forward again in a long and silent line. Phil's heart began to throb. The desert wind was still stinging his face with the fine impalpable dust that seemed to excite every nerve. As they advanced, the red tint on the southern horizon broadened and deepened. It was apparent that it stretched far to east and west.

"It iss a great army, and it means much harm," said Arenberg softly, more to himself than to anybody else.

Nearer and nearer rode the bold horsemen, stopping often to watch for the Mexican lancers who would surely be in advance of the army, beating up the country, despite the darkness, but they did not yet see any. They rode on so far that they heard the occasional sound of a trumpet in the Mexican camp, and the fires no longer presented a solid line.

"Captain," asked Bill Breakstone, "what do you think the sound of those trumpets means at an hour like this?"

"I'm not sure, Bill," replied Middleton, "but it must signify some movement. The Mexicans, like many other people, love color and parade and sound, but they would scarcely be indulging in such things at midnight just for their own sakes. It is some plan. Santa Anna is a man of great energy and initiative. But we must discover what it is. That is what we came for."

A WIND OF THE DESERT

The advance was renewed, although they went slowly, guarding as well as they could against the least possible sound from their horses. They were now so near that they could see figures passing before the fires, and the dark outline of tents. They also heard the hum of many voices, the tread of hoofs by hundreds, and the jingling of many spurs and bridle bits. Phil watched almost breathless, and the desert wind still blew on his face, stirring him with its fine, impalpable powder, and adding new fire to the fire that already burned in his veins. And Phil saw that Middleton shared in this excited interest. The officer's gloved hand on his bridle rein quivered with eagerness.

"Yet a little nearer, my lads," he whispered. "We must risk everything to find out what Santa Anna is intending at so late an hour."

Screened by a narrow thicket of strange, cactuslike plants, they rode so close that they could see between the leaves and thorns directly into the camp. Here they sat on motionless horses, but Phil heard a deep "Ah!" pass between Middleton's closed teeth. The boy himself had experience and judgment enough to know now what was going forward. All this jingling of bits and spurs meant the gathering of the Mexican cavalry. The Mexican camp fires burned along a front that seemed interminable, and also scores of torches were held aloft to guide in the work that was now being done.

Phil saw the Mexican horsemen wheel out by hundreds, until there was a great compact body of perhaps two thousand men, gaudily dressed, well mounted, and riding splendidly. Many carried rifles or muskets, but there were at least a thousand lancers, the blades of their long weapons gleaming in the firelight. Officers in gorgeous uniforms were at their head. Presently the trumpet blew again, and the great force of cavalry under General Minon began to move.

"An advance at midnight," breathed Middleton, but

THE QUEST OF THE FOUR

Phil heard him. "And there go infantry behind them. It is an attack in force. I have it! I have it! They are going toward Agua Neva. Santa Anna thinks that our whole army is there, and probably he believes he can get in our rear and cut us off. Then he'll compress us between his vast numbers as if we were in the jaws of a vise."

Then he added, in a slightly louder tone:

"Come, my lads, we ride to Agua Neva, but we must be as careful as ever. We know now what our task is, and we will do it."

They turned and rode away. Fortune was with them. No horse neighed. Perhaps the sound of their hoofs might have been heard now, had it not been for the great Mexican column marching toward Agua Neva, where the rear guard under Marshall was hurrying the stores, that had been left there, northward to Taylor. Middleton swung his little troop to one side, until they were well beyond the hearing of Minon's cavalry.

"There can no longer be any doubt that they are heading for Agua Neva," he said, "and we must beat them there, no matter what happens. Ride, boys, ride!"

They broke into a gallop, sweeping in a long line across some open fields, riding straight for a few points of light behind which they knew was Agua Neva. They were now well ahead of the great column, and Middleton took the chance of meeting any stray band of Mexican scouts and skirmishers. They did meet such a band, but it was small, and, when the Mexican hail was answered with a shout in a foreign tongue, it quickly scattered and gave the Americans free passage. A few shots were fired, but nobody in Middleton's troop was touched, and none in the other. Without breaking line the Americans rode on. The lights grew clearer and increased in number. In a few moments they clattered down on Agua Neva, and ready sentinels, rifle in hand, halted them.

"Friends!" cried Middleton. "I am Captain Middleton, with scouts from General Taylor. I must see your commander at once!"

But Marshall was there as he spoke, and Middleton exclaimed in short words, surcharged with emphasis and earnestness:

"Santa Anna is coming down upon you! We have seen his cavalry marching, and the infantry are behind them! They will soon be here! They must think that our whole army is in Agua Neva, and evidently they intend to surround it."

"All right," said Marshall calmly. "Most of the wagons are already on the way to the pass. We cover their retreat, and the General told us to hold on here as long as we could. We mean to do it. Are you with us, Captain?"

"Certainly," replied Captain Middleton briefly. "You can depend on us to the last."

"Minon's cavalry must be coming now," said Marshall. "It seems to me that I hear the tread of many horsemen."

"It is they," said Middleton. Marshall's men and his then fell back toward the little town. They were only a few hundred in number, but they had no idea of retreating without a fight. They were posted behind some stone walls, hedges, and a few scattered houses. The last of the wagons loaded with stores were rumbling away northward toward the Pass of Angostura.

Phil sat on his horse behind a stone wall, and all was silence along the line. The wind still blew, and stung his face with the dust of the desert. His heart throbbed and throbbed. He saw Middleton open his watch, hold it close to his face in order that he might see the hands in the moonlight, and then shut it with a little snap.

"Midnight exactly," he said, "and here they come!"

The heavy tread of many men was now in their ears, and the lances gleamed in the moonlight, as the great Mexican force swung into the open space about the little town. They came on swiftly and full of ardor, but a sheet of fire blazed in their faces. The long rifles of the Americans were well aimed, despite the night—they could scarcely miss such a mass—and horses and riders went down together.

While they were still in confusion, Marshall's little force loaded and fired again. A terrible uproar ensued. Men groaned or shouted, horses neighed with fright or screamed with pain. Many of them ran riderless between the combatants. Phil heard the Mexican officers shouting orders and many strange curses. Smoke arose and permeated the night air already charged with the dust of the desert. The Mexicans fired almost at random in the darkness, but they were many, and the bullets flying in showers were bound to strike somebody. Two or three Americans dropped slain from their horses, or, on foot, died where they were struck, behind the walls. The Mexicans in a vast half circle still advanced. Marshall and Middleton conferred briefly.

"How many men have you?" asked Marshall.

"Thirty."

"I have about fifty more cavalrymen. Take them and charge with all your might. They may think in the darkness that you have a thousand."

"Come!" said Middleton to his men, and he and the eighty rode out into the open. They paused there only an instant, because the great half circle of the Mexicans was still advancing. Phil, in the moonlight, saw the enemy very distinctly, the lances and escopetas, the tall conical hats with wide brims, and the dark faces under them. Then, at the command of Middleton, they fired their rifles and galloped straight at the foe.

Phil could never give any details of that wild moment. He was conscious of a sudden surge of the blood, the thudding of hoofs, the blades of lances almost in his face, fierce, dark eyes glaring into his own, and then they struck. The impact was accompanied by the flashing of sabers, the falling of men and horses, shouts and groans, while the smoke from the firing to the right and left of them drifted in their faces.

Phil felt a shock as his horse struck that of a Mexican lancer. The lance-blade flashed past his face, and it felt cold on his cheek as it passed, but it did not touch him. The Mexican's horse went down before the impact of his, and he saw that the whole troop, although a few saddles were emptied, had crashed through the Mexican line. They had cut it apart like a knife through cheese. While the Mexicans were yet reeling from the shock, Middleton, a born cavalry leader, wheeled his men about, and they charged back through the Mexican line at another point. The second passage was easier than the first, because Minon's men had been thrown into disorder, yet it was not made without wounds. Phil was slightly grazed in the side by a bullet, and a lance had torn his coat on his shoulder. If the cloth had not given way he would have been thrown from the saddle. As it was, he nearly dropped his rifle, but he managed to retain both seat and weapon.

"All right!" shouted a voice in his ear. It was that of Breakstone, who was watching over him like a father.

"All right," returned Phil confidently, and then they were back with Marshall's men, all but a dozen, who would ride no more.

"Good work," said Marshall to Middleton. "That startled them. They will ride back a little, and our riflemen, too, are doing almost as good work in the moonlight as they could in the sunlight."

The blood was pounding so heavily in Phil's ears after the double charge that he did not realize until then that the heavy firing had never ceased. The little American force reloaded and pulled the trigger so quickly that the volume of their firing gave the effect of numbers three or four times that of the real. The darkness, too, helped the illusion, and the Southerners and Westerners replied to the shouts of the Mexicans with resounding cheers of their own. An officer galloped up, and Phil heard him shout to Marshall above the crash of the firing:

"The last of the wagons is beyond the range of fire!"

"Good," said Marshall. "Now we, too, must fall back. The moment they discover how few we are they can wrap us in a coil that we cannot break. But we'll fight them while they follow us."

The little force was drawn in skillfully, and the horsemen on either flank began to retire from Agua Neva. The Mexicans, urged by Minon, Torrejon, Ampudia, and Santa Anna himself, pushed hard against the retiring force, seeking either to capture or destroy it. More than once they threatened to enfold it with their long columns, but here the horsemen, spreading out, held them off, and the long range rifles of the Americans were weapons that the Mexicans dreaded. As on many another battlefield, the Westerners and Southerners, trained from their boyhood to marksmanship, fired with terrible accuracy. The moonlight, now that their eyes had grown used to it, was enough for them. Their firing, as the slow retreat northward toward the Pass of Angostura went on, never ceased, and their path was marked by a long trail of their fallen foes. Santa Anna and his generals sought in vain to flank them, but the darkness was against the greater force. It was not easy to combine and make use of numbers when only moonlight served. Regiments were likely to fire into one another, but the small compact body of the Americans kept easily in touch, and they retreated practically in one great hollow square blazing with fire on every side. "Hold on as long as you can," Taylor had said to Marshall, but Marshall, in the face of twenty to one, held on longer than any one had dreamed.

Santa Anna had expected to get his great cavalry force in the rear of Taylor at Agua Neva, but at midnight, finding Taylor not there and only a small detachment left, he had hoped to capture or destroy that in a few minutes.

A WIND OF THE DESERT

Instead, half his army was fighting a most desperate rear guard action with a few hundred men, and every second Marshall saved was precious to the commander back there at the Pass of Angostura.

Phil was grazed by another bullet, and his horse was stung once. Arenberg was slightly wounded, but Breakstone was untouched, and the three still kept close together. The boy could not take note of the passage of time. It seemed to him that they had been fighting for hours as they gave way slowly before the huge mass of the Mexican army. Great clouds of smoke from the firing had turned the moonlight to a darker quality. Now and then it drifted in such quantities that the moon was wholly obscured, and then it was to the advantage of the Americans, who could fire from their hollow square in every direction, and be sure that they hit no friend.

They had now left the town far behind and were well on the way to the Pass. Phil noticed that the fire of the Mexicans was slackening. Evidently Santa Anna had begun to believe that it would not pay to follow up any longer a rear guard that stung so hard and so often. This certainly was the belief of Bill Breakstone.

"The pursuit is dying," he said, "not because they don't want us, but because our price is too high.

> It is not right
> To fight at night
> Unless you know
> Right well your foe.
> The darkness cumbers
> Him with numbers;
> The few steal away,
> And are gone at day.

"My verse is a little ragged this time, Phil, but it is made in the heat of action, and it at least tells a true tale. See how their fire is sinking! The flashes stop to the right, they stop to the left, and they will soon stop in the center. It's a great night, Phil, for Marshall and his men. They were ordered to do big things, and they've filled the order twice over. And we came into it, too, Phil, don't forget that! There, they've stopped entirely, as I told you they would!"

The firing along Santa Anna's front ceased abruptly, and as the retreat continued slowly the columns of the Mexican army were lost in the darkness. No lance heads glittered, and the bugles no longer called the men to action. Bill Breakstone had spoken truly. Santa Anna found the rear guard too tough for him to handle in the darkness, and stopped for the rest of the night. When assured of this, Marshall ordered his little force to halt, while they took stock of the wounded and dressed their hurts as best they could at such a hurried moment. Then they resumed their march for the pass, with the wagons that they had defended so well lumbering on ahead.

After the exertion of so much physical or mental energy the men rode or walked in silence. Phil was surprised to find that his hands and face were wet with perspiration, and he knew then that his face must be black with burnt gunpowder. But he felt cold presently, as the chill night wind penetrated a body relaxed after so great an effort. Then he took the blanket roll from his saddle and wrapped it around him. Breakstone and Arenberg had already done the same. Looking back, Phil saw a few lights twinkling where the Mexicans had lighted their new camp fires, but no sound came from that point. Yet, as of old, the desert wind blew, and the fine dust borne on its edge stung his face, and brought to his nostrils an odor like that of battle. Under its influence he was still ready for combat. He gloried in the achievement of this little division in which he had a part, and it gave him strength and courage for the greater struggle, by far, that was coming. Breakstone shared in his pleasure, and talked lightly in his usual fashion, but Arenberg was sober and very thoughtful.

"Well, we burnt old Santa Anna's face for him, if we

did do it in the dark," said Bill, "and we can do it in daylight, too."

"But did you see his numbers?" said Arenberg. "Remember how vast was his camp, and with what a great force he attacked us at Agua Neva. Ach, I fear me for the boys who are so far from their home, the lads of Kentucky and Illinois and the others!"

"Don't be downhearted, Hans, old boy," said Breakstone with genuine feeling. "I know you have things on your mind—though I don't ask you what they are—that keep you from being cheerful, but don't forget that we've the habit of victory. Our boys are Bonaparte's soldiers in the campaign of Italy, they don't mean to be beaten, and they don't get beaten. And you can put that in your pipe, too, and smoke it, Sir Philip of the Horse Battle and the Night Retreat. Look, we're approaching the Pass. See the lights come out one by one. Don't the lights of a friend look good?"

Phil agreed with him. It was a satisfying thing to come safely out of a battle in which they had done what they had wanted to do, and return to their own army. It was now nearly morning, but the troops still marched, while the last wagons rumbled on ahead. Scouts came forward to hail them and to greet them warmly when they found that they were friends. There was exultation, too, when they heard the news of the fine fight that the little division had given to Santa Anna. Lieutenant Washington, who was in charge of the division that commanded the road, met Middleton and Marshall a hundred yards from the mouths of his guns, and Phil heard them talking. General Taylor had not yet returned from Saltillo, where he had gone to strengthen and fortify the division at that place, as he greatly feared a flank movement of Santa Anna around the mountain to seize the town and cut him off.

Wool, meanwhile, was in command, and he listened to the reports of Marshall and Middleton, commending them highly for the splendid resistance that they had offered to overwhelming numbers. Phil gathered from their tone, although it was only confirmation of a fact that he knew already, that their little force was in desperate case, indeed. Never before had the omens seemed so dark for an American army. For in a desolate and gloomy country, with every inhabitant an enemy and spy upon them, with an army outnumbering them five to one approaching, brave men might well despair.

It struck Phil with sudden force that the odds could be too great after all, and that he might never finish his quest. In another hour or two he might see his last sunrise. He shook himself fiercely, told himself that he was foolish and weak, and then rode toward the pass. They tethered their horses on the edge of the plateau, and at the advice of Middleton all sought sleep.

But the boy's nerves were yet keyed too highly for relaxation. His weary body was resting, but his heart still throbbed. He saw the sentinels walking back and forth. He saw the dark shapes of cannon posted on the promontories, and above them the mountains darker and yet more somber. Several fires still burned in the ravines, and the officers sat about them talking, but most of the army slept.

As Phil lay on the earth he heard the wind moaning behind him as it swept up the pass, but it still touched his face with the fine impalpable dust that stung like hot sand, and that seemed to him to be an omen and a presage. He lay a long time staring into the blackness in the direction in which Santa Anna's army now lay, where he and his comrades had fought such a good fight at midnight. He saw nothing there with his real eye, but with his mind's eye he beheld the vast preparations, the advance of the horsemen, and the flashing of thousands of lances in the brilliant light.

When the morning sun was showing over the ridges and peaks of the Sierra Madre, and pouring its light into the nooks and crannies of the ravines, he fell asleep.

CHAPTER XIV

BUENA VISTA

PHIL did not sleep long, only an hour perhaps, and then it was Breakstone's arm on his shoulder that awakened him. He had laid down fully clothed, and he sprang at once to his feet. His nerves, too, had been so thoroughly keyed for action that every faculty responded at once to the call, and he was never more wide awake in his life. Quickly he looked about him and saw that it was a most brilliant morning. The sun was swinging upward with a splendor that he had not before seen in these gorges of the Sierra Madre. The mountains were bathed in light. The bare ridges and peaks stood out like carving, and the sunbeams danced along the black lava.

"It is Washington's Birthday, and the sun is doing him honor," said Breakstone. "But look there, Phil."

He pointed a long straight finger into the south.

"See that tiny cloud of dust," he said, "there where rock and sky meet. I'll wager everything against nothing that it was raised by the hoofs of Minon's cavalry. Santa Anna and his whole army are surely advancing. Watch it grow."

Phil looked with eager eyes, and he saw everything that Bill Breakstone had predicted come to pass. The cloud of dust, so small at first that he could scarcely see it, grew in height, and began to spread in a yellow line along the whole horizon. By and by it grew so high that the wind lifted the upper part of it and sent it whirling off in spirals and coils. Then through the dust they saw flashes, the steel of weapons giving back the rays of the sun like a mirror.

The American scouts and sentinels had been drawn in —no need for them now—and the whole army was crouched at the mouth of the pass. Almost every soldier could watch Santa Anna unroll before them the vast and glittering panorama of his army. But Taylor himself did not see this first appearance. He had not come from Saltillo, and Wool, the second in command, waited, troubled and uneasy.

Phil was still dismounted, and he stood with his friends on one of the promontories watching the most thrilling of all dramas unfold itself, the drama in which victory or defeat, life or death are the stakes. It was at best a bare and sterile country, and now, in the finish of the winter, the scanty vegetation itself was dead. The dust from the dead earth and the dust from the surface of the lava, ground off by iron-shod hoofs, rose in clouds that always increased, and that seemed to thicken as well as to rise and broaden. To Philip's mind occurred the likeness of a vast simoon, coming, though slowly, toward the American lines. But he knew that the heart of the simoon was a great army which considered victory absolutely sure.

"Looks as if Santa Anna had a million down there in the dust," said Breakstone. "Dost thou remember, Sir Philip of the Mountain, the Ravine, and the Lava, that passage in Macbeth in which Birnam Wood doth come to Dunsinane? It is in my mind now because the dust of New Leon seems coming to the Pass of Angostura."

"They are at least as well hid as Macduff's army was by the wood," said Phil. "That huge cloud seems to roll over the ground, and we can't see anything in it but the flashes of light on the weapons."

They waited awhile longer in silence. The whole American army was watching. All the preparations had been made, and soldiers and officers now had little to do but bide the time. Presently the great wall of dust split apart, then a sudden shift of wind lifted it high, and whirled it over the plain. As if revealed by the sudden lifting of a curtain, the whole magnificent army of Santa Anna stood forth, stretching along a front of two miles, and more than twenty thousand strong. A deep breath, more like a murmur, rose from the soldiers in the pass. They had known long before that they were far outnumbered. The officers had never concealed from them this fact, but here was the actual and visible presence.

"Five to one," said Bill Breakstone, softly and under his breath.

"But they haven't beaten us," said Phil.

The Mexican army now halted, the cavalry of Minon in front and on the flanks, and, seen from the pass, it was certainly an array of which Mexico could be proud. Everything stained or worn was hidden. Only the splendor and glory appeared. The watchers saw the bright uniforms, the generals riding here and there, the numerous batteries, and the brilliant flags waving. Evidently they were making a camp, as if they held the rat in their trap, and would take their time about settling his fate. The sound of bugles, and then of a band playing military airs, came up, and to those in the pass these sounds were like a taunt. Arenberg, a man of few words, uttered a low guttural sound like a growl.

"They are too sure," he said. "It iss never well to be too sure."

"That's the talk, Old Dutch," said Breakstone. "First catch your army."

They waited awhile longer, watching, and then they heard a cheer behind them in the pass. It was General Taylor, returning from Saltillo and riding hard. He emerged upon the plateau and sat there on his horse, overlooking the plain, and the great curve of Santa Anna's army. Phil was near enough to see his face, and he watched him intently.

THE QUEST OF THE FOUR

There was nothing romantic about old Zachary Taylor. He had neither youth nor distinction of appearance. He was lined and seamed by forty years of service, mostly in the backwoods, and the white hair was thick around his temples. Nor was anything splendid about his uniform. It was dusty and stained by time and use. But within that rugged old frame beat the heart of a lion. He had not retreated when he heard the rumors that Santa Anna was coming, and he would not retreat now that Santa Anna was here with five to his one. Perhaps he recognized that in his sixty-two years of life his one moment for greatness had come, and he would make the most of it for himself and his country.

Long the general sat there on his horse, looking down into the plain, and the more important officers clustered in a group a short distance behind him. The brightness of the day increased. It seemed bound to make itself worthy of the great anniversary. The colors of the sunlight shifted and changed on the ridges and peaks, and the thin, luminous air seemed to bring Santa Anna's army nearer. A breeze sprang up presently, and it felt crisp and fresh on the faces of the soldiers. It also blew out the folds of a large and beautiful American flag, which had been hoisted on one of the promontories, and as the fluttering and vivid colors glowed in the sun's rays, a cry of defiance, not loud, but suppressed and rolling, passed through the army.

"Santa Anna will not come to any picnic," said Bill Breakstone.

"He means much harm, and he will suffer much," said Arenberg.

"Our army is not frightened," said Breakstone. "I have been among the troops, and they are cheerful, even confident."

Phil saw that the officers had been watching something intently with their glasses, and now he was able to see it himself with the naked eye.

"A messenger with a white flag is coming from Santa Anna," he announced. "Now what can he want?"

"He can want only one thing," said Breakstone; "but we'll wait and let him tell it himself."

The herald, holding his white flag aloft, rode straight toward the American army. When within three hundred yards of the American line he was met by skirmishers, who brought him forward.

"Don't you see something familiar in that figure and face, Phil?" asked Bill Breakstone.

"Yes, I know him," replied Phil. "I thought I knew him when he rode over the first ridge, but there can be no doubt now. It is our old friend de Armijo."

"It is he," said Breakstone, "and it is a safe thing to say that no man was ever more stuffed with pride, vanity, and conceit than he is now. Let's press forward and see him as he passes. Maybe, too, we can hear what he and General Taylor say."

De Armijo rode up the ravine at the edge of which Phil and his comrades stood. He saw them, and his look was not one of friendship.

"Good morning, Señor de Armijo," said the irreverent Bill Breakstone, "have you come to announce the surrender of Santa Anna's army?"

The Mexican glared, but he made no answer, riding on in silence toward General Taylor. He was magnificently mounted, his uniform was heavy with gold lace, and a small gold-hilted sword hung at his side. Evidently the nephew of the governor of New Mexico was not ashamed of himself. It was also evident that the wound Phil had given him was very slight. An officer met de Armijo, and they saluted each other with punctilious courtesy. The Mexican produced a note which was handed to General Taylor.

Old Rough and Ready did not dismount, but rested the note on his saddle-horn and read it. This note, signed by General Antonio Lopez de Santa Anna. President of the Mexican Republic and Commander-in-Chief of its armies, was written in rounded sentences. It stated that the American army was surrounded by twenty thousand men and could not possibly escape. Hence Santa Anna demanded General Taylor's immediate and unconditional surrender. "I will treat you well," he added in generous conclusion.

Phil thought that he could see the white hair around old Rough and Ready's temples fairly bristle with defiance. He did see him lean over and say to de Armijo: "Tell him to come and take me." But the next instant he called to Middleton and dictated to him a short answer, more polite but of the same tenor. He looked over it once, folded it, and handed it to de Armijo.

"Take that to your master."

De Armijo saluted with all the pride and haughtiness of his race. He would have liked well a few minutes to look about and take note of the enemy's army for his general, but they had brought him up a narrow ravine, and they allowed him no chance. Now Middleton rode back with him that the Americans might not be lacking in courtesy, and Phil and his comrades again stood by as they passed. De Armijo merely gave them a malignant glance, but as he entered the plain that low rolling sound, almost like a roar, burst forth again from the army. Nearly every soldier had divined the nature of the errand, and nearly every one also had divined the nature of old Rough and Ready's reply.

Phil watched de Armijo and Middleton riding onward under the white flag toward the gorgeous tent where Santa Anna and his generals were gathered. He saw Middleton disappear and, after awhile, come riding back again. All these demands and refusals, ridings and returns took time, and the two armies meanwhile rested on their arms. The afternoon came, and the sun still blazed on on a scene of peace. For awhile it reminded Phil in many of its aspects of a vast spectacle, a panorama. Then he saw clouds of dust rise on both the east and west wings of the Mexican army. Horsemen moved in columns, fluid sunlight shifting and changing in colors flowing over lances and escopetas. He also saw horses drawing cannon forward, and the bronze and steel of the guns glittered.

A little after noon a heavy force of cavalry, led by Ampudia, moved forward toward an advanced knoll held by some of Taylor's pickets. Phil thought it was the herald of the battle, but the pickets retired after a few shots, and the Mexicans took the knoll, making no attempt to pursue the pickets who fell back quietly on the main army.

Then the silence was resumed, although they could see much motion in the Mexican army, the constant movement of horsemen and the shifting of regiments and guns. A multitude of brilliant flags carried here and there fluttered in the wind. But the American army remained motionless, and the soldiers, when they talked, talked mostly in low tones.

"Phil, you didn't eat any breakfast," said Bill Breakstone, "and if I didn't remind you of it, you would skip dinner. A soldier fights best on a full stomach, and as they're serving out coffee and bacon and other good things now's your time."

"To tell you the truth, I hadn't thought of it," said the boy.

"Well, think of it, Sir Philip of the Spectacle and the Panorama. It isn't often that you'll have a chance to sit on a front seat in an open air theater like this, and see deploying before you an army of twenty thousand men, meaning business."

Phil ate and drank mechanically almost, although the food gave him new strength without his being conscious of it, and he still watched. The long afternoon waned, the sun passed the zenith, and the colors still shifted and changed on the bare peaks and ridges, but, save for the seizing of the lone knoll, the army of Santa Anna did not yet advance, although in its place it was still fluid with motion, like the colors of a kaleidoscope. It seemed to Phil that Bill Breakstone's theatrical allusions applied with peculiar force. Apparently they were setting the scenes down below, this color here, this color there, so many flags at this point, and so many at that point, bands and trumpets to the right, and bands and trumpets to the left. It was a spectacle full of life, color, and movement, but the boy grew very impatient. Great armies did not march forward for that purpose, and for that purpose alone.

"Why don't they attack?" he exclaimed.

"Having the rat in the trap, I suppose that Santa Anna means to play with it a little," replied Bill Breakstone. "There's nothing like playing with a delicious mouse a little while before you eat it."

"Did you ever see anything more hateful than the manner of that fellow de Armijo?" asked Phil. "He bore himself as if we were already in their hands."

"Doubtless he thought so," said Breakstone, "and it is equally likely that his thought is also the thought of Santa Anna, Minon, Torrejon, Pacheco, Lombardini, and all the rest. But states of mind are queer things, Phil. You can change your mind, it may change itself, or others may change it for you. Any one of these things can happen to Santa Anna or to your genial young friend, de Armijo."

"It iss well to be patient," said Arenberg.

The sun went on down the heavens. The light came more obliquely, but it was as brilliant as ever. In two more hours the sun would be gone behind the mountains, when Phil, still watching the Mexican army, saw a flash of fire near the center of the line. A shell rose, flashed through the air, and burst on the plateau held by the Americans. Phil, despite himself, uttered a shout, and so did many other youthful soldiers. They thought the battle would now begin. A battery of Mexican howitzers also opened fire, and the smoke rolled toward the north. The Mexican general, Mejia, on the American right, began to press in, and Ampudia, on the left, threatened with great force. But there was not yet any reply from the American line. Old Rough and Ready rode along the whole battle front, saw that all was in order, and at times surveyed the Mexican advance through powerful glasses.

But the Mexican movements were still very slow, and Phil fairly quivered with impatience. If they were going to fight, he was anxious for the fighting to begin, and to have it over. Up from the plain came the calls of many bugles, the distant playing of bands, and the beat of drums, broken now and then by the irregular discharges of the cannon and the crackling of rifle shots.

But it was not yet a battle, and the sun was very low, threatening to disappear soon behind the mountains. Its parting rays lighted up the plateau, the ravines and promontories, and the pass with a vivid red light. Phil saw the general turn his horse away from the edge of the plateau, as if convinced that there would be no battle, and then suddenly turn him back again, as a great burst of cannon and rifle fire came from the left. Ampudia, having attained a spur of the mountain, was making a fierce attack, pushing forward both horse and foot and trying to get around the American flank. The firing for a little while was rapid. The rifle flashes ran in a continuous blaze along both lines, and the boom of the cannon came back in hollow echoes from the gorges of the Sierra Madre. The black smoke floated in coils and eddies along the ridges and peaks.

Phil and his comrades had nothing to do with this combat except to sit still and listen.

"They are merely feeling for a position," said Bill Breakstone. "They want a good place from which they can crash down on our left flank in the morning, but I don't think they'll get it."

THE QUEST OF THE FOUR

Already the sun was gone in the east, and its rays were dying on the mountains. Then the night itself came down, with the rush of the south, and the firing from both cannon and rifles ceased. Ampudia had failed to secure the coveted position, but presently the two armies, face to face in the darkness, lay down to rest, save for the thick lines of pickets almost within rifle shot of one another. Once more the night was heavy with chill, but Phil did not feel it now. He and his comrades looked to their horses and secured places for rest. The General, still deeply anxious about his rear guard at Saltillo and fearing a flanking movement by Santa Anna, around the mountain, rode back once more to the town, under the escort of Jefferson Davis, leaving the army, as before, under command of Wool. In this emergency an officer past three score showed all the physical energy and endurance of a young man, spending two days and two nights in the saddle.

Phil slept several hours, but he awoke after midnight, and did not go to sleep again. He, Arenberg, and Breakstone were under the immediate command of Middleton, who allowed them much latitude, and they used it for purposes of scouting. They crept through gullies and ravines and along the edges of the ridges, the darkness and the stone projections giving them shelter. They passed beyond the outermost American pickets, and then stopped, crouching among some bushes. All three had heard at the same time low voices of command, the clank of heavy wheels, and the rasping of hoofs over stones. The three also divined the cause, but Breakstone alone spoke of it in a whisper:

"They are dragging artillery up the side of the mountain in order that they may rake us to-morrow. That Santa Anna calls himself the Napoleon of Mexico, and he's got some of the quality of the real Napoleon."

By raising up a little they could see the men and horses with the guns, and they crept back to their own camp with the news. The American force was too small to attempt any checking movement in the darkness, and that night Santa Anna dragged five whole batteries up the mountainside.

It was about 4 o'clock in the morning when the three returned from their scout, and they sat down in one of the ravines about a small fire of smoldering coals. Some of the Kentuckians were with them, including Grayson, and now and then a brisk word of the coming day was said. In those cold dark hours, when vitality was at its lowest, they were not as confident as they had been. The numbers of the Mexicans weighed upon them, and Phil had not liked the sight of all those cannon taken up the side of the mountain. Their talk ceased entirely after awhile, and they sat motionless with their blankets wrapped around their bodies, because the blasts were very chill now in the Pass of Angostura. The moaning of the wind through the gorges was a familiar sound, but to-night it got upon one's nerves.

Those last few hours were five times their rightful length, but all things come to an end, and Phil saw in the east the first narrow band of silver that betokened the dawn. Day, like night, in that southern region came fast. The sun shot above the mountain rim, its splendor came again in a flood, and up rose the two armies.

There was no delay now. On the left the heavy brigades of Ampudia opened fire at once with cannon, muskets, and rifles. They pressed forward, and at that point the American front, also, blazed with fire.

"It's here, Phil," cried Breakstone. "This is the battle at last!"

Cool as he usually was, he had lost his calm now, and his eyes glowed with excitement. The rosy face of Arenberg was also flushed a deeper hue than usual.

"They come!" he exclaimed.

The whole Mexican army seemed to lift itself up and advance in a vast enfolding curve, but Ampudia still pressed the hardest, endeavoring to crush in the American left, and the five batteries that had been taken up the mountainside in the night poured in a heavy fire. In five minutes a great cloud of smoke from the cannon, rifles, and muskets floated over the field. The Mexicans advanced with courage and confidence. At dawn Santa Anna had made a great address, riding up and down the lines, and they deemed victory a matter of certainty.

Phil, Breakstone, and Arenberg had left their horses in the rear, and at this moment Middleton appeared also dismounted.

"Stay with the Kentuckians there," he said, pointing to the ravine. "They will need every man. You can be cavalrymen later if the chance comes."

The three at once fell into line with Grayson and the others who had welcomed them to their camp, and they saw the truth of Middleton's words. Ampudia had accumulated a great force on the ridge above the plateau, during the night, and now they were coming down in heavy masses upon the thin lines of the Kentuckians.

"It's not just five to one. It's eight to one," muttered Bill Breakstone, as he looked at the long and deep columns which they were so soon to meet.

Phil felt his muscles quivering again, while a red light danced before his eyes. But it was not fear. The time for that had passed. The Kentuckians in the front rank kneeled down, with their hands on the triggers of their rifles. Clouds of dust and smoke floated over them and stung their eyes, and the deepening roar of the battle swelled from right and left. Phil knew that this great force of Mexicans was coming forward to crush them in order that another large division might pass along the plateau and flank the American army. He was good enough soldier to know that if they succeeded the trap would indeed close down so firmly upon the defenders that they could not burst from it.

The boy never took his eyes from the advancing Mexi-

BUENA VISTA

can column. He saw, or thought he saw, the dark faces, the glowing eyes, and he was quite sure that he heard the heavy tread of the approaching thousands. Some one gave the order to fire, and, with a mechanical impulse, he pulled the trigger. All the Kentuckians fired together, aiming with their usual coolness and precision, and the front rank of the Mexican advance was blown away. The Mexicans wavered, the Americans reloaded and fired again with the same deadly precision, and then from their right came the flash of cannon fire, sending the shells and heavy balls into the thick ranks of Ampudia's men. The hesitation of the Mexicans turned into retreat, and, hurrying back, they sought refuge along the slopes of the mountains, while the Kentuckians uttered a derisive shout.

"Draw an extra breath or two, Phil," said Bill Breakstone, "because you won't have another chance for some time. We've driven back the flank, but the main army of the Mexicans will be on us in a few minutes."

Phil did as he was bid. He was glad to see those Mexicans gone from their front, and, for the moment at least, he felt the thrill of victory. Yet, while there was rest for him, at that instant the battle was going on all about him. He seemed to hear somewhere the distant notes of a band playing, cheering the soldiers on to death. Now and then came the call of a bugle, shrill and piercing, and the rifles crashed incessantly. The air quivered with the roar of the cannon, and the echoes came rolling back from the gorges.

Now that he was really in the great battle, Phil felt an abnormal calmness. His heart ceased to beat so fast, and his blood cooled a little. He saw that the main army of the Mexicans was advancing in three columns. Two of these columns, one under Lombardini, and the other under Pacheco, came straight toward the little plateau by the side of the pass, upon which most of the American army now stood. The front of each column was a mass of lancers, and rumbling batteries of twelve-pounders came behind. The third column advanced toward the pass.

It was now about nine o'clock in the morning. General Taylor had not yet arrived from Saltillo, but General Wool, his second, had thrown the whole American force in a line across the plateau and the pass, where, less than forty-five hundred in number, it awaited the full impact of twenty thousand Mexican troops. The moment was more than critical. It was terrible. It required stout hearts among the young volunteers, not trained regulars at all, as they watched the Mexican masses heave forward. Lucky it was for them that they had been born in new countries, where every boy, as a matter of course, learned the use of the rifle. And it was lucky, too, that the battery of O'Brien, a most daring and skillful officer, was on their flank to help them.

"Have you drawn those easy breaths yet, Phil?" asked Breakstone.

"Yes."

"Good, because the chance is gone now. Hark, there go our cannon! Look, how the balls are smashing into them!"

The American battery opened at a range of only two hundred yards, and the balls and shells tore through the Mexican lines, but the Mexicans are no cowards, and they were well led that day. Their ranks closed up, and they marched past the fallen, their flags still flying, coming with steady step toward the plateau. Now their own artillery opened, and their numerous guns swept the plateau with a perfect hurricane of shot and shell. The volunteers began to fall fast. The Mexican gunners were doing deadly work, and the Kentuckians where Phil stood raised their rifles again.

"Fire, Phil! Fire as fast as you can reload and pull trigger. It's now or never!"

Phil again did as he was bid, and the others did the

BUENA VISTA

same, but this was a far more formidable attack than the one that they had driven back earlier. The Mexicans never ceased to come. The fire from their cannon grew heavier and more deadly, and the lancers were already charging upon the front lines, thrusting with their long weapons. It was only inborn courage and tenacity that saved them now. Phil saw the glittering squadrons wheeling down upon them.

"Kneel and fire as they come close," shouted Middleton, "and receive them on the bayonet!"

It seemed to Phil that the lances were almost in their faces before they fired. He saw the foam on the nostrils of the horses, their great, bloodshot eyes, and their necks wet with sweat. He saw the faces of the riders wet, too, with sweat, but glowing with triumph, and he saw them, also, brandishing the long lances with the glittering steel shafts. Then the rifles crashed so close together that they were blended in one volley, and the lancers who did not fall reeled. But they quickly came on again to ride directly upon a hedge of bayonets which hurled them back. Once more the triumphant shout of the Kentuckians rose, but it was quickly followed by a groan. At different points the volunteers from another state, daunted by their great losses and the overwhelming numbers that continually pressed upon them, were giving way. Their retreat became a panic, and the helpful battery was left uncovered. The brave O'Brien was compelled to unlimber and retreat with his guns. The flying regiment ran into another that was coming up and carried it along in its panic of the moment.

Phil and his comrades had full cause for the groan that they uttered. The day seemed lost. The column of Lombardini was on the southern edge of the plateau and was pressing forward in masses that seemed irresistible. The lancers had recovered themselves and were slaying the fugitives, while the Mexican cannon also hailed shot and shell upon them.

Burning tears rose to Phil's eyes—he could not help it, he was only a boy—and he turned appealingly to the faithful Breakstone.

"Shall we, too, have to retreat?" he shouted.

"Not yet! Not yet, I hope!" Breakstone shouted back. "No, we don't retreat at all! See the brave Illinois boys turning the current!"

An entire Illinois regiment had thrown itself in the path of pursuers and pursued, and two fresh cannon began to cut through the Mexican masses. The fugitives were protected and saved from wholesale slaughter, but Bill Breakstone claimed too much. It was impossible for a single regiment and two guns to withstand so many thousands crowded at that point, and the Illinois lads did retreat. But they retreated slowly and in perfect order, sending volley after volley into the advancing masses. Nor did they go far. They halted soon in a good position and stood there, firing steadily into the Mexican columns. Yet they seemed lost. The Mexicans in vast numbers were pouring down upon the plateau, and the Illinois men were now attacked in the flank as well as in the front.

"Time for us to be doing something," said Breakstone, and at that moment the order came. The Kentuckians, also, retreated, turning, as fast as they reloaded, to fire a volley, aiming particularly at the lancers, whose weapons were so terrible at close quarters. Phil looked more than once through all the fire and smoke for de Armijo, but he didn't see him until the battle was a full hour old. Then it was only a passing glimpse, and he knew that his shot had missed—he had fired without remorse, as he now regarded de Armijo as so much venom. After the single shot the columns of smoke floated in between, and he saw him no more.

Phil knew that the battle was at a most critical stage, that it was even worse, that all the chances now favored the Mexicans. An inexperienced boy even could not doubt it. The charge of the lancers had driven back a small detachment of mounted volunteers, the American riflemen posted on the slopes of the mountain were forced out of their positions, and the great columns of infantry were still pressing on the left, cutting their way to the rear of the army.

It seemed to Phil that they were completely surrounded, and, in fact, they nearly were, but the men of Illinois and Kentucky redoubled their efforts. The barrels of their rifles grew hot with so much firing. The mingled reek of dust and sweat, of smoke and burned gunpowder, stung their nostrils and filled their eyes, half blinding them. The shell and grape and bullets of the Mexicans now reached the Kentuckians, too. Phil, as the smoke lifted now and then, saw many a comrade go down. He, Arenberg, and Breakstone were all wounded slightly, though they were not conscious then of their hurts.

Worse came. The great enclosing circle of the Mexicans drove them into a mass. The regiment that had broken in panic could not yet be rallied, although their officers strove like brave men to get them back in line, and, like brave men, died trying. Phil saw officers falling all around him, although Middleton was still erect, sword in hand, encouraging the men to fight on.

"It can't be that we are beaten! It can't be!" cried the boy in despair.

"No," said Breakstone, "it's not a beating, but it's a darned fine imitation. Come on, boys! Come on, all of you! We'll drive them back yet!"

Phil felt some one strike against him in the smoke. It was Dick Grayson, of Paris.

"Looks hot, Phil!" said that ingenuous youth. There was a tremendous discharge of artillery, and Grayson went down. But he promptly sprang up.

"It is hot," he shouted, "hotter than I thought. But I'm not hurt. It was only the wind from a cannon-ball.

Look out, here come the lancers again, and our rifles are unloaded!"

The long glittering line of lancers appeared through the smoke, and Phil thought that their day was done. It seemed to him that he could not resist any more, but, at that moment a mighty crash of artillery came from the pass. The third column of Mexicans had just come within range of Washington's guns, and the gunners, restrained hitherto, were pouring shot and shell, grape and canister, as fast as they could fire, into the Mexican mass. The column was hurled back by the sudden and terrific impact, and, breaking, it fled in a panic. The Mexicans on the plateau were affected by the flight of their comrades, and they, too, lancers and all, wavered. The Illinois troops came pouring back. With them were more Kentuckians and Bragg's battery, and then Sherman's battery, too. Never were cannon better served than were the American guns on that day. When the guns began to thunder in front of them and between them and the enemy, the fugitives were rallied and were brought back into the battle.

Both batteries were now cutting down the Mexicans at the foot of the mountain, but Breakstone, cool as always, pointed to the columns of Ampudia's infantry, which were still pressing hard on the flank, seeking to reach the rear of the American army.

"If they get there we are lost," he said.

"There is dust behind us now," exclaimed Phil. "See that column of it coming fast!"

"Good God, can they have got there already!" cried Breakstone, despair breaking at last through his armor of courage.

The cloud of dust rose like a tower and came fast. Then a shout of joy burst from the Americans. Through that cloud of dust showed the red face and white hair of Old Rough and Ready, their commander, returning from Saltillo, and with him were Davis's Mississippians and

BUENA VISTA

May's mounted men. Wool galloped forward to meet his chief, who rode upon the plateau and looked at the whole wide curve of the battle as much as the dust and smoke would allow.

"The battle is lost," said Wool.

"That is for me to say," said Taylor.

Yet it seemed that Wool, a brave and resolute leader, was right. A great percentage of the American army was already killed or wounded. Many of its best officers had fallen, and everywhere the Mexicans continually pressed forward in columns that grew heavier and heavier. Santa Anna worthily proved that day that, whatever he may have been otherwise he possessed devouring energy, great courage, and a spark of military genius. And the generals around him, Lombardini, Pacheco, Villamil, Torrejon, Ampudia, Minon, Juvera, Andrade, and the rest were full of the Latin fire which has triumphed more than once over the cold courage and order of the North.

The crisis was visible to every one. Ampudia and his infantry passing to the rear of the American army must be stopped. Davis gathered his Mississippians and hurled them upon Ampudia's men, who outnumbered them five to one. They fired, then rushed down one slope of a ravine that separated them from the enemy, and up the other slope directly into the ranks of the Mexicans, firing another volley almost face to face. So great was their impact that the head of the Mexican column was shattered, and the whole of it was driven back. Ampudia's men, by regiments, sought shelter along the slopes of the mountain.

The battle was saved for the moment, but for the moment only. Few battles have swung in the balance oftener than this combat at Buena Vista, when it seemed as if the weight of a hair might decide it.

"We can breathe again, Phil," cried Breakstone. "They haven't flanked us there, but I don't think we'll have time for more than two breaths."

THE QUEST OF THE FOUR

The battle, just in front of them, paused for an instant or two, but it went on with undiminished fury elsewhere. While Phil let his heated rifle cool, he watched this terrible conflict at the mouth of the grim pass, a combat that swung to and fro and that refused to be decided in favor of either. But, as he rested, all his courage came back anew. The little army, the boy volunteers, had already achieved the impossible. For hours they had held off the best of the Mexican troops, five to their one. More than once they had been near to the verge, but nobody could say that they had been beaten.

Phil's feeling of awe came again, as he looked at the great stage picture, set with all the terrible effects of reality. The smoke rose always, banking up against the sides of the mountain, but dotted with red and pink spots, the flame from the rifles of the sharpshooters who lurked among the crags. From the mouth of the pass came a steady roaring where the cannon of Washington were fired so fast. The smoke banked up there, too, but it was split continually by the flash of the great guns. Out of the smoke came the unbroken crash of rifles, resembling, but on a much larger scale, the ripping of a heavy cloth. Now and then both sides shouted and cheered.

Bill Breakstone was a shrewd judge of a battle that day. The crisis had passed, but in a few minutes a new crisis came. For in their rear began another fierce conflict. Torrejon's splendid brigade of lancers made its way around the mountain and fell upon the small force of Arkansas and Kentucky volunteers under Yell and Marshall at the hacienda of Buena Vista. Yell was killed almost instantly, many other men went down, but the volunteers held fast. Some, their horses slain or wounded, reached the roofs of houses, and with their long rifles emptied saddle after saddle among the lancers. It was a confused and terrible struggle, but, in an instant or two, American dragoons came to the rescue. The

BUENA VISTA

lancers gave way and fled, bearing with them their leader, the brave Torrejon, who was wounded badly. Again the army was saved by courage and quick action. If Torrejon and his men had been able to hold Buena Vista, the American force would have been destroyed.

Phil knew nothing of the conflict at Buena Vista itself until the day was done, because he was soon in the very thickest of it again himself. He and his comrades stood among the decimated squares on the plateau, where the battle had shifted for a moment, and where the smoke was rising. Looking over the field, littered with men and horses, it seemed that half of his countrymen had fallen. Everywhere lay the dead, and the wounded crawled painfully to the rear. Yet the unhurt could give little aid to the hurt, because the Mexican battle front seemed as massive and formidable as ever.

"Load, Phil, load!" whispered Bill Breakstone. "See, they're coming again!"

Masses of lancers were gathering anew on the plateau, among them many of Torrejon's men, who had come back from the other side of the mountain, and the lifting smoke enabled Phil and his comrades to see them clearly. The defenders—they were not many now—were more closely packed. The men of the West and South were mingled together, but with desperate energy the officers soon drew them out in a line facing the lancers. Sherman with his cannon also joined them. In the shifting fortunes of the day, another critical moment came. If the charge of the lancers passed over their line, the Americans were beaten.

The battle elsewhere sank and died for the time. All looked toward the two forces on the plateau, the heavy squadrons of cavalry advancing, and the thin line of infantry silent and waiting. The Mexican bugles ceased to sound, and the firing stopped. Phil and the men with him in the front rank knelt again. Arenberg, as usual, was on one side of him, and Breakstone on the other. Middleton was not far away. Phil glanced up and down the American line and, as he saw how few they were, his heart, after a period of high courage, sank like a plummet in a pool. It did not seem possible to stop the horsemen. Then his courage rose again. They had done a half dozen wonders that day, they could do another half dozen.

It was one of the most vivid moments of Phil's life, fairly burnt into his soul. The smoke, lifting higher and higher, disclosed more and more of the field, with its dead and dying everywhere. The mountains were coming out of the mists and vapors, and showing their bare crags and peaks. There was no sound but the hoofbeats of the horsemen and an occasional cry from the wounded, but Phil did not even hear these. There was to him only an awful and ominous silence, as the heavy columns drew nearer and nearer and he saw the menacing faces and ready weapons. The blood quivered in his veins, but he did not give back. Nor did the others, most of whom were boys not much older than he.

"I think this will tell the tale," whispered Bill Breakstone. "Look how steady our lads are! Veteran regulars could not bear themselves better in the face of five to one."

Nearer and nearer came the lancers. Something in the aspect of the steady troops that awaited the shock must have daunted them, because already on that day they had shown themselves brave men more than once. The hoofbeats ceased, their line stopped and wavered, and at that instant the American rifles fired, pouring forth a stream of lead, a deadly volley.

Phil saw the blaze from a long line of muzzles, the puff of rifle smoke, and then as it lifted he tried to shut his eyes but could not. The whole front of the Mexican column was destroyed. Men and horses lay in a heap, and other riderless horses galloped wildly over the plateau. The second line of the lancers stood for a moment, but when the cannon, following up the rifles, hurled shot and shell among them, they, too, broke and fled, while the bullets from the reloaded rifles pelted them and drove them to greater speed.

A shout arose from the scanty ranks of the defense. Another critical moment had passed, and for the first time fortune shifted to the American side. Now the defenders followed up their advantage. They pressed forward, pushing the Mexicans before them, attacking them on two sides and driving them against the base of the mountain.

The whole battle now surged back toward the direction whence Santa Anna had come. The scanty division of the Americans, after so long a defense, a defense that seemed again and again to be hopeless, massed themselves anew and attacked the Mexican army with redoubled vigor. Phil felt the song of victory singing in his ears, the blood leaped in his veins, and a great new store of strength came from somewhere, as he, with Breakstone and Arenberg yet on either side of him, marched forward now, not backward.

The great division of Ampudia which had threatened to surround the American force was now penned in at the foot of the mountain. This single division alone greatly outnumbered the whole American army, but panic and terror were in its ranks. The Southern and Western riflemen were advancing on three sides, sending in showers of bullets that could not miss. Nine cannon, manned by gunners as good as the world could furnish, cut down rank after rank.

Earlier in the day Phil would have thrilled with horror at the scene before him, but in such a long and furious battle his faculties had become blunted. It was nothing to see men fall, dead or wounded. The struggle for life at the expense of another's life, the most terrible phase of war, had now come. His only conscious thought at that moment was to destroy the mass of Mexicans pressed against the mountain, and he loaded and fired with a zeal and rapidity not inferior to that of anybody.

The Mexican mass seemed to shrink and draw in upon itself. The officers encouraged the men to return the terrible fire that was cutting them down. Some did so, but it was too feeble a reply to check Taylor's advance. Santa Anna, farther down, saw the terrible emergency. Vain, bombastic, and treacherous, he was, nevertheless, a great general, and now the spark of genius hidden in such a shell blazed up. In the height of the battle, and with five thousand of his best men being cut to pieces before him, a singular expedient occurred to him. He knew the character of the general opposed to him; he knew that Taylor was merciful and humane, and suddenly he sent forward a messenger under a white flag. Taylor, amazed, nevertheless received the messenger and ordered the firing on the trapped Mexicans to cease. He was still more amazed when he read the Mexican commander's note. Santa Anna wished to know in rhetorical phraseology what General Taylor wanted. While Taylor was considering and preparing the reply to so strange a question at such a time, and the messenger was riding back with it, Ampudia's whole division escaped from the trap up the base of the mountain. Then the Mexicans at the other points instantly reopened fire. It was a singular and treacherous expedient, but it succeeded.

A cry of rage rose from Phil's company, and it was uttered by others everywhere. The boy had seen the herald under the white flag, and, all the rest, too, had wondered at the nature of the message he brought. He did not yet know what was in Santa Anna's note, but he knew that a successful trick had been played. The blood in his veins seemed to turn to its hottest. His pulses were beating the double quick, and he felt relief only when Taylor, enraged at Santa Anna's ruse, ordered the Kentucky and Illinois men to pursue Ampudia's fleeing division.

BUENA VISTA

Forward they went, scarcely a thousand, because very many comrades had fallen around them that day, but they had never been more eager for the charge. The smoke thinned out before them and they advanced swiftly with leveled rifles. They reached the southern edge of the plateau, and then they recoiled in horror. Santa Anna had not only saved a division by a trick, but he had used the same opportunity to draw in his columns and mass the heaviest force that had yet converged upon a single point. Ten thousand men appeared over the uneven ground and approached the single thousand. To face such numbers advancing with great guns was impossible. Again it seemed that the day, after a brilliant success, was lost.

The Americans at once turned and rushed into a gorge for shelter and defense.

The side of the gorge was so steep that Phil slipped and rolled to the bottom. But he quickly sprang up, unconscious of his bruises. Breakstone and Arenberg, with pale faces, were at his side. The gorge was not as much of a shelter and defense as it had seemed. It was instead a trap, the worst into which they had come that day. From the cliffs on both sides of the gorge the Mexicans sent down a continuous rain of bullets and shell. Santa Anna, exulting in his success, urged them on and, his seconds, Ampudia, Pacheco, Lombardini and the others, ran from point to point, encouraging their troops and crying that the battle was now won.

The Americans fired upward at their enemies, but they were pressed together in great confusion. Men and officers went down so fast that it looked to Phil like hay falling before the scythe. Here fell the brave Colonel Clay, the son of the great Henry Clay, and with him McKee and Hardin and many other gallant sons of Kentucky and Illinois.

A great horror seized Phil. Penned in that awful gorge, with that continuous shower of steel and lead from above, he felt as if he were choking. He and others rushed for the mouth of the gorge, but the wary Santa Anna had closed it with a great body of lancers, who were now advancing to assist in the complete destruction of the Americans.

The defenders reeled back, and Santa Anna, thinking the time had come to deliver the final blow, sent the Mexican infantry in thousands down the sides of the gorge, where they attacked with the bayonet the few hundreds that yet fought. Phil was quite sure that no hope was left. Before, at every critical moment there had always been a slender chance of some kind or other, but now he could see absolutely none. A million red motes danced before him, and he struck almost blindly with his clubbed rifle at a Mexican who was trying to bayonet him.

But from a point above, not yet taken by the Mexicans, the brave O'Brien and Thomas, as brave, were still firing their cannon and sending the shot and shell into the Mexican masses, where they were not mingled with the Americans. But they themselves were exposed to a deadly fire. One by one their gunners fell. They were compelled to fall back step by step. Not enough men were left to load and fire the pieces. Soon all the gunners were killed or wounded except O'Brien himself. Presently he, too, was wounded, and the guns were silent. Now, truly, it seemed that the last moment had come!

Phil, when he struck with his clubbed rifle, knew that he hit something, because the Mexican with the eager bayonet was no longer there. He saw Breakstone and Arenberg yet beside him, both wounded, but both erect and defiant. He saw Grayson a little distance away, still alive, and farther on a little group of Kentuckians and Illinoisans, fighting to the last. He had an instant's vision of the whole awful gorge, filled with men driven on by the rage of battle, the dead and wounded strewed all about, the smoke hovering above like a roof, and the

BUENA VISTA

masses of Mexicans who completely encircled them now closing in for the final blow.

It was all a real panorama, passing in an instant, and then from above, and at a new point, came the crash of great guns, the shot and shell striking among the Mexicans, not among the Americans. Not even at this, the last crisis, when the battle seemed lost beyond redemption, had fortune, or rather courage and energy, failed. Bragg, coming on a run with his battery, suddenly opened at short range, and with awful effect, into the Mexican masses. In another minute Sherman arrived with his guns, and close behind, coming as fast as breath would allow, were infantry with the rifle, and, to make the surprise complete, Washington's guns suddenly appeared on the right and began to sweep away the lancers who held the mouth of the gorge.

Never had fortune made a quicker and more complete change. The Mexicans who had suddenly trapped the Kentuckians and Illinoisans had been entrapped themselves with equal suddenness.

The fire now rose to the greatest height of the day. They had been fighting on the plateau, in the ravines, on the slopes, and through the pass for hours. Vast quantities of smoke still hung about and lay like a blanket against the side of the mountain. The sun was far down the western slope.

The Kentucky and Illinois men drew themselves into a close body near the upper end of the gorge. There they fired as fast as exhaustion would allow, but salvation was coming from above, and now they knew it. Closer and closer crept the American artillery. Heavier and heavier grew its fire. The riflemen, also, sent in the bullets like hail. Taylor himself, a half dozen bullets through his clothing, stood on the brink directing the attack. The gorge where the Mexicans stood was swept by a storm of death. Santa Anna, from the other side, watched in dismay. Lancers and infantry alike, unable to stand such a sleet, rushed for the mouth of the gorge. Few of the lancers, who made the larger target, escaped, and the infantry suffered almost as much.

The gorge was cleared, and the Americans held the plateau. Everywhere the Mexicans fell back, leaving the whole field in possession of the little force that had fought so long and so fiercely to hold it. The Mexican bugle sounded again, but now it was the command to retire. The sun dipped down behind the mountains, and the shadows began to gather in the Pass of Angostura. The impossible had happened. Mexico's finest army, five to one, led by her greatest general, had broken in vain against the farmer lads of the South and West, and the little band of regulars. The victory was won over the greatest odds ever faced by Americans in a pitched battle.

CHAPTER XV

THE WOMAN AT THE WELL

PHIL was still in a daze. He and those around him, exhausted by such long and desperate efforts, such a continuous roar in their ears, and such a variation of intense emotions from the highest to the lowest, were scarcely conscious that the battle was over. They knew, indeed, that night was falling on the mountains and the pass, that the Mexicans had withdrawn from the field, that their flags and lances were fading in the twilight, but it was all, for a little while, dim and vague to them. The night and the silence coming together contained a great awe. Phil felt the blood pounding in his ears, and he looked around with wonder. It was Breakstone who first came to himself.

"We've won! We've won!" he cried. "As sure as there is a sun behind those mountains, we've beat all Mexico!"

Then Phil, too, saw, and he had to believe.

"The victory is ours!" he cried.

"It is ours, but harm has been done," said Arenberg in a low voice. Then he sank forward softly on his face. Phil and Breakstone quickly raised him up. He had fainted from loss of blood, but as his wounds were only of the flesh he was soon revived. Breakstone had three slight wounds of his own, and these were bound up, also. Phil, meanwhile, was hunting in the gorge for other friends. Grayson was alive and well, but some that he had known were gone. He was weak, mind and body alike, with the relaxation from the long battle and all those terrible emotions, but he helped with the wounded. Below them lay the army of Santa Anna, its lights shining again in the darkness, and, for all Phil knew, it might attack again on the morrow, but he gave little attention to it now. His whole concern was for his comrades. The victory had been won, but they had been compelled to purchase it at a great price. The losses were heavy. Twenty-eight officers of rank were among the killed, regiments were decimated, and even the unhurt were so exhausted that they could scarcely stand.

Phil sat down at the edge of the gorge. He was yet faint and dizzy. It seemed to him that he would never be able to exert himself again. Everything swam before him in a sort of confused glare. He was conscious that his clothing was stained red in two or three places, but when he looked, in a mechanical way, at the wounds, he saw they were scratches, closed already by the processes of nature. Then his attention wandered again to the field. He was full of the joy of victory, but it was a vague, uncertain feeling, not attaching itself to any particular thing.

The twilight had already sunk into the night, and the black wind, heavy with chill, moaned in the Pass of Angostura. It was a veritable dirge for the dead. Phil felt it all through his relaxed frame, and shivered both with cold and with awe. Smoke and vapor from so much firing still floated about the plateau, the pass, and the slopes, but there was a burning touch on his face which he knew did not come from any of them. It was the dust of the desert again stinging him after the battle as it had done before it. He obeyed its call, summoned anew all his strength, both of body and mind, and climbed out of the gorge, where friend and foe still lay in hundreds, mingled and peaceful in death.

He found more light and cheer on the plateau and in the pass. Here the unhurt and those hurt slightly were building fires, and they had begun to cook food and boil

THE WOMAN AT THE WELL

coffee. Phil suddenly perceived that he was hungry. He had not tasted food since morning. He joined one of the groups, ate and drank, and more vigor returned. Then he thought of the horse which he had left tethered in an alcove, and which he had not used at all that day. The horse was there unharmed, although a large cannon-ball lay near his feet. It was evidently a spent ball which had rolled down the side of the mountain, as it was not buried at all.

The horse recognized Phil and neighed. Phil put his hand upon his mane and stroked it. He was very glad that this comrade of his had escaped unhurt. He wondered in a dim way what his terror must have been tied in one place, while the battle raged all day about him. "Poor old horse," he said, stroking his mane again. Then he led him away, gave him food and water, and returned to his comrades and the field. He knew that his duty lay there, as the Mexican army was still at hand. Many thought that it would attack again in the morning, and disposition for defense must be made. He did not see either Breakstone or Arenberg, but he met Middleton, to whom he reported.

"Scout down at the mouth of the pass and along the mountain slopes, Phil," he said, and the boy, replenishing his ammunition, obeyed. It was not quite dark, and the wind was exceedingly cold. The mercury that night went below the freezing point, and the sufferings of the wounded were intense. Phil kept well among the ravines and crags. He believed that the Mexican lancers would be prowling in front of their camp, and he would not have much chance if he were attacked by a group of them. Moreover, he was tired of fighting. He did not wish to hurt anybody. Never had his soul inclined more fervently to peace.

He passed again into the gorge which had witnessed the climax and deadliest part of the battle. Here he saw dark-robed figures passing back and forth among the wounded. He looked more closely and saw that they were Mexican nuns from a convent near Buena Vista, helping the wounded, Americans and Mexicans alike. Something rose in his throat, but he went on, crossing the pass and climbing the slopes of the Sierra Madre. Here there was yet smoke lingering in the nooks and crannies, but all the riflemen seemed to have gone.

He climbed higher. The wind there was very cold, but the moonlight was brighter. He saw the peaks and ridges of the Sierra Madre, like a confused sea, and he looked down upon the two camps, the small American one on the plateau and in the pass and the larger, still far larger, Mexican one below. He could trace it by the lights in the Mexican camp, forming a great half circle, and he would have given much to know what was going on there. If Santa Anna and his men possessed the courage and tenacity of the defenders, they would attack again on the morrow.

He moved forward a little to get a better view, and then sank down behind an outcropping of rock. A Mexican, a tall man, rifle on shoulder, was passing. He, too, was looking down at the two camps, and Phil believed that he was a scout like himself. The Mexican, not suspecting the presence of an enemy, was only a dozen feet away, and Phil could easily have shot him without danger to himself, but every impulse was against the deed. He could not fire from ambush, and he had seen enough of death. The Mexican was going toward his own camp, and presently, he went on, disappearing behind a curve of the mountain, and leaving Phil without a shadow of remorse. But he soon followed, creeping on down the mountainside toward the camp of Santa Anna.

The rocks and gullies enabled him to come so near that he could see within the range of light. He beheld figures as they passed now and then, dark shadows before the blaze, but the camp of Santa Anna did not show the life and animation that he had witnessed in it when he spied upon it once before. No bugles were blowing, no bodies of lancers, with the firelight shining on glittering steel, rode forth to prepare for the morrow and victory. Everything was slack and relaxed. He even saw men lying in hundreds upon the ground, fast asleep from exhaustion. As far as he could determine, no scouting parties of large size were abroad, and he inferred from what he saw that the Mexican army was worn out.

He could not go among those men, but the general effect produced upon him at the distance was of gloom and despair among them. An army preparing for battle in the morning would be awake and active. The longer he looked, the greater became his own hope and confidence, and then he slowly made his way back to his own camp with his report. Lights still burned there, but it was very silent. After he passed the ring of sentinels he saw nothing but men stretched out, almost as still as the dead around them. They slept deeply, heavily, a sleep so intense that a blow would not arouse. Many had lain down where they were standing when the battle ceased, and would lie there in dreamless slumber until the next morning. Phil stepped over them, and near one of the fires he saw Breakstone and Arenberg, each with his head on his arm, deep in slumber.

He made his report to Middleton, describing with vivid detail everything that he had seen.

"It agrees with the reports of the other scouts," said Middleton. "I think the enemy is so shattered that he cannot move upon us again, and now, Phil, you must rest. It will be midnight in an hour, and you have passed through much."

"It was a great battle!" said Phil, with a look of pride.

"And a great victory!" said Middleton, he, too, although older, feeling that flash of pride.

Phil was glad enough now to seek sleep. The nervous excitement that kept him awake and alert was all gone.

THE QUEST OF THE FOUR

He remembered the fire beside which Bill Breakstone and Arenberg slept, and made his way back there. Neither had moved a particle. They still lay with their heads on their elbows, and they drew long, deep breaths with such steadiness and regularity that apparently they had made up their minds to sleep for years to come. Four other men lay near them in the same happy condition.

"Six," said Phil. "Well, the fable tells of the Seven Sleepers, so I might as well complete the number."

He chose the best place that was left, secured his blanket from his saddlebow, wrapped himself thoroughly in it, and lay down with his feet to the fire. How glorious it felt! It was certainly very cold in the Pass of Angostura. Ice was forming, and the wind cut, but there was the fire at his feet and the thick blanket around him. His body felt warm through and through, and the hard earth was like down after such a day. Now victory came, too, with its pleasantest aroma. Lying there under the stars, he could realize, in its great sense, all that they had done. And he had borne his manly part in it. He was a boy, and he had reason for pride.

Phil stared up for a little while at the cold stars which danced in the sky, myriads of miles away, but after awhile his glance turned again toward the earth. The other six of the seven sleepers slept on, not stirring at all, save for the rising and falling of their chests, and Phil decided that he was neglecting his duty by failing to join them at once in that vague and delightful land to which they had gone.

He shut his eyes, opened them once a minute or two later, but found the task of holding up the lids too heavy. They shut down again, stayed down, and in two minutes the six sleepers had become the seven.

Phil slept the remainder of the night as heavily as if he had been steeped in some eastern drug. He, too, neither moved hand nor foot after he had once gone to oblivion. The fire burned out, but he did not awake.

THE WOMAN AT THE WELL

He was warm in his blanket, and sleep was bringing back the strength that body and mind had wasted in the day. It was quiet, too, on the battlefield. The surgeons still worked with the wounded, but they had been taken back in the shelter of the pass, and the sounds did not come to those on the plateau. Only the wind moaned incessantly, and the cold was raw and bitter.

About half way between midnight and morning Bill Breakstone awoke. He merely opened his eyes, not moving his body, but he stared about him in a dim wonder. His awakening had interrupted a most extraordinary dream. He had been dreaming that he was in a battle that had lasted at least a month, and was not yet finished. Red strife and its fierce emotions were still before him when he awoke. Now he gazed all around, and saw only blackness, with a few points of light here and there.

His eyes, growing used to the darkness, came back, and he saw six stiff figures stretched on the ground in a row, three on each side of him. He looked at them fixedly and saw that they were the figures of human beings. Moreover, he recognized two of them, and they were his best friends. Then he remembered all about the battle, the great struggle, how the terrible crisis came again and again, how the victory finally was won, and he was glad that these two friends of his were alive, though they seemed to be sleeping as men never slept before.

Breakstone sat up and looked at the six sleepers. The blankets of two of them had shifted a little, and he pulled them back around their necks. Then he glanced down the valley where the lights of Santa Anna's army flickered, and it all seemed wonderful, unbelievable to him. Yet it was true. They had beaten off an army of more than twenty thousand men, and had inflicted upon Santa Anna a loss far greater than their own. He murmured very softly:

THE QUEST OF THE FOUR

> "Dreadful was the fight,
> Welcome is the night;
> Fiercely came the foe,
> Many we laid low;
> Backward he is sent,
> But we, too, are spent.

I believe that's about as true a poem as I ever composed," he said, "whatever others may think about the rhyme and meter, and to be true is to be right. That work well done, I'll go back to sleep again."

He lay down once more and, within a minute, he kept his word. Phil and his comrades were awakened just at the break of day by Middleton. Only a narrow streak of light was to be seen over the eastern ridges, but the Captain explained that he wanted them to go on a little scout toward the Mexican army. They joined him with willingness and went down the southern edge of the plateau. A few lights could be seen at the points that Phil had marked during the night, and they approached very cautiously. But they saw no signs of life. There were no patrols, no cavalry, none of the stir of a great army, nothing to indicate any human presence, until they came upon wounded men, abandoned upon the rugged ground where they lay. When Phil and his comrades, belief turned into certainty, rushed forward, Santa Anna and his whole army were gone, leaving behind them their dead and desperately wounded. Tents, supplies, and some arms were abandoned in the swift retreat, but the army itself had already disappeared under the southern horizon, leaving the field of Buena Vista to the victors.

They hurried back with the news. It spread like fire through the army. Every man who could stand was on his feet. A mighty cheer rolled through the Pass of Angostura, and the dark gorges and ravines of the Sierra Madre gave it back in many echoes.

The victory, purchased at so great a price, was complete. Mounted scouts, sent out, returned in the course of

THE WOMAN AT THE WELL

the day with the information that Santa Anna had not stopped at Agua Neva. He was marching southward as fast as he could, and there was no doubt that he would not stop until he reached the City of Mexico, where he would prepare to meet the army of Scott, which was to come by the way of Vera Cruz. The greatness of their victory did not dawn upon the Americans until then. Not only had they beaten back a force that outnumbered them manifold, but all Northern Mexico lay at the feet of Taylor. The war there was ended, and it was for Scott to finish it in the Valley of Mexico.

The following night the fires were built high on the plateau and in the Pass of Angostura. Nearly everybody rested except the surgeons, who still worked. Hundreds of the Mexican wounded had been left on the field, and they received the same attention that was bestowed upon the Americans. Nevertheless, the boy soldiers were cheerful. They knew that the news of their wonderful victory was speeding north, and they felt that they had served their country well.

Phil did not know until long afterward that at home the army of Taylor had been given up as lost. News that Santa Anna was in front of him with an overwhelming force had filtered through, and then had come the long blank. Nothing was heard. It was supposed that Taylor had been destroyed or captured. It was known that his force was composed almost wholly of young volunteers, boys, and no chance of escape seemed possible.

In the West and South, in Kentucky, Illinois, Indiana, Arkansas, and Mississippi, the anxiety was most tense and painful. There, nearly every district had sent some one to Buena Vista, and they sought in vain for news. There were dark memories of the Alamo and Goliad, especially in the Southwest, and these people thought of the disaster as in early days they thought of a defeat by the Indians, when there were no wounded or prisoners, only slain.

THE QUEST OF THE FOUR

But even the nearest states were separated from Mexico by a vast wilderness, and, as time passed and nothing came, belief settled into certainty. The force of Taylor had been destroyed. Then the messenger arrived literally from the black depths with the news of the unbelievable victory. Taylor was not destroyed. He had beaten an army that outnumbered him five to one. The little American force held the Pass of Angostura, and Santa Anna, with his shattered army, was flying southward. At first it was not believed. It was incredible, but other messengers came with the same news, and then one could doubt no longer. The victory struck so powerfully upon the imagination of the American people that it carried Taylor into the White House.

Meanwhile, Phil, in the Pass of Angostura, sitting by a great fire on the second night after the battle, was thinking little of his native land. After the tremendous interruption of Buena Vista, his mind turned again to the object of his search. He read and reread his letter. He thought often of the lava that had cut his brother's feet and his own. John was sure that they had gone through a pass, and he knew that a woman at a well had given him water. The belief that they were on the trail of those forlorn prisoners was strong within him. And Bill Breakstone and Arenberg believed it, too.

"Our army, I understand, will go into quarters in this region," he said, "and will make no further advance by land into Mexico. We enlisted only for this campaign, and I am free to depart. I mean to go at once, boys."

"We go with you, of course," said Bill Breakstone. "Good old Hans and I here have already talked it over. There will be no more campaigning in Northern Mexico, and we've done our duty. Besides, we've got quests of our own that do not lead toward the valley of Mexico."

Phil grasped a hand of each and gave it a strong squeeze.

THE WOMAN AT THE WELL

"I knew that you would go with me, as I'll go with you when the time comes," he said.

They received their discharge the next morning, and were thanked by General Taylor himself for bravery in battle. Old Rough and Ready put his hand affectionately on Phil's shoulder.

"May good fortune follow you wherever you may be going," he said. "It was such boys as you who won this battle."

He also caused them to be furnished with large supplies of ammunition. Middleton could go no farther. He and some other officers were to hurry to Tampico and join Scott for the invasion of Mexico by the way of Vera Cruz.

"But boys," he said, "we may meet again. We've been good comrades, I think, and circumstances may bring us together a second time when this war is over."

"It rests upon the knees of the gods," said Arenberg.

"I know it will come true," said the more sanguine Breakstone.

"So do I," said Phil.

Middleton rode away with his brother officers and a small body of regulars, and Phil, Arenberg, and Breakstone rode southward to Agua Neva. When they had gone some distance they stopped and looked back at the plateau and the pass.

"How did we ever do it?" said Phil.

"By refusing to stay whipped," replied Arenberg.

"By making up our minds to die rather than give up," replied Bill Breakstone.

They rode on to the little Mexican town, where Phil had an errand to do. He had talked it over with the other two, and the three had agreed that it was of the utmost importance. All the time a sentence from the letter was running in Phil's head. Some one murmuring words of pity in Mexican had given him water to drink, and the voice was that of a woman.

THE QUEST OF THE FOUR

"It must have been from a well," said Phil, "this is a dry country with water mostly from wells, and around these wells villages usually grow. Bill, we must be on the right track. I can't believe that we're going wrong."

"The signs certainly point the way we're thinking," said Bill Breakstone. "The lava, the dust, and the water. We've passed the lava and the dust, and we know that the water is before us."

They came presently to Agua Neva, a somber little town, now reoccupied by a detachment from Taylor's army. The people were singularly quiet and subdued. The defeat of Santa Anna by so small a force and his precipitate flight made an immense impression upon them, and, as they suffered no ill treatment from the conquerors, they did not seek to make trouble. There was no sharpshooting in the dark, no waylaying of a few horsemen by guerillas, and the three could pursue without hesitation the inquiry upon which they were bent.

Wells! Wells! Of course there were wells in Agua Neva. Several of them, and the water was very fine. Would the señors taste it? They would, and they passed from one well to another until they drank from them all. Breakstone could speak Spanish, and its Mexican variations, and he began to ask questions—chance ones at first, something about the town and its age, and the things that he had seen. Doubtless in the long guerilla war between Texas and Mexico, captives, the fierce Texans, had passed through there on their way to strong prisons in the south. Such men had passed more than once, but the people of Agua Neva did not remember any particular one among them. They spent a day thus in vain, and Phil, gloomy and discouraged, rode back to the quarters of the American detachment.

"Don't be downhearted, Phil," said Breakstone. "In a little place like this one must soon pick up the trail. It will not be hard to get at the gossip. We'll try again to-morrow."

THE WOMAN AT THE WELL

They did not go horseback the next morning, not wishing to attract too much attention, but strolled about the wells again, Breakstone talking to the women in the most ingratiating manner. He was a handsome fellow, this Breakstone, and he had a smile that women liked. They did not frown upon him at Agua Neva because he belonged to the enemy, but exchanged a gay word or two with him, Spanish or Mexican banter as he passed on.

They came to a well at which three women were drawing water for the large jars that they carried on their heads, and these were somewhat unlike the others. They were undoubtedly of Indian blood, Aztec perhaps, or more likely Toltec. They were tall for Mexican women, and it seemed to Phil that they bore themselves with a certain erectness and pride. Their faces were noble and good.

Phil and his comrades drew near. He saw the women glance at them, and he saw the youngest of them look at him several times. She stared with a vague sort of wonder in her eyes, and Phil's heart suddenly began to pound so hard that he grew dizzy. Since the letter, coming out of the unknown and traveling such a vast distance, had found him in the little town of Paris, Kentucky, he had felt at times the power of intuition. Truths burst suddenly upon him, and for the moment he had the conviction that this was the woman. Moreover, she was still looking at him.

"Speak to her, Bill! Speak to her!" he exclaimed. "Don't let her go until you ask her."

But Breakstone had already noticed the curious glances the woman was casting at Phil, and in the Spanish patois of the region he bade them a light and courteous good morning. Here all the charm of Breakstone's manner showed at its very best. No one could take offense at it, and the three women, smiling, replied in a similar vein. Breakstone understood Phil's agitation. The boy might be right, but he did not intend to be too headlong. He must fence and approach the subject gradually. So he spoke of the little things that make conversation, but presently he said to the youngest of the women:

"I see that you notice my comrade, the one who is not yet a man in years, though a man in size. Does it chance that you have seen some one like him?"

"I do not know," replied the woman. "I am looking into my memory that I may see."

"Perhaps," said Breakstone smoothly, "it was one of the Texan prisoners whom they brought through here two or three years ago. A boy, tall and fair like this boy, but dusty with the march, bent with weariness, his feet cut and bleeding by the lava over which he had been forced to march, stood here at this well. He was blindfolded that he might not see which way he had come, but you, the Holy Virgin filling your heart with pity, took the cup of cool water and gave it to him to drink."

Comprehension filled the eyes of the woman, and she gazed at Breakstone with growing wonder.

"It is so!" she exclaimed. "I remember now. It was three years ago. There was a band of prisoners, twelve or fifteen, maybe, but he was the youngest of them all, and so worn, so weak! I could not see his eyes, but he had the figure and manner of the youth who stands there! It was why I looked, and then looked again, the resemblance that I could not remember."

"It is his brother who is with me," said Breakstone. "Can you tell where these prisoners were taken?"

"I do not know, but I have heard that they were carried into the mountains to the south and west, where they were to be held until Texas was brought back to Mexico, or to be put to death as outlaws."

"What prisons lie in these mountains to the south and west?"

"I do not know how many, but we have heard most of the Castle of Montevideo. Some of our own people have gone there, never to come back."

THE WOMAN AT THE WELL

She and her companions shuddered at the name of the Castle of Montevideo. It seemed to have some vague, mysterious terror for them. It was now Bill Breakstone who had the intuition. The Castle of Montevideo was the place. It was there that they had taken John Bedford. He translated clearly for Phil, who became very pale.

"It is the place, Phil," he said. "We must go to the Castle of Montevideo to find him."

He drew from his pocket a large octagonal gold piece, worth fifty dollars, then coined by the United States.

"Give this to her, Bill," he said, "and tell her it is for the drink of water that she gave to the blindfolded boy three years ago."

Bill Breakstone translated literally, and he added:

"You must take it. It comes from his heart. It is not only worth much money, but it will be a bringer of luck to you."

She took it, hesitated a moment, then hid it under her red reboso, and, the jars being filled, she and her two companions walked away, balancing the great weights beautifully on their heads.

"To-night," said Phil, "we ride for the Castle of Montevideo."

CHAPTER XVI

THE CASTLE OF MONTEVIDEO

THE Castle of Montevideo, as its name indicates, commanded a magnificent view. Set in a niche of a mountain which towered far above, it looked down upon and commanded one of the great roads that led to the heart of Mexico, the city that stood in the vale of Tenochtitlan, the capital, in turn, of the Toltecs, the Aztecs, the Spaniards, and the Mexicans, and, for all that men yet knew, of races older than the Toltecs. But the Spaniards had built it, completing it nearly a hundred and fifty years ago, when their hold upon the greater part of the New World seemed secure, and the name of Spain was filled with the suggestion of power.

It was a gloomy and tremendous fortress, standing seven thousand feet above the level of the sea, and having about it, despite its latitude, no indication of the tropics.

Spain had lavished here enormous sums of money dug for her by the slaves of Mexico and Peru. It was built of volcanic pumice stone, very hard, and of the color of dark honey. Its main walls formed an equilateral triangle, eight hundred feet square on the inside, and sixty feet from the top of the wall to the bottom of the enclosing moat. There was a bastion at each corner of the main rampart, and the moat that enveloped the main walls and bastions was two hundred feet wide and twenty feet deep. Fifty feet beyond the outer wall of the moat rose a *chevaux de frise* built of squared cedar logs twelve feet long, set in the ground and fastened together by longitudinal timbers. Beyond the *chevaux de frise* was another

THE CASTLE OF MONTEVIDEO

ditch, fourteen feet wide, of which the outer bank was a high earthwork. The whole square enclosed by the outermost work was twenty-six acres, and on the principal rampart were mounted eighty cannon, commanding the road to the Valley of Tenochtitlan.

Few fortresses, even in the Old World, were more powerful or complete. It enclosed armories, magazines, workshops, and cells; cells in rows, all of which were duly numbered when Montevideo was completed in the eighteenth century. And, to give it the last and happiest touch, the picture of Ferdinand VII., King of Spain, Lord of the Indies and the New World, was painted over the doorway of every cell, and they were many.

Nor is this the full tale of Montevideo. On the inner side of each angle, broad wooden stairways ascended to the top, the stairways themselves being enclosed at intervals by wooden gates twelve feet high. The real fortifications enclosed a square of nearly five hundred feet, and inside this square were the buildings of the officers and the barracks of the soldiers. The floor of the square was paved with thick cement, and deep down under the cement were immense water tanks, holding millions of gallons, fed by subterranean springs of pure cold water. By means of underground tunnels the moats could be flooded with water from the tanks or springs.

It has been said that the Spaniards are massive builders, the most massive since the Romans, and they have left their mark with many a huge stone structure in the southern part of the New World. What Montevideo cost the kings of Spain no one has ever known, and, although they probably paid twice for every stick and stone in it, Peru and Mexico were still pouring forth their floods of treasure, and there was the fortress, honey colored, lofty, undeniably majestic and powerful.

When Mexico displaced Spain, she added to the defenses of Montevideo, and now, on this spring day in 1847, it lowered, dark and sinister, over the road. It was occupied by a strong garrison under that alert and valiant soldier, Captain Pedro de Armijo, raised recently to that rank, but still stinging with the memories of Buena Vista, he was anxious that the Americans should come and attack him in Montevideo. He stood on the rampart at a point where it was seventy feet wide, and he looked with pride and satisfaction at the row of eighty guns. Pedro de Armijo, swelling with pride, felt that he could hold the castle of Montevideo against twenty thousand men. Time had made no impression upon those massive walls, and the moat was filled with water. The castle, mediæval, but grim and formidable, sat in its narrow mountain valley with the Cofre de Montevideo (Trunk of Montevideo) behind it on the north. This peak was frequently covered with snow and at all times was gloomy and forbidding. Even on bright days the sun reached it for only a few hours.

While Pedro de Armijo walked on the parapet, looking out at the range of mountain and valley and enjoying the sunlight, which would soon be gone, a young man stood at the window of cell No. 37, also looking out at the mountain, although no sunlight reached him there. He gazed through a slit four inches wide and twelve inches high, and the solid wall of masonry through which this slit was cut was twelve feet thick. The young man's ankles were tied together with a chain which, although long enough to allow him to walk, weighed twenty-five pounds. Once he had been chained with another man. Formerly the prisoners who had been brought with him to the Castle of Montevideo had been chained in pairs, the chain in no case weighing less than twenty pounds, but, since only John Bedford was left, Pedro de Armijo concluded that it was his duty to carry the chain alone.

John Bedford was white with prison pallor. Although as tall, he weighed many pounds less than his younger brother, Philip. His cheeks were sunken, and his eyes were set in deep hollows. The careless observer would

THE CASTLE OF MONTEVIDEO

have taken him for ten years more than his real age. He had shuffled painfully to the slit in the wall, where he wished to see the last rays of the daylight falling on the mountainside. The depth of the slit made the section of the mountain that he could see very narrow, and he knew every inch of it. There was the big projection of volcanic rock, the tall, malformed cactus that put out a white flower, the little bunch of stunted cedars or pines—he could never tell which—in the shelter of the rock, and the yard or two of gully down which he had seen the water roaring after the big rains or at the melting of the snows on the Cofre de Montevideo.

How often he had looked upon these things! What a little slice of the world it was! Only a few yards long and fewer yards broad, but what a mighty thing it was to him! Even with the slit closed, he could have drawn all of it upon a map to the last twig and pebble. He would have suffered intensely had that little view been withdrawn, but it tantalized him, too, with the sight of the freedom that was denied him. Three years, they told him, he had been gazing out at that narrow slit at the mountainside, and he only at the beginning of life, strong of mind and body—or at least he was. Never in that time had he been outside the inner walls or even in the court yard. He knew nothing of what had happened in the world. Sometimes they told him that Texas had been overrun and retaken by the Mexicans, and he feared that it was true.

They did not always put the chains upon him, but lately he had been refractory. He was easily caught in an attempt to escape, and a new governor of the castle, lately come, a young man extremely arrogant, had demanded his promise that he make no other such attempt. He had refused, and so the chains were ordered. He had worn them many times before, and now they oppressed him far less than his loneliness. He alone of that expedition was left a prisoner in the castle. How all the others had gone he did not know, but he knew that some had escaped. Both he and his comrade of the chains were too ill to walk when the escape was made, and there was nothing to do but leave them behind. His comrade died, and he recovered after weeks, mainly through the efforts of old Catarina, the Indian woman who sometimes brought him his food.

John Bedford's spirits were at the bottom of the depths that afternoon. How could human beings be so cruel as to shut up one of their kind in such a manner, one who was no criminal? It seemed to him that lately the watch in the castle had become more vigilant than ever. More soldiers were about, and he heard vaguely of comings and goings. His mind ran back for the thousandth time over the capture of himself and his comrades.

When taken by an overwhelming force they were one hundred and seventy in number, and there were great rejoicings in Mexico when they were brought southward. They had been blindfolded at some points, once when he walked for a long time on sharp volcanic rock, and once, when, as he was fainting from heat and thirst, a woman with a kind voice had given him a cup of water at a well. He remembered these things very vividly, and he remembered with equal vividness how, when they were not blindfolded, they were led in triumph through the Mexican towns, exactly as prisoners were led to celebrate the glory of a general through the streets of old Rome. They, the "Terrible Texans," as they were called, had passed through triumphal arches decorated with the bright garments of women. Boys and girls, brilliant handkerchiefs bound around their heads, and shaking decorated gourds with pebbles in them, had danced before the captives to the great delight of the spectators. Sometimes women themselves in these triumphal processions had done the zopilote or buzzard dance. At night the prisoners had been forced to sleep in foul cattle sheds.

THE CASTLE OF MONTEVIDEO

Then had come the Day of the Beans. One hundred and fifty-three white beans and seventeen black beans were placed in a bowl, and every prisoner, blindfolded, was forced to draw one. The seventeen who drew the black beans were promptly shot, and the others were compelled to march on. He remembered how lightly they had taken it, even when it was known who had drawn the black beans. These men, mostly young like himself, had jested about their bad luck, and had gone to their death smiling. He did not know how they could do it, but it was so, because he had seen it with his own eyes.

Then they had marched on until they came to the Castle of Montevideo. There the world ended. There was nothing but time, divided into alternations of night and day. He had seen nobody but soldiers, except the old woman Catarina, who seemed to be a sort of scullion. After he recovered from the prison fever of which his comrade of the chains died, the old woman had shown a sort of pity for him; perhaps she liked him as one often likes those upon whom one has conferred benefits. She yielded to his entreaties for a pencil for an hour or so, and some paper, just a sheet or two. She smuggled them to him, and she smuggled away the letter that he wrote. She did not know what would happen, but she would give it to her son Porfirio, who was a vaquero. Porfirio would give it to his friend Antonio Vaquez, who was leading a burro train north to Monterey. After that was the unknown, but who could tell? Antonio Vaquez was a kind man, and the Holy Virgin sometimes worked miracles for the good. As for the poor lad, the prisoner, he must rest now. He had been *muy malo* (very sick), and it was not good to worry.

John tried not to worry. It was such easy advice to give and so very hard for one to take who had been buried alive through a time that seemed eternity, and who had been forgotten by all the world, except his jailers. That letter had gone more than a year ago, and, of course, it had not reached its destination. He ought never to have thought such a thing possible. Very likely it had been destroyed by Porfirio, the vaquero, old Catarina's son. He had not seen old Catarina herself in a long time. Doubtless they had sent her away because she had been kind to him, or they may have found out about the letter. He was very sorry. She was far from young, and she was far from beautiful, but her brief presence at intervals had been cheering.

He watched the last rays of the sun fade on the volcanic slope. A single beam, livid and splendid, lingered for a moment, and then was gone. After it came the dark, with all the chilling power of great elevation. The cold even penetrated the deep slit that led through twelve feet of solid masonry, and John Bedford shivered. It was partly the dark that made him shiver. He rose from the stool and made his way slowly and painfully to his cot against the wall, his chains rattling heavily over the floor.

He heard a key turning in the lock and the door opening, but he did not look around. They usually came with his food at this hour, and the food was always the same. There was no cause for curiosity. But when he heard the steps of two men instead of one he did look around. There was the same soldier bringing his supper of frijoles and tortillas on a tin plate, and a cup of very bad coffee, but he was accompanied by the new governor of the castle, Captain Pedro de Armijo, whom John did not like at all. The soldier drew up the stool, put the food on it, and also a candle that he carried.

John began to eat and drink, taking not the slightest notice of de Armijo. The man from the first had given him the impression of cold, malignant cruelty. John Bedford had often thought that his own spirit was crushed, but it was far from being so. Pride was strong within him, and he resolved that de Armijo should speak first.

THE CASTLE OF MONTEVIDEO

De Armijo stood in silence for some time, looking down at the prisoner. He was not in a good humor, he had seldom been so since that fatal day when the whole army of Santa Anna was hurled back by the little force from the North. He knew many things of which the prisoner did not dream, and he had no thought of giving him even the slightest hint of them. In him was the venomous disposition of the cat that likes to play with the rat it has caught. A curious piece of mockery, or perhaps it was not wholly mockery, had occurred to him.

"Bedford," he said, speaking good English, "you have been a prisoner here a long time, and no one loves captivity."

"I have not heard that any one does," replied John, taking another drink of the bad coffee.

"You cannot escape. You see the impossibility of any such attempt."

"It does not look probable, I admit. Still, few things are impossible."

De Armijo smiled, showing even white teeth. He rather liked this game of playing with the rat in the trap. So much was in favor of the cat.

"It is not a possibility with which one can reckon," he said, "and I should think that the desire to be free would be overpowering in one so young as you."

"Have you come here to make sport of me?" said John, with ominous inflection. "Because if you have I shall not answer another question."

"Not at all," said de Armijo. "I come on business. You have been here, as I said, a long time, and in that time many changes have occurred in the world."

"What changes?" asked John sharply.

"The most important of them is the growth in power of Mexico," said de Armijo smoothly. "We triumph over all our enemies."

"Do you mean that you have really retaken Texas?" asked John, with a sudden falling of the heart.

De Armijo smiled again, then lighted a cigarette and took a puff or two before he gave an answer which was really no answer at all, so far as the words themselves were concerned.

"I said that Mexico had triumphed over her enemies everywhere," he replied, "and so she has, but I give you no details. It has been the order that you know nothing. You have been contumacious and obstinate, and, free, you would be dangerous. So the world was to be closed to you, and it has been done. You know nothing of it except these four walls and the little strip of a mountain that you can see from the window there. You are as one dead."

John Bedford winced. What the Mexican said was true, and he had long known it to be true, but he did not like for de Armijo to say it to him now. His lonesomeness in his long imprisonment had been awful, but not more so than his absolute ignorance of everything beyond his four walls. This policy with him had been pursued persistently. Old Catarina, before her departure, had not dared to tell him anything, and now the soldier who served him would not answer any question at all. He had felt at times that this would reduce him to mental incompetency, to childishness, but he had fought against it, and he had felt at other times that the isolation, instead of weakening his faculties, had sharpened them. But he replied without any show of emotion in his voice:

"What you say is true in the main, but why do you say it."

"In order to lay before you both sides of a proposition. You are practically forgotten here. You can spend the rest of your life in this cell, perish, perhaps, on the very bed where you are now sitting, but you can also release yourself. Take the oath of fealty to Mexico, become a Mexican citizen, join her army and fight her enemies. You might have a career there, you might rise."

THE CASTLE OF MONTEVIDEO

It was a fiendish suggestion to one who knew nothing of what was passing, and de Armijo prided himself upon his finesse. To compel brother to fight against brother would indeed be a master stroke. He did not notice the rising blood in the face before him, that had so long borne the prison pallor.

"Have you reconquered Texas?" asked John sharply.

"What has that to do with it?"

"Do you think I would join you and fight against the Texans? Do you think I would join you anyhow, after I've been fighting against you? I'd rather rot here than do such a thing, and it seems strange that you, an officer and the governor of this castle, should make such an offer. It's dishonest!"

Blood flashed through de Armijo's dark face, and he raised his hand in menace. John Bedford instantly struck at him with all his might, which was not great, wasted as he was by prison confinement. De Armijo stepped back a little, drew his sword, and, with the flat of it, struck the prisoner a severe blow across the forehead. John had attempted to spring forward, but twenty-five pounds of iron chain confining his ankles held him. He could not ward off the blow, and he dropped back against the cot, bleeding and unconscious.

When John Bedford recovered his senses he was lying on the cot, and it was pitch dark, save for a slender shaft of moonlight that entered at the slit, and that lay like a sword-blade across the floor. His head throbbed, and when he put his hand to it he found that it was swathed in bandages. He remembered the blow perfectly, and he moved his feet, but the chains had been taken off. They had had the grace to do that much. He strove to rise, but he was very weak, and the throbbing in his head increased. Then he lay still for a long time, watching the moonbeam that fell across the floor. He was in a state of mind far from pleasant. To be shut up so long is inevitably to grow bitter, and to be struck down thus by de Armijo, while he was chained and helpless, was an injury to both body and mind that he could never forgive. He had nothing to do in his cell to distract his mind from grievous wrongs, and there was no chance for them to fade from his memory. His very soul rose in wrath against de Armijo.

He judged that it was far in the night, and, after lying perfectly still for about an hour, he rose from the bed. His strength had increased, and the throbbing in his head was not so painful. He staggered across the floor and put his face to the slit in the wall. The cold air, as it rushed against his eyes and cheeks, felt very good. It was spring in the lowlands, but there was snow yet on the peak behind the Castle of Montevideo, and winter had not yet wholly left the valley in which the castle itself stood. But the air was not too cold for John, whose brain at this moment was hotter than his blood.

The night was uncommonly clear. One could see almost as well as by day, and he began to look over, one by one, the little objects that his view commanded on the mountainside. He looked at every intimate friend, the various rocks, the cactus, the gully, and the dwarfed shrubs—he still wished to know whether they were pines or cedars, the problem had long annoyed him greatly. He surveyed his little landscape with great care. It seemed to him that he saw touches of spring there, and then he was quite sure that he saw the figure of a man, dark and shadowy, but, nevertheless, a human figure, pass across the little space. It was followed in a moment by a second, and then by a third. It caused him surprise and interest. His tiny landscape was steep, and he had never before seen men cross it. Hunters, or perhaps goat herders, but it was strange that they should be traveling along such a steep mountainside at such an hour.

A person under ordinary conditions would have forgotten the incident in five minutes, but this was an event in the life of the lonely captive. Save his encounter with

THE CASTLE OF MONTEVIDEO

de Armijo, he could not recall another of so much importance in many months. He stayed at the loophole a long time, but he did not see the figures again nor anything else living. Once, about a month before, he had caught a glimpse of a deer there, and it had filled him with excitement, because to see even a deer was a great thing, but this was a greater. He remained at the loophole until the rocks began to redden with the morning sun, but his little landscape remained as it had ever been, the same rocks, the same pines or cedars—which, in Heaven's name, were they?—and the same cactus.

Then he walked slowly back to his cot. The chains were lying on the floor beside it, and he knew that, in time, they would be put on him again, but he was resolved not to abate his independence a particle. Nor would he defer in any way to de Armijo. If he came again he would speak his opinion of him to his face, let him do what he would.

There was proud and stubborn blood in every vein of the Bedfords. John Bedford's grandfather had been one of the most noted of Kentucky's pioneers and Indian fighters, and on his mother's side, too, there was a strain of tenacious New England. By some possible chance he might be able to return de Armijo's blow. He drew the cover over his body and fell into a sleep from which he was awakened by the slovenly soldier with his breakfast. The man did not speak while John ate, and John was glad of it. He, too, had nothing to say, and he wished to be left to himself. When the man left he lay down on the cot again and slept until nearly noon. Then de Armijo came a second time. He had no apologies whatever for the manner in which he had struck down an unarmed prisoner, but was hard and sneering.

"I merely tell you," he said, "that you lost your last chance yesterday. The offer will not be repeated."

John said not a word, but gazed at him so steadily that the Mexican's swarthy face flushed a little. He hesitated, as if he would say something, but evidently thought better of it, and went out. That night he had a fever from his wounded head and the exertion that he had made in standing so long at the loophole. He became delirious, and when he emerged from his delirium a little weazened old Indian woman was sitting by the side of his cot. She had kindly and pitying eyes, and John exclaimed, in a weak but joyous voice:

"Catarina!"

"Poor boy," she said, "I have watched you one day and one night."

"Where have you been all the time before?" he asked in the Mexican dialect that he had learned.

"I have been one of the cooks," she said. "The officers, they eat so much, tortillas, frijoles, everything, and they drink so much, mescal, pulque, wine, everything. Many busy months for Catarina, and I ask for you, but I cannot see you. They say you bad, very bad. Then they say you try to kill the governor, Captain de Armijo, but he strike you on the head with the flat of his sword to save his own life. You have fever, and at last they send me to nurse you as I did that other time."

"Do you believe, Catarina, that I tried to kill de Armijo?" asked John.

She looked about her fearfully, drew the reboso closely across her shrunken shoulders, and answered in a frightened tone as if the thick walls themselves could hear:

"How should I know? It is what they say. If I should say otherwise they would lash me with the whip, even me, old Catarina."

The captive sighed. Nothing could break the awful wall of mystery that enveloped him. Catarina even did not dare to speak, although no one but himself could possibly hear.

"You mind I smoke?" said Catarina.

"No," replied John with a wan smile. "Any lady can smoke in my presence."

THE CASTLE OF MONTEVIDEO

She whipped out a cigarrito, lighted it with a match, held it for a moment between the middle and fore finger, then inserted it between her aged lips. She took two or three long, easy whiffs, letting the smoke come out through her nose. John had never learned to smoke, but he said to her:

"Does it do you good, Catarina?"

"Whether it does me good, I know not," replied the Indian woman, "but it gives me pleasure, so I do it. I have to tell you, Señor John, that my son, Porfirio, has returned from the north. He has been at Monterey and the country about it."

John at once was all eagerness.

"And Antonio Vaquez, the leader of the burro train?" he exclaimed. "Has he heard from him? Does he know if the letter went on beyond the Rio Grande?"

"My son Porfirio has not seen Antonio Vaquez," replied Catarina, "and so he does not know from Antonio Vaquez whether the letter has crossed the Rio Grande or not. But it is a time of change."

"De Armijo told me that."

The old woman looked at him very keenly, and drove more smoke of the cigarrito through her nose. Her next words made no reference to de Armijo, but they startled John:

"You look through the loophole to-night, about midnight," she said. "You see something on the mountain side, fire, a torch, it may mean much. Who can tell?"

Excitement flamed up again in John's veins.

"What do you mean, Catarina?" he exclaimed. "Last night I crawled to the loophole for air. It was bright moonlight, and while I was standing there I thought three human beings passed on the little patch of the mountainside that I can see."

"It is all I know," said Catarina. "I can tell you no more. Now I am *concinero* (cook) again. Now I go. But watch. There have been many changes. Diego, the soldier, will bring you your food as before. Watch that, too."

"Poison!" exclaimed John aghast.

"No! No! No! *Hai Dios* (my God), no! But do as I say!"

She snuffed out the end of the cigarrito, picked up the dishes, and promptly left the cell. She also left the captive much excited and wondering. De Armijo had said there were changes! Truly there had been changes, said Catarina, but she had not told what they were. He made many surmises, and one was as good as another, even to himself. Let a man cut three years out of his life and see if he can span the gulf between. But he was sure, despite his ignorance of their nature, that Catarina's words were full of meaning, and, perhaps among all the great changes that had come, one was coming for him, too.

He slept that afternoon in order that he might be sure to keep awake at night, and long before midnight he was on watch at the loophole. There was still soreness in his head, where the flat of the heavy steel blade had struck, but it was passing away, and his strength was returning. It is hard to crush youth. It was now easier for him, too, as the chains had not been put back upon his ankles.

He waited with great impatience, and, as his impatience increased, time became slower. He began to feel that he was foolish. But Catarina had been good to him. She would not make him keep an idle quest in the long cold hours of the night. And he had seen the three shadows pass the night before. He was sure now from what Catarina had said that they were the shadows of human beings, and their presence there had been significant.

The night was not so bright as the one before, but, by long looking, he could trace the details of his landscape, all the well known objects, every one in its proper place, with the dusky moonlight falling upon them. He stared so long that his eyes ached. Surely Catarina had been talking foolish talk! No, she had not! His heart stopped beating for a few moments, because, as certainly as he was at that loophole, a light had appeared on his bit of landscape. It was but a spark. A spark only at first, but in a moment or two it blazed up like a torch. It showed a vivid red streak against the mountainside, and the heart of the captive, that had stood still for a few moments, now bounded rapidly. The words of Catarina had come true, and he had had a sign. But what did the sign mean? It must be connected in some way with him, and nothing could be worse than that which he now endured. It must mean good.

It was a veritable flame of hope to John Bedford, the prisoner of the Castle of Montevideo. New strength suffused his whole body. Courage came back to him in a full tide. A sign had been promised to him, and it had come.

The light burned for about half an hour, and then went out suddenly. John Bedford returned to his cot, a new hope in his heart.

CHAPTER XVII

THE THREAD, THE KEY, AND THE DAGGER

WHEN John Bedford rose the next morning he was several years younger. He held himself erect, as became his youth, a little color had crept into the pallid face, and his heart was still full of hope. He had seen the light that Catarina had promised. Surely the world was making a great change for him, and he reasoned again that, his present state being so low, any possible change must be for the better.

But the day passed and nothing happened. Diego, the slouching soldier, brought him his food, and, bearing in mind the vague words of Catarina, he noticed it carefully while he ate. There was nothing unusual. It was the same at his supper. The rosy cloud in which his hopes swam faded somewhat, but he was still hopeful. No light had been promised for the second night, but he watched for long hours, nevertheless, and he could not restrain a sense of disappointment when he turned away.

A second day passed without event, and a third, and then a fourth. John Bedford was overcome by a terrible depression. Catarina was old and foolish, or perhaps she, too, had shown at last the cunning and trickery that he began to ascribe to all these people. He would stay in that cell all his life, fairly buried alive. A fierce, unreasoning anger took hold of him. He would have flared out at stolid Diego who brought the food, but he did not want those heavy chains put back on his ankles. His head was now healed enough for the removal of the bandage, but a red streak would remain for some time under the hair. Doubtless the hair had saved him from a fracture of the skull. Every time he put his hand to the wound, which was often, his anger against de Armijo rose. It was that cold, silent anger which is the most terrible and lasting of all.

Although he was back in the depths, John felt that the brief spell of hope had been of help to him. His wound had healed more rapidly, and he was sure that he was physically stronger. Yet the black depression remained. It was even painful for him to look through the slit at his piece of the slope, which he sometimes called his mountain garden. He avoided it, as a place of hope that had failed. On the sixth day, Diego brought him his dinner a little after the dinner hour. He was sitting on the edge of his cot and he bit into a tamale. His teeth encountered something tough and fibrous, and he was about to throw it down in disgust. Then the words of Catarina, those words which he had begun to despise, came suddenly back to him. He put the tamale down and began to eat a tortilla, keeping his eye on Diego, who slouched by the wall in the attitude of a Mexican of the lower classes, that lazy, dreaming attitude that they can maintain, for hours.

Presently Diego glanced at the loophole, and in an instant John whipped the tamale off the plate and thrust it under the cover of the cot. Then he went on calmly with his eating, and drank the usual amount of bad coffee. Diego, who had noticed nothing, took the empty tray and went out, carefully locking the heavy door behind him. Then John Bedford did something that showed his wonderful power of self-restraint. He did not rush to the bed, eager to read what the tamale might contain, but strolled to the loophole and looked out for at least a quarter of an hour. He did not wish any trick to be played upon him by a sudden return of Diego. Yet he was quivering in every nerve with impatience.

When he felt that he was safe, he returned to the cot

and took out the tamale. He carefully pulled it open, and in the middle he found the tough, fibrous substance that his teeth had met. He had half expected a paper of some kind, rolled closely together, that the writing might not perish, and what he really did find caused a disappointment so keen that he uttered a low cry of pain.

He held it up in his hand. It was nothing more than a small package of thread, such as might have been put in a thimble. What could it mean? Of what possible use was a coil of fifty yards or so of thread that would not sustain the weight of half a pound? Was he to escape through the loophole on that as a rope? He looked at the loophole four inches broad, and then at the tiny thread, and it seemed to him such a pitiful joke that he sat down on the cot and laughed, not at the joke itself, but at any one who was foolish enough to perpetrate such a thing.

He tested the thread. It was stronger than he had thought. Then he put it on his knee, took his head in his two hands, and sat staring at the thread for a long time, concentrating his thoughts and trying to evolve something from this riddle. It *did* mean something. No one would go to so much trouble to play a miserable joke on a helpless captive like himself. Catarina certainly would not do it, and she had given him the hint about the food, a hint that had come true. He kept his mind upon the one point so steadily and with so much force that his brain grew hot, and the wound, so nearly cured, began to ache again. Yet he kept at it, studying out every possible twist and turn of the riddle. At last he tested the thread again. It was undeniably strong, and then he looked at the loophole. Only one guess savored of possibility. He must hang the thread out of the loophole.

He ate the rest of the tamale, hid the little package under his clothing, and at night, after supper, when the darkness was heavy, he threw the end of the thread through the long slot, a cast in which he did not succeed

THE THREAD, THE KEY, AND THE DAGGER

until about the twelfth attempt. Then he let the thread drop down. He knew about how many feet it was to the pavement below, and he let out enough with three or four yards for good count. Then he found that he had several yards left, which he tied around one of the iron bars at the edge of the loophole. It was a black thread, and, although some one might see it by daylight, there was not one chance in a thousand that any one would see it at night.

"Fishing," he said to himself, as he lay down on his cot, intending to sleep awhile, but to draw in the thread before the day came. It might be an idle guess, he could not even know that the thread was not clinging to the stone wall, instead of reaching the ground, but there was relief in action, in trying something. He fell asleep finally, and when he awoke he sprang in an instant to the floor. The fear came with his waking senses that he might have slept too long, and that it was broad daylight. The fear was false. It was still night, with only the moon shining at the loophole. But he judged that most of the night had passed, and his impatience told him that if anything was going to happen it had happened already. He went to the window. His thread was there, tied to the bar and, like a fisherman, he began to pull it in. He felt this simile himself. "Drawing in the line," he murmured. "Now I wonder if I have got a bite."

Although he spoke lightly to himself, as if a calm man would soothe an excitable one, he felt the cold chill that runs down one's spine in moments of intense excitement. The moonlight was good, and he watched the black thread come in, inch by inch, while the hand that drew it trembled. But he soon saw that there was no weight at the other end, and down his heart went again into the blackest depths of black despair. Nevertheless, he continued to pull on the thread, and, as it emerged from the darkness into the far end of the loophole, he thought he saw something tied on the end, although he was not sure, it looked so small and dim. Here he paused and leaned against the wall, because he suddenly felt weak in both mind and body. These alternations between hope and despair were shattering to one who had been confined so long between four walls. The very strength of his desire for it might make him see something at the end of the thread when nothing was really there.

He recovered himself and pulled in the thread, and now hope surged up in a full tide. Something was on the end of the thread. It was a little piece of paper not more than an inch long, rolled closely and tied tightly around the center with the thread. He drew up his stool and sat down on it by the loophole, where the moonlight fell. Then he carefully picked loose the knot and unrolled the paper. The light was good enough, and he read these amazing words:

> "Don't give up hope.
> Your brother is here.
> He received your letter.
> Put out the thread
> Again to-morrow night.
> Read and destroy this."

John leaned against the wall. His surprise and joy were so great that he was overpowered. He realized now that his hope had merely been a forlorn one, an effort of the will against spontaneous despair. And yet the miracle had been wrought. His letter, in some mysterious manner, had got through to Phil, and Phil had come. He must have friends, too, because the letter had not been written by Phil. It was in a strange handwriting. But this could be no joke of fate. It was too powerful, too convincing Everything fitted too well together. It must have started somehow with Catarina, because all her presages had come true. She was the cook, she had put the thread in the tamale. How had the others reached her?

THE THREAD, THE KEY, AND THE DAGGER

But it was true. His letter had gone through, and the brave young boy whom he had left behind had come. He was somewhere about the Castle of Montevideo, and since such wonders had been achieved already, others could be done. From that moment John Bedford never despaired. After reading the letter many times, he tore it into minute fragments, and, lest they should be seen below and create suspicion, he ate them all and with a good appetite. Then he rolled up the thread, put it next to his body, and, for the first time in many nights, slept so soundly that he did not awake until Diego brought him his breakfast. Then he ate with a remarkable appetite, and after Diego had gone he began to walk up and down the cell with vigorous steps. He also did many other things which an observer, had one been possible, would have thought strange.

John not only walked back and forth in his cell, but he went through as many exercises as his lack of gymnastic equipment permitted, and he continued his work at least an hour. He wished to get back his strength as much as possible for some great test that he felt sure was coming. If he were to escape with the help of Phil and unknown others, he must be strong and active. A weakling would have a poor chance, no matter how numerous his friends. He had maintained this form of exercise for a long period after his imprisonment, but lately he had become so much depressed that he had discontinued it.

He felt so good that he chaffed Diego when he came back with his food at dinner and supper. Diego had long been a source of wonder to John. It was evident that he breathed and walked, because John had seen him do both, and he could speak, because at rare intervals John had heard him utter a word or two, but this power of speech seemed to be merely spasmodic. Now, while John bantered him, he was as stolid as any wooden image of Aztecs or Toltecs, although John spoke in Spanish, which, bad as it was Diego could understand.

He devoted the last hours of the afternoon to watching his distant garden. It had always been a pleasant landscape to him, but now it was friendlier than ever. That was a fine cactus, and it was a noble forest of dwarf pine or cedar—he wished he did know which. An hour after the dark had fully come he let the thread out again.

"This beats any other fishing I ever did," he murmured. "Well, it ought to. It's fishing for one's life."

He was calmer than on the night before, and fell asleep earlier, but he had fixed his mind so resolutely on a waking time at least an hour before daylight that he awoke almost at the appointed minute. Then he tiptoed across the cold floor to the thread. Nobody could have heard him through those solid walls, but the desire for secrecy was so strong that he unconsciously tiptoed, nevertheless. He pulled the thread, and he felt at once that something heavy had been fastened to the other end. Then he pulled more slowly. The thread was very slender, and the weight seemed great for so slight a line. If it were to break, the tragedy would be genuinely terrible. He had heard of the sword suspended by a single hair, and it seemed to him that he was in some such case. But the thread was stronger than John realized—it had been chosen so on purpose—and it did not break.

As the far end of the thread approached the loophole, he was conscious of a slight metallic ring against the stone wall. His interest grew in intensity. Phil and these unknown friends of his were sending him something more than a note. He pulled with exceeding slowness and care now, lest the metallic object hook against the far edge of the loophole. But it came in safely, slid across the stone, and reached his hand. It was a large iron key, with a small piece of paper tied around it. He tore off the paper, and read, in a handwriting the same as that on the first one:

"This is the key to your cell, No. 37, but do not use it. Do not even put it in the lock until the fourth night from to-night. Then at midnight, as nearly as you can judge, unlock and go out. Let out the thread for the last time to-morrow night."

John looked at the key and glanced longingly at the lock. He had no doubt that it would fit. But he obeyed orders and did not try it. Instead he thrust it into the old ragged mattress of his cot. He resumed his physical exercises the next day, giving an hour to them in the morning and another hour in the afternoon. They helped, but the breath of hope was doing more for him, both mind and body, than anything else. He felt so strong and active that he did not chaff Diego any more lest the Mexican, stolid and wooden though he was, might suspect something.

He let out the thread according to orders, and, at the usual time, drew in a dagger, slender and very light, but long and keen as a razor. He read readily the purpose of this. There would be much danger when he opened the door to go out, and he must have a weapon. He ran his finger along the keen edge and saw that it would be truly formidable at close quarters. Then he hid it in his mattress with the key, wound up the thread, and put it in the same place. All had now come to pass as promised, and he felt that the remainder would depend greatly upon himself. So he settled down as best he could to three days and nights of almost intolerable waiting. Dull and heavy as the time was, and surely every second was a minute, many fears also came with it. They might take it into their heads to change that ragged old mattress of his, and then the knife, the thread, and the key would be found. He would dismiss such apprehensions with the power of reason, but the power of fear would bring them back again. Too much now depended upon his freedom from examination and search to allow of a calm mind.

Yet time passed, no matter how slow, and he was helped greatly by his physical exercises, which gave him occupation, besides preparing him for an expected ordeal.

THE QUEST OF THE FOUR

Hope, too, was doing its great work. He could fairly feel the strength flowing back into his veins, and his nerves becoming tougher and more supple. Every night he looked out at the mountain slope and itemized his little garden there that he had never touched, shrub by shrub, stone by stone, not forgetting the great cactus. He told himself that he did not expect to see any light there again, because the unknown sender of messages had not spoken of another, but, deep down at the bottom of his heart, he was hoping to behold the torch once more, and he felt disappointment when it did not appear.

He tried to imagine how Phil looked. He knew that he must be a great, strong boy, as big as a man. He knew that his spirit was bold and enterprising, yet he must have had uncommon skill and fortune to have penetrated so deep into Mexico, and to preserve a hiding-place so near to the great Castle of Montevideo. And the friends with him must be molded of the finest steel. Who were they? He recalled daring and adventurous spirits among his own comrades in the fatal expedition, but as he ran over every one in his mind he shook his head. It could not be.

It is the truth that, during all this period, inflicting such a tremendous strain upon the captive, John never once tried the key in the door. It was the supreme test of his character, of his restraint, of his power of will, and he passed it successfully. The thread, the dagger, and the key lay together untouched in the bottom of the old mattress, and he waited in all the outward seeming of patience.

The first night was very clear, on the second it rained for six or seven hours. The entire mountainside was veiled in sheets of water or vapor, and John saw nothing beyond his window but the black blur. The third night was clear, but when the morning of the fourth day dawned, John thought, from the clouds that were floating along the mountain slope, it would be rainy again. He

THE THREAD, THE KEY, AND THE DAGGER

hoped that the promise would come true. Darkness and rain favor an escaping prisoner.

The last day was the most terrible of all. Now and then he found his heart pounding as if it would rack itself to pieces. It was difficult to go through with the exercises, and it was still more difficult to preserve calmness of manner in the presence of Diego. Yet he did both. Moreover, his natural steadiness seemed to come back to him as the hour drew near. His was one of those rare and fortunate natures which may be nervous and apprehensive some time before the event, but which become hard and firm when it is at hand. Now John found himself singularly calm. The eternity of waiting had passed, and he was strong and ready.

Diego brought him his supper early, and then, through his loophole, he watched the twilight deepen into the night. And with the night came the rain that the morning and afternoon clouds had predicted. It was a cold rain, driven by a wind that shrieked down the valley, and drops of it, hurled like shot the full width of the slit, struck John in the face. But he liked the cool sharp touch, and he felt sure that the rain would continue all through the night. So much the better.

John's clothing was old and ragged, and he wore a pair of heelless Mexican shoes. He had no hat or cap. But a prisoner of three lonely years seeking to escape was not likely to think of such things.

He waited patiently through these last hours. He was compelled to judge for himself when midnight had come, but he believed that he had made a close calculation. Then he took a final look through the loophole. The wind, with a mighty groaning and shrieking, was still driving the rain down the slopes, and nothing was visible. Then, with a firm hand, he took from the bed the thread, the knife, and the key. It was not likely that he would have any further use for the thread, but for the sake of precaution he put it in his pocket. He also slipped the dagger into the back of his coat at the neck, after a southwestern fashion which allowed a man to draw and strike with a single motion.

Then, key in hand, he boldly approached the door. Some throbbings of doubt appeared, but he sternly repressed them. Giving himself no time for hesitation, he put the key in the lock and turned his hand toward the right. The key, without any creaking or scraping, turned with it. His heart gave a great leap. He did not know until now that he had really doubted. His joy at the fact showed it. But the miracles were coming true, one after another.

He turned the key around the proper distance, and he heard the heavy bolt slide back. He knew that he would have nothing to do now but pull on the door, yet he paused a few moments as one lingers over a great pleasure, in order to make it greater. He pulled, and the door came back with the same familiar slight creak that he had heard it make so often when Diego entered or left. With an involuntary gesture of one hand, he bade farewell to his cell and stepped into the long, dark corridor upon which the row of cells opened. But for the sake of precaution he locked the cell door again and put the key in his pocket.

Then he drew the slender dagger, clutched it firmly in his right hand, and stepped softly back against the wall, which was in heavy shadow, no light entering it from the narrow barred window at either end. John's heart beat painfully, but he did not believe that the miracles which were being done in his behalf had yet ended. With his back still toward the wall, and his hand on the hilt of the dagger, he slipped soundlessly along for a few feet. His eyes, growing used to the darkness, made out the posts at the head of a stairway.

Evidently this was the way he should go, and he paused again. Then his blood slowly chilled within him. A human figure was standing beside one of the posts. He saw it distinctly. It was the figure of a tall man in a long black serape, with a dark handkerchief tied around mouth and chin after the frequent Mexican fashion, and a great sombrero which nearly met the handkerchief. He could see nothing but the narrowest strip of dark face, and in the dusk the man rose to the size of a giant. He was truly a formidable figure to one who had been three years a captive, to one who was armed only with a slender knife.

But the crisis in John Bedford's life was so great that he advanced straight toward the ominous presence in his path. The man said nothing, but John felt as he approached that the stranger was regarding him steadily. Moreover, he made no motion to draw a weapon. John saw now that one of his hands rested on the post at the stairhead, and the other hung straight down by his side. Surely this was not the attitude of a foe! Perhaps here was merely another in the chain of miracles that had begun to work in his behalf. He advanced a step or two nearer, and the stranger was yet motionless. Another step, and the man spoke in a sharp whisper:

"You are John Bedford?"

"I am," replied John.

"I've been waiting for you. Come. But first take this."

He drew a double-barreled pistol from his pocket and handed it to John, who did as he was told. The stranger then produced from under his capacious serape another serape and a Mexican hat, which John, acting under his instructions, also put on.

"Now," said the man, "follow me, and do what I do or what I tell you."

>"It is the midnight hour,
> They wait us at the gate.
> May Heaven its favors pour,
> Then easy is our fate.

You seem to be a brave fellow like your brother; then

now is the time to show your courage, and remember, also, that I can do all the talking for both of us. Talking is my great specialty."

It seemed to John that the stranger spoke in an odd manner, but he liked the sound of his voice, which was at once strong and kind. Why should he not like a man who had come through every imaginable danger to save him from a living death!

"My brother?" whispered John in his eagerness. "Is he still near?"

"I told you I was to do all the talking," replied the man. "You just follow and step as lightly as you can."

John obeyed, and, after a descent of a few steps, they came to one of the heavy wooden doors, twelve feet high, but the stranger unlocked it with a key taken from the folds of that invaluable Mexican garment, the serape.

"You didn't think I'd come on such a trip as this without making full preparations?" said the man with a slight humorous inflection. Then he added: "You're just a plain, common Mexican, some servant or other, employed about the castle, and you continue to slouch along behind me, who may be an officer for all one knows in this darkness. But first push with me on this door. Push hard and push slowly."

The heavy door moved back a foot or two, but that was all the stranger wanted. He slipped through the opening, and John came after him. Then the man closed and locked the door again.

"A wise burglar leaves no trail behind him," he said, "and, although it is too dark for me to see you very well, I want to tell you, Sir John of the Cell, that your figure and walk remind me a great deal of your brother, Sir Philip of the Mountain, the River, and the Plain, as gallant a lad as one may meet in many a long day."

A question, a half dozen of them leaped to John's lips, but, remembering his orders, he checked them all there.

THE THREAD, THE KEY, AND THE DAGGER

"Ah, I see," said the stranger. "That would certainly tempt any man to ask questions, but, remembering what I told you, you did not ask them. You are of the true metal.

> "Though in prison he lay,
> His spirit was strong,
> He sought a better day,
> And now it's come along.

At least it's a better night, which, for the uses of poetry, is the same as day. This stairway, John, leads into the great inner court, and then our troubles begin, although we ought to return thanks all the rest of our days for the rain and the heavy darkness. The Mexican officers will see no reason why they shouldn't remain under shelter, and the Mexican soldiers, in this case, will be glad enough to do as their officers do."

John now followed his guide with absolute faith. The man spoke more queerly than anybody else that he had ever heard, but everything that he did or said inspired confidence.

They came to the bottom of the stairway and reached the great paved central court, with the buildings of the officers scattered here and there. They stepped into the court, and John fairly shrank within himself when the cold rain lashed into his face. He did not know until then how three years within massive walls had softened and weakened him. But he held himself erect and tautened his nerves, resolved that his comrade should not see that he had shivered.

They saw lights shining from the windows of some of the low buildings, but no human being was visible within the square.

"They've all sought cover," said his rescuer, "and now is our best chance to get through one of the gates. After that there are other walls and ditches to be passed, but, Sir John of the Night, the Wall, the Rain, and the

Moat, we'll pass them. This little plan of ours has been too well laid to go astray. Just the same, you keep that pistol handy."

John drew the serape about his thin body. It was useful for other things than disguise. Without it the cold would have struck him to the bone. His rescuer led the way across the court until they came to one of the great gates in the wall. The sentinel then was pacing back and forth, his musket on his shoulder, and at intervals he called: "Sentinela alerte!" that his comrades at other gates might hear, and out of the wind and rain came at intervals, though faintly, the responding cry, "Sentinela alerte!" John and the stranger were almost upon this man when the cry "Sentinela alerte!" came from the next gate. He turned quickly as the two dark figures emerged from the darker gloom, but the stranger, with extraordinary dexterity, threw his serape over his face, checking any cry, while his powerful hands choked him into insensibility. At the same time the stranger uttered the answering cry, "Sentinela alerte!"

"You haven't killed him?" exclaimed John, aghast, as his rescuer let the Mexican slide to the wet earth.

"Not at all," replied this resourceful man. "The cold rain will bring him back to his senses in five minutes and in ten minutes he will be as well as ever, but in ten minutes we should play our hand, if we ever play it."

He drew an enormous key from the pocket of the Mexican, unlocked the gate, and, after they had passed out, locked it behind them. Then they stood on the edge of the great moat, two hundred feet wide, twenty feet deep and bank full. The man dropped the key into the water.

"Now, Sir John of the Escape," he said, "the drawbridge is up, and if it were down it would be too well guarded for us to pass. We must swim. I don't know how strong you are after a long life in prison, but swim

THE THREAD, THE KEY, AND THE DAGGER

you must. Life is dear, and I think you'll swim. We'll take off most of our clothes and tie them with our weapons on our heads. What a wild night! But how good it is for us!"

Crouching in the shadow of the wall they took off most of their clothes, and then each tied them in a package containing his weapons, also, on his head. They were secured with strips torn from John's rags. Meanwhile, the night was increasing in wildness. John would have viewed it with awe, had not his escape absorbed every thought. The wind groaned through the gorges of the great Sierra, and the cold rain lashed like a whip. The rumblings of thunder came from far and deep valleys between the ridges.

"Now," said the man, "we'll drop into the moat together. But let yourself down by your hands as gently as you can, and make no splash when you strike. Now, over we go!"

The two dropped into the water, taking care not to go under, and then began to swim toward the far edge of the moat. John had been a good swimmer, but the water was very cold to his thin body. Nevertheless, he swam with a fairly steady stroke, until they were about halfway across, when he felt cramps creeping over him. But the stranger, who kept close by his side, had been watching, and he put one hand under John's body. In water the light support became a strong one, and now John swam easily.

They reached the far edge and climbed up on the wall. Here John lay a little while, gasping, while the stranger, who now seemed a very god to him, rubbed his cold body to bring back the warmth. From a point down the bank came the cry "Sentinela alerte!" and from a point in the other direction came the answering cry, "Sentinela alerte!"

"Lie flat," whispered his rescuer to John, "and we'll wriggle across fifty feet of ground here until we come to a wooden wall. We're lost if we stand up, because I think lightning is coming with that thunder."

He spoke with knowledge, as the thunder suddenly grew louder and the air around them was tinted with phosphorescent light. It was not a flare of lightning, merely its distant reflection, but it was enough to have disclosed them, if they had been standing, to any one ten paces distant. The danger itself gave them new strength, and they quickly crossed the ground to the *chevaux de frise*, where they crouched against the tall cedar posts. They lay almost flat upon the ground, and they were very glad of the shelter, because the lightning was coming nearer. Now, when the lightning flashed along the mountain slopes, they saw not far away the dim figure of a soldier, and they heard distinctly his cry: "Sentinela alerte!"

"Wait until he goes back," whispered the stranger. "Then we must climb the wall and climb it quickly. It's fastened with cross timbers which will give us hold for both hand and foot."

The lightning tinted the sky once more with its phosphorescent gleam, and they did not see the soldier.

"Now for it!" said the man in a sharp, commanding whisper. "Up with you and over the wall!"

John seized the crosspiece, and in another instant was on the top of a wall of cedar posts twelve feet high. He did not know until afterward that the strong hand of his rescuer had helped him up. In another instant the man was beside him, and then the lightning flared brightly, showing vividly the huge castle, the stone ramparts, the moats and the two figures, naked to the waist, sitting on top of the cedar wall.

"Sentinela alerte!" was shouted far louder than usual, and "Sentinela alerte!" came the reply in the same tone. Two musket shots were fired, and the two figures, one with a red stain on his side, sprang outward from the cedar fence into the second and smaller moat, which was only fourteen feet wide, although its outer wall was an earthwork rising very high above the water. Two or three strong strokes carried them across, and with desperate efforts they climbed up the high bank. They heard shouts, and they knew that when the lightning flared again more shots would be fired at them. It was then that John noticed the red stain on the side of his comrade, and all the reserves of mental strength that made him so much like his brother, Philip, came to his aid. He snatched the package from his head, tore it apart, threw the serape around his body and stood up, erect and defiant, pistol in hand. He would do something for this man who had done so much for him.

The lightning flared again, a long quivering stroke, and the heads of half a dozen men appeared at the crest of the *chevaux de frise*, not twenty feet away. But John Bedford looked at only one of them. He saw the swarthy, angry face of de Armijo. He seemed to be beckoning with his sword to his men, but a flash like that of the lightning seared John's whole brain. He remembered how this man had struck him down, when he was chained and helpless, and he fired point blank at the angry face. De Armijo fell back with a terrible cry. He was not dead, but the bullet had plowed full length across his cheek, and he would bear there a terrible red weal all the rest of his life.

The lightning passed, and they were in complete darkness, but John felt a hand on his arm.

"Come," whispered his rescuer. "You did that well. Prison hasn't taken any of the manhood from you. We're outside everything now, and the others are waiting for us."

They fled away together in the darkness.

CHAPTER XVIII

THE HUT IN THE COVE

JOHN BEDFORD forgot everything in those moments of wild exultation save the fact that he was free. The miracles had begun, and the whole chain was now complete. After three years in one cell he had left behind him forever, as he believed, the Castle of Montevideo, and he was going straight to his brother and powerful friends. He cast back only a single look, and then he saw the huge dim bulk of the castle showing through the mists and the rain. But presently the woods shut it from view, and he could not have seen it had he looked again. John's exultation, the vast rebound, grew. He had escaped, and he had struck down the enemy who had struck him. He felt equal to anything, and he forgot for the moment that the man who had rescued him in such an extraordinary way was wounded. But the man himself stopped soon.

"We'll wait here, Sir John of the Fleet Foot," he said. "Our friends who are frolicking in this thorny Forest of Arden were to come if they heard the sound of firing, and we must not go far away lest we miss them. Truly that was a fine and timely shot of yours, Sir John of the Bold Escape, and I judged by the look of your face that you had no love for the man at whom you fired."

"I did not," replied John. "He beat me, when I was in chains."

The other man uttered a low whistle.

THE HUT IN THE COVE

"That was a nasty thing to do, but you are even. If he's still alive he'll have a face that will scare a dog.

> "Whate'er you do
> Unto another,
> Some day that other
> Will do unto you.

"Bear that in mind, young sir. In the hour of triumph do not rejoice too much in the fall of the man who has failed, because when he achieves his triumph and you have failed, which is likely to come to pass some time or other, he may make some moments exceedingly bitter unto thee. And now I shall dress myself, as I think I hear the footsteps of visitors."

John remembered that he, too, was clad lightly, and hastily put on his upper garments, while his friend did likewise. He now heard the steps, also, and they were rapidly coming nearer.

"Shouldn't we move?" he whispered. "Those must be Mexicans."

"No, we shouldn't move, because those are not the footsteps of Mexicans. Those sounds are made by the hardy feet of just two persons. One of them is a large brave German man, whose tread I would know a mile away, and the other, the lighter tread of whom is drowned in the volume of sound made by his comrade, is a boy, a strong, healthy boy who comes from a little town in Kentucky, which has the same name as a big town in France."

John began to tremble all over. He knew what these words meant. His friend uttered a low whistle, and quickly a low whistle in reply came from a point not twenty feet away. There was a moment of silence, then the approaching footsteps were resumed, the bushes were parted, and, as the lightning flared once more across the sky, John Bedford and Philip Bedford looked into the faces of each other.

They wrung hands in the darkness that followed the

lightning flash, and, after the Anglo-Saxon fashion, said brief, inconsequential words. Yet the hearts of the two were full, and both Bill Breakstone, who had done the last miracle, and Hans Arenberg were moved deeply.

"Your letter came, John," said Phil simply, "and we are here. These are the best friends I ever had or that anybody ever could have. The man who brought you out of the castle was Bill Breakstone, and the one with me is Hans Arenberg. Without them I never could have reached you in the castle."

"You talk too much, young sir," said Bill Breakstone.

Then John suddenly remembered.

"Mr. Breakstone is wounded," he exclaimed. "We took off most of our clothes to swim the moat and I remember seeing a red spot on his side."

"Like your brother, you talk too much," said Bill Breakstone. "It seems to be a family failing with the Bedfords. It's a mere scratch."

"No harm iss done where none iss meant," said Arenberg sententiously. "It iss also well for us soon to be away from where we now are."

"That is true," said Breakstone. "The Mexicans undoubtedly will make some sort of a search and pursuit, though I don't think they'll carry it far on such a night. Come on boys, I'll lead, and the reunited family will bring up the rear. But no talking is best. You can't tell what we might stir up."

He led the way, and the others followed in silence. They crossed a valley, reached a mountain slope and began to climb. Up they went for at least two hours, pausing at times for John to take breath and rest. Meanwhile the storm continued, with cold rain, an alternate groaning and whistling of the wind through the valley, deep rumblings of thunder, and now and then a bright flare of lightning. John caught only one other glimpse of the huge, ominous bulk of the Castle of Montevideo, but it was far below him now. He knew, too, that it was impossible for anybody to follow a mountain trail in such darkness and storm. But, despite his great joy, he was feeling an exceeding weariness of the body. The long confinement had told heavily, but he would utter no complaint.

A half hour more, and they turned into a deep cove which led three or four hundred yards into the Sierra. At its end stood a small cabin, built of logs and almost hidden under the overhang of the cliff.

"Welcome to our home, Sir John," said Bill Breakstone, "we have no title to it, and it probably belonged to some Mexican sheep herder or hunter, but since our arrival none has appeared to claim it.

He threw open the door, and all went inside into the dry dark. John heard the door close behind him, a bar fell into place, and then the striking of a match came to his ear. A little blue flame appeared and grew. Arenberg, who had struck the match, lighted a pine torch, which he stuck at an angle in a hole in the wall, and a fine red flame lighted up the whole interior of the little cabin. Cabin! It was no cabin to John Bedford. It was a gorgeous palace, the finest that he had ever seen, and he was surrounded by the most devoted and daring friends that man ever had. Had they not just proved it?

The little torch disclosed a hard earthen floor, upon which the skins of wild animals had been spread, log walls with wooden hooks and pins inserted here and there, evidently within recent days, a strong board roof, rafters from which skins and some tools hung, a fireplace with a stone hearth, and four narrow skin couches, three of which had been often occupied, the fourth never. Outside, the wind still wailed, and the cold rain still beat upon the logs, but here it was warm, dry, and light. The greatness of it all suddenly overwhelmed John, and he sank forward in a faint.

THE QUEST OF THE FOUR

Phil instantly seized his brother and raised him up, but Breakstone and Arenberg told him not to be alarmed, that it was merely the collapse of a weakened frame after tremendous tension, both physical and mental. Breakstone brought water in a gourd from a pail that stood in the corner, and soon John sat up again, very much ashamed of himself, and offering many apologies, at all of which the others laughed.

"Considering all you've been through to-night," said Bill Breakstone, "it's a wonder that you held out so long. I wouldn't have believed that you could do it, if I hadn't known your brother so well. Good thing I learned to be an actor. I was always strong in those Spanish parts. Wide hat brim, big black cloak coming up to meet the hat brim, terrible sword at my thigh, and terrible frown behind the cloak and the hat brim. Now, Hans, I think you can light the fire on the hearth there. No chance that anybody will see the smoke on a night like this, and there's no reason why we shouldn't dry our clothes and have a gay party. We've carried through our great adventure, and we'll just royster over it awhile."

Arenberg, without another word, took down the pine torch from its hole in the wall and ignited the heap of dry pine boughs that lay in the fireplace. They caught at once, crackled, and blazed pleasantly. Warm red shadows were soon cast across the floor, and a generous heat reached them all. They basked in it, and turned about and about, drying all their clothing and driving the last sign of chill from their bones. Arenberg also made coffee over the coals, and cooked venison, which they had in abundance. When John ate and drank in plenty, he felt that life did not have much more to offer. He sat on one of the skins, leaned comfortably against the wall, and contemplated his younger brother.

"You have grown a lot, Phil," he said.

"You didn't expect him to stand still, just because you were away locked up in a castle?" asked Bill Break-

THE HUT IN THE COVE

stone. "He had to grow up, so he could come and rescue you. Such tasks are too big for little children."

John Bedford smiled indulgently.

"It was certainly a big job," he said. "I am the one who ought to appreciate most its size and danger. It was a big thing to get through Texas even. Of course I learned while I was a prisoner in the castle that the Mexicans had retaken it. It made me feel mighty bad for a long time."

Phil and Bill Breakstone looked at each other. Arenberg pushed one of the pine-knots back into the fire. For a little while there was silence. Then Breakstone said:

"You tell him, Phil."

John Bedford looked in wonder at the three, one by one. Their silence impressed him as ominous, and he, too, was silent.

"The Mexicans have not retaken Texas, John," said Philip Bedford. "They will never retake Texas. They could never beat the Texans alone, and the Texans are not alone. There has been war between the United States and Mexico for a year. An American army under General Taylor beat the Mexican army at Palo Alto, at Resaca de la Palma, and took the city of Monterey by storm. Then most of his army were drawn off to help General Scott, who is invading Mexico by the way of Vera Cruz. General Taylor, with the rest of his force, between four and five thousand men, nearly all volunteers, many from our own state, John, and some you knew, advanced to Saltillo and beyond. He was attacked in the Pass of Angostura by Santa Anna, the President of Mexico, with more than twenty thousand men, the best of the Mexican troops, but, John, he won the victory over odds of five to one. It was long and hard and desperate, and a half dozen times we were within an inch of losing the battle, but we won at last, John! We won at last! And we know, because we three were there, all through it! all day long! Bill Breakstone, Hans Arenberg, and I!"

THE QUEST OF THE FOUR

John looked at them and gasped. It had all been poured upon him so suddenly that he was overpowered.

"War between Mexico and the United States!" he exclaimed, "and we've been winning battle after battle! Why, they never said a word to me about it in the castle. De Armijo made me think that the Mexicans had retaken Texas."

"I forgot to tell you," said Bill Breakstone to the others, "that de Armijo knocked John down, when he was chained, but John got back at him to-night when he plowed his face with a bullet. In fact, I think John has the better of the bargain:

> "A blow—
> He'll rue it.
> A bullet—
> That pays it.

"Now, I propose, as it's pretty near toward morning, and this is about the snuggest hotel I know of anywhere in the Sierras, that John and I, who have been through a lot, go to sleep. Phil, you and Arenberg can toss coins, or decide in any other way you choose, who's to keep watch. There's your bed, John; it's been waiting for you quite awhile."

He pointed to the skin couch that had never been occupied, and John lay down upon it. Complete relaxation of both mind and body had now come. The room was warm and dry, his friends were near, and, in two minutes, he was buried in a deep and dreamless sleep. Phil rose and looked at him. His neck and wrists were thin, his face was wasted wofully. Arenberg watched Philip with sympathy.

"Much harm has been done to him," he said, "but he will overcome it all in a month. You have fared wonderfully well in your quest, Herr Philip, and I take it as an omen that we shall do as well in mine. I come next, you know, Philip."

THE HUT IN THE COVE

"It is true," said Phil, with a great stirring of the heart. "Nobody ever had such help as you and Breakstone have given to me, and now I will help you, and John, too, as soon as he is strong enough, to our utmost power in whatever task you may have."

He held out his hand, and Arenberg took it in a powerful grasp.

"Now you sleep! I will watch," he said. "No, I will not let you stay awake, because I wish to do so instead. I intend to think much with myself."

Phil saw that the German was in earnest, and he took his place on his own couch. Soon he was asleep. Arenberg sat on a piece of wood before the coals which were now almost dead. He clasped his knees in his hands, and his rifle, which was between his knees, projected above his shoulder. So long as the light from the coals endured he cast a black and almost shapeless shadow on the wall. But the last coal went out by and by, and he sat there in the darkness, never stirring. He watched automatically through the faculty of hearing, but his thoughts were not on that little cabin nor any of its occupants. In the darkness his chest heaved, and a big tear from either eye rolled down his cheek. But he did not move. After awhile he felt the dawn, and went to the single shuttered window, which he opened slightly.

The rain and wind had ceased, but drops of water, turned into a myriad of glittering beads by the rising sun, hung from trees and bushes. The air of the mountains at that early hour was crisp and cold, and it felt good to Arenberg's face. He glanced at his three comrades. They were still absorbed by that absolute sleep which is the mortal Nirvana. Then Arenberg took from the inside of his coat something small, which he looked at for a long time. Again a big tear from either eye rolled down his cheek and fell on the floor. But the face of Hans Arenberg, in that brilliant Mexican sun which now shone straight upon it, was curiously transformed. For the first time in many days it was illumined with hope.

"It's my turn now! It's my turn!" he murmured. "We have succeeded in everything so far, and we will succeed again. I feel it. All the omens are good."

There is something mystic in the German nature, a feeling derived, perhaps, from the unknown ages passed by the Teutonic tribes in the dark forests of the Baltic. They were as prolific as the Greeks in seers and priestesses, and some of this feeling was in Arenberg now, as he gazed at the dripping forest and the blazing sun rising over a peak ten thousand feet high. Below him he knew lay the Castle of Montevideo, but before him the mountains were unrolled, peak after peak, and ridge after ridge. To his German mind came visions of Valhalla and the great gods that were.

Hans Arenberg yet felt the great uplift of the spirit. The premonition of success, of a triumphant end to his quest was very strong within him. He kissed the little package and replaced it within the inside of his waistcoat. Then he looked again at his comrades. They were still in Valhalla.

The German was very kindly and very pitiful. He had noticed the wasted frame of John Bedford, and he knew how much he needed sleep. Bill Breakstone, too, had gone through a tremendous ordeal, and Phil Bedford was but a boy, who had waited, tense and strained, all through the night.

"Let them sleep," murmured Hans Arenberg. "I will still watch."

He left the window open a little so that the fresh air might come in, and resumed his seat. The other three slept on soundly. An hour or two later he opened the door softly and went out into the cove, which he scouted carefully. It was as silent and desolate as if man had never been there. At forty yards the cabin itself was invisible in the foliage and against the dark, volcanic cliff.

THE HUT IN THE COVE

The German was quite sure that no one would come, but, for precaution, he examined every bush and projection of rock. Then he climbed one of the cliffs, and, sheltering himself well, looked down the valley. There, far below, was the huge, honey-colored Castle of Montevideo, seeming singularly vivid and near in the intense sunlight. Arenberg thought that he could make out a figure or two on its walls, but he was not sure. He also examined the slopes, but he could not detect human life. Then he returned to the cabin and found his comrades still sound asleep. Arenberg smiled.

"Let them sleep on," he murmured, "until the sleep that is in them is exhausted." He opened the door a little in order that he might let in more fresh air, and also because it gave him a complete view down the valley. No one could approach the cabin without being seen by Hans Arenberg, who had uncommonly good eyes.

The German sat there all the morning and listened to the hours as they ticked themselves away. He listened literally, and he heard the ticking literally, because he carried a large silver watch in his waistcoat pocket, and in the dead silence, he could hear it very well. His comrades slept on, each on his couch. Once Arenberg rose and looked at John Bedford.

"A fine young man," he murmured. "He iss worthy of his brother."

It was fully an hour after noon when Bill Breakstone began to squirm about on his couch and yawn mightily.

Then he opened his eyes, sat up, and stared at Hans Arenberg, who sat placidly by the fireplace, looking down the valley.

"Hans!" said Bill Breakstone.

Arenberg looked at him and smiled.

"I'm thinking," said Bill Breakstone, "that we've overslept ourselves a bit. I guess from the looks of the light there at the door that the sun must be up at least an hour."

"It has been up seven hours," replied Arenberg.

"Then we're that much ahead," said Bill Breakstone calmly, "and at least one of those two has needed it badly."

He looked at the sleeping brothers.

"It iss so," said Arenberg. "The captive who iss a captive no longer iss, I take it, a good youth, like his brother."

"He surely is," said Breakstone with emphasis, "and I have given him the honor of knighthood, along with Phil. Besides, he's as smart as a steel trap. He read the meaning of the thread that we sent him, and he did everything else exactly as we wished. It's all the more wonderful because so long a time in prison is apt to make one dull and stupid in some ways. Anything happen on your long watch, Hans?"

"Nothing. I made a scout all the way up the cove. I am sure there iss no human being except ourselves on this mountain."

"I move that we boil a little coffee and fry a little venison for the youngsters. John, in particular, needs it, because he's got to be built up. I don't think there's any danger."

"Then we'll light the fire and let the cooking wake them up."

John Bedford, in a dream, as it were, felt a delicious aroma in his nostrils. It was singularly pleasant to a poor prisoner in a bleak stone cell in the Castle of Montevideo, and he did not wish to destroy the illusion. In the early morning the air that came through the loophole was very cold, and there was no reason why he should rise. Perhaps he was really dreaming, and, since it was such a pleasant dream, he would let it run on. But that odor in his nostrils grew more and more powerful, and it was not like the odor of the frijoles and tortillas that Diego brought him. He also heard, or thought he heard, the voices of men, and not one of them bore any resemblance to the harsh Mexican tones of Diego. Then he remembered it all, and the truth came in such a sudden flood of delight that he sat up abruptly and looked around that wonderful cabin, the finest cabin in the world.

Arenberg had just brought the coffee to a boiling point, the strips of venison, under the deft handling of Bill Breakstone, were just becoming crisp. Phil was coming in with a canteen of fresh water, and at the wide-open door, through which he might pass as he pleased, the sunshine was entering like a golden shower.

"Morning, Sir John the Sleeper," said Bill Breakstone cheerily. "It's well along in the afternoon, but, if you were to ask me, I'd tell you that you hadn't slept a minute too long. Phil here has been up only five minutes before you, but, by running for the water, he's trying to make you believe that he's an early riser."

John said not a word, but rose to his feet—they had all lain down fully dressed—and looked at the open door with a gaze so fixed and concentrated that all stared curiously at him. Something was working in John's mind, something deep and vital. He walked in a perfectly straight line across the cabin floor until he came within a foot of the open door. Then he stood there for a little space, gazing out.

The curiosity of the others deepened. What was passing in his mind? But John said never a word. Instead, he stepped out in the sunshine and crisp air, went two or three yards, and then came back again into the cabin. But he did not stay there. He went out once, came back once more, and repeated the round trip four more times. All the while he said never a word, and, at each successive trip, the look of pleasure on his face grew. At the sixth that look was complete, and he turned to the three who were staring at him open-eyed and open-mouthed.

"I'm not crazy, as you think, not the least bit of it," he said. "It's been three years since I could go out of a door and come in at it as I pleased. I wanted to prove to myself that it was no dream, and to enjoy it at the same time. I'll never have such an acute joy again in this world, I suppose. As you haven't been where I've been, you'll never know what it is to go in and come out when you like."

"We don't know, but we can guess," said Phil.

A little lump came into the throat of Bill Breakstone.

"I was never cooped up like that," he said, "but if I were, I guess I couldn't stand it. But the coffee and the venison are ready, and while we set to and keep at it, Phil, you tell your brother how it all came about."

Phil was willing. He was so full of the story himself that he was anxious John should hear it all. He recounted how the letter had reached him at Paris in Kentucky, his journey to New Orleans, and his successive meetings there with Arenberg, Middleton, and Bill Breakstone; how they had joined the Santa Fé train and their encounter with the Comanches, led by Santana and Black Panther, the deeds of de Armijo, their long trail southward to join Taylor's army, and a description, as far as he saw it amid the flame and smoke, of the great battle of Buena Vista. He told of the sharp lava, the pass, and of the woman at the well who had given the cup of water to the weary prisoner who was but a boy.

"I remember her, I remember her well," said John, a thrill of gratitude showing in his tone. "I believe I'd have died if it hadn't been for that water, the finest that anybody ever tasted. I knew from the voice that it was a woman."

"We felt sure then," continued Phil, "that we were on the right trail, and we believed that, with patience and method, we'd be sure to find you if you were living. We knew that the letter had been brought to the Texas frontier by Antonio Vaquez, a driver who had received it in turn from one Porfirio, a vaquero, and we knew from your letter that you were confined in some great stone

THE HUT IN THE COVE

prison or castle. We learned of Montevideo, which is perhaps the greatest castle in Mexico, and everything pointed to it as the place.

"The Mexican army retreated in great haste southward after Buena Vista, in order to meet Scott, who was advancing on Mexico by the way of Vera Cruz. That left the country comparatively clear for us, and we came through the mountains, until we saw the Castle of Montevideo. When we saw it, we believed still more strongly that this was the place, but we knew that the biggest part of our work was before us. We would have to spy, and spy, and keep on spying before we could act. Any mule driver or sheepherder might carry news of us, and we must have a secure hiding-place as a basis. After a long search we found this cabin, which I don't think had been occupied for several years. We soon fixed it up so it was comfortable, as you can now see. There's a little spring at the west edge of the cove, and on the other side of the ridge there's a little valley with water and grass, but with walls so steep that a horse won't climb 'em unless he's led. Our horses are there now, having perhaps the best time of their lives.

"When we were located, good and snug, we began to spy. I believed after we met the woman at the well that fortune was favoring us. Arenberg here talked a lot about the spirits of the forest and the stream, some old heathen mythology of his, to which Bill and I didn't pay any attention. But anyway, we had luck. We scouted about the castle for weeks, but we didn't learn a thing, except that de Armijo was now governor there. We could find no more trace of you than if you had been on the moon.

"At last our lucky day came. We ran squarely upon a good-looking young Mexican, a vaquero. There wasn't time for us to get away or for him to get away. So we, being the more numerous, seized him. I suppose he thought he was going to be killed at once, as we were

Americans, looking pretty tough from exposure and hardships, and so to make a play on our good feelings—Bill Breakstone could understand his Spanish—he said that once he'd tried to help a Gringo, a prisoner, in the great castle in the valley. He said he'd carried a letter from him, asking for help, and that the prisoner was not much more than a boy, taken in a raid from Texas three years ago.

"It flashed over us all at once that we had found the right man. Everything fitted too well together to permit of a mistake, and you can believe that we treated Porfirio, the vaquero, the finest we knew how, and made him feel that he had fallen into the hands of the best friends in the world. Were you still alive? We waited without drawing breath for the answer. You were still alive he answered, and well, so far as a prisoner could be. He knew that positively from his mother, Catarina, who was a cook at the castle, although he himself would not stay there, as, like a sensible man, he liked the mountains and the plains and the free life. He did not tell us of the blow that de Armijo had given you, perhaps because Catarina had said nothing of it to him, but we learned that he hated de Armijo, who had once struck him when he was at the castle, for some trifle or other—it seems that de Armijo had the striking habit—and after that we soon made our little plot. Catarina, of course, was the center of it, and her duties as a cook gave her the chance.

"It was Catarina who put the thread in the tamale. She might have put the letter there, but the writing on it would have been effaced, and even if it could have remained she did not dare. If the paper had been discovered by the Mexicans, she, of course, would have been declared guilty, but thread, even a package of it, might have found its way into the loose Mexican cooking, and if it had been discovered none of the sentinels or officers could have made anything out of such a slender thing. We trusted to your shrewdness that you would drop the

THE HUT IN THE COVE

thread out of the window, because there was nothing else to do with it, and you didn't fail us."

"But who tied the note on it?" asked John.

"Catarina, again—that is, she was at the end of the chain, Porfirio was in the middle, and we were at the other or far end. He passed the letter in to her—he works about the castle at times—and she tied it on the end of the thread. The key and the dagger reached you by the same route. Then we knew that, although you might unlock the door of your cell, you could never go outside the castle without the aid of some one within. For that reason we told you the night on which to unlock it, and the very hour, in order that the right man might be waiting for you at the head of the stairway. Bill Breakstone had to be that man, because he can speak Spanish and the Mexican dialects, and because, lucky for you, he's been an actor; often to amuse others he has played parts like the one that he played last night in such deadly earnest.

"Catarina got the keys—there are duplicates to all the cells—so we sent that up early, and on the day before your escape she stole the one to the big gate that guards the stairway. It was easy enough to steal the clothes for Breakstone, take him in as a servant, and his nerve and yours did the rest. But we must never forget Catarina and her son Porfirio, the vaquero. Without them we could have done nothing."

"I'm prouder of it than of any other thing in which I ever took part," said Bill Breakstone.

"It was not one miracle, it was a chain of them," said John Bedford.

"Whatever it was, here we all are," said Phil.

CHAPTER XIX

ARENBERG'S QUEST

IT was necessary for several reasons to remain some days in the cove. John Bedford's strength must be restored. After the long confinement and the great excitement of his escape, he suffered from a little fever, and it was deemed best that he should lie quiet in the cabin. Phil stayed with him most of the time, while Breakstone and Arenberg hunted cautiously among the mountains, bringing in several deer. They incurred little risk in their pursuit, because the mountaineers, few in number at any time, were all drawn off by the war.

John had a splendid constitution, and, with this as a basis, good and abundant food and the delight of being free built him up very fast. On the fourth day Bill Breakstone came in with news received through the Porfirio-Catarina telegraph that the escape of John had caused a great stir at the castle. Nobody could account for it, and nobody was suspected. De Armijo was suffering from a very painful wound in the face, and would leave on the following day for the capital to receive surgical treatment.

"I'm going to see Porfirio for the last time to-morrow," said Breakstone, "and as we have some gold left among us, I suggest that we make a purse of half of it and give it to him. Money can't repay him and his mother for all they've done, but it may serve as an instalment."

All were willing, and Breakstone departed with a hundred dollars. He reported on the day following that Porfirio had received it with great gratitude, and that, as they were now rich, he and his mother were going to buy a little house of their own among the hills.

"And now," said Breakstone, "as John here has been gaining about five pounds a day, and is as frisky as a two year old just turned out to pasture, I think we'd better start."

It was late in the afternoon when he said these words, and they were all present in the cabin. Three pairs of eyes turned toward Arenberg. A sigh swelled the chest of the German, but he checked it at the lips. Without saying a word he drew a little packet from the inside of his waistcoat and handed it to Phil, who was nearest.

Phil looked at it long and attentively. It was the portrait of a little boy, about seven, with yellow hair and blue eyes, a fair little lad who looked out from the picture with eyes of mirth and confidence. The resemblance to Arenberg was unmistakable. Phil passed it to Breakstone, who, after a look, passed it on to John, who in his turn, after a similar look, gave it back to Arenberg.

"Your boy?" said Breakstone.

Arenberg nodded. The others, sympathetic and feeling that they were in the presence of a great grief, waited until he should choose to speak.

"It iss the picture of my boy," said Arenberg at last. "Hiss name is William—Billy we called him. I came to this country and settled in Texas, which was then a part of Mexico. I married an American girl, and this iss our boy. We lived at New Braunfels in Texas with the people from Germany. She died. Perhaps it iss as well that she did. It sounds strange to hear me say it, but it iss true. The Comanches came, they surprised and raided the town, they killed many, and they carried away many women and children. Ah, the poor women who have never been heard of again! My little boy was among those carried off. I fought, I was wounded three times, I was in a delirium for days afterward.

THE QUEST OF THE FOUR

"As soon as I could ride a horse again I tried to follow the Comanches. They had gone to the Northwest, and I was sure that they had not killed Billy. They take such little boys and turn them into savage warriors, training them through the years. I followed alone toward the western Comanche villages for a long time, and then I lost the trail. I searched again and again. I nearly died of thirst in the desert; another time only luck kept me from freezing in a Norther. I saw, alas! that I could not do anything alone. I went all the way to New Orleans, whence, I learned, a great train for Santa Fé was going to start. Perhaps among the fearless spirits that gather for such an expedition I could find friends who would help me in my hunt. I have found them."

Arenberg stopped, his tale told, his chest heaving with emotion, but no word passing his lips. Bill Breakstone was the first to speak.

"Hans," he said, "you have had to turn aside from your quest to help in Phil's, which is now finished, and you have done a big part; now we swear one and all to help you to the extent of our lives in yours, and here's my hand on it."

He solemnly gave his hand to Arenberg, who gave it a convulsive grasp in his own big palm. Phil and John pledged their faith in the same manner, and moisture dimmed Arenberg's honest eyes.

"It will be all right, Hans, old man," said Breakstone. "We'll get your boy sure. About how old is he now?"

"Ten."

"Then the Comanches have certainly adopted him. They'd take a boy at just about the age he was captured, six or seven, because he would soon be old enough to ride and take care of himself, and he's not too old to forget all about his white life and to become a thorough Indian. That logic is good. You can rely on it, Hans."

"It iss so! I feel it iss so!" said Arenberg. "I feel

that my boy iss out there somewhere with the Comanche riders, and that we will find him."

"Of course we will," said Breakstone cheerfully. "Phil, you see that a place is registered in this company for one William Arenberg, blue eyes, light hair, fair complexion, age ten years. Meanwhile I want to tell you, John Bedford, that we were so certain of getting you, in spite of the impossible, that we brought along an extra rifle, pistol, and ammunition, and that we also have a horse for you over in the valley with the others."

"It's like all that you have done for me," said John, "thorough and complete."

They went over into the valley the next day, saddled and bridled the horses, and, well provided with food and ammunition, started for the vast plains of Northwestern Texas, on what would have seemed to others a hopeless quest, distance and space alike were so great. When they came out upon one of the early ridges John had a sudden and distinct view of the Castle of Montevideo lying below, honey-colored, huge, and threatening. A shudder that had in it an actual tinge of physical pain passed through him. One cannot forget in a moment three years between stone walls. But the shudder was quickly gone, and, in its place, came a thrill of pure joy. Freedom, freedom itself, irrespective of all other good things, still sparkled so gloriously in his veins that it alone could make him wholly happy.

They rode on over the ridge. John looked back. The Castle of Montevideo was shut from his view now forever, although he never ceased to remember the minutest detail of Cell 37 and the little patch of mountainside that could be seen from the deep loophole of a window.

But they were all joyous, Phil because he had found and rescued his brother, John because he had been found and rescued, Bill Breakstone because he had helped in great deeds ending in triumph, and Hans Arenberg because they were now engaged upon his own quest, the quest that lay next to his heart, and these comrades of his were the best and most loyal that a man could ever have for such a service. Three or four years rolled away from Hans Arenberg, the blue eyes grew brighter, the pink in his cheeks deepened, and Phil, looking at him, saw that he was really a young man. Before, he had always made upon his mind the impression of middle age.

They rode steadily toward the northwest for many days without serious adventure. Once or twice they encountered small bands of Mexican guerillas, with whom they exchanged distant shots without harm, but the war was now south of them, and soon they passed entirely beyond its fringe, leaving the mountains also behind them. They met various American scouts and trappers, from whom they bought a couple of pack horses, two good rifles, and a large supply of fresh ammunition. It was explained by Bill Breakstone, who said:

> "More than enough
> Merely makes weight,
> Less than enough,
> You're doomed by fate."

The two extra horses were trained to follow, and they caused no trouble. They carried the supplies of spare arms and ammunition and also of dried venison for the intervals in which they might find no game. They also found it wise to take skin bags of water, buying the bags at a village occupied by American troops, which they passed. They found Northern Mexico almost at peace. Resistance to the Americans there had ceased practically, and in the towns buying and selling, living and dying went on as usual. They had nothing to guard against but sudden ambushes by little bands of guerillas, and they were now all so experienced and so skilled with the rifle that they feared no such trap.

It was wonderful at this time to watch John Bedford

grow. He had already reached the stature and frame of a man, but when he came from the Castle of Montevideo he was a frame, and not much more. Now the flesh formed fast upon this frame, cords and knots of muscle grew upon his arms, his cheeks filled out, the prison pallor disappeared and gave way to a fine healthy brown, the creation of the Southern sun, his breath came deep and regular from strong lungs, and he duly notified Bill Breakstone that within another month he would challenge him to a match at leaping, wrestling, jumping, boxing, or any other contest he wished. They had also bought good clothes for him at one of the villages, and he was now a stalwart young man, anxious to live intensely and to make up the three years that he had lost.

Meantime, leaving the Mexican mountains and the alkali desert of the plateau behind them, they came to the Rio Grande, though farther west than their first passage. Here they stopped and looked awhile at the stream, a large volume of water flowing in its wide channel of sand. Phil felt emotion. Many and great events had happened since he saw that water flowing by the year before, and the miracle for which he hoped had been accomplished. To-day they were upon a quest other than his own, but they pursued it with an equal zeal, and he believed that all the omens and presages were in their favor.

They found a safe passage through the sandy approaches, swam the river upon their horses, and stood once more upon the soil of Texas. Phil felt that they would have little more to do with Mexicans, but that they must dare the formidable power of the Comanches, which now lay before them.

They camped that night in chaparral, where they were well concealed and built no fire. The weather was quite warm again, save for those sudden but usually brief changes of temperature that often occur in West Texas. But there was no sign of storm in the air, and they felt that their blankets would be sufficient for the night—however hot the day might be, the nights were always cool. Bill Breakstone had first beaten up the chaparral for rattlesnakes, and, feeling safe from any unpleasant interruption from that source, they spread out their blankets and lay comfortably upon them while they discussed the plan of their further march.

They felt quite sure that, with the passage of American troops south, the Comanches had gone far to the westward. The Indians had already suffered too much from these formidable invaders to oppose their southward march. Besides, they had received definite information that both Santana and Black Panther with their bands had gone almost to the border of New Mexico. The sole question with the four was whether to search over a wide belt of territory at once, or to go straight westward until they struck the Rio Grande again.

"I favor the long trip before we begin the hunt," said Bill Breakstone. "The chances are all in favor of the Comanches being out there. The buffalo herds, which will soon be drifting southward, are thickest in that part of the country."

Breakstone's logic seemed good to the others, and the next morning they began the long march through a region mostly bare but full of interest for them all. They passed a river which flowed for many miles on a bed of sand a half mile wide, and this sand everywhere was thick with salt. From the bluffs farther back salt springs gushed forth and flowed down to the river.

Then they came upon the southern edge of the Great Staked Plain of Texas, known long ago to the Spaniards and Mexicans as the Llano Estacado. John Bedford, who was a little in advance, was the first to see the southern belt of timber. It had been discovered very soon that John's eyes were the keenest of them all. He believed himself that they had been strengthened by his long staring through the loophole at the castle in order to make out every detail of his little landscape on the far mountainside. Now he saw a faint dark line running along the horizon until it passed out of sight both to east and west. He called Breakstone's attention to it at once, and the wise Bill soon announced that it was the southern belt of the Cross Timbers, the two parallel strips of forest growing out of an otherwise treeless country which for hundreds of miles enclose a vast plain.

"It's the first belt," said Bill Breakstone, "and, while it's not as near as it looks, we're covering ground pretty fast, and we'll strike the timber before nightfall. How good it looks to see forest again."

Even the horses seemed to understand, as they raised their heads, neighed, and then, without any urging from their masters, increased their pace. Phil rode up by the side of his brother John, and watched the belt of timber rise from the plain. He had often heard of this strange feature of the Texas wilds, but he had never expected to see it.

A little before nightfall they rode out of a plain, perfectly bare behind them for hundreds of miles, into the timber, which grew up in an arid country without any apparent cause, watered by no rivers or creeks and by no melting snows from mountains. Phil and John looked around with the greatest interest. The timber was of oak, ash, and other varieties common in the Southwest, but the oak predominated. The trees were not of great size, but they were trees, and they looked magnificent after the sparse cottonwoods and bushes along the shallow prairie streams that they had passed.

The foliage had already turned brown under the summer sun, but there was fresh grass within the shadow of the trees, upon which the horses grazed eagerly when they were turned loose. The four meanwhile rejoiced, and looked around, seeking a place for a camp.

"How long is this belt, Bill?" asked Phil of Breakstone.

THE QUEST OF THE FOUR

"I don't know, but maybe it's a thousand miles. There's two of them, you know. That's the reason they call them the Cross Timbers. After you pass through this belt you cross about fifteen miles of perfectly bare plain, and then you come to the second belt, which is timbered exactly like this. One belt is about eight miles wide, the other about twelve miles wide, and, keeping an average distance of about fifteen miles apart, they run all the way from the far western edge of these plains in a southeasterly direction clean down to the Brazos and Trinity River bottoms, where they come together and merge in the heavy timber. It's a most wonderful thing, Sir Philip of Buena Vista and Sir John of Montevideo, and it's worthy of any man's attention."

"It has mine, that's sure," said Phil, as he walked about through the forest. "It's an extraordinary freak of nature, but the roots of the two belts of timber must be fed by subterranean water, though it's strange that they should run parallel so many hundreds of miles, always separated by that strip of dry country fifteen miles wide, as you say, Bill."

"I can't account for it, Phil," replied Breakstone, "and I don't try. The people who don't believe in queer things are those who stay at home and sit by the fire. I've roamed all my life, and I've had experience enough to believe that anything is possible."

"Look!" exclaimed Phil in delight. "Here's our camp, just made for us!"

He pointed to a tiny spring oozing from beneath the roots of a large oak, flowing perhaps thirty yards and then losing itself beneath the roots of another large oak. It looked clear and fresh, and Phil, kneeling down and drinking, found it cold and delightful. Bill Breakstone did the same, with results equally happy.

"Yes, this was made for us," he said, confirming Phil's words. "There are not many such springs that I ever heard of in the Cross Timbers, and our luck holds good."

ARENBERG'S QUEST

They called the others, who drank, and after them the horses. It was an ideal place for a camp, and they felt so secure that they lighted a fire and cooked food, venison, and steaks of antelope and deer that they had shot by the way.

"It might be a good idea," said Breakstone, "to rest here in the shade a part of to-morrow. All of us have been riding pretty hard, and you know, Hans, old man, that if you go too fast you are not strong enough to do what you must do when you get there."

It was Arenberg whose feelings were now consulted most, and, when they looked at him for an answer, he nodded assent.

Hence they took some of their supplies from the pack horses, and made themselves more comfortable on the grass about the little spring. Lengthy scouting, done by Arenberg and Breakstone, showed that there was no danger from Comanche, Lipan, or any other Indian tribes, and they could take their rest without apprehension. They also dared to build a fire for the cooking, a luxury which they enjoyed much, but which was usually dangerous in the Indian country. Fallen and dry timber was abundant, and when they had cooked a plentiful supply of venison and buffalo strips they fell to and ate with the appetite which only life under the stars can give. By and by Bill Breakstone gazed at John in admiration. But John took no notice. He ate steadily on, varying the course with an occasional tin cup of water.

"Sir John Falstaff," said Bill Breakstone, "I've read a lot about you in Shakespeare, and on two or three memorable occasions I have played you. You have been renowned two hundred and fifty years for your appetite, and I want to tell you right now that your fame isn't up to the real thing by half. Say, Sir John, they didn't give you much to eat in that Castle of Montevideo, did they?"

"Tortillas, frijoles, tamales, tortillas, frijoles, tamales," replied John in a muffled voice, as he reached for another delicate piece of fried deer.

"Go right on," said Bill Breakstone, "I've no wish to stop you. Make up for all the three years that you lost."

John, taking his advice, stuck to his task. Although imprisonment had greatly wasted him, it had never impaired his powerful and healthy constitution. Now he could fairly feel his muscles and sinews growing and the new life pouring into heart and lungs.

After supper they lay upon their blankets in a circle, with their feet to the fire, and spoke of the land that stretched beyond the two belts of trees, the Great Staked Plain.

"We'll find it hot," said Breakstone, "and parts of it are sandy and without water, but we should get through to the Rio Grande, especially as we have, besides the sand, a big region of buffalo grass, and then the land of gramma grass, in both of which we can find plenty of game. Game and water are the things for which we must look. But we won't talk of trouble now. It's too fine here."

They spent the next day and the following night among the trees, and were fortunate enough to find in the oaks a number of fine wild turkeys which abounded in all parts of the Southwest. They secured four, and added them to their larder. The next day they rode through the belt, and across the twelve miles of bare country into the second belt, which was exactly like the first, with the oak predominating.

"Makes me think of the rings of Saturn," said Phil, as they entered the timber once more.

But they passed the night only in the inner belt, and emerged the next morning upon the great plain that ran to the Rocky Mountains.

"Now," said Bill Breakstone, "we leave home and its comforts behind."

Phil felt the truth of his words. He understood now why the Bible put so much value upon wood and water. To leave the belt of trees was like going away from a wooded park about one's house in order to enter a bleak wilderness. It was very hot after they passed from the shade, and before them stretched the rolling plains once more, without trees, reaching the sky-line, and rolling on beyond it without limit. The sun was pouring down from a high sky that flamed like brass. Bill Breakstone caught the look on Phil's face and laughed.

"You hate to give up an easy place, don't you, Phil?" he said. "Don't deny it, because I hate it just as much as you do. Arenberg alone forgets what lies before us, because he has so much to draw him on."

Arenberg was too far ahead to hear them. He always rode in advance now, and the place was conceded to him as a right. They passed through a region of gramma grass which stood about three feet in height, and entered a stretch of buffalo grass, where little clumps of the grass were scattered over the brown plain.

"It doesn't look as if great buffalo herds could be fed on tufts like that," said Phil.

"But they can be," said Bill Breakstone. "It looks scanty, but it's got some powerfully good property in it, because cattle as well as buffalo thrive on it as they do on nothing else. We ought to see buffalo hereabouts."

But for two days after entering this short grass region they saw not a single buffalo. Antelope, also, were invisible, and they began to be worried about their supplies of food. Both Breakstone and Arenberg believed that there were hunting parties of Indians farther westward, and they kept a sharp watch for such dangerous horsemen. Fortunately they had been able to find enough water for their horses in little pools and an occasional spring, and the animals retained their strength. Finally they encamped one evening by the side of a prairie stream so slender that it was a mere trickle over the sand. It also contained a slight taste of salt, but not enough to keep both men and horses from drinking eagerly.

After supper Phil took his rifle and walked up the little stream. It had become a habit with the four, whenever they camped, to look about for game. But they had been disappointed so often that Phil's quest now was purely mechanical. Still he was alert and ready. The training of the wilderness compelled any one with wisdom to acquire such quantities quickly. He walked perhaps half a mile along the brook, which was edged here and there with straggling bushes, and at other points with nothing at all. It was twilight now, and suddenly something huge and brown rose up among a cluster of the dwarf bushes directly in Phil's path. In the fading light it loomed monstrous and misshapen, but Phil knew that it was a lone bull buffalo, probably an old and evil-tempered outcast from the herd. He saw that the big brute was angry, but he was a cool hunter now, and, taking careful aim, he planted a bullet near the vital spot. The buffalo, head down, charged directly at him, but he leaped to one side and, as the mortally stricken beast ran on, he reloaded and sent in a second bullet, which promptly brought him to earth.

Still practicing that wilderness caution which never allows a man's rifle to remain unloaded, he rammed home a third bullet, and then contemplated his quarry, an enormous bull, scarred from fights and undoubtedly tough eating. But Phil was very happy. It was in this case not the pride of the hunter, but the joy of the commissary. Tough though this bull might be, there was enough of him to feed the four many a long day.

While he was standing there he heard the sound of running feet, and he knew that it was the others coming to the report of his shots. Bill Breakstone first hove into view.

"What is it, Phil?" he cried, not yet seeing the mountain of buffalo that lay upon the ground.

"Nothing much," replied Phil carelessly, "only I've killed a whole buffalo herd while you three lazy fellows were lying upon the ground playing mumble peg, or doing something else trivial. I'll get you trained to work after awhile."

Breakstone saw the buffalo and whistled with delight. The four set to work, skinned him, and then began to cut off the tenderest parts of the meat for drying. This was a task that took them a long time, but fortunately the night was clear, with a bright moon. Before they finished they heard the howling of wolves from distant points, and Phil occasionally caught slight glimpses of slender dark forms on the plain, but he knew they were prairie wolves that would not dare to attack, and he went on with his work.

"They'll have a great feast here when we leave with what we want," said Bill Breakstone. "They're not inviting creatures, but I'm sorry for 'em sometimes, they seem so eternally hungry."

After the task was finished, three went back for the horses to carry their food supply, and Phil was left to guard it. He was tired now, and he sat down on the ground with his rifle across his knee. The moon came out more brightly, and he saw well across the prairie. The slender, shadowy forms there increased in numbers, and they whined with eagerness, but the boy did not have the slightest fear. Nevertheless, he was glad they were not the great timber wolves of the North. That would have been another matter. At last he took a piece of the buffalo that his comrades and he would not use and flung it as far as he could upon the prairie.

There was a rush of feet, a confused snarling and fighting, and then a long death howl. In the rush some wolf had been bitten, and, at the sight of the blood, the others had leaped upon him and devoured him.

Phil, who understood the sounds, shuddered. He had not meant to cause cannibalism, and he was glad when his comrades returned with the horses. They spent two days jerking the buffalo meat, as best they could in the time and under the conditions, and they soon found the precaution one of great wisdom, as they did not see any more game, and, on the second day afterward, entered a region of sand. The buffalo grass disappeared entirely, and there was nothing to sustain life. This was genuine desert, and it rolled before them in swells like the grassy prairie.

The four, after going a mile or so over the hot sand, stopped and regarded the gloomy waste with some apprehension. It seemed to stretch to infinity. They did not see a single stalk or blade of vegetation, and the sand looked so fine, or of such small grain, to Phil that he dismounted, picked up a handful of it, and threw it into the air. The sand seemingly did not fall back, but disappeared like white smoke. He tried it a second and a third time, with the same result in each case.

"It's not sand," he said, "it's just dust."

"Dust or sand," said Bill Breakstone, "we must rush our way through it, and I'm thinking that we've got to make every drop of water we have in the bags last as long as possible."

They rode on for several hours, and the very softness of the sand made the going the worst that they had ever encountered. The feet of the horses sank deep in it, and they began to pant with weariness, but there was no relief. The vertical sun blazed down with a fiery splendor that Phil hitherto would have believed impossible. The whole earth shimmered in the red glare, and the rays seemed to penetrate. All of them had broad brimmed hats, and they protected their eyes as much as possible. The weariness of the horses became so great that after awhile the riders dismounted and walked by the side of them. Two hours of this, and they stopped in order that Breakstone might take the direction with a little compass that he carried in a brass box about two inches in diameter. He had made the others buy the same kind, but they had not yet used them.

"This is the best kind of compass to put in your baggage on such a trip as this," he said, "and it says that we're going straight on in the way we want to go. Come, boys, the more sand we pass the less we have in front of us."

They staggered bravely on, but the glare seemed to grow. The whole sky was like a hot, brassy cover that held them prisoners below. It scarcely seemed possible to Phil that trees, green grass, and running water had ever existed anywhere. A light wind arose, but, unlike other winds that cool, this wind merely sent the heat against their faces in streams and currents that were hotter than ever. It also whirled the fine sand over them in blinding showers. Acting on the advice of Breakstone, they drew up their horses in a little circle, and stood in the center, shielding their eyes with their hands. Peering over his horse's back, Phil saw hills of sand four or five feet high picked up and carried away, while hills equally high were formed elsewhere. Ridges disappeared, and new ridges were formed. The wind blew for about two hours, and then the four, covered with sand, resumed their march, noting with joy that the sun was now sinking and the heat decreasing. The very first shadows brought relief, but the greatest solace was to the eye. Despite the protection of hand and hat-brims, they were so burnt by the sand and glare that it was a pain to see. Yet the four were so weary of mind and body that they said nothing, as they trudged on until the edge of the sun cut into the western plain on the horizon. Phil had never before seen such a sun. He had not believed it could be so big, so glaring, and so hot. He was so glad now that the earth was revolving away from it that he raised his clenched hand and shook his fist in its very eye.

"Good-by to you," he exclaimed. "And I was never before so glad to see you go!"

THE QUEST OF THE FOUR

Phil spoke in such deadly earnest that Bill Breakstone, despite his aching muscles and burning throat, broke into laughter.

"You talk as you feel, Phil," he said, "but it's no good to threaten the sun. It's just gone for a little while, and it will be back again to-morrow as bright and hot as ever."

"But while it iss gone we will be glad," said Arenberg.

Down dropped the shadows, deeper and deeper, and a delicious coolness stole over the earth. It was like a dew on their hot eyeballs, and the pain there went swiftly away. A light wind blew, and they took the fresh air in long, deep breaths. They had been old three or four hours ago, now they were young again. The horses, feeling the same influence, raised their lowered heads and walked more briskly.

The shadows merged into the night, and now it was actually cold. But they went on an hour or more in order to find a suitable place for a camp. They chose at last a hollow just beyond a ridge of sand that seemed more solid than usual. On the slope grew a huge cactus with giant arms, the first that they had seen in a long time.

"Here we rest," said Bill Breakstone. "What more could a man ask? Plenty of sand for all to sleep on. No crowding. Regular king's palace. Water in the waterbags, and firewood ready for us."

"Firewood," said John Bedford. "I fail to see it."

Breakstone pointed scornfully to the huge cactus.

"There it is, a whole forest of it," he said. "We break down that cactus, which is old and dry, and it burns like powder. But it will burn long enough to boil our coffee, which we need."

But they took a good drink of water first, and gave another to every one of the horses. Then they chopped down the giant cactus and cut it into lengths. As Breakstone had said, it burned with a light flame and was rapidly consumed, leaving nothing but thin ashes. But they were able to boil their coffee, which refreshed them even more than the food, and then they lay on their blankets, taking a deep, long rest. The contrast between night and day was extraordinary. The sun seemed to have taken all heat with it, and the wind blew. They could put on coats again, draw blankets over their bodies, and get ready for delicious sleep. They knew that the sun with all its terrors would come back the next day, but they resolved to enjoy the night and its coolness to the full.

The wind rose, and dust and sand were blown across the plain, but it passed over the heads of the four who lay in the narrow dip between the swells, and they soon fell into a sleep that built up brain and muscle anew for the next day's struggle.

CHAPTER XX

THE SILVER CUP

THEY awoke at the coming dawn, which began swiftly to drive away the coolness of the night, and, using what was left of the giant cactus, they boiled coffee and heated their food again. This was a brief task, but by the time it was finished the whole world was enveloped once more in a reddish glare. All that day they advanced, alternately riding and walking through an absolutely desolate land. The single cactus that they had burned loomed in Phil's memory like a forest. The water was doled out with yet more sparingness, and, a few minutes after they drank it, throat, tongue, and lips began to feel as parched as ever.

Phil did not see a living thing besides themselves. No rattlesnake, no lizard, no scorpion dwelled in this burning sand. Two or three of the horses began to show signs of weakness.

"If we only had a tent to shelter us from this awful glare," said Breakstone, "we could camp for the day, and then travel at night, but it will be worse standing still than going on. And get on we must. The horses have had no food, and they cannot stand it much longer."

They slept on the sand that night until a little past twelve o'clock, and then, to save time, resumed the march once more. The air was cool and pleasant at that time, but the desert looked infinitely weird and menacing under the starlight. The next day they entered upon a region of harder sand and in one or two places found a patch of scanty herbage, upon which the horses fed eagerly, but

THE SILVER CUP

there was not a sign of water to ward off the new and formidable danger that was threatening them, as the canteens and water-bags were now almost empty.

"To-morrow they will be empty," said Bill Breakstone.

His dismal prophecy came true. At noon of the following day the last drop was gone, and John and Phil looked at each other in dismay. But Bill Breakstone was a man of infinite resource.

"I mean to find water before night," he said. "Not any of your Mississippis or Missouris, nor even a beautiful creek or brook, not anything flowing or pretty to the eye, but water all the same. You just wait and see."

He spoke with great emphasis and confidence, but the others were too much depressed to believe. Nevertheless, Bill Breakstone was watching the ground critically. He noticed that the depressions between the swells had deepened, and that the whole surface seemed to have a general downward slope. Toward the twilight they came to a deeper depression than any that they had seen before. Two or three slender trees, almost leafless grew in it. The trees themselves seemed to cry aloud: "I thirst! I thirst!" But Bill Breakstone was all cheeriness.

"Here is our water!" he cried briskly. "Get ready all!"

He himself took out a stout shovel from the baggage on his horse, and began to dig, with great vigor, in the lowest part of the bowl.

"I see," said Phil, "you're going to dig a well."

"I am, and you're going to help me do it, too."

"But will we find anything at the bottom of it?"

"We will. Many a man has died of thirst in the desert, with plenty of water not twenty feet away. Some men are born without brains, Phil. Others have brains, but never use them, but I am egotistical enough to think that I have some brains, at least, and some will and capacity to use them. Now I've thrown up a pretty good pile of sand there, and I'm growing tired. You take that shovel and see what you can do, but make it a wide hole. You don't want a ton of sand caving in on you."

Phil took the shovel and worked with energy. John and Arenberg with tin cups also leaped down into the hole and helped as much as they could. As the sand was soft they descended fast, and Phil suddenly uttered a shout. He drew up a shovelful of wet sand, and, after that, sand yet wetter.

"That will do," said Breakstone a minute or two later. "Stand aside now and watch the water come into our well."

They had reached an underground seepage or soakage, draining from the higher ground above, and slowly a pool of water gathered at the bottom. The four uttered a shout of joy, entirely pardonable at such a time. The water was muddy, and it was warm, but it was pure water without any alkali, and, as such it meant life, life to men and beasts in the desert.

"The horses first," said Breakstone, "or they'll be tumbling in here on our heads, and they are entitled to it, anyhow."

They filled their kettles and pans with water, climbing out again and again. The horses drank greedily and uttered deep sighs of satisfaction. It took a long time to give them enough by this method, but when they were satisfied the men took their tin cups and drank.

"Slowly now," said Breakstone. "Don't you be too eager there, John, you escaped convict! Phil, you accidental buffalo killer, just hold that cup of yours steady, or you'll be dashing its contents into your mouth before the rest of us. Now then, you sun-scorched scamps, drink!"

The four drank together and at the same pace. Never in his life had anything more delicious trickled down Philip Bedford's throat. That yellow, muddy water

THE SILVER CUP

must have been the nectar that Jupiter and the rest of the gods drank, when they were lounging about Olympus. Four empty cups came back, and four heartfelt sighs of satisfaction were uttered. The cups were filled again, but Bill Breakstone held up a warning finger.

"I know you want it bad," he said, "because I want it myself just as bad as any of you, but remember that it's never good for the health to drink too fast, especially when you're nearly dead of thirst."

Phil appreciated the wisdom of his words. Yet he was terribly thirsty. On the burning desert the evaporation was so rapid that his system was already dry again through and through.

"Now," said Bill Breakstone, "fill again, gentlemen, and drink. Not quite so fast as before. Just let it linger a little, like an epicure over his wine, while the delicious taste tickles your palate, and the delicate aroma fills your nostrils."

The yellow water was all of these things to them, and they did as Bill bade while they drank. After that, they took more cups of it from time to time, and noted with satisfaction that, as they dipped the water out of the pit, more trickled back in again. Toward night they watered the horses a second time, and Arenberg suggested that they spend both the night and the day there, since the water seemed to be plentiful. In the day they could at least sit in the shadow of their horses, and, if pushed hard by the sun, they could sit in their well. As the suggestion came from Arenberg, who had the most reason for haste, it was adopted unanimously and quickly.

In the night, when it was cool and work was easy, they deepened the well considerably, securing a much stronger and purer flow of water. They also gave a greater slope to the sides, and then they went to sleep, very well contented with themselves. The next day, either in reality or imagination, was hotter than any of the others, and they felt devoutly thankful for the well, by which they could stay as long as they chose. When the sun was at its hottest they literally took refuge in it, sheltering themselves against the sandy bank and putting their hands in the water.

"My hands must be conductors," said Bill Breakstone, "because, when I hold them in the water, I can feel the damp coolness running all through my system. Now, Sir John, you escaped convict, without the striped clothes, did you ever see such a fine well as this before?"

John laughed.

"I'd rather have this well and freedom," he said, "than my cell in the Castle of Montevideo and all the beautiful mountain springs about there "

"Spoken like a man," said Bill Breakstone; "but this well is a beauty on its own account, and not merely by comparison. Look at the flowers all around its brink. Look at the beautiful white stone with which it is walled up. Look at the clearness of the water, like silver, in which my lily white hand now laves itself.

> "Our thirst rages:
> Water is found;
> Out of Hades
> At one bound.

"Can you better that descriptive poem, Phil?"

Phil shook his head.

"No, Bill," he replied, "I can't. We're all of us poets at heart, but you're the only one that can give his poetry expression. One poet is enough, another is too many."

At sundown they watered all the horses again, filled every canteen and skin bag with water, bade farewell to the well that they had digged and loved, and again marched westward over the sand. But they were now vigorous and full of hope, the sand was harder, and in the long cool night hours they traveled fast. Their most pressing need now was to secure food for the horses, which

THE SILVER CUP

were relatively weaker than their masters, and by the moonlight they watched anxiously for some dim line which would indicate the approach of forests or mountains. They saw no such line, but the country was undoubtedly growing hillier. The sand was also packed much harder. At times it seemed to resemble soil, but as yet there was neither grass nor bushes.

They plodded along in silence, but hopeful. All the horses were weak from the lack of food, and the four walked by the side of them throughout the night. But the night itself was beautiful, a dusky blue sky sprinkled with a myriad of silver stars. The weakness of the horses increased, and the four human beings were much alarmed for their brute comrades, who were so important to them. But toward morning all the horses raised their heads, thrust out their noses, and began to sniff.

"Now what can the matter be?" exclaimed John Bedford.

"They smell water," replied Bill Breakstone. "They can smell it a long way off, and, as it's bound to be surface water, that means grass. I'm of the opinion, boys, that we're saved."

The horses, despite their weakness, advanced so rapidly now that the four ran in order to keep up.

"Jump on their backs," exclaimed Bill Breakstone, when they had gone about a quarter of a mile. "It's water sure, and they won't mind a little extra weight now."

They sprang into the saddles, and the horses, seeming to take it as a hint, broke into a run. They ascended a slope and saw a dark outline before them.

"Trees! Pines! Fine, good pines!" exclaimed Arenberg. "The sight iss much good!"

They galloped among the pines, which were without undergrowth, and then down the other slope. Phil caught a glimpse of something that set all his pulses beating. It was a surface of dark blue water.

"Yes, the pines are good," he said, "but this is better! A lake, boys! A lake of pure cold water, a precious jewel of a lake, set here among the hills of the desert, and just waiting for us!"

Phil was right. It was a little lake set down among hills, with a rim of tall forest. It was almost circular, and about a hundred yards in diameter. They rode into it until their horses were up to their bodies. They let them drink copiously, and then rode back to the bank, after which they were out with the tin cups again and took their fill, finding the water not only pure but cold. Then Philip Bedford sat down on the grass and looked at the lake. A light wind was making silver lacework of its surface. Beyond it, and apparently for some distance, fine, tall trees stood. Abundant grass, sheltered by the hills, grew in the open places. At the far edge of the lake a dozen wild ducks swam, evidently not yet understanding human presence. The silver of the water and the green of the grass were like a lotion to the boy's eyes, used so long to the brazen sun and the hot sand. He looked and looked, and then he cried:

"I think this must be heaven!"

Nobody laughed. Every one had the same feeling. They had come from the desert, and the power of contrast was so great that the little lake with its trees and grass was, in truth, like a foretaste of heaven. They took everything from the horses, even the bridles, and turned them loose. There was no danger that they would wander from such a place. Then John Bedford began to take off his clothes.

"I'm going to have a swim," he said. "I haven't had a real bath in more than three years, and, after this last march of ours, I think I'm carrying at least a hundred pounds of unpleasant desert about my body."

"Me, too," said Phil. "Bet you ten thousand acres of desert that I beat you into the water."

"Go ahead, boys," said Breakstone, "and Hans and

I will watch and decide. Remember that you mustn't have on a single garment when you jump, or you'll be disqualified."

Breakstone had scarcely finished the words when two white bodies flashed through the air and struck the water with two splashes that were one in sound. Both disappeared beneath the surface and then came up, spluttering and splashing and swimming with bold strokes.

"A tie," said Bill Breakstone.

Hans Arenberg nodded.

The brothers found the water much colder than they had expected, but they swam so vigorously that they were soon in a fine glow. Bill Breakstone looked at Hans Arenberg. Hans Arenberg looked at Bill Breakstone.

"Why not?" said Bill.

"It iss what we ought to do," said Arenberg.

In two minutes they also were in the lake, enjoying a greater luxury than any Roman ever found in his marble and perfumed bath. All the dust and dirt of the desert were quickly swept from them, and the cold water infused new life into their veins and muscles. Toward the center they found by diving that the lake had a depth of at least twenty feet. As they saw no stream flowing into it, they were of the opinion that it was fed by underground springs, probably the snow water from distant mountains, which accounted for its coldness. At the far side they found the outlet, a rivulet that flowed between rocks and then descended swiftly toward the plain. They marked its course by the rows of trees on either side, and they knew that after its passage from the hilly country it would enter the desert, there to be lost among the sands. To the north of them the country seemed to rise considerably, and Breakstone believed that the faint blue haze just under the horizon indicated mountains.

"If so," he said, "we're not likely to suffer much more from the desert, because the mountains in this part of the Southwest generally mean trees and water. Meanwhile, we'll take the goods the gods provide us, while the lovely lake is here beside us; which bears a little resemblance to more famous lines, and which fits the case just now."

After a splendid swim they lay on the grass and let the sun dry them, while they soothed their eyes with the view of the lakes and the woods and the horses grazed in peace near the water's edge. It was idyllic, sylvan, and at this moment they felt at peace with everybody, all except Arenberg, who rarely let his boy and the Comanches go out of his thoughts.

"Maybe we're the first white people who have ever seen this lake," said John Bedford.

"Not likely," replied Breakstone. "Hunters and trappers have roved through this region a lot. People of that kind generally see things before the discoverers come along and name 'em."

"At any rate," said Phil, "we've never seen it before, and since it's the color of silver, and it's set here in this bowl, I propose that we call it 'The Silver Cup.'"

"Good," said Breakstone, and the others, also, approved. They were silent for awhile longer, enjoying their rest, and then Hans Arenberg spoke gravely:

"It iss likely," he said, "that the Comanches know of this lake, and that warriors in time may come here. We are sure that their bands went westward to avoid the American troops. Wherever there iss good water they will come sooner or later, and this water iss the best. It may be that it will pay us to stay here awhile and seek some clue."

"I think you're right," said Bill Breakstone, speaking for all the others. "We don't know just where we are going, and we've got to stop and catch hold to something somewhere. And, as you say, in this part of the world good water is bound to draw people."

Now that they were thoroughly refreshed they dressed and made a very careful inspection of the country. On

THE SILVER CUP

all sides of "The Silver Cup" but the north the belt of wood was narrow, but northward it seemed to extend to a considerable distance. Looking from an elevation there, they were positive that the blue haze under the horizon meant mountains. There was timber as far as they could see in that direction, and this view confirmed them in their resolution to stay where they were for awhile.

They also took into account another consideration. It had been many months since the battle of Buena Vista. Much had happened since then, and the summer was waning. With winter approaching, it was more than likely that the Comanches would either hug the warm plains or return toward them. It was an additional reason why warriors might come to The Silver Cup. Such coming, of course, brought danger, but the likelihood of success increased with the danger.

They found a sheltered place on the north side of the lake, but about forty yards distant. It was a kind of rocky alcove, sloping down toward the water, with great trees growing very thickly on every side. They put their supplies in here and made beds of dry leaves. Just above them was a fine open space richly grassed, into which they turned the horses.

"Those four-footed friends of ours will be our sentinels to-night," said Bill Breakstone. "I don't think any creeping Comanche could pass them without an alarm being raised, and, as we all need rest, we'll leave the watching to them and take the chances."

They did not light any fire, but ate their supper cold, and quickly betook themselves to The Dip, as they called this shelter. There, wrapped in their blankets, they lay down on the soft beds of leaves, and deemed themselves fortunate. Phil could just see between two great tree-trunks a narrow strip of The Silver Cup, which flashing in the moonlight with a luminous glow, looked like a wonderful gem. The water rippled and moved softly. Beyond was the fringe of trees, and beyond that the vast blue sky with a host of friendly stars. Then Phil fell into the sleep of the just, and so did all his comrades. The only one of them who awoke in the night was Hans Arenberg. He looked at his friends, saw they were sleeping so soundly that they did not move, and he arose very gently. Then he stepped out of The Dip and walked down to the edge of The Silver Cup. There he stood looking at the waters which still shifted and moved like molten metal under the wind.

There was a spell upon Hans Arenberg that night. The soul of the old Teuton was alive within him, of the Teuton who lived in the great forests of Germany far back of the Christian era. It was his inheritance, like that of the Americans who, also, grew up in the shadow of the vast wilderness. The forest and lake were alive to him with the spirits of his primitive ancestors, but they were good spirits. They whispered in chorus that he, too, would succeed, and he began to whistle softly a quaint melody, some old German folk song that he had whistled to his boy. His mood grew upon him. All things were mystic. The seen were the unseen, and the things around him had no place. Even the lake vanished as he softly whistled the little melody, and it seemed to him after awhile that an answer to it came out of the forest, the same melody whistled more softly yet, and from childish lips. Arenberg knew that he was dreaming awake, but from that moment he never doubted.

He came from the spell, slipped back into The Dip, and was the first next morning to awake. But he built the fire and did all the cooking, and he was uncommonly cheerful, whistling at times a peculiar but beautiful melody that none of them had ever heard before.

"Arenberg must have had a fine dream last night," said John Bedford to Phil.

"Looks so," replied Phil, "but I'm not going to ask him about it."

Arenberg and John remained and watched at the lake

THE SILVER CUP

that day, devoting themselves at the same time to the improvement of their camp, by means of a roof of bark and poles at the upper edge of The Dip, which would protect them from the infrequent rains. Phil and Bill Breakstone mounted the best of the horses and made a great scout northward. They found that the thick woods extended four or five miles. Beyond that the timber became scattering, and they also saw patches of open country with the succulent buffalo grass. Farther on lay the great mountains, clearly visible now.

"That's our water supply," said Bill, pointing to the blue range. "As we guessed, The Silver Cup is certainly fed from them, and I think that we've seen enough for the present. We've established the fact that we've got about the best base to be found in this country, and these woods will surely contain game."

Their luck continued high, for within fifteen minutes they flushed a black-tailed deer, which Phil, from his horse's back, brought down with a fine running shot. It was a fat doe, and, skinning and cleaning it there, they put it upon one of the horses and carried it back to camp. They did not arrive until nearly sundown, and their spoils made them doubly welcome to their comrades.

"You have done good work," said Hans Arenberg, "and this deer is very welcome. There are more where it came from, and to-morrow I think, also, that I will shoot some of the foolish ducks that are swimming around on the lake."

Arenberg was as good as his word; the next day they added a half dozen fine ducks to their larder. On the following day Arenberg and John rode northward, making the great scout. They had resolved to do this day by day, two to ride for enemies, and two to watch and work at the camp until something happened. Thus nearly two weeks passed and The Silver Cup remained untouched by any human beings save themselves. It was so peaceful that apparently it would remain forever so. Nor did they find anything in the forest except game, although they threshed up the country at least thirty miles to the north. Still they clung to their camp, knowing that they must have patience.

The hot days passed fast, and the coolness of autumn came upon them. One night it rained heavily, but the thatched roof did its duty, and they did not suffer. The waters of the lake grew colder, but they rarely missed their daily swim. Breakstone thought it likely that it was already snowing on the distant mountains.

They continued to beat up the country in circles that widened steadily, still without any sign of Comanches or any other Indian tribe, but Arenberg was resolute in his desire to stay, and the others thought it right to defer to him in the matter that concerned him most. The German held to the theory that sooner or later Comanches would pass that way, since water, wood, and game, the three requisites of savage life, were found there.

Hence they made ready for winter. They had two axes in their baggage, and they built a strong shack in The Dip, one quite sufficient to protect them from the winter storms which were likely to occur here, as they were at a great elevation above the sea. They made rude fish traps, with which they caught excellent fish in the lake, and they could increase the supply indefinitely. The black-tailed deer were numerous in the forest. They also found wild turkeys, and they shot two buffaloes on the plains below. The horses grazed in a sheltered little valley, and they judged that grass could be found there all through the winter.

There would be no trouble about living. Beyond a doubt, they could find ample supplies of food, and so long a time passed without the appearance of an enemy that they began to feel quite safe at their home in The Dip and in the region about it. As they sat there late one afternoon and watched the twilight come over The

THE SILVER CUP

Silver Cup, Hans Arenberg spoke the thoughts that had been heavy in his mind that day.

"See what a misty twilight it iss," he said. "It iss too cold for rain, and so I think it means snow. The Comanches will come with the snow. While the weather was warm, and they could sleep on the open plain, they rode there, hunting the buffalo. Now the western bands will seek shelter and they will come here."

He walked from the hut and stood looking down at the lake, the surface of which had turned from silver to gray. The three followed him with a gaze which was of blended curiosity and sympathy.

"I more than half believe him," said Breakstone in a whisper to the others.

"It seems to me that sometimes he talks like a prophet," said John Bedford.

"He is a prophet sometimes," said Bill Breakstone, "or at least he's got second sight. Now he's looking at that lake, but he doesn't see it at all. He sees the Comanches, riding, riding, always riding toward this place, and maybe they have with them some one for whom he is looking. Maybe, and maybe not, but we'll see, don't you forget that, Phil, you and John, and somehow I'm thinking that he sees true."

It rapidly grew colder, and they were glad enough, when they came back from hunting and scouting, to seek the shelter of the thatched hut in The Dip. There, while the coals glowed on the stone hearth that they had made, and the smoke passed out through the vent in the wall, they speculated much on what was passing far to the southward of them. The great battle at the mouth of the Pass of Angostura was still so vivid in the minds of Phil, Breakstone, and Arenberg that they did not have to shut their eyes to see it again, and John often dreamed that he was still in the Castle of Montevideo, sitting by that deep loophole, looking out upon his mountain landscape.

"I guess they're closing in on the City of Mexico,"

said Bill Breakstone. "It's in a rough and mountainous country, easy to defend, but after the battle of Buena Vista I don't believe anything in Mexico can defeat our soldiers, no matter what the odds."

"And Middleton is with them," said Phil. "I'd like to see the Captain again. He was a fine man."

"Maybe we will," said Breakstone. "The West is a mighty big place, but there are not many white men in it, and when you shuffle them around some you are likely to meet them more than once."

The next morning The Silver Cup had a cover, a beautiful clear cover of ice an eighth of an inch thick. The following morning the cover was a little thicker, and it thickened perceptibly every succeeding morning, until it would bear the weight of Phil or John. The trees were heavy with frost, and the wind sometimes blew so sharply from the mountain that they made rude ear-muffs of deerskin and helped out their clothing as skillfully as possible with skins and furs.

Then the snow came. Looking northward, they saw a whitish mist over the forest. The mist gradually turned to dark blue clouds hanging very low. The snow fell, at first, in slow, solemn flakes, and then swiftly. They filled the air, all the forest was hidden, and nothing marked the presence of The Silver Cup but the level expanse of the snow. It fell to the depth of six or seven inches, then the skies cleared away, became crystal blue, and the cold increased, promising no more snow for the present, but a long continuance of that which lay on the ground. They visited the horses the next morning and found them well protected in their valley. Large spaces there were but thinly covered with the snow, and the horses could easily get at the grass. Assured on this point, John and Breakstone returned to The Dip, while Phil and Arenberg, mounting the strongest two horses, rode northward.

CHAPTER XXI

THE NOTE OF A MELODY

PHIL and Arenberg were undertaking this journey because they wished to make one of their usual thorough scouts. It merely happened to be their day, as John and Breakstone had gone on the day preceding. They were well wrapped up, with their ear-muffs on and with big moccasins that they had made to go over their shoes. The snow was very light and dry, and offered little obstacle to the horses, which were fat and strong with good feeding.

"We certainly leave a fine trail, Hans," said Phil, looking back at the impressions made by their horse's hoofs.

"It iss so," said Arenberg, "but since we hunt people it iss not our object to hide ourselves. Do you notice how beautiful iss the forest, Herr Philip? All the trees are white with the snow. It iss a great tracery, silver sometimes and gold sometimes as the sun falls, and it extends farther than we can see. It must often have been such as this in the great Teutonic forest where my ancestors dwelled thousands of years ago. Here in these woods I have this feeling at times, as if the centuries were rolled back, and last night I dreamed a strange dream."

"What was the dream?"

"I don't know. That was the strange part of it. I awoke and I knew that I had dreamed a strange dream which was not unpleasant, but, try as hard as I would,

I could not remember anything about it. What do you think that portends, Herr Philip?"

"I do not know. Perhaps when we want a thing so much and think about it so much the imagination, while we are asleep and the will is dead, forms a picture of it that remains in our possession when we awake. But it's just surmise. I don't know anything about it."

"Nor do I," said Arenberg, "but sometimes I believe. Now I suggest that we ride toward the northwest. I believe that good hunting grounds are in that direction beyond this forest, and perhaps the Comanches may have been on the plain there, and may now be seeking shelter in this wilderness."

"It's as good a theory as any," said Phil, "and we'll try it."

They rode for several hours toward the northwest, passing from the region of heavy forest into that of the scrub timber, and again into heavy forest as they approached the slopes of the higher mountains. They were now at least twenty miles from The Silver Cup, and it was past midday. They had brought jerked venison with them, and they ate their noon meal on horseback. But Phil wanted water, and he saw a clear white line leading among the trees, which he thought might indicate a brook flowing under the ice and snow. He dismounted, scraped away the snow and found that he was right. He broke the ice, took a good drink, and then noticed a trail on the far side of the brook. It was unmistakably that of a single horse, and he called excitedly to Arenberg.

"Look, Hans," he said. "Doesn't this show that an Indian pony has passed here?"

Arenberg came at once, and when he looked down at the trail his eyes sparkled with a kind of exultant joy. But he showed no excitement otherwise.

"It iss the trail of a single Indian pony," he said. "We will follow it. It iss not likely that a lone warrior rides in this region. He goes to join others."

THE NOTE OF A MELODY

Phil looked closely at Arenberg. He was quite sure that his comrade considered this a sign, the first sign that had come in the long, long search. He knew how the stout heart must be throbbing within the German's powerful chest.

"Lead on, Hans," he said. "I think you're right."

The two followed the trail at a good walk. It lay before them in the snow as plain as a railroad track. There was but little undergrowth here, and they saw far among the stems of the trees. They were quite sure that danger lay before them, since they might ride at any moment into an ambush, but they kept on without hesitation, although they watched well with two pairs of unusually keen eyes. In this manner they rode about five miles, and then Arenberg's eyes began to scintillate again. The pony's trail was merged into that of three or four more coming from the north.

"It iss so! It iss so!" he said softly, although excitement now showed in his tone. "The Comanches have come! Presently more riders will enter the trail, and beyond will lie their camp. Now, young Herr Philip, it iss for us to go with great care."

A mile farther the trail was merged with that of at least twenty horsemen. Phil himself did not doubt that the new Indian camp lay before them. The forest was now heavy with undergrowth here and there, for which he was thankful, since it afforded hiding for Arenberg and himself, while the trail was so broad that they could not possibly miss it. There was another fortunate circumstance. They had been longer on the trail than they had realized, and the twilight was now coming fast. It already lay in deep shadows over the vast, lonely wilderness. Although he was very near, Phil saw Arenberg's figure enveloped in a sort of black mist, and the horse's feet made but little sound on the soft snow. At intervals the two stopped to listen, because there was no doubt now in the mind of either that they were close to a large Indian camp. A half hour of this, and they stopped longer than usual. Both distinctly heard a low chant. Arenberg knew that it was the song of Indian women at work.

"Phil," he said, "we are close by. Let us leave our horses here and steal forward. We may lose the horses or we may not, but we cannot scout on horseback close up to the Indian camp."

Phil did not hesitate. They fastened the horses to swinging boughs in dense thickets, trusting them to the fortune that had been kind thus far, and then crept through the snow and among the trees toward the low sound of the chant. At the edge of a thicket of scrub cedar they knelt down and looked through the snow-laden branches into an Indian village that lay in the valley beyond.

It was a broad valley, with a creek now frozen over running through it, and the village, a large one, was evidently not more than a day or two old, as many of the lodges were not yet finished. All these lodges were of buffalo skin on poles, and the squaws were still at work on some of them. Others were beating buffalo meat or deer meat before the cooking fires, and yet others dragged from the snow the dead wood that lay about plentifully. Many warriors were visible here and there amid the background of flame, but they merely lounged, leaving the work to the squaws.

"It may be the band of Black Panther," said Phil.

"I think it iss," said Arenberg, "but I also think it has been swollen by the addition of another band or two."

The two were lying so close under the dwarf pines that Phil's arm was pressed against Arenberg's side, and he could feel the German trembling all over. Phil knew perfectly that it was not fear, but a powerful emotion that could thus shake the strong soul of his friend. Evidently the Indians had no thought of a foreign presence in a region so far from any settlement. A feeling of good-humor seemed to pervade the village. It was obvious

THE NOTE OF A MELODY

that they had found game in abundance, and thus the Indian's greatest want was filled.

Some of the Indian women continued the low humming chant that Phil and Arenberg had first heard, and others chattered as they worked about the fires. But Arenberg's eyes were for neither men nor women. He was watching a group of children at the outskirts. They were mostly boys, ranging in years from eight to thirteen, and, despite the darkness and the distance, he followed them with a gaze so intense, so full of longing, that it was painful to Phil who saw it. But it was impossible to distinguish. It was merely a group of Indian lads, half at play, half at work, and it would have been folly for the two to go closer.

But only hope was in the soul of Arenberg. The mystic spell of the great woods was on him, and he did not believe that he had come so far merely to lose at last. Phil suddenly felt his great frame shake under a stronger quiver of emotion than before. About a third of the Indian boys, carrying tin pails or stone jars, moved up the creek.

"Come," whispered Arenberg, in intense excitement. "They're going after water, where it is not defiled by offal from the village! We'll follow them on this side of the creek! See, the dwarf pines continue along the bank indefinitely!"

Arenberg led the way, treading softly in the snow. He was now the director, and Phil obeyed him in everything. Besides his own perception of the critical, Phil caught some of the intense excitement that surcharged every pore of Arenberg's being. He felt sure that something was going to happen. The thought was like fire in his brain.

The boys moved on toward a point where the ice had been broken already. The creek curved, and the village behind them passed out of sight, although its sounds could yet be heard plainly. Directly they came to the water hole and filled the pails and jars. Arenberg's excitement was increasing. He was much closer to them now, and again he studied every figure with a concentration of vision that was extraordinary. Yet the night was already dark, the figures were indistinct, and, to Phil at least, one figure, barring size, looked just like another.

The boys turned away, walked perhaps a dozen paces, and then Phil heard by his side a soft whistle, low, melodious, a bar of some quaint old song. It might have been mistaken in a summer night for the song of a bird. The boys stopped, but moved on again in a moment, thinking perhaps it was only fancy. Another ten feet, and that melodious whistle came again, lower than ever, but continuing the quaint old song. The third boy from the rear stopped and listened a little longer than the others. But the sound had been so faint, so clever an approach to the sighing of the wind among the pines, that the other boys seemed to take no notice of it. Arenberg was moving along in a parallel line with them, keeping behind the pines. Phil followed close behind him, and once more he put his hand on his arm. Now he felt, with increasing force, that the man was shaken by some tremendous internal excitement.

The file of Indian boys moved on, save the one who had been third from the last. He was carrying a pail of water, and he lingered, looking cautiously in the direction whence the low whistle had come. He was a small, strong figure, in Indian dress, a fur cap on his head. He seemed to be struggling with some memory, some flash out of the past. Then Arenberg, rising above the breastwork of pines, his head showing clearly over the topmost fringe, whistled a third bar of the old German folk song, so low, so faint that to Phil himself it was scarcely more than the sighing of the wind. The boy straightened up and the pail of water dropped from his hands upon the soft snow. Then he pursed his lips and whistled softly, continuing the lines of the melody.

THE NOTE OF A MELODY

An extraordinary thrill, almost like the chill of the supernatural, ran down Phil's back, but it was nothing to the emotion that shook the German. With a sudden cry: "It iss he!" Arenberg leaped entirely over the pine bushes, ran across the frozen creek, and snatched up the boy in his arms. It was Phil then who retained his coolness, luckily for them both. He seized the fallen rifle and called:

"Come! Come, Hans, come with the boy, we must ride for our lives now!"

Arenberg came suddenly back to the real world and the presence of great danger, just when he had found his son. He lifted the boy in his arms, ran with him across the creek, up the slope, and through the bushes. Little Billy scarcely stirred, but remained with his arms clasped around his father's neck. Already hostile sounds were coming from the Indian camp. The Indian boys, at the sound of Arenberg's footsteps, had turned back, and had seen what had happened.

"We must reach the horses," cried Phil, retaining his full presence of mind. "If we can do that before they wing us we'll escape. Run ahead. I'll bring your rifle."

Arenberg, despite the weight of his boy, rushed toward the horses. Phil kept close behind, carrying the two rifles. From the village came a long, fierce cry, the Comanche war whoop. Then it came back from the snowy forest in faint, dying echoes, full of menace. Phil knew that in a few moments the alert warriors would be on their ponies and in full pursuit.

"Faster, Hans! Faster!" he cried. "Never mind how much noise we may make now or how broad a trail we may leave! To the horses! To the horses!"

The little boy was perfectly silent, clinging to his father's neck, and Arenberg himself did not speak now. In a minute they reached the horses, untied them, and sprang upon their backs, Billy, as they always called him hereafter, sitting with a sure seat behind his father. Phil handed Arenberg his rifle:

"Take it," he said. "You may need it!"

Arenberg received the weapon mechanically. Before, he had been the leader. Now Phil took the position. He dashed away in the forest, turning toward the east, and the hoofs of Arenberg's horse thudded on the snow at his flank. They heard behind them the second shout of the Comanches, who had now crossed the creek on their ponies. Arenberg suddenly lifted his boy about and placed him in front of him. Phil understood. If a bullet came, it was now Arenberg instead of his boy who would receive it.

But it was not in vain that their horses had rested and eaten the sweet, clean grass so long. Now they obeyed the sudden call upon accumulated strength and energy, and, despite the double burden that Arenberg's horse bore, raced on at a speed that yet held the Indian ponies out of rifle shot.

"We must keep to the east, Hans," said Phil, "because if we brought them down on our friends at The Silver Cup we'd all be overpowered. Maybe we can shake them off. If so, we'll take a wide curve to our place. You ride a little ahead now. I can use the rifle better, as you have to look out for Billy besides yourself."

Arenberg urged his horse to greater speed and continued about a length ahead of Phil. Fortunately the forest was open here, and they could go at good speed without the dangers of tripping or becoming entangled. Phil looked back for the first time. He saw at some distance a half dozen Comanches on their ponies, mere shadowy outlines in the dusk, but he knew that more were behind them. His heart sank a little, too, when he remembered the tenacity of the Indians in pursuit.

"They're not gaining, Hans," he said, "and if they do I'll shoot at the first who comes up. Keep a watch for a good path, and I'll follow."

THE NOTE OF A MELODY

They galloped on an hour perhaps, and then the Indians began to yell again. Two or three fired their rifles, although the bullets fell short.

"Don't worry, Hans," called Phil. "They're merely trying to frighten us. They have not gained."

He sent back a taunting cry, twirled his own rifle in defiance, and then remembered that it was the slender, long-barreled Kentucky weapon, the highest of its type. He took another glance backward, but this was a measuring one. "It will reach," was his thought. He turned his whole body from the hips up in his saddle, took swift aim at the leading Comanche, and fired. The white smoke puffed from the muzzle of his rifle, the report was uncommonly loud and sharp in the night, and the bullet went home. The leading Indian fell from his pony in the snow, and the pony ran away. A fierce cry of rage came from the Comanches.

"It was well done, Herr Philip," said Arenberg. He did not look back, but he knew from the cry of the Indians that Phil's bullet had struck its target. The Comanches dropped back somewhat, but they were still near enough to keep the two flying horses in sight. Phil and Arenberg maintained their course, which was leading far from The Silver Cup. Phil's brain was cooling with the long gallop, and his nerves were becoming steadier. The change in himself caused him to notice other changes around him.

The air felt damp to his face, and the night seemed to have grown darker. He thought at first that it was mere fancy, but when he looked up he knew that it was the truth. He could not see the moon, and, just as he looked, the last star winked and went out. The damp touch on his face was that of a snowflake, and, as he still looked, the dark clouds stalked somberly across the sky.

"The snow! the snow," he murmured in eager prayer. "Let it come! It will save us!"

Another and larger flake dropped on his face, and,

after it, came more, falling fast now, large and feathery. He looked back for the last time. Not a single pursuer could be seen in the heavy gloom. He felt that their chance had come. He rode up by the side of Arenberg.

"Hans," he said, "turn sharp to the south. Look how the snow comes down! It is impossible for them to follow us now. It does not matter how we blunder along except that we must keep close together."

"It iss good," said Arenberg, as he turned his horse's head. "The great God is putting a veil about us, and we are saved!"

He spoke with unaffected solemnity, and Phil felt that his words were true. He felt, too, that they would not have escaped had it not been for the great snow that was now coming down. Surely a power had intervened in their behalf.

They rode southward for about an hour through forest, comparatively free from undergrowth, the two horses keeping so close together that the knees of their riders touched. The snow continued to fall, and they went on, always in a dense white gloom, leaving to their horses the choice of the path. They stopped finally under a huge tree, where they were sheltered, in some degree, from the snow, and Arenberg made the boy more comfortable on the saddle behind.

"Hello, Billy," said Phil. "Do you know that you've been away from home a long time? Your father was beginning to fear that you'd never come back."

The boy smiled, and, despite the Indian paint on his face, Phil saw there the blue eyes and features of Arenberg. He guessed, too, that the black hair under the cap would become gold as soon as the paint wore off.

"I not know at first," said Billy, speaking slowly and hesitatingly, as if it were difficult for him to remember the English language, "but the song when I hear it one, two, three times, then it come back and I answered. I knew my father, too, when he picked me up."

THE NOTE OF A MELODY

Arenberg gave him a squeeze, then he produced from his pocket some jerked venison, which Billy ate eagerly. "He's strong and hearty, that's evident," said Phil. "And, since we cannot leave any trail while the snow is pouring down in this way, I suggest that we let our horses rest for awhile, and then ride as straight as we can for The Silver Cup."

"It iss well," said Arenberg. "Nothing but one chance in a thouand could bring them upon us now, and God iss so good that I do not think He will let that chance happen."

Arenberg spoke very quietly, but Phil saw that the words came from his heart. The boy still preserved the singular stillness which he seemed to have learned from the Indians, but he held firmly to his father. Now and then he looked curiously at Phil. Phil chucked him under the chin and said:

"Quite a snow, isn't it, Billy?"

"I'm not afraid of snow," rejoined the boy, in a tone that seemed to defy any kind of a storm.

"Good thing," said Phil, "but this is a fine snow, a particularly fine snow. It has probably saved us all."

"Where are you going?" asked Billy.

"Where are we going?" said Phil. "Well, when this snow lightens a little we are going to ride a long distance through the woods. Perhaps we'll ride until morning. Then, when morning comes, we'll keep on riding, although it may not be in the forest. We'll make a great circle to the south, and there, at the edge of the forest, we'll come to a beautiful clear little lake that four men I know call The Silver Cup, only you can't get at the contents of that cup just now, as it has a fine ice covering. But overlooking The Silver Cup is a fine rocky hollow with a neat little thatched cabin in it. We call the hollow and the cabin The Dip, and in it are two of the four persons, your father and I being the other two.

"It's a fine little place, a snug little place, Billy, and

there isn't any lodge anywhere on this whole continent of North America that is equal to it. There is a big flat stone at one end on which we build our fire, and just above it is a vent to carry off the smoke.

"Hanging about that cabin are some of the most beautiful skins and furs you ever saw. And then we have rifles and pistols and knives and hatchets, and a shovel and an ax or two, and big soft blankets, and, when we are all in the hut at night, every fellow rolled in his warm blanket, as you will be, being a brave new comrade, and when the wind roars outside, and the hail and the snow beat against it and never touch you, then you feel just about as fine as anybody can ever feel. It's surely a glorious life that's ahead of you, Billy Arenberg. Those other two fellows who are waiting for you, Billy, are as good as any you ever saw. One of them is my brother, who has just escaped from a great prison, where wicked men held him for a long time, just as you have escaped, Billy, from the savages, to whom you don't belong, and the other is the bravest, oddest, wisest, funniest man you ever saw. You can't help liking him the very first moment you see him. He talks a lot, but it's all worth hearing. Now and then he makes up queer rhymes. I don't think he could get them printed, but we like them all the same, and they always mean just what they say, which isn't generally the way of poetry. I see right now, Billy, that that man and you are going to be great friends. His name is William, just like yours, William Breakstone, but he's Bill and you are Billy. It will be fine to have a Bill and a Billy around the camp."

The boy's eyes glistened. All sorts of emotion awoke within him.

"Won't it be fine?" he said. "I want to see that camp."

Phil had spoken with purpose. He had seen what Arenberg, thinking only of his recovered son, had failed to see, that the boy, taken in his early childhood and

THE NOTE OF A MELODY

held so long, had acquired something of the Indian nature. He had recognized his father and he had clung to him, but he was primitive and as wild as a hawk. The escape from the Indian village had been no escape for him at all, merely a transference. Phil now devoted himself to the task of calling him back to the white world to which he belonged.

All the time as they rode forward in the snow, Phil talked to him of the great things that were to be seen where the white men dwelled. He made their lives infinitely grander and more varied than those of the Indians. He told of the mighty battle in which his father had been a combatant. Here the boy's eyes glistened more than ever.

"My father is a great warrior," he exclaimed happily.

"One of the greatest that ever lived," said Phil. "There were more men, Billy, at that place we call Buena Vista than all the Comanche warriors put together several times over. And there were many cannon, great guns on wheels, shooting bullets as big as your head and bigger, and the battle went on all day. You couldn't hear yourself speak, the cannon and rifles roared so terribly and without ever stopping, and the smoke was greater than that of the biggest prairie fire you ever saw, and thousands of men and horses, with long lances, charged again and again. And your father stood there all day helping to beat them back."

Phil did not wish to speak so much of battle and danger, but he judged that this would appeal most to the boy, who had been taught by the Comanches that valor and fighting were the greatest of all things. The boy exclaimed:

"My father is one of the greatest of all warriors! He is a chief! He and you and I and the other two of whom you speak will go with a great army and beat the Mexicans again!"

Phil laughed and turned the talk more to the chase.

the building of cabins in the wilderness, and of great explorations across the prairies and through the hills. He still held the interest of the boy, and Phil saw the soul of the white race growing stronger and stronger within him. Arenberg listened, too, and at last he understood. He gave his comrade a look of gratitude. That, Phil always considered one of the greatest rewards he ever received.

They finally found a partial shelter in a ravine protected by trees, and here they dismounted in order to rest the horses and shake the snow from themselves. But they were not suffering from the snow. They were all warmly clad, and, as usual in the West in winter, Phil and Arenberg carried heavy blankets at their saddle horns. One of these had already been wrapped around Billy, and when they dismounted he remained clad in its folds. The fall of snow was lightening somewhat, enabling them to see perhaps twenty feet farther into it, but it was still a vast white gloom.

"I think it will stop before morning," said Arenberg, "and then we can make much greater speed. Are you sleepy, Billy?"

"I do not sleep when we are in danger," replied the boy.

He spoke with such youthful pride that Phil smiled. Yet the boy meant it. His wild life had certainly harmed neither his spirit nor his body. He was taller and heavier than most boys of his age, and Phil could see that he was as wiry and sinewy as a young panther. He seemed to endure the hardships of the night quite as well as Phil or his father.

"Snow is warm if there is something between you and it," said Phil. "Let's scrape out a place here against the bank, throw up the snow around us in walls, and rest until daylight. It will be a little hard on the horses, but they seem to be doing fairly well there against the trees."

"It iss wisdom that you speak," said Arenberg.

THE NOTE OF A MELODY

They threw back the snow until they made a den against the cliff, and the three, wrapped from head to foot in their heavy blankets, crouched in it close together. The snow fell upon the blankets, and, at times, when it lay too thick, they threw it all off. Billy seemed perfectly contented. Either he had no awe of the wilderness, or the presence of the others was enough for him. He had all the quietness and taciturnity of a little Indian lad. He did not speak at all, and did not move. By and by his eyes closed and he slept soundly. Arenberg drew the blanket a little more closely, until only the mouth and nose showed from the blanket, his breath making a white rim around the aperture. Then Arenberg said in a whisper to Phil:

"Young Herr Philip, you have helped me to get back my own. I cannot repay you."

"I am repaying *you*," said Phil. "You have *already* helped me."

After that they did not speak for a long time. The snow became lighter and lighter, then it ceased entirely. The horses were quiet in the shelter of the trees, and Phil was so snug and warm that he fell into a beautiful sleep, from which he was aroused by Arenberg.

"It iss day, Herr Philip," he said. "Look how the sun shines on the snow."

Phil drew himself out of the hole and looked at a white world, tinted silver in the early dawn.

"Yes, it is time for us to go," he said. "Wake Billy, and we'll ride."

But Billy was already awake, his small face illumined with curiosity and interest.

"Now we will ride," he said to Phil, "and see the men of whom you have told me."

They had some food left, and, after eating it to the last particle, they mounted their horses and rode with as much speed as was wise in the deep snow. Both Phil and Arenberg had an excellent idea of direction, and, guided by the sun, they rode straight toward The Silver Cup. But the snow was so deep and heavy that they were compelled to stop often to let their horses rest, and nearly a whole day passed before they saw the familiar trees and slopes that marked the approach to The Silver Cup. It was a glad sight. They were thoroughly exhausted with a day of plowing through the snow, and the horses were in the same condition. A trace of smoke marked the point at which The Dip lay.

"They're at home to callers, or at least one of them is," said Phil, "and I'll be glad to be on the inside of that hut again, with real red coals before me on a stone hearth."

In order to give the horses an equal chance, Billy, through the day, had ridden alternately behind Phil and his father. Now he was behind Arenberg, and he leaned forward eagerly to see. Before him lay a sort of path trampled in the snow, and, suddenly leaping from the horse, he ran forward with the agility and speed of a deer.

Bill Breakstone and John Bedford were inside the little thatched hut, and the red coals of which Phil had spoken in fancy were really burning on the hearth. They had made no search for Phil and Arenberg in the deep snow, knowing that such a thing was useless. There was not one chance in a thousand that they could find them, while Phil and Arenberg, strong, capable, and brave, were sure to come back. So they took their rest and made the place as comfortable as possible for the return of their partners, who would certainly be cold and hungry.

"John, keep that coffee ready to put on," said Bill Breakstone. "You know that your brother loves coffee when he comes in out of the snow and the cold."

"It will be ready any minute," replied John Bedford. "And I'm glad, Bill, you thought of that little pot of tea for Arenberg. You know he loves to have it about once a week."

THE NOTE OF A MELODY

"So I do," said Bill Breakstone. "Good old Hans. I suppose that he and Phil made a burrow somewhere in the woods, and slept in it last night. Naturally it's slow traveling back here through such a deep snow. Now what under the sun is that?"

The rude door of their little thatch was suddenly thrown open, and a small painted face thrust in. But the eyes in the painted face staring at them so intently, were blue, although they did not then notice the fact.

"A little Indian boy," said Bill Breakstone, rising. "Probably he got lost from a band in the storm and has stumbled upon us. We wouldn't welcome a lot of warriors, but we won't repel one boy. Come in, Red Jacket, Tecumseh, Powhatan, or whatever your name may be. We won't hurt you."

To his immense surprise the boy walked boldly in, came straight up to him, and said, in excellent English:

"I know that you are Bill Breakstone, and I want to hear you make rhymes."

Bill stared and stared. It was perhaps the first and last time in his life that he was dumfounded. But two larger figures came in immediately behind the boy, and Phil said:

"Mr. William Breakstone, I wish to introduce our new friend and comrade, Master William Arenberg. As 'William' seems a trifle pompous, he is to be known as Billy to distinguish him from you, who remain the Bill that you always have been. Look this way, Billy, and you will see my brother, John Bedford."

Hans Arenberg stood by, so happy that tears rose in his eyes. But Bill Breakstone came at once from his cloud of surprise. He snatched the boy up in his arms and gave him a big hug.

"Well, Billy," he cried, "here you are at last! I don't know how they got you, but they've brought you. Now my first duty as housekeeper is to wash our little boy's face."

He took water from a pail and promptly cleaned all the paint off Billy's face. Then Billy stood forth a white and not an Indian boy, and, with the departure of the paint, nearly all that was left of his acquired Indian nature seemed to go, too. While Phil and Arenberg told the story of the new miracle, he made himself easily at home, examining everything in the hut with minute care, and, by his actions, notifying Bill Breakstone and John Bedford that he was ready at once for a cordial friendship.

"Tea is ready! So is coffee," announced Bill Breakstone presently. "Now sit down, eat, drink, and be merry, for to-morrow you may not have such a good chance."

They charged with avidity, and little Billy Arenberg proved that he was already a mighty trencherman in the making.

"I wish I had some German blood in me, then I could eat with a fair appetite," said Bill Breakstone, as he reached for a huge buffalo steak.

CHAPTER XXII

BREAKSTONE'S QUEST

IT was nearly night, and they quickly agreed that they must not remain any longer in The Dip, however comfortable it might be. The Comanches were bound to find them in time, and the longer their lead the better.

"The night is going to be clear," said Breakstone, "and we must leave just as soon as we can pack our things on our horses. Everything indicates that the country toward the west slopes down rapidly, and we may soon pass out of the area of deep snow. Besides, we want to go toward the west. It's my turn now, and my search lies there."

"It iss so," said Arenberg with deep feeling. "You have helped all the rest of us, and we would not be fit to live if we did not now help you."

"I knew that you would not think of anything else," said Breakstone simply. "I'll tell you about it a little later, but now we'll start as soon as we can, and maybe we can come back some day and enjoy The Silver Cup again."

The horses were brought from the sheltered valley, and their provisions and other supplies were strapped on them. They soon discovered that Billy knew how to ride very well, and the gentlest of the horses was assigned to him, although he slept during the early part of the night. But when he was roused he was full of zeal and interest, and he was also so alert and active that he proved himself a help instead of a burden.

At midnight, they put out the fire and left a cold

hearth. Then, with some reluctant glances backward at The Dip and the snowy cover of The Silver Cup, they rode away in single file, Breakstone leading, Phil next, followed by John, behind whom came Billy, with Arenberg at the rear. It was cold, but they were sufficiently clad, and they rode on until daylight, the dry snow crunching beneath the hoofs of their horses.

The descent proved to be sharp, and when daylight came they were in a region where the snow was very light. They saw the plains before them and below them, and they believed that by noon they would be entirely beyond the expanse of snow.

"By the time those Comanches discover our abandoned home," said Bill Breakstone, "it's likely that we'll be days and days away. We'll never see them again because our journey leads west and always west, far beyond the Comanche country."

"I learned from Billy," said Phil, "that it was really Black Panther who was in command back there. Billy had been with another band, farther west, which last spring was incorporated into the more powerful force of Black Panther. The chief was treating Billy well, and was going to adopt him as his son."

"Then I am glad that we shall fight no more with Black Panther," said Arenberg.

"So am I," said Breakstone thoughtfully. "I suppose the chief has acted according to his lights. If we'd been roaming over the country for ages, we'd fight for it, too. Well, good-by to you, Black Panther, I wish you many a good buffalo hunt, but that no white people may fall into your hands."

At noon, as they had expected, they passed through the last thin sheet of snow and entered warm country. But it was not desert here. It was a region of buffalo grass, with shallow streams and scattered timber. It was very pleasant after so much riding through the snow, and, after resting an hour by the side of one of the rivulets, they kept on until night. They were not compelled to spend any time in hunting a camp, but stopped under a clump of trees, turned the horses loose to graze on the plentiful grass, and spread their own blankets on the turf. They were too tired to light a fire, but they ate heartily of the cold food, and then lay back comfortably on the blankets. Billy fell asleep in a few minutes, but the others did not yet feel the desire for slumber. The ride of a day and half a night had not been hard, but, as much of that ride had been downward, the change was wonderful. Gone was the deep snow, gone the biting winds. They wrestled with neither the ice nor the desert, but lay upon a carpet of pine needles and breathed an air that came, crisp with life, from the mountains. Bill Breakstone luxuriated in it, and finally, observing that the others were not asleep, he sat up.

"Boys," he said, "I think the time has come for me to tell you about the errand that has brought me so far, and that's going to take me a lot farther. I haven't said anything about the nature of it before, because it was the one that could wait longest. Sit up and look at what I'm going to show you."

They sat up on their blankets, and he took from his pocket a little package which he unwrapped and looked at a moment or two. Then he poured the contents out upon his blanket. They looked like gravel or grains of stone, but the moon was good then, and from some of the grains came a slight metallic glitter, like pin-points of light.

"That," said Bill Breakstone in deeply impressive tones, "is gold."

"It looks more like gravel to me," said John Bedford.

"It is gravel, too," said Breakstone, "gravel, and gold in the gravel."

"About how much iss your gold worth?" asked Arenberg skeptically.

"Fifty cents, maybe," replied Bill Breakstone.

"Which wouldn't carry you far."

"No, it wouldn't," said Breakstone genially. "But see here, my merry Dutchman, a man may have a million dollars in the bank, and carry only a dime in his pocket. That's me. This is my sample, my specimen. It came from a spot far away, but there's a million more, or something like it, there waiting for us. Listen to me, Sir Philip of the River and the Plain, Sir Hans of the Forest and the Snow, and even you, Sir John of the Castle and the Cell, and I will tell you a glittering tale which is true."

Every one moved forward a few inches on his blanket, and their figures grew tense with interest. The moon sent a broad shaft of light through an opening in the trees directly upon the face of Bill Breakstone, showing eyes that sparkled with the pleasure of one who held a great secret that he was willing to tell to others.

"I'm not joking," continued Bill Breakstone earnestly. "I'm a rover, but I find when I rove. There's gold, lots of it, far west across the great mountains in California. You find it in the sand and gravel along the edges of streams which are dry most of the year. A man can generally do the work all by himself, with water and a pan, sifting the gold dust from the baser stuff.

"It's a terribly wild country of hills and of tremendously high mountains covered with snow. When the snow melts and the water comes down into these dry creek and river beds it comes with a mighty rush, and it washes the gold from the rocks along with it. At least, that's my theory, and the gold has been piling up for ages in dust and grains along the edges of these beds in the valleys below. I found this dust in a wild country about a thousand miles from here, but I can go straight back to the place."

The others were continually creeping a little nearer and a little nearer on their blankets, and the moonlight which found new openings through the trees showed three more pairs of eyes sparkling with excitement.

"Why did you come away after you found the gold?" asked Phil.

"Because I lacked supplies. Because I was alone. Because California belonged to the Mexicans. Because the Indians were dangerous to one man. Any of these reasons was good enough, but we can take supplies in abundance. I will not be alone. I doubt very much whether California now belongs to the Mexicans, or will belong to them much longer, and it is very likely that the Indians have wandered off into some other region. Boys, after so many dangers we'll all be rich."

"But, Bill," said Phil, "we can't take your gold, which you found after so much hardship and danger."

Bill Breakstone gave Phil Bedford a threatening look.

"I wish you to listen to a few words of wisdom," he said in a menacing tone, "and take care that you listen well. If I hear any more such foolishness from you, Sir Philip of the River and the Plain, you'll lose your golden spurs and your silver breastplate and your steel helmet and all your titles. You'll be degraded into the position of a common varlet to pull off my shoes, to bring me the mead to quaff, and to have a spear shaft broken over your wooden head when you're not bright and lively. And to you, Hans Arenberg, I give the same advice. I'll make you the King's Jester, and, with that solemn Prussian face of yours and that solemn Prussian mind of yours, you'll find jesting for me about as hard a task as any man ever undertook. And you, John Bedford, I will deliver bound hand and foot to your friend Captain Pedro de Armijo with the great red scar across his face which you put there. What a crisp little revenge he would take! I can see you now frying over the coals."

"But, Bill," persisted Phil, "it's your find."

"I know it, but you needn't think that ends everything. It's only the beginning. We've got to get back to that dead river of mine, and for that I need comrades. We've got to do weeks and weeks of work, and for that I need comrades. We've got to fight off danger, Indians perhaps, Mexicans perhaps, outlaws perhaps, and for that I need comrades. After we get the gold we've got to bring it safely to civilization, and for that I need comrades. Also, there is so much of the gold in the bed of the dead river that I could not spend it all alone, and for that I need comrades. Now will you come willingly and share and share alike with me, or shall I have to yoke up together and drive you unwillingly?"

"We'll come," said Phil, and John and Arenberg added their assent.

"I wish the Captain was with us, too," said Bill Breakstone. "He belongs in this crowd, and he ought to have some of the gold."

Phil and Arenberg echoed his regret at the absence of Middleton.

"Now that it is all settled," said Bill Breakstone, "I'm going to sleep."

In five minutes he was sound in slumber, and the others soon followed him to that pleasant land.

They resumed their journey the next morning, but they advanced in leisurely fashion. Breakstone warned them that there were other high ranges ahead, and they agreed that it would not be wise to attempt their passage in winter. Hence, they must find a winter home in some sheltered spot, where the three requisites of wild life, wood, water, and game, could be found. It did not take them long to find such a place, and they built a rude cabin, using it as their base during the remainder of the winter, which was mild, as they were not at a great elevation. Although they made an occasional scout, they never found any Indian sign, and the cold weather passed in comparative ease and safety. Little Billy developed at a remarkable rate, and here he sloughed off the last vestige of the Indian. But he had learned many cunning arts in hunting, trapping, and fishing which he never forgot, and there were some things pertaining to these in which he could instruct his elders.

Not a single hunter, trapper, or rover of any kind passed through during the winter months, and they often wondered what was going on in the world without.

"I'd surely like to see the Captain again," said Bill Breakstone one cold evening as they sat by their fire. "Just to think of all that he went through with us, and now he's vanished into thin air. Maybe he's dead, killed in some battle a thousand miles down in Mexico."

"I don't believe the Captain is killed," spoke up Phil promptly. "I don't believe that he's the kind of man who would be killed. But a lot of things must have happened since we left. There must have been some big fighting away down there by the City of Mexico. Do you think we could have been whipped, Bill?"

"Phil, I've half a mind to take away all your titles without another word," replied Breakstone reprovingly. "How could you think of our being whipped, after what you saw at Buena Vista?"

"That's so," said Phil, his cheerfulness coming back at once.

Late in the spring they began the passage of the ranges, and although it was a long, hard, and sometimes dangerous task, they got safely across with all their horses, coming again into a plains country, which merged farther west into a desert. Here they were about to make a great loop northward, around the Mexican settlements, when they met an American soldier carrying dispatches. They hailed him, and, when he stopped, they rode forward, all eagerness. It was deputed to Bill Breakstone to ask the momentous question, and he asked it:

"How is the war going on?"

The soldier looked at them, amused little crinkles at the corners of his mouth. He knew by their appearance that these were people who had been long in the wilderness.

"It isn't getting on at all," he replied.

"What!" cried Bill Breakstone appalled.

"It isn't going on, because it's all over. General Scott marched straight to the City of Mexico. He fought a half dozen terrible battles, but he won every one of them, and then took the City of Mexico itself. A treaty of peace was signed February 2 last. You are riding now on American soil. New Mexico, Arizona, California, and vast regions to the north of us have been ceded to the United States."

"Hurrah!" they cried together, Billy joining in with as much enthusiasm as the others.

"What about Santa Fé?" asked Bill Breakstone.

"It's occupied by an American garrison, and there is complete peace everywhere. The only danger is from wandering Indians."

"We know how to fight them," said Bill Breakstone. "Boys, we ride for Santa Fé."

The soldier continued northward, and they turned the heads of their horses toward the New Mexico capital, reaching, in good time and without loss, the queer little old Spanish and Indian town from which the flags of Spain and then of Mexico had disappeared forever. They intended to remain only two or three days in order to obtain more horses and fresh supplies. Then they would slip quietly out of the town, because they wished their errand to be known to nobody. On the second day Bill Breakstone and Phil were walking together, when a man in sober civilian dress suddenly seized a hand of each in a firm grasp, and exclaimed in joy:

"Why, boys, when did you come here?"

"The Captain!" exclaimed Bill Breakstone. "How things do come around!"

It was Middleton, his very self, thinner and browner, but with the same frank open countenance and alert look.

BREAKSTONE'S QUEST

Bill and his comrade explained rapidly about the rescue of John Bedford, the recovery of little Billy Arenberg, and their passage through the mountains.

"And now," said Breakstone, "you tell us, Captain, how you happen to be up here in Santa Fé in civilian dress."

Middleton smiled a little sadly as he replied:

"The war is over. We won many brilliant victories. We were never beaten once. And I'm glad it's over, but there is nothing left for the majority of the younger officers. I should probably remain a captain all the rest of my life at some obscure frontier station, and so I've resigned from the army."

A light leaped up in Bill Breakstone's eyes, but he asked very quietly:

"And what are you meaning to do now, Captain?"

"I don't know, but I've been hearing talk about gold in California, and perhaps I'll go there to hunt it."

"Of course you will!" exclaimed Bill Breakstone, letting himself go. "You're going to start to-morrow, and you're going with us. I know right where that gold is, and I'm going to lead you and the rest of the boys to it. You remember that every one of us had a quest that drew us into the West. The secret of the gold is mine. We need you and we share alike. As I've told the others, there's enough for all."

Middleton was easily persuaded, and they left Santa Fé the next morning before daylight, taking little Billy Arenberg with them. They traveled a long time toward the northwest, crossing mountains and deserts, until they reached the mighty range of the Sierra Nevada. This, too, they crossed without accident or loss, and then Bill Breakstone led them straight to the dead river and up its channel to the hidden gold. Here he dug in the bank and showed them the result.

"Am I right or am I wrong?" he asked exultantly.

"Right!" they replied with one voice.

THE QUEST OF THE FOUR

At first they washed out the gold, but afterward they used both the cradle and the sluice methods. The deposits were uncommonly rich, and they worked there all through the summer and winter. The next spring, Middleton and Arenberg carried a great treasure of gold on horses to San Francisco. They also took Billy Arenberg with them, but on their way back they left him, to his huge regret, at a good school in Sacramento, while they rejoined their comrades on the great Breakstone claim. They exhausted it in another year, but they were all now as rich as they wished to be, and they descended into the beautiful valley of California, where they expected to make their homes.

THE END